# THE COACH

A. K. STEEL

The Coach
Copyright ©2022 by A. K. Steel

All rights reserved. No part of this book may be reproduced or transmitted in either electronic, paper hard copy, photocopying, recorded, or any other form of reproduction without the written permission of the author. No part of this book either in part or whole may be reproduced into or stored in a retrieval system or distributed without the written permission of the author.

This book is a work of fiction. Characters, names, places and incidents are products of the author's imagination. Any resemblances to actual events, locations, or persons living or dead is purely coincidental.

The author acknowledges the trademark status and owners of products referred to in this fiction which have been used without permission. The publication and use of these trademarks is not authorised, associated with, or sponsored by the trademark owners.

Published by A.K. Steel

Edited by Contagious Edits

Blurb by Contagious Edits

Cover Design by Opium House Creatives

## ABOUT THE BOOK

Love is all fun and games... until someone gets hurt.

I'm Andrea Harper, top striker for the LA Angels. I play hard, party hard, and I don't do relationships. I sleep with who I want, when I want. I'm out to have fun. The only important thing in my life is soccer. I have spent my entire life dedicated to the game. And I'm on track to be one of the best female soccer players in the country, if not the world. Being the best is the only thing that matters.

But life has a way of throwing you a curveball when you least expect it, and in my case, it was love.

One night with my childhood hero was all it took. Brad Swift. He's nearly ten years older and used to be one of the best professional soccer players in the world before he got injured. He was my childhood hero until we slept together and messed all that up. I thought I could put it down to just another stupid mistake, that he would go back to England and I would never see him again.

That was until he turned up at training as our new soccer coach.

The attraction we share is undeniable, but he's off limits. It's strictly forbidden for a coach to date a player. Too bad I've never been one to follow the rules and the temptation is just too much... So we slip up, make a pact to keep it fun. Nobody needs to know.

But secrets this good have a way of getting into the wrong hands. And when they do, danger is the name of the game.

* Content warning: contains elements of violence and self-harm.

# CHAPTER ONE

### ANDY

The beat of the music reverberates through my body. My eyes are closed, and I move with no care for what I might look like to those surrounding me. This song is sick; I think it's a David Guetta remix, Love Tonight, or something like that. This is my happy place, when everything else in my life feels overwhelming. This is what I need to calm the crazy.

My girl gang, Darcy and Luna, are by my side. We're out at one of the trendiest clubs in LA, and we've been dancing up a storm for at least an hour. I have a ridiculous amount of energy and find it hard to sit still at the best of times. That's part of why I became a professional athlete.

The three of us play for the Angels here in LA, one of the best women's soccer teams in the country. We're super close friends and have been since we met in college. After four years of college, we all luckily got signed to the same team, and they both came to live with me and my sister Jasmine. These girls are my people, and man, we have a blast when we're together.

"This bar is seriously epic," screams Luna over the loud

music on the dance floor. Her long black hair is down and sways around her waist as she moves her arms above her head.

"Totally," agrees Darcy, grinning. I'm not even sure how she's moving in the tight red number she has on. The girl loves to show off what God gave her. Why wouldn't you when you look like Darc, thick brown curls, olive skin, and a body that looks like a Victoria Secret model. She moves around me provocatively, putting on a show, I'm sure trying to gain the attention of any cute guy around us.

I grin and nod in agreement as I dance along to the beat. They're right, I adore this bar. It's the perfect combination of all the things that I need to make me feel good on a Saturday evening: dance music, hot-as-fuck men, and whiskey. I'm in my own little world, just feeling the music vibrating through my body. With our hectic training schedule, it feels like it's been so long since we've had a night out, and I really need to let loose and have a little fun. If I don't, the pressure all gets to be too much.

And tonight, we're celebrating this week's big win against Louisville. It seems like as the season goes on, we're just getting better and better. There is no way I'm going to let what happened last year go down again. This is our year to win the National Women's Soccer League championships.

The song changes and my eyes flicker open to see my sister Jasmine walking through the crowd. I wave her over, and she dashes through the crowd to our group. "Jassy," I squeal as I wrap my arms around her in a clumsy hug. "You came! I thought you were on a date," I yell so she can hear me over the music.

She pulls a disgusted face. "Yeah, that didn't go so well, so I ditched him for my girls."

I'm upset for her. I know how excited she's been all week about meeting this guy. She found him on one of those online dating sites. I can see the disappointment in her features. My sister is a hopeless romantic, always on the search for her perfect prince. All she seems to find are slimy frogs—no, worse than that, I would say toads! The guys she finds are the worst. But with every blow, she gets back up and tries again.

My sister is tenacious. I am too, it's a family trait, but I use my persistent energy to be the best soccer player possible. I don't date. I gave up on chasing the perfect man back in college when I realized they were all assholes, good for a screw when I'm horny and that's it. Pouring everything I have into my career is a much more satisfying option.

"Good choice," I tell her. "Come on, let's get you drunk." I take her hand and drag her along with me to the bar. She struggles to keep up in her tall pumps and little black dress. She looks beautiful all dressed up for her date, and I can never understand how she ends up with the losers she does. She is stunning, super intelligent, and so much fun.

I'm one of four sisters, but she's the one I'm closest to. I adore her and wish I knew how to turn her frown into a smile, but this is becoming a usual occurrence with her. She needs to have some fun and stop trying so hard to meet men.

I lean over the bar, smiling flirtatiously at the nice-looking bartender. He flashes a smile in my direction and comes to stand in front of us. "Two Jamesons, please," I ask super sweetly.

Jasmine gives me a worried look. "Andy, this seems like a bad idea. You know when I drink whiskey I get really trashed and end up doing something stupid. Remember what happened last time?"

I grin at my sweet big sister. She should know me well

enough to know I'm not out tonight to sit and drink cocktails and gossip with all the pretty girls. I need to let loose and have some fun. "Yeah, I remember." I burst out laughing at the thought of my sweet innocent sister so drunk she stripped off her clothes and ran down the main street of our hometown. I did it with her, but that's not so unusual for me, I have no shame. "That's the idea, let's do something really stupid." I grin at her. Trying to convince her to come over to the dark side with me. She is the sensible voice of reason in our group, but every so often she concedes, and that's when we really have some fun.

The bartender places the drinks in front of us. Jas narrows her eyes at me, faking a filthy look. "You're the worst little sister ever, such a bad influence on me." She laughs, taking her drink from the bar and having a small sip.

I drain my glass, setting it back on the bar and signaling to the bartender for another. "That's why you love me." I give her a wink.

She shakes her head, following my lead, polishing off her drink and ordering another. She would be lost without me. Stuck in her boring, goody-two-shoe life trying to please our parents, but because of me, she gets out and has a little fun. I'm good for her and she knows it.

Darcy and Luna have ditched the dance floor and found their way to a table along the back of the club. We make our way back across the busy club to join them.

I sip my next drink, looking around for something fun to do—or some*one*. That would get rid of all of this nervous energy I have. I can't sit for too long, my body needs to move. "I'm bored. I think we should play a little game," I suggest to the others.

Darcy throws me a look. There's a little twinkle of

mischief shining in her eyes. She likes this idea too. "What do you have in mind, my wild friend?"

The other two look between each other and shrug. They are more the followers, happy to wait for me and Darcy to come up with a plan, then they play along. And I'm doing this for Jasmine. She needs a distraction from her shitty date. Who knows, she might even find someone special tonight. I mean, I doubt it, but she might.

"How about we give each other fake identities, we pick someone to chat up, and the first one to get a number wins?" I suggest. Because I can't see anyone worth my time, I need to make this a game. It'll be more fun that way.

"You mean like, different jobs?" asks Luna, fiddling with her hands, a little unsure of my brilliant idea.

I grin over to her. "Yes. Like a different identity for the night, something fun and sexy."

Darcy smirks at me. She gets it, she's always up for some fun. The two of us have gotten ourselves into some real trouble together. At times I would say we have even gone a little too far in the name of fun. "I'm in." She claps her hands excitedly. I see her scanning the room already, looking for her target.

"What will the winner get?" asks Luna, always concerned with the prize.

"I don't know, bragging rights? Loser has to buy the next round?" I shrug. Who cares what they get?

Jasmine assesses me and I think she has had just enough whiskey to be over her awful date and ready to loosen up a little. "Yeah, alright. I guess I could do with an Andy distraction." Her eyes narrow in on me and she smirks. "I'm picking your persona, though."

"Okay, Sissy, shoot. Who am I then?"

She looks me over, tapping a finger to her lips, considering me. "Well, I would like to make you something totally out of your comfort zone, like a beautician, but I don't think you could get away with it with those nails and that hair." The look she gives me with a roll of her eyes.

You'd think I would be hurt by the way she says it, but nope. I look at my nails, and shrug. She's right, I'm not a girly girl at all. My nails are short. My waist-length, Viking-blonde hair hasn't been brushed in a couple of days and is in a messy bun held together loosely with a few bobby pins. I'm not like most of the other girls strutting around this club, or even my friends really, in their tight little dresses and high heels. I don't give a fuck about making myself up to attract the opposite sex—or the same sex, for that matter. I am who I am.

I'm wearing skinny black jeans with a black tank and my leather jacket, teamed with my comfy combat boots. This is me, unless I'm in my sweats to work out or soccer uniform to play. And I have never had any problem picking up guys, so why put in all the effort the other girls do?

"You would be more suited to a beautician, actually," I say. "Ooh, I know what you can be." I smirk, coming up with a profession she will hate.

"What?" She rolls her eyes at me.

"A fashion model." She shrieks, and I laugh. I knew she would hate that, but now I bet she's thinking about how annoying I am and not about her failed date, so I don't really care.

She shakes her head. "Oh God, no! I'm so far from a fashion model it's not even funny, no guy would believe it."

"Jas, you're gorgeous," Darcy adds. "Tall, slim, stylish. Andy's right, you make the perfect fashion model." She wraps her arm around Jas, giving her a squeeze. My sister has no idea just how beautiful she really is, and Darcy's description of her is very accurate.

"Well, that's you sorted, Jas," says Luna. "You're a fashion model, just finished a shoot for Vogue Magazine, and I think that guy over there, the one who has been eye-fucking you since you sat down." She's looking over my shoulder.

Jasmine glances in the direction Luna is looking and blushes, covering her face. "What? No, he hasn't," she whispers. Ooh, she likes the look of him already, good.

I peek over my shoulder at who Luna is talking about and he so is watching her. "Lucky you, Jas, he's hot as fuck!" She's beetroot red now, her perfect porcelain skin giving her away.

"What about me?" says Luna. "Make me something good, like a flight attendant or a sex shop owner," says Luna. She is our cute pocket rocket, one of the fastest on our soccer team, with stunning features and long almost-black hair. The girl is also obsessed with sex; you name it she's done it. She might look shy, sweet, and innocent, but she is most certainly not.

Darcy turns to her. "You are so going to be a sex shop owner, that's perfect for you, with the blond dude over there." She tilts her head in his direction.

Luna rubs her hands together. "Ooh, thanks, he is mighty fine, I can work with that. And Darcy, you should be a flight attendant, with him." She points and we all look. Just as we do, he glances our way, and we all burst out laughing, totally busted.

Darcy locks eyes with him, not caring for a second that she's been caught checking him out. "Perfect, I can do that. A flight attendant just back from Paris, and the scrummy man in the suit, who is now wondering why we're staring at him and laughing." She grins, giving him a wave, always up for the challenge. He raises a brow and smirks. Damn, she's already ahead of the rest of us.

"What's it going to be for our girl Andy, Jasmine? Cause I have just spotted the perfect guy for her," Darcy says with a devilish grin. This is going to be good. I can't see who she's talking about, but I don't really care either. I'll chat up anyone for a challenge.

We all watch Jasmine while she thinks it over. "A mechanic," she announces, looking proud of herself.

I roll my eyes at my sister. A mechanic? At least it's not some girly job. I guess I can pull off mechanic. "Who's the guy, Darcy?"

"Him." She tilts her head in the direction of the bar to a guy who is sitting on his own, drink in hand. I recognize him immediately as Brad Swift. He used to be one of the best strikers in the game, played for Chelsea. When I was younger, I worshiped him, and Darcy fucking knows that. That was until he got injured a couple of years back and I haven't heard a thing about him since. She has to have picked probably the only person in here I would feel intimidated to talk to, and she knows it. She is just as competitive as me and she wants to win this little game.

"You fucking bitch." I laugh.

She grins back. "Good luck, baby, may the best girl win." She holds out her hand for me, and I give it one quick shake.

Even with the most impossible challenge for me, I'm all in. I never back down from a challenge and a chance to win. "See you losers when you're buying me drinks," I call, rising from my seat before the others have the chance, and I take off across the room toward the hottie the girls have picked out for me.

Brad Swift. In a club here in LA. Not just any club but

the same one that we chose to come to tonight. What are the chances?

My heart is pounding, so unlike me, and for a split second as I get a little closer, I have second thoughts. He's mighty fine, and he's in a suit, all clean-cut and swoony. I can feel my lady parts wake up, the throb with need already thumping through me. I could never resist a handsome man in a suit, especially this one.

I take a deep breath to get my nerves under control. I give myself a pep talk. *Andy, we don't get nervous, remember? He is just a guy, no one special. You've got this.* Checking behind me, I see my friends have all taken up the challenge as well and are heading to their selected guys.

Game on, girlfriends.

I sway my way through the club with an air of relaxed confidence, my eyesight set just past him to the bartender, but I take him in with my peripheral vision. And that's enough to trigger a hot flush of excitement, knowing how close I am to him, Brad Swift. This guy used to be a poster on my bedroom wall for fuck's sake, that's how obsessed with him I was. I wanted to be every bit as good a player as he was. It's why I started playing striker position in the first place and practicing scoring goals became an obsession. And he was mighty fine to look at, my first proper celebrity crush.

What am I going to say to him? Part of me wants to drop at his feet, thank him for being such an inspiration, tell him he's my hero and the reason I'm one of the top soccer players in the country. But that's not going to work here, not tonight, anyway. I'm playing a game, one I made up. And tonight, I'm a mechanic, thanks to Jasmine.

This guy would be used to getting the attention of any girl he wants, so I decide to ignore him instead. I walk straight past him to the bar, smiling at the cute bartender from earlier. I fix my hair, tucking a strand behind my ear in a flirtatious way. Standing close enough to Brad that he can't miss me, I lean over to get the bartender's attention. "Another Jameson, thanks," I purr.

He smiles with a nod of the head and pours my drink, placing it in front of me. I take it, swirling the amber-colored liquid around a few times, then taking a small sip. I turn toward Brad, who is now unashamedly checking me out. I raise a brow in his direction, like, *what the fuck are you looking at?* Then I lean back on the bar, sipping my drink as I take in my surroundings. Playing it as cool as I can, even though my heart is pounding out of my chest. I'm close enough that I can smell his aftershave, and it's intoxicating.

"Nice choice." He smiles my way, then turns to the bartender. "Another Jameson on the rocks." The bartender places his drink down in front of him. He has a swig then looks back to me. "You're not like the other girls hanging around here tonight."

That Australian accent... fuck, he sounds so sexy. I take another sip of my drink, trying to stay calm. He's going to come on to me. Acting uninterested works every time. Guys like this have overly inflated egos, and they can't stand the fact that a pretty girl might not be interested in them.

"Oh yeah, how's that?" I ask, keeping my face unemotional, trying to look bored, glancing around the club like I'm on the hunt for something better, rather than giving him the attention I can tell he craves.

"I've been sitting alone at the bar for an hour, and so far, I've had a line-up of overdone girls asking for my autograph or a photo." Out of the corner of my eye, I can see his brow knit together, displeased at the thought, and I'm glad I didn't come over here with my hero speech.

I feign shock, placing a hand over my chest, finally looking his way. "Oh, that sucks to be you. Wait, autograph? Who are you? Don't tell me you're on one of those reality TV shows or something." I laugh internally, trying my best not to blow my cover when I see the look on his face. He's not used to girls not knowing who he is, it's so obvious. It's one thing to be good at what you do, but this guy is that and sexy as hell as well. Everyone knows who Brad Swift is!

He frowns. "No, not TV. You really don't know who I am?"

I think for a minute, tapping my finger to my mouth. Then shake my head. "Sorry, can't place you. Oh, I've got it. Were you in Crocodile Dundee? You have that Aussie accent going on."

He throws his head back, laughing, and fuck, it's the best sound ever. "Crocodile Dundee, that movie is really fucking old. But you got me, I'm from Australia originally."

"So you're Australian, but it's not a full Aussie accent, though. Where else have you lived?" I ask, trying not to stare at him too intently, which is hard. He is truly the most beautiful man I have ever seen in real life. Short chestnut-colored hair, warm brown eyes, his skin is golden, and his lips—fuck, they look perfect for kissing. I glance at them for a second longer than I should, and he notices, his lips turning into a cheeky smile. Damn.

"You know your Aussie ascents?"

I shrug. "Yeah, a bit, I guess. My mom is an Aussie. She's been here for nearly forty years, but she still sounds like one."

"I've been in England for the past ten years playing soccer for the premier league. That's the difference you were hearing."

I fake a smile. "Oh, you play sports, cool," I say like it's the most uninteresting thing in the world.

He tilts his head, his eyes roaming leisurely over me. This whole uninterested thing is working like a charm. The look he gives me is like he wants to eat me up, and man, I want him to. "What do you do?" he asks, a smile playing on his lips.

"I'm a mechanic." I shrug like it's no big deal. God, I hope he doesn't know anything about being a mechanic, or cars, cause all I have on the topic is, *yeah, I fix cars*.

I glance around the room to see how the other girls are doing. They're all still chatting, no one has a number yet, that I can tell. Good, I still have a chance to win this.

He gives me a sidewise grin. "Of course you are. What's your name, pretty mechanic?"

He thinks I'm pretty. My heart almost skips a beat. One of my idols thinks I'm pretty. "Andy. What about you? Or should I just call you Dundee?"

"It's Brad," he says, unimpressed by my joke. He really is ticked off that I don't recognize him. It's hilarious.

I hold out my hand for him to shake. "Nice to meet you, Brad. This was interesting, but I need to be getting back to my friends now." I tilt my head to the side, trying to read him. His gaze holds mine as he continues to grasp my hand. I blink back at him, all of a sudden forgetting what I'm here to do and losing my words, completely lost in his gaze.

"Yes, pretty girl? What did you want to say?" His eyes flick to my lips and I get a vision of his lips pressed to mine, his hands in my hair as my eyes flutter closed, so caught up in the moment of passion between us. I snap out of my daze. *You want to win, Andy, concentrate.* "I was just going to ask for your number. Maybe we can do coffee sometime and you can tell me what it's like to play sports."

He laughs at my comment, but his eyes don't leave mine. "Why exchange numbers to have coffee sometime when I can talk to you now? Tonight?"

I shrug, words to voice my argument not coming because I don't want to stop talking to him. But damn, if I can't get the number, I won't win. But the longer I stand here with him, the less I care about the silly game.

"I'm only in town for the night, then I fly back to London. You want to have a drink with me, you're going to have to come back to my room tonight," he adds, trying to persuade me to leave with him.

Smooth, Brad. You can see how hard he normally has to try, or rather, not at all. I'm sure most girls fall at his feet with such an offer, but I'm not most girls. The offer is tempting, though, so much so I'm really struggling with how to turn him down. "Does that line normally work on the overdone girls that were bothering you before?" I reply, cocking a sassy brow.

"Every time." He smirks cheekily, and I believe him. A guy like him wouldn't even have to try. He could get any girl in this bar, but he wants to take me back to his room.

I pull out of his grip, realizing I'm still holding his hand. "Like you said, baby, I'm not like most of the girls in here. That's not going to work on me." I finish my drink, placing the empty glass down on the bar, making it obvious I'm about to leave.

He stands, finishing his drink and placing it on the bar. He takes a step closer to me; he is so much taller in real life than he seems on the TV playing soccer. I have to kink my neck to look up at him, and I'm not short for a girl.

He assesses me, his eyes dancing with delight, and I wonder what he's thinking. "What would work on you, Andy?"

I swallow the lump in my throat—standing this close to him, the way he's looking at me. *That's what works for me*, my lady parts are screaming at me. But I'm not telling him that. "A girl can't give away all her secrets, Brad." I pause, racking my brain for something good to come back with. "How about this? Why don't you tell me exactly what you have in mind for this evening, you know, if I were to come back to your hotel room. Then I'll decide if it sounds worth my time or not." I almost whisper the words. I'm trying to act my confident self, but I'm melting from the heat he's radiating, and my mind is turning to mush.

He leans down, his mouth nearly touching my ear. "The hottest fucking night of your life, pretty girl. I promise, you won't regret it." He pulls back from me, the sexiest fucking smile ever crosses his face, and I know I'm screwed.

I'm not getting this guy's number to win a bet against my girlfriends.

I'm leaving here with him, and he knows it.

# CHAPTER TWO

### ANDY

No sooner have the doors to the elevator closed are Brad's hungry eyes set upon me. My mouth is dry, my heart pounding as he closes the gap between us, slamming me into the wall like he couldn't have waited another second to get his hands on me.

Fuck. He's so hot, the way his large frame dominates mine as he grabs me, holding me in place as his lips devour mine, his tongue invading my mouth. He tastes of whiskey, and it's such a massive turn-on.

My hands run through his short hair while his skate down my back, sending shivers in their wake. He stops when he reaches my butt, dragging me even closer to his hot body. Letting me feel the effect I have on him, with his hard length pressed into me. He lifts me, and my legs wrap around him as he pins me to the wall behind us, our bodies pressed even closer together.

Our kiss is feverish. I bite his lip and grind against him. I'm not one to hold back in the bedroom. I go after what I want, and right now, I couldn't care less that we're in a hotel elevator—I want him now.

I arch my back, pressing my breasts toward his chest, and his hand skims my tank, palming my breast, my nipples already hard and aching for his touch. I groan into his mouth as he rolls my nipple between his fingers.

The elevator dings and another couple enters. Shit. We must have forgotten to actually press the button for his floor, and we're still just sitting in the lobby. Whoops.

We pull our mouths away from each other and I slide my legs back down to the ground. "Sorry, we got a little carried away," I offer to the bitch death-staring us. She turns up her nose and looks to the front of the elevator.

I try to stifle my giggle, but when I look at Brad, his face says it all—he thinks this is just as funny as I do. It's pretty hilarious. We just got caught practically dry-humping in the elevator. I burst out laughing, and he pulls me back toward him, hugging me from behind. "Behave, pretty girl. They don't look impressed," he says softly into my neck.

"I'm sorry," I whisper, trying to get the laughter bubbling up inside of me under control. He wraps his arms around me. I can feel his hard cock pressed into my butt. My lady parts throb with anticipation of what is about to come. When are we going to get to his room already and away from these stuck-up snobs, who have probably never had a fun day in their lives, judging by their stone-cold expressions?

His hotel was just a short walk up the street from the club, and I'm glad. The sexual tension between us wasn't going to last much longer before I pulled him into an alley and asked him to fuck me up against a wall. It was a real possibility. I texted the girls to say where I was headed. I'm a little reckless in life but I don't have a death wish, and I knew they would worry.

We arrive at the third floor and the other couple steps

out, though not before giving us another dirty look. The poor dude is probably just jealous his missus is so stuck up he doesn't get to have any fun. "Try finding her clit tonight, she looks like she needs a release. An orgasm would help," I call to them as the doors close. The woman looks murderous, and the guy tries to calm her.

"Andy." Brad pulls me toward him.

"What? I don't know what her problem was, I was trying to help." I laugh.

I spin back in Brad's arms, locking our lips again. I need another taste of him. The next floor is his, and we clumsily make our way out, bumping into walls, still attached to each other. God, I have never wanted anybody so badly in my life.

His door is right across the hall, and he pulls a key card from his pocket and swipes us in, our bodies still intertwined. I stumble backward, but he holds onto me, slamming the door behind us.

Alone in his room at last.

His lips are back on mine, and I kiss him like I could die if I don't get another taste of him. I shrug out of my jacket, letting it fall to the floor so he can touch me. His hands run up my arms then settle in my hair. He pulls back from me, his gorgeous eyes looking straight into mine. He slips the bobby pins from my hair, letting it fall down my back, long and thick. His hands comb through the messy strands as he gazes at me.

I pant, trying to catch my breath from that kiss. Something strange is happening here, and I pull back from him, completely dropping my eyes. His stare is intense, and it scares the shit out of me. What was that look? It was way too intense for a quick fuck, and that's all this is because that's all I do, and he's off back to England in the morning.

He shouldn't be looking at me like that. My heart is pounding, this is all so extreme.

Teenage-me fantasized about what it would be like to kiss him, but this was so much more than I could have imagined. I need a little space for a second. My head is swimming with the alcohol I consumed and the deep need I have for him.

I stroll around the room, taking in my surroundings. It's fancy, large, with floor-to-ceiling windows framed with luxurious drapes, and sliding doors that open onto a wraparound balcony. The color pallet is neutral with a hint of blue, and it looks ultra-modern and trendy. I'm not new to expensive hotels or luxurious accommodation; my family did plenty of travel when I was growing up, and it was usually in the nicest places money could buy. This place would have cost a bit, even if it is just for the night.

Brad kicks off his shoes, removing his jacket and placing it over a chair. I can't help but watch him as he moves around the room. He has so much confidence, one of the things I find sexiest in a man. I know he's quite a bit older than me, must be close to ten years, but tonight, like this, it's not like you can even tell—and besides, I don't care. I like older guys, they know what they're doing. Not like guys my age who only seem to care about themselves in the bedroom.

"Drink?" he asks, taking two glasses and pouring himself a whiskey from a bottle at the bar.

"Nah, I'm good." I'm already a little drunk, and I want to remember every second of this.

I can hardly believe I'm in Brad Swift's hotel room. Sixteen-year-old Andy would be high-fiving me, freaking, if she knew. I take a seat on the end of the plush bed and remove my boots. Then pad over the super-soft carpet to the glass doors, sliding them open and exploring the balcony, stopping to lean on the railing and admire the view. The view of Los Angeles is lovely at this hour, lights twinkling. The night air is also mighty refreshing after the heat we had today.

I hear Brad follow me out and place his glass on the outdoor table. His warm arms wrap around me. "Nice view, hey?"

"It's beautiful."

"You're beautiful," he says, and the way he says it does things to my insides. He thinks I'm attractive. I don't think it's just a line so I'll sleep with him, I'm pretty sure he already knows I'm a sure thing. It feels like he really believes it.

I feel a flutter within, and I don't like it. This is supposed to be just a quick opportunistic fuck, that's all, I have to remind myself. I don't do anything more than that, ever, with anyone.

I turn around in his arms, reaching up on my tippy-toes. I kiss him, distracting myself from the feelings inside. His tongue swipes through my mouth. I run my hands over his chest. I can feel how muscular he is through the cotton fabric of his baby-blue shirt. This is what I need to concentrate on. His hot fucking body and what it can do for me.

I reach his top button, wanting to see what's underneath. As we kiss, I unbutton each of the buttons then push his shirt over his shoulders and down his arms, forcing it to the floor. My hands drift straight back to his hard chest. His body is insane. I knew it would be.

I push him back to the balcony till he hits the edge, then lower to my knees, unbuckling his suit pants. They fall to his ankles, and I drag his briefs down his legs. His massive erection springs free. He leans back on the balcony railing, looking every bit the Adonis he is. I will distract him and the way he's making me feel by doing the thing we're really here for.

"What's your plan, pretty girl? You're happy to do this out here on the balcony?"

"If you are." I lick the tip of his cock, tasting him.

He reaches down, cupping my chin so I'm forced to look into his eyes. "You like the thought someone might see us?"

"I just don't care if they do." I roll my tongue over my lips as my hands massage his hardened length. Fuck, he feels good, so hard. Pre-cum beads at the tip, and I reach down to lick it off, tasting his salty arousal. He lets out a low growl, and I take him into my mouth. I tip my head back farther, taking all of him in, sucking back and forth as he watches my every move with dark eyes.

"You look so hot like that, my cock filling your mouth." His hands drop to the back of my head, and he eases me onto him. I love the tight grip he has on my hair, his dominance. He feeds his cock into my mouth a few times then pulls my hair back, pulling me off him completely. "What you're doing is unbelievable, but I need to be buried deep in you now."

He pulls me to standing in front of him. "Is that right?"

"Yes. Get these clothes off now." He tugs at my tank top, pulling it over my head, and I quickly unbuckle the fly on my jeans, pushing them down my legs and kicking them to the side.

He gives me a slow, sexy smile. "No underwear."

"Nope." I should be cold, being that we're outside in the night air, but I'm so hot for him I don't even feel the temperature. He stands back, admiring me, and I smirk at him. "Like what you see, baby?"

His eyes scan over my body, eating me up, and I love it.

I'm not shy. I want his attention on me. To see the way my naked body affects him makes me just as hot for him. I run my hands up my side, cupping my breasts and squeezing.

"You have no idea. Your body is scorching, Andy."

Before I know it, his hungry lips are back on mine, roughly kissing me as his hands roam over my skin, following the path I just took. It feels like they're everywhere, over my butt, up my torso to my breasts. He palms them roughly, plucking my nipples. I need to touch him just as badly. I reach for his hardened length, stoking him, desperate to have him inside me but not wanting to rush anything either.

His kiss moves down my neck to my breast as he takes a nipple in his mouth and sucks hard, with a pop when he pulls back. My back presses into the balcony behind me and I moan loudly in pleasure. He moves to the other, doing the same. Then he travels back up to my lips, his hand falling between my legs, exploring my slick folds.

As his kiss deepens, he plunges two thick fingers inside, and I cry out at the sudden movement. He swallows my sounds with his kiss, still working his fingers back and forth savagely, and I cling to him, enjoying every thrust. He's rough and skilled with his fingers and continues to pump me, and it feels unbelievable, but I need more.

"Protection," I cry. Telling him where I need this to go. He pulls his fingers free and grabs up his suit pants, pulling his wallet out and removing a foil packet. I take it from him. Of course he was prepared tonight. This is what he would do on the regular. I try to push that thought away. Why should I care? It's what I do as well.

My hands return to him, rolling it onto his large length, then pulsing it a couple of times. He's rock hard, throbbing with need for me, and I love it. The way his body craves mine in the moment before our bodies meet.

With one more dark, lustful look, he spins me around so I'm looking out over the balcony, then spreads my legs wider. I flick my hair over my shoulder, turning my face so I can watch him as he grabs my hip with one hand, his cock with the other. He lines himself up and slams straight in. I hang on to the balcony as a scream escapes me, and his hand comes to my mouth, covering it.

He pulls me back into his hard body. "Shh, pretty girl, we're outside, the people below will be able to hear you," he whispers into my ear, sending a wave of excited goosebumps over my skin. Right now, I couldn't give a fuck if anyone else hears. He's massive, and he just slammed straight into me.

I whimper into his palm. He places kisses down my neck, giving me time to adjust to his size. I roll my hips back on to him, slowly circling, stretching myself, and he gives me the time I need to catch up.

Leaving his hand across my mouth as he moves in short, sharp thrusts, his other hand comes around the front, playing with my throbbing clit. I'm locked into place against his strong body. He has all the control here, and I love it.

The sounds of people chattering below becomes obvious as a rowdy group walks past. We're four stories high, behind a balcony, I'm sure they can't quite see what we're doing, but I love the idea of getting caught. It makes it all the more exciting.

I close my eyes, concentrating on what Brad is doing to me, the circular motion sending thrills through my whole body as he rubs my most sensitive spot with his skilled fingers. The sensation is almost too much to take. I get the familiar tell sweep over me, and my body convulses around his cock, waves of pleasure throbbing through me. Again, I scream into his hand, unable to control myself.

When I'm done quivering, he pulls his hand away from my mouth, bending me over farther. I don't even care what he does right now, I'm having an out-of-body experience. This is all so hot, so much more than I could have envisioned when I agreed to come back here tonight.

Grabbing me with both hands around my hips, his fingertips bite into my flesh as he really lets me have it, pumping me hard a few times before I feel his body tense and he slams into me one last time, filling me. I whimper out a cry, but I loved every last bit of it.

"Fuck, that was hot." He stills, pulling out of me, and I turn around and drop my head to his chest, searching for words.

"Oh my God," I pant, trying to catch my breath. That was so...

He scoops me up in his muscular arms and carries me inside to the bed where he lays me down carefully. His passionate gaze hasn't lost its intensity. I pull the comforter back and climb into bed. He's right there with me, rolling on top of me, his lips back on mine.

I can't stop kissing him. I don't want to. I feel this crazy amount of attraction to him, one that can't be satisfied with just one round. That scene on the balcony was insane, and I get the impression we're far from done here tonight. I want so much more and so does he.

I have just met my match on the soccer field and in the bedroom. It's almost a shame I only get to have him for one night. I could definitely get used to this.

. . .

I wake in the early hours of the morning, the sky just lightening in pale pinks and oranges. The view is just as stunning at this hour. I stretch a little, trying not to wake up the gorgeous man next to me. My body aches, but it's a delicious pain, one of being more satisfied than I think I have ever been.

Last night was something else. Brad convinced me to stay the night with a promise of buffet breakfast this morning, and how could I resist? I love my food. And I wouldn't mind taking that massive jet tub for a spin before we get out of here as well.

Not to mention that, for the first time in a really long time, I didn't feel like running straight from the room after we finished fucking. I wanted to stay and have his arms wrapped around me as I slept. He is someone entirely different from who I thought he would be, and I liked whatever it was we shared.

I know he'll go back to England today and I will never see him again, but having that night together was amazing and something I will cherish forever. Because honestly, I've never experienced that level of connection with another human before. It was something else.

I tiptoe to the bathroom, and on the way back, I grab my phone from my bag. There are two missed calls and a text from Jasmine, all from last night. I flick open the message and feel the color drain from my face. My euphoric buzz is gone instantly as I read her words.

**Jasmine:** Abort mission, the asshole is married!!

My hands tremble. Brad's married? My actual worst-case scenario with a one-night stand. What the actual fuck.

Why didn't I look at my phone last night? I don't remember ever hearing about him getting married in the tabloids, but I suppose it could be more recent, when he dropped off their radar.

I glance over to where he's sleeping. He is fucking perfect, of course he's married. I cover my mouth so I don't cry out loud and wake him. I need to get the hell out of here before he wakes up and I kill him. Angry tears prick at my eyes. If there is one thing I hate in this world, it's fucking cheaters. And to think this guy has had hero status in my mind for years. That two-timing piece of shit. Oh God, his poor wife. I'm the worst person in the world.

Shit, shit, shit, I need to get out of here.

I scoop up my clothes from the bedroom floor and take them to the bathroom, rushing to pull them on. I grab a lipstick from my bag and leave a note on the bathroom mirror for the adulterating dickhead. Because I can't help myself. I don't want to face him, but I fucking want him to know why I'm taking off. He won't get away with this completely.

When I'm done, I rush back into the room, grabbing my boots and slamming the door as I go. I hope it wakes him with a fright. My hands are shaking I'm so mad with him, with myself.

How did I let this happen? I just spent the night with someone else's husband. I know I'm not perfect. I sleep around a lot but never with someone else's man. I feel dirty, cheap, and used. I try to think back to last night. I definitely didn't see a wedding band on his hand. He must have planned to do the dirty on his wife while he was out of town and took it off.

I storm down the hall of the hotel, not caring who I wake up at the early hour, and decide to take the stairs. I don't need to relive the memory of the elevator. He's lucky I don't know where his car is or I would mess it up and go all Carrie Underwood on it.

His line from last night comes back to me: *I promise you won't regret it*. My fucking ass! I have never regretted anything more in my life. I let him use me, and what's worse, he got under my skin in more ways than just physically. I felt something for someone for the first time in forever, and that makes me the biggest idiot ever, because I fucking know better.

# CHAPTER THREE

### BRAD

It's 4pm when I arrive at the main soccer training field for the Angels, Los Angeles's professional women's team. It's been a month since I was here last for my interview with the club's general manager, about a job at the time I wasn't even sure I wanted.

This wasn't the plan for my career. My entire life had been set up to play soccer at the highest level until I could retire, then I would work out the rest. And that's exactly what I did for ten years. I played for Chelsea as the striker, one of the best players in the league. I still hold the record for the highest goals scored in a year. But I was forced into early retirement two years ago when I was injured playing the season final. I was taken out completely with an illegal kick to the back of my knee. The blow shattered my kneecap and any hope of me ever playing again. My team went on to win the final with the penalty goal kick they got because of it, but that was it for me. Even after reconstructive surgery. I can walk on it fine, but I won't ever play again —not at the level I would like to, anyway.

I was completely devastated. Soccer was my life, and I

couldn't see what my next move should be, so I took two years off to concentrate on the life I was building with my then girlfriend Madeline.

I'd been in limbo since, until a good friend of mine and the assistant coach here, Ava, told me about the coach position opening up for one of the top women's teams in the National Women's Soccer League of America. So I jumped on a plane to find out more. Turns out they thought I was a perfect match, and here I am, relocated across the world for a second time and starting all over again.

I seek out the current coach and move to stand with him, where he's making calls from the sidelines. "Hi, Mitch."

He turns to me with surprise. "Brad, you made it. I thought you wouldn't be here until next week." He holds out his hand for me to shake.

"There was nothing keeping me in England, and besides, I figured the sooner I get to know the team the better, right? The season has already started."

He gives me a nod, but I can tell he's conflicted. "It's good to have you here. The girls have been kept in the dark about the change. I thought it was for the best until you got here. They don't know I'm sick," he says quietly.

I feel for him, I really do. This must be hard, handing over his team. And for this reason, as well, but he needs to focus on getting better. "Understandable. I can just shadow you until you're ready to tell them," I offer, trying to ease the blow for him.

"No, man, we can tell them tonight. I need to take a step back. I start treatment next week, and the doctors don't know how it's going to go, so it's best you're here to support them." I'm sure the news will go down badly. Mitch has been the coach of this team for twelve years, and he is extremely respected by his players. They have been getting consistently better, and last year even made the final, losing in a penalty shootout.

"Alright, mate, no worries. I'm ready to take over. Give me a rundown on your players." I watch the team running drills from the sidelines. They're not bad, but I can still see room for improvement if we're going to win the comp this year. We'll need to bring something truly exceptional, because all the other teams will be watching us as the ones to beat. The pressure is high for a new coach, but pressure isn't something that has ever bothered me before. I thrive on it.

"Girls, let's break into defense and attack. Luna, I want to see you running the sideline then crossing it to either Darcy or Andrea." The team takes off into the drill he was talking about. I watch them, taking notes in my head with the names he's giving me. It's hard to make out faces, as the light is low. There's a blonde, the striker. She has a great boot on her, and her accuracy is spot-on. "Who's the blonde with the braids?" I ask Mitch.

"Andrea Harper, she's the one to watch. She's a firecracker, full of sass, and runs her mouth when things don't go her way, but she's one of the best in the game. A massive fan of yours, as well."

The way she plays, she reminds me of myself. You can tell she gives it everything she has, absolutely no fear. But attitude is something I won't stand for. I'll need to work closely with her, because I know she will be our key to winning this year.

The team finishes running drills and makes their way back into the training shed for a rundown of this week's game. They chat among themselves noisily. The vibe for this team is positive, and why wouldn't it be? They're having a great year so far. It's a good thing, but from my experience, you're only as good as your last game. Things can change quickly.

We make our way up to the meeting room and I see a familiar face as soon as I walk in. Ava runs over to me, throwing her arms around me in an embrace.

"Brad, it's so good to see you," she says warmly.

"You too." I hug her back. Ava is the assistant coach and the one who told me about this job. When she heard about the opening, she knew she wanted someone she could work with, and she also knew I was available. We lean against the tables at the back, waiting for Mitch to talk to his team.

In the light of the shed, it's the first time I've a chance to see the players' faces. I try to take them in and ask Mitch names and position. He points them out, and I take it all in as best I can. When he points out Andrea, my jaw nearly hits the floor. *I'm a mechanic who knows nothing about soccer* my ass. It's the girl I met at the club when I came to LA for my interview. Now I know exactly what Mitch was talking about with the attitude. This girl has it in spades. And worse, after the night we shared, I already know she fucking hates me with a passion.

I massage the back of my neck uncomfortably. This situation is not ideal. I just hope she doesn't say anything or this new job might be in jeopardy before I even start.

"You nervous or something?" asks Ava, giving me a look.

"Nah, I'm good."

She gives me a look then turns her attention back to Mitch as he addresses the group. I stand back, leaning up against a table, giving him the space to say what he needs to. "Girls, I have some news. I have been given some unfortunate health news. I have been diagnosed with Non-Hodgkin's Lymphoma. My prognosis is good, but I need to start treatment immediately. Meaning I need to take a step

# THE COACH

back from actively coaching the team." The gasps and mutters of concern for their leader are voiced. You can see how much the team adores him. They're going to be some very big shoes to fill.

Ava gives my arm a squeeze of encouragement. And I'm glad she's here. I get the feeling I'm going to need someone on my side for this adjustment.

I watch Andrea; she looks like she's going to cry. The girl beside her takes her hand and laces it with hers. As another comes to stand with them, the three of them huddle together, exchanging looks as Mitch explains what he needs to say. What a terrible situation.

Andrea's expression changes to anger immediately as her gaze finds me and she connects the dots. What are the chances that the one and only girl I've slept with since my marriage fell apart is the best player on the new team I'm going to be coaching? Pretty fucking low, I would say, and yet somehow, this is the scenario playing out before me.

Andy—or Andrea—bumps arms with the small black-haired girl next to her, and she narrows her eyes at me as well, with her best death stare. She has clearly filled her friend in on what happened. Fuck, I'm screwed. My team is going to hate me before I've even started.

And it's all just a misunderstanding.

The note she left in red lipstick on my bathroom mirror, the morning after the night we spent together, was enough to tell me why she left in the early hours with a hard slam of the hotel door. She thinks I was cheating on my wife with her. But that couldn't be further from the truth. Yes, I'm still technically married, but we're separated, so much so that we're now living in different countries. Me in America, trying to start over again, and her with my ex-best friend and teammate, Byron, back in England.

Mitch continues, "But it's not all bad news. We have been lucky enough to gain the best striker in the game as your new coach. He will be working closely with Ava as he learns the ins and outs of our team dynamics. Girls, meet Brad Swift. Your new coach."

All sets of eyes are now on me, and the enormity of the situation I have signed up for really settles in. I plaster on a confident smile and step forward to introduce myself to the team. Somehow, standing in front of twenty fierce female athletes is one of the most intimidating things I have ever done. Their eyes are all glued to me. They've just been dealt the devastating blow that their coach is leaving them, and I'm supposed to somehow tell them I know what I'm doing and it's all going to be okay. When really I have no fucking idea what I'm doing. I've never coached before. I know how to play, and yes, I was the captain for many years, and I'm great at encouraging others, but it's not the same thing.

I take a deep breath. "Ladies, I'm sure the news of losing such a wonderful coach is devastating, to say the least, but if you put your trust in me, I'm sure we will be able to work together and bring home a win this year."

The scowl I get from Andy and her friends tells me she's not on board with this at all. I'm going to have my work cut out for me to win her over. Or she will just have to get over herself and realize I'm in charge now, and she's going to have to do what I say or suffer the consequences. But most of the others on the team offer warm, friendly smiles, and I relax a little.

There's chatter among the girls, and I flip over the white board to explain how we're going to win our next game. Ava gives me a nod of approval, and Mitch agrees with me, and most of the team looks satisfied with what I have to say. Mitch dismisses them and they start to filter out.

Some of the players come and introduce themselves, excited to be on my team. Maybe this won't be so bad after all.

My line of sight keeps tracking back to her. I had hoped I would be able to contact her once I officially moved here. That night we had together was unlike anything I have ever experienced, and now I guess it makes more sense. She's more like me than I even knew that night. Younger than I had guessed, not because she looks older but because she just came across with such confidence, I couldn't have imagined she was only twenty-four. And she left such an impression on me, I was determined to track her down when I had everything sorted.

But now this changes everything. And even more than I already wanted to, I need to set her straight tonight before this gets any more out of hand.

---

ANDY

After practice, our coach Mitch gathered us all and explained that he's unwell and will be stepping down as our coach. I'm devastated. He is the most amazing mentor I have ever had. I've grown so much in the last two years, all because of him. I'm not one to show my emotions openly, but I can feel tears collecting in my eyes. I try to blink them away. He's too sick to train us. Luna takes my hand, giving it a squeeze, and Darcy comes to stand by our side looking just as upset.

Then I notice him. An uncomfortable flush of heat sweeps over me. I didn't think I would ever see him again. But it's the devil himself—or at least that's how I have painted him in my head for the last four weeks. Fucking Brad Swift. What is he doing here standing behind our coach next to Ava, all relaxed, leaning up against a table, with that stupid smug smirk on his face? I want to slap it off.

He looks so cool and calm and gorgeous, and I hate him even more. My pulse increases. That teamed with the burning feeling of my skin makes me feel like I need to get out of here. Why is my body reacting to the sight of him, like I want to jump his bones, when I know what an asshole he is? I'm more messed up than I originally thought.

Mitch says the words I knew were coming. Brad is our new coach.

I glance at the girls, with fear in my eyes, I'm sure. This is too much, and I bite the inside of my mouth to stop the tears. My beautiful friends' faces say it all. Fuck, this cheating asshole is our new coach. I want to die or kill him. I'm being dramatic, I know, but I don't even want to look in his direction, much less see him four times a week at practice, then games, and have him tell me what to do. He can't be my mentor like Mitch has been. This is total bullshit.

He steps forward and I send daggers with my eyes. "Ladies, I'm sure the news of losing such a wonderful coach is devastating to say the least, but if you put your trust in me, I'm sure we will be able to work together and bring home a win this year." He's smooth and charming as hell, and the other members of my team eat up his every word. They'll all be swooning over him. If I didn't know the truth about him, I would be the same. But I do!

I narrow my eyes at him, burning a hole through his skull, and right on cue, he glances my way. I'm not going to make this easy for him, not at all. I'm going to make him suffer for what he did to his wife and me. I've thought a couple of times over the last few weeks about contacting her and telling her what he did—what *we* did—but how do you even do that?

He tells us his game plan for this weekend then dismisses us.

Luna grabs me by both hands. "Oh my fucking God! What are you going to do, babe?"

I blink back at her, my mind totally blank. "I think I'm in shock. Let's get out of here, I need time to process this before I work out what to do."

I grab my bag and approach Mitch, throwing my arms around him in an embrace. "I know I'm a major pain in your ass but thank you for everything you've done for me. I wouldn't be the player I am if it weren't for you," I tell him.

I wish I could do something to help him. He has been so influential in my life, I wish I could do something to give back to him. Saying thank you doesn't really seem good enough.

"Thanks, Coach," says Luna shyly from next to me.

He pats me on the back, probably feeling awkward as fuck that I'm hugging him. So I pull back before I start blubbering on his shoulder.

He smiles proudly at us both. "Andrea, you have the ability to go far, just don't let your attitude affect your game. And be nice to the new guy, I saw the look you gave him. He deserves a chance, just like you gave me."

"I didn't go easy on you when I first started here either." I smirk, remembering what I was like. People have to earn my respect, and Mitch has. But Brad definitely has not! "I'll try." It's the best I can offer to him, and I'm saying that for Mitch's sake and not Brad's, because fuck that. Brad is on my shit list, and I intend to give him hell.

"Good. I'll still be around if you need me."

He turns his attention to Luna. "You were on fire tonight. Keep that up this season."

"Thanks. Good luck with everything, Coach." She smiles, and we go to walk away. I want out of this room before I have to look at Brad again. He makes my blood boil.

"Andrea, can I see you for a sec before you go?" Brad's deep voice calls across the room. Ahh, that accent. He sounds fucking sexy, and it makes me hate him even more. Damn it. I don't want it to, but it takes me back to that night, before I knew he was married. His voice has a seriously dangerous effect on me. But then I remember I hate this man.

I roll my eyes at Luna. "I'll catch a lift with Darcy and see you back home," she says, offering me a sympathetic smile.

I turn and stalk reluctantly over to him, folding my arms over my chest in an overly dramatic fashion. I wait for whatever it is he just has to say to me. He looks serious, so uptight and more his age, different to the fun-loving guy I met that night. He can't seem to find his words, and I wonder why when he's now confronted with his shitty decision.

"What do you want?" I snap, giving him the death stare of the century. He might have just been announced as our new coach, but it doesn't mean I have to be happy about it. Or play nice.

He looks completely unfazed by my attitude, and I want to push him, piss him off just like he has me. "Just a quick chat. I think unfortunately I have given you the wrong first impression." His gaze takes me in, and I can't tell from the way he looks at me what he's thinking, but it feels like there's more swirling in the air between us than just my hate for him.

I glance around the room; it's empty, just the two of us left. Good, I can actually speak my mind without being overheard. My eyes return to his and I place my hands on my hips. "I think you're fucking right about that."

His stare heats even more, and I can see how easy it's going to be to push his buttons. "Andrea. I'm your coach, do not speak to me like that. While we are at training and the games, you are to respect me, no matter how you might feel."

I narrow my eyes at him, hoping I match his intensity. It kills me that he has authority over me. But I'm also not scared enough to rein in my crazy. This dude deserves everything I throw at him. "You weren't my coach when you bent me over your hotel balcony and fucked me from behind, though, were you." I poke him again. "When you cheated on your wife with me." I growl, the heat radiating off my face the madder I get with him. I want to storm out of here, make a scene, now that I've said my piece, but then I wouldn't get to know what it is that he feels the need to say to me. And part of me wants to hear it, what his pathetic excuse could possibly be to sleep around on his poor wife.

He crosses his arms and straightens his stance. He is all dominating male. His eyes darken and he talks down to me. It's not hard when he's so tall, but I hate it just the same. "I understand you're angry, but things aren't always what they seem. You don't know my situation. And let's get one thing straight right now—I didn't cheat on my wife with you, like you think."

He didn't? But Jasmine worked out that he had a wife, I don't get it. I blink back at him. I look to his hand. Still no wedding band. Lies, I'm sure, to get me back on his side now that he's a part of my team. "How could that be possible? I know you're married," I snap. It was all there online, pictures of him and his stunning wife.

He doesn't answer right away, just stares right back at me, as if contemplating what to say next. I notice a flash of hurt in his eyes, then he answers me. "If you must know, we're separated. She left me two months ago for my best mate, another player on my team, Byron Stanford." His face softens when he says it, and I see a glimpse of the real him, not the stuffy coach trying to put on an act. This Brad is vulnerable, he's been hurt. Really hurt, by the sounds of it.

I take a step back, feeling like a mega bitch for my snarky attitude and the way I just walked out on him that morning. This was not what I was expecting him to say at all. I came over here so prepared for a fight, because over the last month, I have painted him as the bad guy in my head. Hated him for what I thought he'd done. But the bitch cheated on him with Byron Stanford.

The name rings a bell straight away; he's often in the tabloids for having a reputation for dating beautiful high-society women. I don't know a lot about him other than he also plays for Chelsea, so it must have really stung when Brad worked it out.

I guess I was quick to judge because, from my experience, men can't be trusted. And in this case, I guess women can be just as bad. One of the reasons I don't do relationships. Not once did I think this could have been a misunderstanding. *Good one, Andy.*

I look at his features and take him in properly for the first time tonight. I can see the pain he carries. What do I say to what he just told me? It was too personal for a coach to be telling one of his players, and I feel like we have already crossed too many lines.

I swallow the lump in my throat. I'm not going to apologize, cause I don't do that, but I do feel bad for him. "Well, that's shitty," I offer.

"Yeah, it was." He sighs, and the way he does makes me feel like me believing him was really important to him. That was weighing heavily on him. He looks me over and I wonder what he's thinking. I really don't know anything about him at all, except he was an exceptional soccer player and he is fucking insane in bed. And that attraction I felt that night, it's still swirling through the air between us. My body feels alive in a strange way just standing this close to him.

Maybe it would have been better if he was the asshole I thought, would have made it easier to ignore this chemistry. Now I have to get through this year knowing my coach has seen me naked. Not only that, he was the best fuck of my life. And even worse, he made me feel things I have never felt before, and that alone is very, very dangerous.

He drops his arms, looking a little more relaxed. "I think you owe me some sort of explanation." He takes one of my braids and flicks it over my shoulder. "Andy, the mechanic who knows nothing about soccer?" He raises a brow, a small smile playing on his lips. He has me there. I was lying through my teeth.

I laugh a little. "Ahh, yeah. About that. Well, my friends call me Andy, not Andrea, and it was a kind of stupid drunk challenge thingy between me and my roommates."

"Elaborate," he says with a little smirk.

"You know when you get a bit drunk and play games with your friends? This one was who could get the first phone number from a guy while using a fake identity." I pull a face because this must look ridiculously immature to him.

"Can't say I have ever played a game like that, but I

guess that explains the identity change. Just tell me one thing. You knew who I was, didn't you?"

I give him a sassy smile. He was really worried some random girl didn't know who he was. What an ego. "Yeah, I love soccer. I knew who you were." I'm not telling him he was the poster boy on my wall. There is no way he needs his head inflated that badly.

He grins, as if proud that I did. "I knew it." He grows a little more serious. "Are we going to be okay?" he asks, a little uncertain. "Or is this going to be a problem?" He gestures between us, and I have to wonder if he's referring to the one-night stand we had or the fucking hot tension I can feel radiating between us just being so close to him again.

"Yeah." I shrug, but there's no confidence to my voice or my stance. I don't know if we are going to be alright this year at all. How can I answer that tonight? But we have to be. I will just have to forget about that night, pretend it didn't happen. "Let's just start fresh right now. Whatever happened that night, it wasn't us, just two strangers," I offer, because in all honesty, I don't really know what else to do. I've never been in this type of situation before, and it's uncomfortable as fuck. And the truth is, the last thing I need is the rest of my team thinking I have anything going on with him and that I'm getting special treatment. Other than my two besties, the rest of my team aren't as friendly with me. Jealously is a curse when you're the best. And I don't need more drama.

He gives an understanding nod. "Okay, if that's what you want to do?"

The way he asks it, what is that? I thought I was making this easy for him, letting him off the hook. Isn't that what he wants to do? I'm pretty positive he doesn't want anyone else to know what happened. I mean, we didn't know each other at all, but it doesn't look good to the club. "Yes, this definitely needs to be left in the past and never talked about again," I say with more confidence in my voice.

"Alright, Andy. Guess I will see you at training tomorrow."

I offer a smile. The use of my nickname isn't lost on me. Does he think we're friends? And why do I kinda hope he does. "Yes, tomorrow," I mutter.

I know I'm supposed to be walking away from him, but I can't remove my eyes from his. He breaks eye contact first and slowly leaves the room, me watching his every step. I'm left wondering what the fuck that just was. It felt like a meaningful moment between us, when it really shouldn't have.

One minute I fucking hated his guts, and now I'm back to feeling, I don't know... confused? How the hell am I going to get through this year now?

## CHAPTER FOUR

ANDY

I drove home in a bit of a daze, the conversation I just had with Brad running through my head on repeat. The way he looked at me... made me feel by just being close to him. And I could see he was just as thrown by all of this. Now I'm sitting in the driveway of the modern four-bedroom house I share with my sister and two friends. I think I'm still in shock.

Brad Swift is my new coach. And not a cheating asshole. And the sexiest man on the planet. My body is still swirling with excitement from just talking to him.

I guess I should get moving, go inside. The other girls are probably wondering where I am. I grab my bag and make my way up the driveway. Our house is very modern, all white rendered walls on the outside with a garden of cacti lining the driveway. I'm not one of those spoiled brats who doesn't know how lucky she is to have a privileged upbringing. I know how blessed I am. I have always had whatever I needed and wanted, no questions asked, and my sisters are the same. My parents bought this place for me and Jas a few years back, and we pay rent to them, but one day it will be ours to divide up and share the profits between us.

My family have always been quite well off because my dad was a movie producer in the eighties and nineties and made a shit ton of money. My parents are trying to teach us how to make it on our own but giving us a hand at the same time, cause there is no way Jas and I would be able to afford a place like this if they didn't buy it.

Once inside, our place is all polished concrete floors and exposed-timber-beam ceilings with white-washed walls. It's light and bright and airy. Jassie and I have decorated with lots of house plants and warm furnishings in mustards and pinks. We love this place.

I drop my bag in the entry hall. I really need to take a shower, but first, I need to know what they make of the whole situation, cause I can't wrap my head around it.

I make my way through the house to the kitchen in search of what the girls are cooking that smells so delicious.

My sister is standing in the large fully equipped kitchen stirring something on the stove. She must hear me walk in and turns to me with a massive cheeky grin. Looks like she's already heard the latest development from the girls.

Luna is sitting at the breakfast bar, and Darcy must be in the shower. I can hear the water running. It makes me wish I hadn't told them all about what happened that night. But I'm not good at keeping stuff from my friends. If I were, it could have just been my dirty little secret—well, mine and Brad's. Now every practice until the end of the year is going to be awkward as fuck.

"So, what's new?" Jasmine smirks.

"Oh, nothing much," I sass, throwing Luna a look for telling her already.

"Not what I heard. Spill, Sissy. What was his pathetic

excuse for doing what he did?" She narrows her eyes at me, and I feel the anger still radiating off her. Cheating assholes are a very sore point with us Harper girls after what our older sister Amelia just went through with her husband.

I look at them both, wondering what I should actually say here. This has all gotten so weird so quickly that I'm not quite sure what the correct protocol in this area is. Brad is our coach now, and I'm pretty sure he wouldn't want the entire team knowing his personal business. He seemed reluctant to tell even me. "It's not really my story to tell, and if he is our coach now, we're going to need to respect his privacy. But let's just say he's not the cheating man-whore we all thought he was."

Luna raises a brow. "And you believe whatever story he told you?"

I shrug. "Yeah, it seemed legit," I say, trying not to get into it too much.

Swanning over to the big pot that Jasmine is stirring on the stove, I take a spoon to it. She swats me away. But not before I get a taste in. It's good, but I knew it would be. My sister can cook.

"I can't believe he's our new coach, and poor Mitch," says Luna.

"Have you girls seen the group chat that's erupted on messenger from the rest of the team?" calls Darcy from her bedroom.

I run back into the front hall where I dumped my bag and grab my phone, swiping up. The long list of messages flash up on my screen. Shit, the entire team is talking about Brad like he's some kind of man candy. I mean, he is, but not for any of them.

I walk back into the kitchen, sulking a little. He was supposed to be a fun one-night stand, and even then, I knew he was more than that. That's why I was so angry when I thought he was married. There was something there between us I haven't ever felt with anyone else. I didn't want to admit it until today, but now that I know he's no longer in a happy marriage because he has a cheating whore of a wife, I want to feel what we had again.

I'm glad he's separated from his wife and the night we had doesn't have to be tarnished, but I'm a little sad that now he's my coach, and that means it will have to be it for us. We can never share a night like that again. Now he belongs to my team, and our relationship can only ever be a work one.

"Everyone wants a little bit of what you had, Andy," snips Darcy, and if I didn't know better, I would say she was jealous for some reason. But she was the one who picked him for me that night, so I know that can't be the case.

I'm sure the look I throw her says it all. *Well, they can back the fuck off, he's mine.* And as soon as I think it, I wonder what on earth is going through my head. He is most certainly not mine. And he never will be. I had him for one night only.

"Too bad he's our coach, hey, babe? And it's completely against club policy for him to lay a finger on one of the girls on his team. No dating or sex, only coaching for Mr. Swift."

I glare at her, because what's her point? I didn't want to date him anyway. I wonder if that's even the true policy or if she's just full of shit. I make a note to look into that further, just because it would be good to know. Not because I'm thinking of fucking him again.

Can he get in trouble for what we've already done? No, he couldn't. He wasn't even our coach then. And he had no idea I even played. "Well, that's good, didn't want to go there again anyway. You of all people know I only do one-time things. Just tell the rest of the team about the policies and all this should be over with quickly!" I raise my brow to Darcy to emphasize what I'm saying.

The rest of the team seems to follow along with what she says, so she's the one to keep them in line. "Also, what you girls know about that night, it stays in this room. Do not tell anyone else on the team." I point between them. Jasmine zips her lips. Luna nods, and Darcy comes over to where I'm standing and wraps her arms around me in a hug.

"Stop getting your panties in a twist, babes, your secret is safe with us." She gives me a squeeze then pulls back with a laugh. "I'm so glad I picked him for you that night. This year is going to be so much fun now."

Luna laughs as well. Bitches. They like watching me suffer. I would be the same if the roles were reversed.

I shake my head at both of them. "Yeah, fun for you guys. I'm going to die every time I see him," I groan.

"You know we're only joking, babe. It's all going to be fine. Just pretend like it never happened. I'm sure he was a shitty lay anyway, wasn't he? All inflated ego and shit, it would have been all about him."

"Yeah, something like that," I huff, slumping down to sitting at the dinner table, knowing that it was most definitely not what it was like with him. God, every time I think about that night my insides clench and I get that weird fluttery feeling.

Jasmine plates up our food and places my bowl in front of me. "Hey, don't sulk. You'll be on to the next cute thing by the weekend and saying, Brad who?"

Darcy takes a seat beside me. "Speaking about this weekend, are we going out? I need to have a little fun."

Jasmine gives us a sneaky smile. "Sorry, ladies, I can't. I have another date lined up."

"Ooh, tell me all about the lucky guy." I'm trying not to

get my hopes up for her too much, but I just want her to be happy. If anyone deserves a nice relationship, it's her.

"No, not this time. I don't want to jinx anything." I give her a look like fuck, she'll be telling me all about it later when it's just the two of us.

I turn to my friend. "Okay. Luna?"

"Not this weekend. After our game, I'm spending the weekend with Rick."

We all look at her, confused. I haven't heard her talk about a Rick before.

"The guy who thinks I work at the sex shop." She laughs. "He wants to test out some of the new toys that have just arrived in." I shake my head at her. She ends up with a sex maniac out of that night, and I end up with a total mess. Typical.

"Looks like it's just the two of us then, girlfriend," Darcy says. "It'll be more fun that way."

I smirk at her, wondering what exactly she has in mind. Even after knowing her for nearly six years, Darcy is still a bit of a mystery to me. She never talks about anything too profound or serious, not her family or life back home. I know literally nothing about her past at all. She's not the deep conversation kind of girl who you really know well. Luna is the total opposite. She's an open book and I know every little detail about her life. But we love Darcy because she's the fun one, always up for a night out, so really, what does it matter if that's all we know about her?

## CHAPTER FIVE

### BRAD

THIS MORNING I'M WORKING WITH OUR ASSISTANT coach, Ava. Mitch was going to be here as well, but he ended up in the hospital last night, so she can give me the rundown. We will need to work closely together this year, anyway.

Ava and I go back a while. She did some work with Chelsea when I was playing for them. So I think we'll make the perfect team to bring home the victory this year.

Since finding out I had the job, I've been watching over last year's games and working on some new ideas for areas where we can improve, and I'm looking forward to sharing them with her and the team. I'm not sure the girls are going to be stoked about some of the changes, but they'll adapt, and I'm sure we'll be able to see the benefits before too long.

Ava hands me a clipboard with a flick of her hair and a smile. "Are you ready for today, Coach?"

I flip through the attached papers. There's the team roster with the positions they play and some of the drills she's been working on. Everything is very organized. She specializes in set pieces, for corners, free kicks, and penalties. As a new coach, I'm lucky to have her experience. "Yeah, I'm ready."

"I can take charge this morning if you want to observe, then you can take over this afternoon," she offers.

"Sounds good to me." It will give me a better chance to see what's going on and the team dynamics as well. Stuff I couldn't pick up by watching their games on a screen.

The girls filter into the parking lot, and I can't help but look for her. Andrea Harper. I know I need to put what happened behind me and move forward, but that's easier said than done when that night together was the first time I really connected with another person in a really fucking long time. I had plans for her, and finding out she was on my team last night was more than just disappointing. I know I should have picked up on it sooner, I've been studying this team for weeks, but somehow, I didn't connect the dots. Her name in soccer is Andrea, and mostly she goes by her surname Harper, and she looks so different in her sports gear to the all-black badass look she had going on the night I met her.

I don't see her getting out of her car and making her way to the field like the other players. Why am I not surprised that she can't be here on time like the rest of the team? Even Mitch said she has attitude that needs to be kept in check.

I stroll down to the field with Ava. A few of the players say hi and offer welcoming smiles. "You're certainly getting a lot of attention this morning," Ava says with a smirk. "I take it the team are happy about you being a new addition to our coaching staff."

"I'm sure they're all just being friendly with their new coach." I give her a look back that tells her I won't put up with anything else.

"Yes, all new coaches get that kind of flirtatious smile

and wave." She rolls her eyes, and if I didn't know better, I would think she is jealous.

We take our place on the side of the field, clipboard in hand. It feels odd to be on the sidelines, not taking the field with my team. My feet itch to play, it's all I've known. But I guess now I get to know something else, a new way of enjoying my favorite game.

As if Ava can read my mind, she offers me a sympathetic smile. "It must be strange for you not being one of the players."

"Yeah, it is. All I ever wanted to do, from the youngest age, was to be a professional soccer player. I guess life had other plans."

"And you were one of the best, not many can say that." She gives my arm a squeeze.

I offer her half a smile. I was the best; that's what hurts the most. The only dream I ever had for my life was to be the best soccer player possible.

I can remember practicing kicking for goal. My poor older sister, who was left in charge of me until Mum got home from work, would be dragged along to the local sports field, and I would shoot goals at her till she had enough of it, or it was dark and Mum called us home. Lucky for me my sister was a sick player herself. She was the top goalie in our area in the juniors. I like to think because of me.

The last two years since my accident have been the most difficult of my life. First my injury then surgery and rehab so I could walk on it again. Then coming to terms with the fact that I would never play again. I was miserable, and I know it's one of the reasons my new marriage suffered so much. Well, that and I should have known right from the start that Madeline only wanted to marry me for the status and money it gave her, and once I wasn't the top soccer star anymore, she was bored and went looking for something more exciting. She didn't go far to find it! When I caught her in bed with my best mate and the player who benefited most from my injury because he was now the top striker, that was it, my marriage was over as well.

My mum and sister begged me to come home to Australia, and I thought about it, starting over somewhere quiet away from the limelight, but I would never have been happy with that. That would feel like running away. Soccer is my life, and if the only way I can still be a part of this world is to coach, then that's what I'm going to do.

As I watch the girls warm up, I know I've made the right choice. A fresh start in a new country where I don't have to be haunted by the past, because I will never run into Madeline, and I can move on.

Ava runs the girls through the drill for this morning. Today we have to work on cardio. The girls follow her instructions and split into two groups, starting the drill.

I glance back to the parking lot. Where is she? I check my watch. She's now twenty minutes late. She is supposed to be the best player on the team, the captain, and she can't bother to show up on time to train.

A black motorbike speeds into the lot, and the rider parks then runs toward the changing shed, removing her helmet. I can see it's Andy, her blonde braids running down her back. She turns to me and mouths *sorry*. Of course she rides a bike. She is like the female equivalent of me ten years ago. And I'm not sure why that bothers me so much, but it might be the way she looks so fucking hot doing it.

And I'm her coach now so I can't be thinking of her like that.

I give her a stern look in return. She might have had her last coach wrapped around her little finger, but if she thinks she can get away with this kind of behavior with me, she is mistaken. Cocky soccer players who think they know it all and don't have to follow the rules like the rest of the team don't go far. I should know, I was one of them, until I was pulled into line by a coach who knew better. And this girl has the chance to go really far, but only if she gets out of her own way and listens to those around her who have the experience.

Moments later, she comes running down the hill. She's ditched the leather jacket and is in her training shirt and shorts, barefoot, with socks, boots, and shinpads in her hands. The way my body reacts to her instantly needs to change. We had that one night, and as she said yesterday, it has to stay in the past. It can never happen again.

"Sorry I'm late, I'm having a shitty morning," she says as she drops down beside me and starts to get her boots on. I notice the way Ava looks her over with a disapproving stare.

I return my gaze to the girls on the field in front of me, trying not to focus on her more than I need to. "I don't know what Mitch let you girls get away with, but you turn up late again, you won't play the next game," I say sharply.

I can feel her eyes flick back up to me angrily, even though I give her no attention. "You're kidding me, right? You know I'm the best player on the team, and they won't win without me," she says smugly, standing. I can feel the heat coming off her as she glares at me.

I tilt my head to her. "I don't care how good you think you are, Andrea. If you can't follow my rules, you won't play. So don't let it happen again."

She glares at Ava, and I wonder if there's some sort of bad blood between them because the two of them don't seem very fond of each other. Then she gives me one last look before she takes off to join the rest of the team. Mumbling under her breath that I'm an asshole.

"Andrea," I shout, loud enough for everyone on the field to hear.

She turns back to look at me, fire in her eyes. The rest of the team stop what they're doing and glance our way.

"Give me three laps of the field," I snap.

She narrows her eyes at me. "For fuck's sake," she mutters.

"Four," I demand.

She growls in frustration, shooting me one last scowl, and takes off around the field. The rest of the team return to what they were doing, but their murmurs can be heard across the field.

I walk over to stand with Ava. "You trying to piss off our best player?" she asks, brow raised.

"No. Just making sure she knows she's not going to get away with the attitude with me. She carries on like a spoiled brat and sets a bad example for the whole team."

She smirks at me. "You're right. I think this is going to be a good change for our team. We can do so much better if we focus on the game as a team instead of one superstar player."

I give her a nod. I may have just made an enemy of Andy, but I'm not here to make friends. I'm here to help them win this year. And I might be overcompensating a little for the fact that when it comes to this fiery little blonde, all I want to do is fuck her, and I can't.

## ANDY

I'm jogging the perimeter of the field like I've been instructed, almost finished my fourth lap. Fuck this shit. My morning has gone from bad to worse and it's not even 9am.

After yesterday, I thought maybe he wasn't the jerk I had painted him to be. He may have been able to explain himself and wasn't cheating on his wife, but after the last five minutes, my opinion has gone straight back to thinking he is a total asshole. I hate coaches who dictate rather than work with the players, and I can see that is going to be his style. He probably gets off on the power he has over us. What a fucking asshole.

I don't even remember what I saw in him that night. I thought he was fun and charming. Must have been the alcohol. Made him more likeable. Worst part is he probably thinks I'm late all the time like a total slacker, but I'm not. Soccer is the most important thing in my life, and I take it very seriously.

When I'm done, I jog over to join in with Luna and Darcy. I can feel his eyes on me, and I hate it.

"What happened to you, thought you were leaving right behind us this morning?" says Darcy.

"My car wouldn't start, so I tried to work out what the problem was and ended up with grease on my shirt so had to change. Still didn't get the car fixed, so I jumped on my bike. I knew I was cutting it fine and was going a little faster than I probably should have, took a corner too quick and nearly collided with an oncoming car. I'm still a little shaken from the whole thing. I'm lucky to be alive, and this fucker rips into me as soon as I get here." I'm babbling, getting the whole story out quickly. I'm still feeling a bit upset from the whole thing. My hands are still trembling, and I try to shake it off.

"Shitty morning to be late," Luna offers with a sympathetic smile.

"Don't I know it. It's just my luck." I roll my eyes.

We finish the morning session with no more drama and break to have lunch. Sitting with Luna and Darcy, I dig into my chicken salad. It's the last thing I feel like after the morning I've had. I could go for a burger and fries, something fatty. Something I know I shouldn't be eating when I need to be in top condition. But I'm also a massive comfort eater, and I know a burger and fries would make me feel better right now. I still have no idea what's wrong with my car. It's new, only bought for me last year, so it shouldn't be having any issues.

Darcy looks up from her lunch, watching me aggressively stab my salad with my fork. "You okay, babes?"

"Nope. Tell me, Darc, would you be? How am I supposed to do this with him? I'm going to have to change teams," I whine dramatically.

"Stop being a drama queen. You're going to be fine. It's just a small adjustment. He has to come in here all tough and set his boundaries. Things will settle down in a few weeks. Anyway, it's a good thing he's showing his true colors early. That way you can go back to hating him and be over him already." She smirks, the bitch. Why she thinks this is funny I have no idea.

"Yeah, just unlucky for you," offers Luna. "You pissed him off first so you're the example."

"Just my luck." I shovel in another mouthful of my salad. What is Darcy even talking about, be over him? I was never into him, not really. It was just sex.

Luna grabs my hand. "If it was me, I'd flirt with him and

drive him crazy. Use your assets. You know he's hot as sin for you or he wouldn't have taken you home that night, and now that he can't have you, it'll be killing him. You could have some fun." She winks.

And I know that's what she would be doing in my place, but that's not my style. I glare in his direction, hoping he might just burst into flames.

Brad and our assistant coach Ava are sitting together having their lunch. They seem to be getting on well, all chatty like they know each other. So I give her a death stare as well.

She would be lapping up every second of his attention, I'm sure. In her mid-thirties, she is as single as they come. Pretty, with long dark hair, and she's fit as well. They would probably be a good match, and she's more his age. I guess for an assistant coach she's nice enough most of the time, been here since I started with the team and worked well with Mitch, but she has pulled me aside a few times about my attitude, so she would have loved me getting in shit this morning, I'm sure.

As I watch them enjoying their food and conversation, I find myself becoming more jealous by the second. I don't even know why, I fucking hate him after the way he made me feel this morning.

He glances my way, catching me watching him, and I can see by his expression that he's assessing me. What's his fucking problem? I give him the same look back, narrowing my eyes. I don't care that I've been caught staring at him.

His lips turn up at the side into a bit of a smirk. Is this some joke to him? I glare harder but can't help but notice how nice he looks today, his hair neat and trimmed short on the sides, a little longer on top. His chiseled jaw is freshly shaven, and the skin that I can see on his bare arms is tanned. It has me remembering what his body looked like under his clothes, chest muscular, with just a light dusting of hair. Why does he have to be so handsome?

He laughs at something Ava says and his gaze drops back to her. I remember that laugh. It does something to my insides. I'm totally fucking screwed around him, and I need to cut it out. I don't know what that weird staring contest was between us, anyway.

Luna is right, though, I want to mess with him. Not how she suggested, but I have a better idea of something much more my style, and I already know how it'll drive him crazy.

The afternoon session starts, and Brad announces he will be taking over and running some new drills. Great, this should be fun! I look over my shoulder to the girls and roll my eyes, and they smirk back at me. I follow instructions just like the others and work harder than I have in a long time. Not trying to impress, just proving to him how much he needs me. I mean, the *team* needs me.

I also make an effort never to look his way or make eye contact, no matter how much the rest of my team fusses over him. I'm here to train, and he is nothing more than the guy giving instructions on how best to do that.

The afternoon session wraps up, and I make my way to the changing room to ditch my cleats, switching them for my combat boots and leather jacket. I say goodbye to the girls, and with my helmet under my arm, I hightail it straight for my bike. I don't want to have to see that jerk again today.

I throw my leg over my bike and secure my helmet in place. Just before I take off, he walks in front of me so I can't. I kill the engine. "What?" I snap at him, irritated.

"Andy, I wanted to see you before you left for the day, but you took off so fast I nearly didn't catch you."

"That was the point. I have somewhere to be. Don't want to be late now, do I?" *And don't think I didn't notice the use of my nickname, dick.* I glare at him. What could he possibly need to say to me that couldn't have waited until tomorrow?

"Fast learner," he says with a smug smile.

I give him a fake smile back. Was that supposed to be funny? Cause I'm not laughing. I take off my helmet and wait for him to talk. He looks more uncomfortable than he was before. I knew it, he hates not having the attention on him. He is so used to having the limelight on him, and he can't stand that I don't want to suck up to him like the rest of them.

"I just wanted to say that despite a rocky start this morning, you did a good job this afternoon."

I don't know why, I think his comment was supposed to be encouraging, but I see red. "I work my fucking ass off at practice, and I will do the same in a game. I'm not some slacker like you think! And this morning, that was the first time I have ever turned up late to practice, and it wasn't because I don't give a shit. It was because my car wouldn't start, and I nearly got killed rushing to get here on time. Thanks for making a bad morning worse by not hearing me out and just making assumptions." Wow, I even surprised myself, I really gave it to him.

He eyes me suspiciously, like he's not sure whether to believe me or not. "I'm sorry to hear you had a bad morning, and I was probably a little harder on you than I should have been."

"You think?" I sass, not giving him anything more than my resting bitch face.

He runs a hand through his hair, and I can't help but notice how the late-afternoon sunlight highlights the golden tones. "This is new to me, and I don't know how to navigate this with you." He pleads with his eyes for me to understand where he's coming from.

I'm not exactly sure what he means, but I get the feeling it's not about coaching me. I cross my arms over my chest protectively. "Navigate what? I told you yesterday, we forget what happened. It's simple."

"Is that how you really feel?"

The way he looks at me, his gaze dropping to my mouth as he says the words, I can hardly stand it. I can't have feelings for my soccer coach. I won't fucking let it happen, no matter how gooey my insides turn when he talks to me in that accent and looks at me like he wants to eat me. "Yes. Now if that's all, I need to get going." Like right now, before I change my mind and do something stupid like kiss his fucking irresistible lips.

He takes a step to the side, and I place my helmet back on. I can feel his eyes glued to me as I take off. What exactly did he want me to say, I have feelings for him after one hot night of fucking? Is that what he was getting at? It doesn't matter how either of us feels, anyway. He is my coach, and we could both get in a lot of trouble if anything was ever to happen between us again.

So it won't. Ever.

## CHAPTER SIX

ANDY

The rest of the week I try to ignore my new awkward situation and concentrate on improving my game, while my team carries on over Brad and how swoony he is. Insert eye roll. I mean, he's not that good. He just thinks he is. I bet they don't even realize how stupid they look sucking up to him. It pisses me off, not because I'm jealous but because we're here to play soccer, not ogle our coach. I'm completely over him, anyway. He's turning out to be a pain in my ass. All bossy and shit, and I hate that.

I stayed on a little after everyone else tonight because I needed to work on my shots at goal. The penalty kick I missed in the finals last year still haunts me. I won't let the same thing happen, never again.

I jump out of the shower, grabbing my towel and drying off. Suddenly, the lights flicker off and I'm left in complete darkness. Fuck! I wrap my towel around myself and sneak out to the front of the room, feeling for the light switch on the wall. Finding it, I try to flick it on, but nothing happens.

My heart kicks up a beat. I know it's probably just a power outage or something like that, but I hate the dark. It gives me the creeps. I hear movement from one of the other shower stalls. Maybe I'm not alone like I thought. "Is someone there?" I call, hoping it's just one of the other girls.

No answer. My mind must be playing tricks on me because of the dark. I start walking carefully back to where my bag is, feeling my way along the wall. There isn't even the slightest bit of light coming in from outside. I reach my bag and hear it again. There is definitely someone in here. I'm not sticking around to find out who, if they won't answer me.

I grab my bag and move quickly toward where I know the door is. My heart races and I hug my bag to my chest. Swinging open the door quickly, I run out and smack straight into someone. Strong hands catch me and stop me from falling over completely, and when I regain my balance, I glance up to see who it is. Brad. Of course it is.

I step back from him, frustrated that he's the one to see me all flustered. And mostly naked, just in my towel.

"Are you okay? You look like you've seen a ghost," he asks, concern in his features.

I blink up at him awkwardly. I've been avoiding him all week and he is the last person I want to see right now while I'm having my mini freak-out. "Just gave myself a scare. The lights went out while I was changing. The switch wouldn't work, and I swear it sounded like there was someone in the room with me, but I thought everyone else had left." I hug my bag to my chest a little closer, hoping I'm covered up.

His glance roams over me, his eyes staying a little longer than they should. "I think everyone else is gone for the night. I only came back to grab my phone. I left it in the office. You must have had quite the scare to run out of there like that."

"Well, wouldn't you if the lights went off on you like that?" I snap. I don't need him being a smartass right now.

"Are you afraid of the dark, Andy?"

What a stupid question. "Isn't everyone?"

He shrugs. "Come and get changed in my office, then we can investigate the light situation," he offers, and right now it's probably the best option I have. Either that or change in my car, cause I'm not going back in there.

"Okay," I say, following him into his office reluctantly. But the truth is, right now I don't really want to be alone, even if the alternative is Brad.

He flicks on the light in his office no problem at all, closing the door for me so I have privacy. The look he gives me, I feel like a silly child.

I dress quickly into my jeans and T-shirt, then throw on my boots. Tossing my towel back in the bag, I swing open the door quickly, ready to take off and avoid any more of this awkward situation.

Brad is waiting for me, leaning up against the wall. I want to slap that smug fucking look off his face. I hate that he was the one to see me vulnerable tonight. No one ever sees me panicked or out of control. Why did it have to be him here?

"Let's check out the fuse box," he suggests, and as much as I just want to take off, my curiosity is piqued as to why the lights went off in the first place, so I follow him to where the panel is located around the back of the building. He pulls back the cover, holding his phone up so he can see the switches. "That's strange, one of them is turned off." He says it like he didn't believe my story in the first place.

"I told you it was. Did you think I came running out in next to nothing just for fun?" I snap.

He raises a brow at me, then turns back to the board and flicks it back on. "I wouldn't put it past you, Andy. I know you like a bit of public nudity in the name of fun." The look he gives me. This is not the time or the place for looks like that, but I can see it, he's right back there on the balcony with me. I give him nothing. He's right, under different circumstances I would be up for it. But right now, I'm freaked out, and as if realizing just how much, his face turns serious again. "So, you really think someone might have been in there with you?"

"I don't know. I was freaked out, so maybe my ears were playing tricks on me? But it sounded like it."

"Maybe, but this is odd. If you were the only one in the room and you were just showering, you couldn't have been doing anything that would have tripped the power. Someone must have turned it off."

So he believes me now? "You think? Why would they have done that?" I give him a look. This is a little strange, and it's probably nothing, but I don't like it.

"Come on, I'll walk you to the parking lot. You probably shouldn't be back here so late by yourself anyway." He offers me a smile.

I drop my resting bitch face, the look I normally reserve for him, and half smile back. He's trying to be nice; it's hard to keep hating him. "I stay late here by myself all the time, it's fine."

As we walk, I give him a sideways look, taking him in properly. He's changed from what he was wearing today and is in a T-shirt and black jeans. He looks casual and relaxed, different to what he's been here all week while we train. He's so serious, so hard to judge as our coach. Standing so close to him, I get a flashback to that night. The way he smells, so comforting and familiar, so sexy.

The man as a coach drives me nuts, but when I see him like this, I forget why.

"Why stay late?" he asks. He looks to me, puzzled. I'm not sure why he would be, though. I thought it would be obvious.

"So I can train in the quiet, focus my mind, you know."

He nods. "Yeah, I get it. I thought you might be trying to impress the new coach or something." He smirks, his brow raising. He's trying to be cheeky with me. He looks like the guy I met that night at the club. Younger and more relaxed. Why can't he be more like this all the time?

He stops when we arrive at the women's changing room. "I just want to check the lights are back on." He pushes the door open and flicks on the lights. "They're working, but I don't think this was just a tripped circuit." He stops what he was going to say, and I see why. The mirror has a note scribbled on it in lipstick.

*Some of us can see what's going on even when kept in the dark. Remember who you belong to, because girls who forget find themselves in more trouble than they can handle.*

"I... I don't understand." I look at Brad who seems just as confused as me. "Do you think this message is for me?"

"You were the only one back here tonight. Maybe there's something we're missing, but it would appear that someone is trying to leave you a message. Have you just split up with someone or something?"

"No, not at all, I don't do relationships. I don't get it at all. This message doesn't mean anything to me."

"Maybe it's just someone mucking around. Come on, let's get you to your car."

We enter the lot, and my hands still hold a tremble. I'm so confused about all of it. It couldn't have been a note left for me, it makes no sense. It is strange that it's exactly like the note I left for Brad the morning after we slept together, red lipstick scribbled on a mirror. I'm sure that's just a weird coincidence.

I stop walking when I arrive at my car.

"Your car's fixed?" he says, looking over my red SUV.

I lean against the door, not quite sure why I'm not just getting in and taking off, but something about him tonight makes me want to stay a little longer. It could just be the fact that I'm a little creeped out still. "Yeah, my dad took a look at it. Turns out the spark plugs weren't connected." Still not quite sure what happened there. As soon as Dad had a look under the hood, he had it worked out. The whole thing is strange. I shrug, trying to brush it off.

"That's odd... they somehow detached themselves?" His face looks etched with concern, the little frown lines he gets on his forehead more prominent. It's much the same as my dad's when he realized what was wrong with it. We did some research and there is no way they came off by themselves. If my dad and now Brad are so concerned, it makes me wonder if I should be more worried than I am about it.

"More likely someone removed them on purpose," I say, eyebrow hitched, waiting for his reaction.

He takes a step toward me, closing the gap, his face deadly serious as he assesses me.

My body reacts to him in such close proximity, my heartbeat quickening, my nipples hardening, and I get that dull throb between my legs. This isn't even a sexy conversation. What the fuck is wrong with me? Why do I react like this around him?

"Have you had any trouble like this before? Your stuff being messed with?" he asks quietly, his eyes never leaving mine.

I blink back at him, not sure what's going on here. "It's

nothing, probably just some punk kids playing a prank or something. I'm not worried," I say, trying to brush it off. I don't want him being all concerned about it like my folks are. But I'm a little worried, I would be stupid not to be.

He rests a hand on my shoulder, in the way an older, wiser mentor type would to show their support. But something about the contact feels like it means more. His touch on my bare shoulder is almost electric. "Andy, you need to be careful. You're getting a name for yourself, and sometimes those beneath you don't take well to it. Or fans could become obsessed with you in a bad way. This sounds like a deliberate act to me. You should report it to the police. Especially now after what happened tonight. This isn't a coincidence." He looks so worried, and I can't help but wonder if his concern is because he's my coach or because he's worried about me?

I blink back at him, wondering if he's right, but dismiss the thought just as quickly. I'm no one interesting. Really, this isn't some threat against me, why would it be? "It's okay, Brad. Don't get your knickers in a knot. If anyone is stupid enough to want to be my weird stalker, I'm a big girl and I'll be able to protect myself. I'm not concerned at all, and you shouldn't be either."

His hand stays on my shoulder, his thumb brushing back and forth. His eyes don't leave mine. His stare is intense, willing me to do things I know I shouldn't. I can't, not with him again anyway. But I gaze longingly back at him just the same.

"Yeah, maybe. But I have seen stuff like this before. It starts out like a simple little thing, like a prank, then gets out of control quickly. Give me your phone."

I follow his instructions and reach into my pocket, retrieving my phone for him. Why, I don't know.

"'This is my mobile number. Promise you will call me if you're ever worried for your safety." He types his number into my phone. Normally it would majorly piss me off if a guy tried to act all protective, but with Brad, I like it. Knowing he wants to look out for me is somewhat comforting. I don't even want to consider why, but it is.

"Okay, but I won't need to," I say softly.

"But if you do, you have it." He smiles, and I get the impression him giving me his number is more than just so I can call if I'm ever in trouble.

He assesses me for a bit longer, and I know I really should be getting home before this unwelcome chemistry buzzing between us takes us somewhere we both know it shouldn't. I'm about to tell him that when he talks first.

"What are you doing now?"

I shrug. "Probably going to get something for dinner, the girls would have already eaten. Why?"

"Have dinner with me?"

I must show the shock on my face as I blink back at him, because he corrects himself. "I mean, do you want to grab something to eat with me? We could go over the plan for this week's game. I have a few ideas I wouldn't mind running past you, since you know the players on the team and their strengths better than I do at this stage. And I feel like you shouldn't be alone right now."

Brad Swift is asking me to dinner. This is a new and strange development.

I really shouldn't, but I can't help myself. Curiosity and all that. "Yeah, okay, why not," I say. I'm going out of interest's sake.

Brad could have taken the lovely Ava to dinner to talk tactics if that's what he really wanted to do. She knows the players just as well as I do. And she has a thing for him, that much is obvious after this week. But he is asking me, and my inquisitive side wants to know more. Maybe the side that still has a major crush on him as well.

I am just as bad as all the other girls on my team.

"It will be purely professional," he adds, though the look in his eyes tells a different story.

"Of course," I agree with a sweet smile. Dinner with Brad Swift, just professional.

I guess the silent treatment I've given him all week worked its magic again. He can't stand me ignoring me. He thinks he's the one in charge here because he's my coach.

Yeah right, Brad.

---

BRAD

We agreed to meet at the wood-fire pizza place in town. I honestly have no idea what possessed me to ask her to dinner. One minute I'm walking her to the car park, just to make sure she gets there safely in the dark after the creepy thing that just happened. The next, I can't stop staring at her lips and thinking about how much I want another taste of them.

The thought of going home to a large empty house doesn't help this situation either. I'm used to having a busy social life, and the silence of my now-boring life is deafening. I know a night spent with Andy will be amusing, and ever since Madeline fucked me over, all I want to do is let loose a little, feel like I did before I settled down and was tied to her.

Every part of me knows dinner with this cute blonde bombshell is a terrible idea. I'm so attracted to her that really spending any time with her outside of training is not ideal. I should be doing my best to stay away, but I can't. I'm drawn to her. She has me sucked in with her don't-give-a-fuck attitude and sassiness. There is something about her that I just want to know more about.

And this week after our chat, she has been doing her best to avoid me. Quite childish, really, no eye contact and that scowl permanently on her face. I think she must be used to getting her own way and doesn't cope well when she's challenged on it. She's a brat.

Honestly, I have enjoyed pushing her buttons and making her squirm a little. She has all the confidence in the world and can handle anything I throw at her. It's sexy as fuck.

Running into her tonight was unexpected, and now that she's started talking to me, even if it was because she was scared, I can't help but want to keep it that way.

I watch as she screams into the parking spot behind me and jumps out of her car. Her long hair is swept into two loose braids, and she flicks one over her shoulder as she moves toward me. I love the look on her, but it tells me what I already know. She's way too young for me. And even if I wasn't her coach, this would never progress to anything more than just a fun flirtation.

She passes me, a small smirk playing on her lips, and I watch her go by. She moves with confidence, and her ass looks amazing in those skinny jeans. I get a vision of my fingers digging into it as I pick her up and slam her against a wall, our mouths pressed together.

I push off the car where I was standing and follow her into the modern-looking Italian restaurant. There's a large wood-fire stove in the center of the room and tables scattered around. The atmosphere is dark and moody, with mostly couples cozily sipping wine at tables for two. Andy walks through the room like she owns the place. I follow her to a table in the back where she takes a seat, scanning the menu with her finger.

She is so different to the type of women I'm used to. Ones who hang on my every word and don't take their eyes off me, women like my ex, who go after professional athletes for the prestige they bring them. They're always done up to the nines, hair and make-up perfect, nails manicured, outfits perfectly put together and high heels. High-maintenance, manipulative, and all kinds of trouble. I learned that the hard way. And now I still have to deal with my ex while we finalize the divorce.

But Andy is in control of her own life. She's hard working and determined and doesn't let anybody stand in her way. She's the type of girl who knows what she wants and goes out of her way to achieve it for herself. I like that about her.

She looks up from the menu. "What do you feel like?" she asks, glancing over me, her eyes sweeping down my body.

I settle into a seat across from her and scan the menu. "I don't know. You pick a couple of pizzas for us to share, I'm not fussy." And right now, I can't even think about food. My mind is on her.

"Well, okay then." She taps her chin as she decides what to order.

A young waitress dressed in a pale blue button-down and tan slacks approaches our table and pulls a notepad from her apron. "What can I get you tonight?" She smiles warmly.

Andy points to the menu. "A bruschetta pizza to start, then a supreme and—" she turns to me. "Do you like olives?"

"They're alright."

"And a caprice. Thanks," she tells the waitress.

"And a bottle of the house red, thanks," I add with a smile.

"Not a problem at all," says the young girl. When she looks me over, her face breaks into a massive grin and she bats her lashes at me. "Oh my God, it's you, isn't it? Brad Swift?"

Andy throws me a look and rolls her eyes, unimpressed, and I smile politely back to the young girl, stifling back a grin at Andy's obvious annoyance. "Yes, that's me."

The girl pulls out her phone. "Can I get a quick selfie? My brother is like your hugest fan, he's never going to believe I served you tonight."

"Sure." I smile, standing to take a photo with the girl. This isn't the first time I've been approached by a fan, but it's awkward doing this in front of Andy. Probably because of the smart-ass smile she's giving me the entire time.

"Thank you so much." The waitress takes a quick snap and scurries back off to the kitchen excitedly.

I take my seat again.

"Oh my God," Andy mocks, her hand over her chest.

I laugh at her. "You're just jealous."

"Nope! Not at all. I couldn't care less if I get noticed or not. That's not why I play, as opposed to some." She gives me a pointed look. Does she really think that?

"You think that's why I played? To get famous?"

The waitress returns with our wine, and I pour two glasses, handing one to Andy.

She sips at it then holds the glass in her hand, swirling the burgundy liquid. "Was it?"

I give her an annoyed look. I can't believe she thinks that little of me. "Not at all. I played because, for as long as I can remember, it's all I could think about. What about you, why do you play?" I throw her question back at her. See how she likes it.

"For the same reason as you, I guess. I'm one of four girls, and my sisters are all a bit more placid than me. I was hard to manage, so my parents put me in soccer as a kid. I was seriously full of energy, they thought it might tire me out. It didn't, but I fell in love with the game and everything about it. So I started practicing every day. I did every holiday camp I could and eventually got scouted. I became obsessed with being the best. I still am."

She looks proud as she says it. You can see what the game means to her. It's her everything. That's how I used to be as well before I got injured.

"I've been watching you this week. You work harder than anyone else on the team. You remind me of myself when I was your age."

"That must have been a long time ago. You're, like, really old now," she teases.

"Funny, try more experienced! And I'm not that much older than you."

She smirks. "I know you're not, but you're old enough that I have a really embarrassing story to tell you." She wrinkles her nose and offers me the first genuine smile since I got here this week. "This is, like, really embarrassing, but I have to tell you anyway."

She buries her head in her hands and giggles. "When I was in the seventh grade, I had your poster on my wall. It was the one from your first season with Chelsea when you scored that winning penalty in the final. I wanted to be you so badly. Well, as good as you anyway—I didn't want to be a dude or anything."

I grin smugly at her as the waitress brings over our

pizzas and places them down on the table in front of us. Taking a little too long, she offers me a flirtatious look before disappearing back to the kitchen.

Andy shakes her head at the waitress, and I chuckle at her. I fucking knew it. The first night we met, she tried to act like she had no idea who I was and as if I wasn't having any effect on her, and all along, she has been crushing on me since she was twelve. "I think that's more embarrassing for me than it is for you." I laugh. "I still can't believe how good you were at lying that first night. Here I was, the poster boy from your wall, and you acted like you had no clue who I was."

"I'm just a good actress."

"That you are." We both grab for the pizza, munching on a piece in silence. She looks deep in thought, and I wonder what's running through her mind. This should be more uncomfortable between us, but it's not.

"So, Andy, I'm curious. You wanted to play like me... or you had a major crush on me?" I ask, picking up another slice and taking a bite. I know I'm getting back into dangerous territory by asking that, but I'm interested to know what the answer is.

She finishes her mouthful then smirks. "Don't go getting a big head or anything, but it might have been a little of both. Can you blame me? I was a hormone-fueled teenager, that's all it was." She shrugs with a cute smile. Her tough exterior wall is coming down, and I'm finally starting to see the real Andrea Harper, and she has a thing for me just as much as I do her.

I'm in trouble if I want to keep my job, but I can't stop what is happening between us, even if I wanted to.

"I can imagine you as a kid. Your poor parents."

She grins as if proud. "Hey!" She acts offended. Then

shrugs. "My parents say I'm the reason they have gray hair and wrinkles, but they did have four of us, so that's their fault. They could have stopped at two."

"Yeah, four kids is a lot. I just have an older sister."

"Is she into soccer like you?"

"Yeah, but not as much. What about your sisters? I know you said they were different to you, but are they into the game?"

"My second sister Jasmine comes to every one of my home games. She also lives with me, Darcy, and Luna, so she likes it by association. My other sisters support me, but sports aren't really their thing."

"Are you still trouble now?" As I ask it, I know I shouldn't. I'm steering the conversation to where I want it to be, pushing her to tell me what she wants to happen here, because I need her to say it. That she has been thinking about me just as much as I have her.

She tilts her head to the side, assessing me as she thinks over what I just said. "Is that what you want, Brad? For me to be a bad girl?" Her teeth sink into her bottom lip, and she bites down, her heated gaze not leaving mine for a second.

The way she looks at me, all I want to do is give in and tell her that's exactly what I want. I have thought of nothing else but her since that night we shared, and the idea of us being very bad together is just too tempting. Her leg brushes mine under the table, and I straighten up in my seat.

"You know exactly what I want, Andy, but you and I both know that's no longer on the table."

"I guess you're just going to have to go home and get yourself off to the thought of just how bad I could be for you then, aren't you, Coach Swift."

This girl is killing me. Did she just say that? It was exactly what I was thinking. "I will be now."

"It's a real shame you're my coach, Brad. We could have had a lot of fun together. I liked you fucking me on that balcony for all to see." She rises from her chair, placing some money on the table. "See you at the game on Sunday," she says with a wink, and before I know what's happening, she struts straight out of the restaurant without even looking back. We were mid-meal, and now I'm left with a hard-on and the mental image of what she just said.

## CHAPTER SEVEN

### ANDY

I jog off the field with the rest of the team. The air is filled with excitement after just claiming another win, this one against the Chicago Red Stars. We huddle together with hugs and pats on the back, congratulating each other for a game well played.

"Sick header, Darcy," I say, hugging her around the shoulders.

She squeezes me back. "Right back at you, sister. And that cross up the side, Luna, man, you can run fast."

Luna smiles, proud of herself, and she should be, she played so well.

Brad joins the group and addresses us. "You were on fire tonight, girls. I couldn't be happier with your performance after just scraping by with the win last week. You all really stepped up and played together as a team. Three-nil is a well-deserved outcome."

He's grinning, his perfectly straight teeth on display. This is the happiest I've seen him since he started with our team. He looks gorgeous, actually, his hair all messy, probably from running his fingers through it while he watched us from the sidelines.

Too bad he's now off limits—it makes him even more enticing. What it would feel like to run my hands through his hair, grip him tightly while he eats my pussy. Oh God, why does my mind keep going there? It's out of control with the dirty thoughts about him. I left him sitting there in the Italian restaurant last weekend because I knew if I stayed even a second longer, I would end up going home with him, and it just can't happen.

Ava stands close by his side, beaming with excitement for us, I guess feeling like her hard work is finally starting to pay off. I have to admit, she and Brad make a good team. Even if she looks at him with sappy lovey-dovey eyes; I know she has a lady boner for him, it's so obvious.

"We will be celebrating tonight at Dine 23 and I would like all of you to join us at 6pm," Ava says to the team.

I turn to Darcy and Luna. "I guess we're going out for dinner with everyone then."

"Looks like it." Luna shrugs.

"I'm seriously exhausted, though, after flying in this morning. I could totally give it a pass and just order in room service. Do you think we would get in shit if we did?" I ask, not really caring that much if I did.

"Probably," Luna says. "Besides, I want to see Coach Swift's reaction when he sees you all dolled up. The man has been staring at you every chance he gets this week, and that's when you're in your sweats." Her eyes go wide as she waits for my response.

I glance around us to make sure no one else just heard what she said, then I give her a slap across the arm for it. "He has not, and can you keep your voice down?" I say quietly to her, the irritation evident in my tone.

She grins cheekily. She loves to ruffle my feathers, and now that she has this over me, she's doing her best every chance she gets. "Oh, come on, Andy, don't tell me you haven't noticed him this week. I've caught you too," Luna whispers, her eyes going to Darcy as if looking for her to agree.

Darcy nods and laughs with Luna. They have clearly already been discussing this and think it's funny. I roll my eyes at the two of them and stalk off to the changing rooms. I have nothing more to say to either of them on the matter. I need a shower and to get away from any talk of me giving Brad looks this week. I have not been. I try and think back over the week. Have I? I have noticed him glancing my way every now and then, but I didn't think it would be obvious to anyone else. I didn't even tell my friends about the dinner Brad and I had. I thought it would be best to keep it to myself, even though nothing happened. It's just better if no one knows. If anything, I was trying to ignore him all week, so they're just trying to rile me up.

Once I'm in the changing room, I flick on the shower and strip off my clothes to stand under the hot water. I close my eyes, relaxing under the scorching stream, allowing my hair to get soaked through.

I'm utterly exhausted. We train for this all week, but the game always takes it out of me in a different way. My muscles ache all over, and I have a bleeding toe from being stomped on. I wasn't joking outside with the girls. I do really wish we could just stay in for the night.

The last week since Brad and I had dinner, we've both done our best to keep our distance, keep it professional around the rest of the team and training staff. But it's not easy. The chemistry between us is fucking crazy, and if my two best friends are noticing it, I'm sure it's not going to be long before others on the team start to as well.

Going out for dinner with everyone tonight when he is going to be there seems like a terrible idea. I just don't know how to handle this situation. I don't normally see my one-night stands again—on purpose—so this has never been an issue I've needed to deal with.

The noisy chatter of some of the other players entering the room interrupts my thoughts.

"How big do you think her ego is going to be after two more goals tonight," I hear from one of the girls. I think it's that bitch Ainsley. I freeze. There's no need to guess who they're talking about.

"Pretty inflated, I'd say! It's bad enough that she had Mitch wrapped around her little finger, now Coach Swift as well. Did you see them yesterday, huddled together on the sidelines? I bet you a hundred bucks she's screwing him already. She's such a slut!"

I feel my face heat with anger. Fucking Cindy; I would know her foghorn voice anywhere. The bitch is just jealous. When I joined the squad, I got her spot, because I had more talent in my little finger than she has in her whole body. She's older and on her way out, mostly on the team as a backup for either me or Darcy, but most games we play all the way through, so she's doesn't get much of a run anymore.

"I can hear you, Cindy," I call out from the shower stall I'm in. I don't care if that bitch knows I just heard her. She needs to be put in her place, and if I weren't soaking wet, I would do it right now.

I hear her whisper something then the two of them chuckle. They must leave the room because the chatter of the others overtakes them and I can't hear them anymore.

Immature high school bullshit and I still have to deal with it. I knew this would happen. That's why I made the girls swear to me they wouldn't tell anyone about what happened between me and Brad. If the rest of the team finds out, then how well I play will be irrelevant. They will all think I'm getting preferential treatment because of our history. Even if it was just one night and I had no idea at the time that he would end up being our coach.

I finish up in the shower, dry myself, and pull on a pair of denim cutoffs and a vintage-looking T-shirt with a faded print of a sunset on the front. It's Friday night and I should feel like getting dressed up and going out with my team after a win, but I feel off. Overhearing that conversation from those bitches and knowing the reality... every time I look at Brad, I swoon like some giddy schoolgirl. I want to be able to pull my shit together and get the hell over this infatuation I have with him, but I can't. Even when he totally pissed me off last week, I still couldn't stop imagining that night we had together and the way he made me feel. I want to experience it again; my body is craving him badly.

I bury my head in my hands and take a deep breath. Get your shit together, Andy, he is just some fucking guy. Stop thinking about him and move on with your life.

As if a light bulb goes off in my head, I get an idea. I know exactly what I need. A distraction. I grab my towel and dry off my hair, running a brush through the tangled mess. I decide to leave it out to dry. I chuck all my soccer stuff in a bag, and with renewed focus, I stalk out of the room to find my friends.

I'm going to find me someone cute to play with tonight and forget about Brad for good.

I find Darcy and Luna together, freshly showered. "You two ready? I need to drop in at the hotel before we go out."

# THE COACH

Luna gives me a look. "Sure thing. You okay, babe?"

"Yep. I've just worked out what's wrong with me this week. I need to get under someone new so I can forget about, well, you know who."

"I'm with you. I need a night of fun as well," she agrees.

"What happened to the guy who thinks you're a sex-shop owner?"

"It fizzled. I'm over it." She looks sad about it, and I get the impression that she quite liked him.

"Sorry, babe. We'll have an awesome night and help you forget."

The girls and I get back to our room in time to quickly get ready for the dinner. I switch out my shorts for a short, fitted skirt and apply some make-up, dark eyeliner and mascara mainly. My hair has dried and is in waves down my back. I scrunch some product into it and leave it.

Grabbing my heeled boots, I make my way to the door. Luna is ready in a stylish black dress, and Darcy has on a short skirt and a black off-the-shoulder top. We look hot. And I'm feeling re-energized with new purpose for tonight. Finding me a scorching-hot distraction.

---

BRAD

I'm sitting at dinner with Ava, the rest of the coaching staff, and team. We're at a trendy rooftop restaurant and bar in Chicago that's just around the corner from our hotel. Most of the team have made it here already and are sitting at a long table running almost the length of the room. There are three spots still left at the table. Why am I not surprised that Andy and her two friends are the last to arrive? I wonder if she's even coming. I didn't see her after the game.

There's laughter by the door and I check for the millionth time to finally see that it's Darcy and Luna, followed by Andy. She looks different tonight, dressed up all pretty in a fitted mini skirt and heeled boots. Her make-up is also more on the heavy side than it normally is, but I guess most of the time I spend with her, she's in her soccer gear, looking cute, and I find her hard to resist like that. But like this... she's sexy as fuck and I can't drag my eyes away from her. Even though I know I should.

Tonight is going to be interesting.

The only seats left are across from myself and Ava, and the three of them slot into the empty spots. I glance Andy's way, hoping to get her attention, but her eyes look anywhere but to me. It seems like something is bothering her, and I have to wonder if this situation is as hard for her as it is me. Because the more time I spend around her, the more difficult it is to avoid the temptation.

We all order and enjoy our meal. The conversation around the table flows easily as the girls chatter excitedly about the win. But as the night goes on, the more I can't help but notice Andy's not her usual self. She's quiet and appears uncomfortable to be here. She could just be tired from today's game, but I don't think that's it.

After dinner, everyone moves down toward the back of the restaurant where there's a bar. I get a drink with Ava and some of the other coaching staff and take a seat at a table. I have only just sat down when my phone rings, and I glance at the screen to see who's calling. The name Madeline lights up the screen, and I hit decline. I have nothing to say to her.

"Madeline?" asks Ava, looking over my shoulder.

She's being nosy, but I don't mind. She's been a good friend to me since I arrived in LA. "Yeah, she's playing hardball with the divorce settlement. We're only in the beginning negotiations but she's already being difficult."

Ava smiles at me sympathetically, not what I was going for by telling her. I hate that people pity me for my failed marriage. It makes me feel even more pathetic than I already do. "I'm not surprised, with everything you've told me about her, but I'm sorry you have to go through it." Her hand drops to my thigh, and she gives it a squeeze.

I glance at her, trying to work out if I'm reading her correctly. She's giving me flirty vibes tonight, and I don't know whether that's just her being friendly after a few drinks or something more. "Thanks, hopefully it'll all be over soon, and I will never have to see her again." I leave it at that, not wanting to elaborate any further tonight.

I'm suddenly very aware that I don't really know much about Ava. She asks a lot of questions about my life, and I'm happy to talk about it, but I haven't really gotten to know her at all. "What about you, anyone special in your life?"

She drops her chin then looks back up at me through long, fluttery lashes. "Not at the moment. I have terrible luck with relationships. I've all but given up, really." The look in her eyes, I can see she hasn't given up completely, though.

My phone starts up again. Madeline's relentless. "Sorry."

"You should answer it," she suggests, a look of disappointment flashing through her eyes.

I feel bad to cut off our conversion, but Madeline isn't going to give up if she wants to talk to me, so I better answer it. "I won't be a sec," I offer to Ava. I take the call and walk away from the table.

"What do you want, Madie?" I snap into the phone, not in the mood for her shit at all.

"Brad, sweetie, so nice to hear your voice. Just a quick call to let you know I'll be in LA next month. I have a photo shoot I'm doing, and I want to catch up with you." Her voice is all sing-songy like she's happy. And it confuses the hell out of me. Has she been drinking?

"Why?" is all I can say, because I can think of no logical reason why I would want to see her in person.

"I have something I need to talk to you about," she says like it's the most normal thing in the world that we would catch up. I haven't talked with her at all since I left. Any communication we've had has gone through my legal team.

"Just tell me over the phone," I demand. I don't like playing her games, and she sounds like she's in a mood to play.

"Brad, don't be that way. I'm coming to see you. It will be better in person, okay?"

I really don't want to see her again. But I guess it must be important if she's called, especially after how we ended things. "If you must," I say, defeated. I have never been able to say no to her.

"Text me your address, and I'll let you know what time works for me. Got to run now, sweetie."

"Yeah, okay." I disconnect the call and wonder how she always gets what she wants from me. I let her walk all over me when we were together, and now, after everything she did, I won't just tell her to fuck off and let the lawyers deal with her. There's no love there anymore, I know that for sure, but she has a hold over me still, and I hate it.

I run a hand through my hair, frustrated with myself, then tuck my phone back in my pocket. I should get back to our group. Making my way back toward our table, the first thing I spot is Andy chatting to some guy. He has his hand slung over her shoulder, and she laughs at something he says.

Her eyes flick to me, noticing that I walk by her. She looks guilty and I'm sure my expression shows her just how unimpressed I am that she's flirting with some young idiot. She shrugs like she doesn't care what I think.

My fists ball at my sides, anger radiating through me. The guy whispers something in her ear, and her gaze lands back on him. Is she trying to piss me off on purpose? She knows how I feel about her. I think I made that obvious last weekend, right before she walked away from me. Then all week, she has been acting like it never happened, but every time I talk to her, I feel it. The sexual tension between us is insane.

This is clearly her attempt to either make me jealous as hell or just piss me off because we can't act on our impulses toward each other. She is succeeding at both. I want to rip his fucking hands off her and drag her back to my room, caveman-style—but I can't.

I am her coach and nothing more.

First Madeline calling, now Andy being overly flirtatious with some dickhead. I know I have no right to be upset with her. We can never be anything other than what we are, coach and player. But I'm internally raging about it. I hate that she is so easily moving on to someone new, when I'm still hung up on her, and she fucking knows it.

I order another scotch from the bar and slump down into the seat next to Ava. "I think this is the last one. I'm nearly done for the night," I tell her.

She gives me a disappointed pout, then places her hand over mine. "Stay a bit longer Brad, for me." Her eyes plead with me, and for the first time with her, I worry about where this is going between us.

I offer her half a smile. "Okay." Part of me wants to keep an eye on that guy with Andy anyway. He looks dodgy, as I'm sure he can't be trusted. What is she even doing with him?

I look back to Ava. Her face is kind, her eyes locked with mine. "Are you okay?" she asks.

I sigh. "Yeah, I just don't want to deal with Madeline anymore and I still have to. She's in town next month for a shoot and is coming to see me, wants to talk about something."

"Sounds interesting." She raises a brow.

"I'm sure it's nothing. Probably just wants to try and screw me out of more money. Show me how much happier she is now." I take a big swig of my drink.

"I'm sorry, Brad, you deserve so much better." She runs her hand up my leg and gives it a squeeze. I look at her. She's so caring and there's a warmth to her, but the way she looks at me with longing and lust—shit, there is something more going on here for her. She wants me to stay because she wants to be more than just friends, I can feel it.

Could tonight get any worse? I need to go back to my room before things escalate with Ava.

I glance across the room, looking for Andy, and spot her just in time to see her leaving through the door to the stairs, with the guy she was talking to. His arm is wrapped around her shoulders and she has her arm around his waist.

Fuck. I spoke too soon, and the night just got worse.

I know I have no right to stop her, but I'm not going to let her leave with some other guy. She's mine, even if she can't be.

I throw back the remainder of my drink. "Thank you,

Ava, I appreciate your friendship. I'm going to call it a night, though," I say, making it blatantly obvious what this is to me.

She looks in the direction I'm studying and frowns. "Oh, okay, I'll see you in the morning then." She sounds disappointed, and I feel bad, but this is just a platonic work relationship, nothing more.

"See you then," I offer with a smile, hopping up and taking off through the restaurant.

I make my way down the stairs and on to the road out front, quickly scanning the street for the direction Andy went. I can't see her, and I turn toward the restaurant and slam my fist up against the wall in frustration. "Fuck."

I notice movement in the side street and turn to see her leaning up against the wall with the guy draped over her. She sees me and looks guilty. "Brad," she mutters.

The guy takes a step back, sizing me up. He's big, but I could take him if it comes to that. I walk toward them, my eyes set on hers. "What are you doing, Andy?" I question her, not quite sure where I'm going with this, only that I want him away from her.

The guy she's with snakes his arm around her, pulling her closer into him. "Who's this guy?" he asks.

She sighs. "My coach," she says with a roll of her eyes. Her gaze hasn't left me, and the attitude she's giving off is more for my benefit than his. She's not into this idiot. I don't know what she's trying to do here. But she has my attention, and I'm sure that was part of it.

I take a few steps closer to them, making it obvious I'm not uncomfortable at all with this situation and I'm not leaving them alone. "I think it's time to call it a night, Andrea. We have an early flight home, remember?" I say sternly, and I know it'll piss her off being told what to do, but right now I don't care. She's acting like a child so I'm going to treat her like one.

"You don't get to tell me what to do off the field, Brad."

"Is he your coach or your dad?" the guy says to her, then turns to me. "She's a big girl, I think she can work out when she's had enough and take herself home," he spits.

Andy looks conflicted with an internal struggle.

I take her hand and she lets me. I look back at her, trying to convince her with my eyes this is a really bad idea. "Is that really what you want, to stay here in an alleyway with this dick? Or do you want me to walk you back to the room, make sure you get home safe?" I suggest, giving her an out.

She looks at me with a small sassy smile and her hand squeezes mine back. I know I've won this standoff. "Sorry, dude, I gotta go. Early flight and all that." She steps away from him, and I pull her closer to me.

"Whatever, slut," he grumbles under his breath, taking off back inside the restaurant.

I feel her flinch as he says it, and I want to thump him. She must feel me tense, because she grips my hand tighter. "Don't, Brad, he's not worth it."

"You need to make better choices, Andy."

"Ha, yeah, I know. What, is it part of the job to save me from myself, Coach?"

"Something like that," I huff, still pissed at her. For what reason, I'm not really sure. Mostly just for putting herself in a shitty situation like that. He could have been anyone.

"Just so you know, I don't make a habit of having men come to my aid. I'm only walking home with you now because I was over it anyway."

"Alright then." She is so independent that she can't accept she was getting herself in over her head and she needed me. "What's going on with you tonight, anyway? You're not yourself."

Realizing our hands are still intertwined, she releases mine, tossing her long hair over one shoulder and combing her hands through it. It looks so pretty tonight with it out and wild. I would like to run my hands through it and hold a handful as I fuck her from behind. A vision of us on that hotel balcony comes back to me, and I have to force it to the back of my mind. I can't be thinking about her like this anymore.

"How would you know how I am usually, anyway?" She assesses my face, and I can't tell if she likes that I care or not.

"Andy, I have watched you and how you interact with others pretty much every day for two weeks now. I know more than you think, and tonight you weren't celebrating like the others. You were sulking."

"I wasn't sulking." She pouts.

I give her a sideways look, eyebrow raised, like *you definitely were*. "And that guy, what was that? That doesn't seem like you."

She rolls her eyes. "You really have no idea about me at all, Brad. None. Why are you paying so much attention to me, anyway?" she sasses.

"I care that you're okay, that's all. I don't like seeing you unhappy, and tonight you are clearly miserable."

She gives me a look that tells me I'm spot-on, then sighs loudly. "Fine, I'll tell you, but it stays between us. I don't want you trying to fix anything, I have it under control. Okay?"

I don't like the sound of this. What would I need to fix? She gives me a stern glare like she won't spill until I agree to her terms. "Alright, just tell me what's going on."

"It's the fucking jealous bitches on our team," she huffs.

I knew there was something going on with her. This is the first I've heard about any jealousy within the team; I thought they were a tight group, supportive of each other. "What's happened with these other girls?"

"After the game, when I was in the shower, I overheard two of them talking about me." She says it calmly, but I can see how upset she is about it. Her entire body is stiff and she looks uncomfortable.

"What did they say?"

"It's not important, they just pissed me off, judging me and shit. I hate girls like that."

We're just out front of the hotel, and I put my hands on her shoulders, stopping her from walking so I can look at her properly. She's really upset about this. Whatever they said, it must have been bad. She doesn't seem like the type to be so easily affected by what others say about her. "What did they say about you?"

Pale blue eyes blink up at me from behind long dark lashes. I brush the hair out of her eyes, tucking the stray strands behind her ear. She's such an attractive girl, her long hair framing her oval-shaped face. I want so badly to bring her lips up to mine and kiss her, tell her just how much I think about her and the night we shared. This moment could be perfect.

She sighs. "That my ego is inflated, because I'm doing well, scoring high."

I look at her, confused. "There's nothing wrong with that. I used to get people saying that about me all the time. Just own it, don't let them upset you."

She looks at me even more intensely, as if willing me to read her mind so she doesn't have to say it out loud. "It's not just that." She hesitates, nibbling her bottom lip nervously. "They think I have all the coaches wrapped around my little finger, Mitch and now you. They made a bet that I was already sleeping with you, because in their words, *I'm such a slut."*

And the flinch from earlier when that dickhead called her a slut makes more sense now. I feel the anger wash over me. I know I said I would just listen and not try and fix this, but this type of bullying shit is not on with my team. These girls need to be called out for this. "Are you fucking kidding me? Who said it, Andy?"

She takes a step back from me. "Nope, I'm not telling you that. I don't need you going in and saving me from them, it will only make all of this worse. I'll deal with it, Brad. Promise me you won't say anything to anyone. Not even Ava, okay?"

I cross my arms across my chest and glare at her. I'm not angry with her; I'm annoyed she won't let me help. This needs to be dealt with. But I can see she's not going to back down with this one. "Okay, I won't," I huff. "But it's bullshit. You shouldn't have to put up with bullying like this," I say, trying to keep my frustration at the situation under control.

"Yeah, but I do. See, that's the difference between men and women. I bet you get celebrated because you're confident and have a healthy sex life, but girls get shamed for the same thing. And we can't be good at what we do, because it's always just assumed that we've slept with someone to get to the top. They all just think I'm chasing you to get an advantage. That's why I walked away last weekend. I have to walk away from you."

She's right, no one ever questioned me. I could sleep with whoever I wanted, and before I got married, I did. And now it makes more sense. She walked not because she wanted to but because she was worried about the consequences on her career if it ever got out. "It's so unfair," I say softly.

"Yeah, but it's reality in our society." She smiles sadly, and I wish I could make her feel better. But after what I just heard, I need to be even more careful about keeping my distance from her. "Thanks for walking me back. I better go before anyone sees us together and starts more rumors. I'll see you tomorrow."

She turns to walk away, and I can't help it, I have to let her know how I feel about her. Even if it can never go any further than this. "Andy, just so you know, if things were different, it would be me chasing you, not the other way around. And you get the game time because you work harder than anyone else. You put in the hours and have more talent. Don't let them get to you."

She offers me a small smile. "Thanks for saying that." She pauses, blinking back at me. She wants to say something else but she's not sure if she should. "Brad, if things were different, you wouldn't have to chase me. I'd already be all yours." She offers a small, sad smile and wanders through the sliding front doors of the hotel.

My heart actually hurts hearing her says those words. Watching her walk away is hard when all I want to do is comfort her and show her exactly how I feel about her. Part of me wishes I didn't take this job, but I needed my fresh start, and this really is a good opportunity for me to have that. I just have to get my feelings for her under control, so I don't mess up her career or mine.

## CHAPTER EIGHT

ANDY

The doorbell rings, waking me from a deep sleep. I'm sure one of the others will get it. I'm a dead weight, there is no way I'm moving for anything right now.

I roll over and close my eyes, getting comfy in my bed. The sunlight streams through the crack at the side of my blinds, and I can feel the warmth of the day calling my name, but I don't have anywhere to be this morning, so a lazy sleep-in it is.

The damn door chimes again. Where are the others? Don't they know it's my birthday and I should deserve to stay in bed this morning? I groan loudly and throw back the covers. I slip into my robe. Sleepily I make my way to the front door, pushing it open to reveal an empty front porch. How odd.

I curse at the annoyance of getting up for nothing. Then my gaze drops down and I see a bunch of flowers leaning against the side wall of the house. I pick them up, my mood improving. Looking them over, the greenery is fresh and beautiful, and they're in soft pale pink wrapping paper with a beautiful silky ribbon at the front.

But it's the flowers themselves that have a sudden uneasy feeling washing over me.

It appears that it should be a dozen roses, but the heads of the flowers have all been removed. What the actual fuck kind of a gift is this? I catch a glimpse of a small note attached to the ribbon. I slip it out and read the card. *Happy birthday, Andrea* is all it says, in black capital letters. Is this a joke from one of my friends? It's not funny if it is, but it looks like something Luna and Darcy would think up together to get a laugh.

I take the weird bunch of flowers into the house and lock the door behind me. I sit them in the kitchen sink, not quite sure what else to do with them. I'm too awake now to bother going back to bed, so I fill the kettle, putting it on and waiting for it to boil. I wonder where the others are.

I don't have to think on it for long. Seconds later, Jasmine, Darcy, and Luna arrive through the front door chatting excitedly about something. "Happy birthday!" they sing together when they see me. Their expressions change from excitement to worry when they catch sight of me.

"What's wrong, Sis? It's just one year older, you don't have to be all pouty about it," says Jasmine.

"Did one of you do this as a joke?" I say, pointing to the headless flowers in the sink.

Darcy comes closer to inspect the bunch of flowers. She scrunches up her nose in disgust. "What the fuck, babe?"

"I know, right?" I say, trying not to show how freaked out I really am. This has to be just some weird joke. They'll break soon and start laughing.

"Flowers with no heads? That's weird as hell," she says to the others, and they come over to look at them as well.

"This definitely wasn't us," the others agree.

They look deadly serious, and I can feel the slight tremble in my hands. "I was hoping it might have been, cause now I'm kinda freaked out about it. Who sends flowers like this?"

Jasmine comes around the counter and places the large box she's holding down, then wraps her arms around me in a supportive hug. "First your car, now this weird gift. Do you think someone is trying to mess with you?"

"Yeah, it's starting to feel like that." I didn't even tell Jas about the lights going out on me at the soccer field, cause until now, I had myself convinced I was just being silly, but now I'm not so sure. And if this is someone messing with me, they know where I train and live. It's really creepy.

"I'm sure we'll work this out. Come on, don't let it get you down. It's your birthday, we need to celebrate. Here, we organized breakfast from your favorite place for you." She hands over a brown paper bag and a to-go coffee.

I inspect what's in the bag. It smells amazing. A breakfast wrap, eggs, bacon, avocado, salsa, and fresh baby spinach. These things are to die for. "Thank you." I take it to the dining table and the others follow.

Food first, then I'm calling my dad, not something I like to do unless I have to. Don't get me wrong, I'm close to my parents, but I also like to show how independent I am, and I have since I was young. It's my other sisters who normally need them the most. But my dad is smart and super protective; he'll know what to do about all of this. I just feel bad because it was only a few weeks ago he was here helping me fix my car. But my entire family are coming to LA this afternoon for my birthday, so he would be here anyway.

. . .

THE GIRLS SPENT THE DAY TRYING TO DISTRACT ME AND making sure I had a good day. We spent the afternoon getting ready for my party, and it definitely helped. I'm in a better mood now. I'm so excited to see everyone I care about this evening. My party is a dress-up at a local venue. I love celebrating my birthday, and every year we make a big fuss about it, any opportunity to dress up and party. This year's theme is Superheroes, cause I'm a nerd at heart and love my comics. Also, it's just fun to dress up as a kickass powerful woman.

The four of us look authentic as hell. Jasmine is Harley Quinn, her hair in high pigtails, with blue on one side, red on the other. She wears a ripped white t-shirt, fishnet stockings, and red-and-blue booty shorts. And carries a baseball bat. She looks seriously fierce and would give Margo Robbie a run for her money.

Luna is Gamora from Guardians of the Galaxy, in tight black leather pants and jacket. It took us forever to paint her skin green, using the body paint she got from the costume shop. It's so worth it, though. She looks totally legit. It's going to be fun for her trying to wash it off, though.

Darcy is Captain Marvel with a blue-and-red bodysuit.

And me, I'm Wonder Woman, of course, with flowing chestnut-brown wig and all.

We strut into the party, all the craziness of this morning almost forgotten. My dad said he will install a security camera and alarm system, and for now, that's all I really think we need to do. None of the things that have happened are really all that bad, but I feel safer knowing I'll have a little extra protection soon.

Everyone is here. Mom, Dad, and my other two sisters, Amelia and Cassie, have made the trip from Palm Springs, my hometown and where they all live. My sisters look adorable. Cassie has her strawberry-blonde hair in a high ponytail and is dressed as Black Widow in a skin-tight black bodysuit. Amelia is sexy Sailor Moon. Her stupid ex-husband would be so fucking jealous if he saw her right now. She is the oldest of the four of us, but you wouldn't know it. She has a rocking body and is the trendiest of us sisters, with her perfect complexion and her pretty, short blonde bob styled to perfection.

"Happy birthday, darling." Mom wraps her arms around me in a warm embrace. She is a beautiful woman, tall and slender, with long pale blonde, almost-gray hair. She's not in costume. Instead, she's in a fitted navy-blue dress that is cinched at the waist, showing off her perfect figure. She's the kind of woman who is always perfectly dressed, and even though I always throw a dress-up birthday party, she has never dressed up for one.

When I pull back from her, I feel almost teary, though I don't even know why. It's been a couple of months since I ventured home, so that could be it.

Dad wraps me a bear hug. He's a big man, tall and imposing with a graying beard. "Happy birthday, baby girl." I take comfort in his embrace.

"Thanks for coming, guys." I beam, so excited to have my entire family under the one roof for the first time since my cousin Drew and his wife Jenna came to visit.

A song I like comes on, and Darcy pulls me by the hand to the dance floor. Luna and my sisters follow us, and we go nuts, dancing like no one is watching.

A few songs in, Amelia wraps her arm around me. "Come and get a drink, Sis." Darcy gives me a look, pissed that I'm leaving her, but she has the others, she's fine. She just likes all the attention on her.

We walk toward the bar and she orders me a scotch.

Drinks in hand, we make our way over to a quiet table and take a seat. "You look amazing tonight, Sis," I tell her. "Being single agrees with you."

"Thanks."

"So, how is everything going? You and the kids settled in at your new place?"

"We are. It's so lovely there, and the kids seem happy enough. I can't imagine what it must be like for them now, growing up without their dad in their lives at all, but they're adjusting better than I thought they would."

"That's good." I take her hand. "How are you? Really, not the bullshit you tell everyone else."

She smiles and it reaches her eyes. "Yeah, actually I'm okay. Moving to our own place was the best thing we could have done. I'm over the initial shock of it all now, and you know what? I really do think it's for the best. He was such a jerk to me the whole time we were married. I was putting up with it for the kids, but now that I don't have to, I can move on with my life. We're all happier without him."

"That's right, Sis. He was a piece of shit and you and the kids are better off."

She gives me a definite nod, like she's still trying to convince herself that this is all true. She takes a swig of her drink then places it back on the table with a thud. "Oh, and I didn't tell you the best part," she says, her face now alight with excitement.

"What's that?"

"My fashion label is just about to expand into another hundred boutiques across the country."

"Oh my God, Amelia, I'm so excited for you!" I squeal and throw my arms around her. This is the best news, after the year from hell. It sounds like her life is taking a massive change for the better.

"That's where you two disappeared to. We were looking for you," calls Cassie as she and Jasmine stride across the room to us, drinks in hand. They take a seat at the table, and we all link hands. We have a super special bond and we always have. They are all so different from me and each other but that has never mattered.

Cassie turns her attention to me. "So, what's the birthday girl got in store for tonight? I'm surprised to see you without a date. Bet you have some hottie you're hiding away from us until Mom and Dad leave."

I fiddle with my hair. She's right, normally I would have someone I had organized to meet up with, or I would already be eyeing someone up at the very least, but this year, no one takes my interest. At least not anyone I'm allowed to go home with anyway. "No, not this year," I say a little sadly, my mind going straight to Brad. He's the hottie I would like to be hiding from everyone, but that's not going to happen.

"What! I can always rely on you to have some fabulous story to tell, so I can live through you when my own life is boring as batshit." Cassie pouts, but I'm sure her life is anything but. She's in college; I bet she's having the time of her life.

"She has a story, alright," says Jasmine with a smirk. She gives me a look like, *can I tell them?* but she doesn't wait for a reply. "She doesn't have a date tonight, because she is pining over her soccer coach," she blurts out.

I shoot her a look for opening her big mouth, when we had an agreement not to say anything. I could kill her right now. If Mom and Dad found out I slept with my soccer coach, Dad would lose his shit. That's a fact. Brad would lose his job for sure, and I would be embarrassed as hell.

She shrugs at me and grins to our other sisters like the

whole thing is funny. Give her a few drinks and she forgets how to keep secrets.

I feel two sets of eyes focus on me. I glance up at them and they're wearing the same stupid grin as Jasmine. "Andy, do tell. I need a good story," says Amelia.

"It's not a good story, it's stupid. And I'm not pining over him. It was a one-time thing before either of us even knew he was going to be my coach. Now it's all out of hand because I have to see him like all the fucking time."

"That's the funny part," Jasmine says, chuckling. "She was hating him, thinking he did the dirty on his wife, then he turns up at her training session as the new coach. Can you imagine? What are the chances?" The other girls' eyes go wide.

"Oh, Andy, it could only happen to you," says Cassie.

"I know, right, I have all the bad luck."

"Now what? Was he cheating on his wife?" asks Amelia, looking worried, and I know why. She's been there and it's awful.

I shake my head. "No, it was a misunderstanding. He's separated from her. She did the dirty on him. He was nursing a broken heart."

"Oh, good. So where does that leave you then?"

I shrug. "He's my coach. What happened is in the past," I say, trying to act as if I believe my own words. Maybe if I can convince them that I have no interest in him anymore, it will actually start to be true.

Jasmine just gives me a look then rolls her eyes, not very subtly. "Yeah, except she's stopped seeing anyone else or even trying to meet other people."

"That's not true. I nearly hooked up with a total babe when I was in Chicago."

Jasmine sips on her drink as she listens to my reply, her

full attention on me. She's assessing me like a pet project, and I don't like it. "Oh yeah? And why didn't you? The old Andy would have." Her eyebrows shoot up in question.

I go to respond then stop and glare at her instead. She's trying to do her psychology bullshit on me, trying to get in my head so I have some grand realization or something. Well, that's not going to happen here tonight, sissy dearest. I can feel the other two watching me as well, and I need to shut this down. "I didn't feel like it, that's all."

She laughs like she has me and she knows it. "Yeah, right. My bet is Brad was watching you, all protective alpha male with his chest puffed out, and you felt guilty because... you love him."

I hit her on the arm. "I do not."

"Andy, you're totally blushing," says Amelia, grinning at me. "You do like this guy. I can see it."

I sigh and cover my face, because it doesn't matter what I say now. They're going to believe what they want to, anyway. And Jasmine is kind of right. I do *like* him, and he was the reason I didn't hook up with that guy like I normally would have.

"It doesn't matter how I feel about him anyway, because he is my coach, and it would be against the rules to do anything. So that's that." I say it with total conviction, like I believe the words coming from my mouth. But I don't. All I want to do is have another taste of him, just a little one, that no one would have to know about. The only thing stopping me is what those bitches said the other day about me, and well, the fact that he would lose his job. I don't want that on me. He's actually turning out to be a good coach, despite how I felt about him that first week. I don't want to be the one to screw that up for my team.

Cassie grabs my arm and drags me from the table.

"Enough of the interrogation. It's her birthday, let her dance," she says, saving me, and I'm grateful, hurrying away with her quickly. "When has some silly rule ever stopped you before, Sis? I know you, you go and get what you want," she says with a wink as we make our way back to the dance floor.

She's right. I normally do.

My birthday party was perfect, and after catching up with my sisters, I danced until everyone else left to go home and the venue kicked me out. Now I'm wandering home alone. Darcy took off early, probably with some random hook-up, knowing her. Luna and Jasmine met brothers and left with them about an hour ago. And the rest of my family all went their own ways back off to Palm Springs.

It's a nice night out so I don't mind the short walk home, even if I feel a little abandoned by my girl gang on my special day. I can't really complain, because if I weren't pining after the soccer coach I can't have, I would have been the same as the rest of them, hooking up with a random guy who I would never see again. But I proved to myself last Friday night that I can't do that at the moment. It felt so wrong. And when Brad came out front to find me, the way he looked at me, I knew I couldn't go through with it. No matter how much I wanted to prove to myself I could, so I could just get over him.

Something huge has shifted for me, something I can't even explain to myself. All I know is no other random dude is going to do. I want Brad, and that's all there is to it.

A text message pings on my phone, and I pull it out of my bag to check who on earth it is at this hour.

**Unknown Number:** Happy birthday, beautiful girl!!

Okay, bit late, but nice. Slightly strange, though. I don't recognize the number.

**Me:** Thank you. Sorry, but your number isn't saved in my phone. Who is this?

**Unknown Number:** An old friend. Did you like my birthday present?

The hairs stand up on the back of my neck. This must be who sent the flowers. No one else fessed up to it today, and as much as I haven't wanted it to ruin my birthday, it's been playing on my mind.

**Me:** What old friend?

**Unknown Number:** I will reveal that at a later date. Today, I just want to make sure you have an extra special day for your birthday.

Yuck, this person is making me feel sick, and I don't have to take it.

**Me:** If you can't tell me who you are, I'm not communicating with you anymore.

There's nothing for a few minutes, and I continue my walk up the street at a faster pace. Hopefully they're done, knowing I'm not continuing to listen to it.

Then another text pops in. I don't even want to look, but my curiosity gets the better of me and I can't help myself.

**Unknown Number:** How's your SUV working? All better?

A nauseous feeling washes over me and settles in the pit of my stomach. The concern my dad and Brad had about what happened with my car being a targeted attack on me now sinks in a little further. This all might be a little more serious than I wanted to believe. Another text pings on my phone.

**Unknown Number:** You make a very sexy Wonder Woman. But a girl like you really shouldn't be wandering home alone. I'm getting off in my car at the sight of you.

Oh my God. I glance around my surroundings, suddenly feeling very panicked and unsafe. The streets are practically empty, just a few random cars parked up a bit farther. No other people to hear me if something was to happen.

My mind starts to race through what I just read. Some fucking creep is in his car watching me? Whoever this is knows what I'm wearing, but any number of people from the party could just be messing with me. They all know what character I'm dressed as. I look up the street and see the flashing neon sign of a twenty-four-hour diner that would be as safe a place as any right now. So I make a run for it, not stopping until I have burst through the front door.

The waitress behind the counter gives me a look. "Sorry," I say, feeling silly to have caused a scene, bursting in here.

She returns to what she's doing when she realizes I'm nothing to worry about.

The place is pretty deserted, and I'm not surprised. I make my way to a booth and slump down in the vinyl seat, trying to catch my breath. My heart is beating so hard I can feel my pulse throbbing through my body.

Shit. Who can I call? I don't want to keep walking home alone. It's late and I'm freaking the fuck out. My family have already driven home, and the girls have gone their own ways. I could call them, but all of us would be over the legal alcohol limit to drive and I don't want to worry them.

I remember what Brad said to me the day I got scared when the lights went out at the soccer field. He offered me his number, so I could call if I was ever worried. Well, I'm fucking worried. Without another thought about it, I hit dial and pray he picks up.

"Hello?" His sleepy voice comes through the phone. Shit, I feel stupid and guilty as soon as he answers. Maybe I should just hang up and think of another way to get home.

"I'm so sorry, did I wake you?" I ask, knowing I did.

"Andy, is that you? What's wrong?" he mutters, his voice now sounding panicked.

"It's probably nothing, but I'm a bit freaked out. I think someone might be watching me."

I can hear movement through the phone, sounds like him throwing on clothes or something. "Where are you?" he demands.

"At some fifties diner on 119th Street."

"Okay, stay there, I'll be there in five." He disconnects the call, and I wonder if that spur-of-the-moment decision was the right one. But right now, I don't care. I'm scared that some creep is stalking me, just like what Brad said had happened to his friend. And for whatever reason, he is the only one I want to come and save me.

---

BRAD

I hurry through the door to the diner and glance around the room for her. She's in a booth toward the back near the jukebox. My anxiety washes away when her eyes connect with mine and I know she's safe. The sight of her surprises me a little. She's wearing a Wonder Woman costume... I think. I can see relief wash over her pretty features, knowing I'm here.

I'm not sure what's appropriate right now, but I don't really care. I slide straight in next to her, wrapping an arm around her and pulling her toward me. She buries her head against my chest. "I'm so sorry to wake you up, I just got really freaked out." I feel the shake in her hands and hear the fear in her voice, no sign of the overconfident sassy girl I know. She's really thrown by whatever happened tonight.

"Hey, hey, it's okay. I told you to call me if you needed me." She pulls back to look at me and I take her hands in mine, trying to stop the way they're shaking.

She offers me a weak smile. "Do you want a coffee or something to eat? It's on me for getting you out of bed."

"Nah, I'm good. Really, don't worry about it, Andy. I told you to call me if you needed me and I meant it," I say, reassuring her.

"You can have some of my pie. I thought I wanted it but I'm feeling too yucky to eat it." She slides it toward me. It looks good, and she's barely touched it, so I dig in.

"So what happened tonight?" I don't want to push her, but I want to know what's going on so I can help her. It was bad enough for her to call.

She nibbles on her bottom lip nervously. "This." She hands her phone over to me with the message thread already up.

I scroll through from the start. The hairs stand up on the back of my neck as I read through. I can see why she's scared. She was walking alone late at night, and this is some creepy shit. I feel irritated that she put herself in danger in the first place. After what we talked about the other week, I thought she would have been more careful. "Why were you walking home alone? Where are the other girls you live with?"

"They all ended up going home with guys for the night. It was my party, so I didn't want to leave till the very end. I thought I would be okay. I do stuff like this all the time."

"Is it your birthday?" I feel like I should have known that about her. But really, how much do we know about each other?

"Yes. Twenty-four." She smiles for the first time since I got here.

Wow, twenty-four. She's so young. When I'm with her, I forget just how young she is. "Happy birthday! So that explains the costume."

She glances down at what she's wearing like she'd forgotten she was dressed as a superhero. "Oh, this old thing? This is just my usual when I go out." She giggles.

"It should be, you look amazing."

"You should have seen it before I took the wig off. I totally looked legit." She wiggles her eyebrows for emphasis.

"I bet. How come you didn't go home with someone, like your friends?" It's none of my business, I know it's not, but I want to know the answer anyway.

She gives me an intense look, like I should know the answer to her question, then she sighs, glancing away from me and down at the table, playing with the wig. "Wasn't feeling it, I guess."

"Because of me?" I know I shouldn't push her. It's not fair to even be talking about this, but at the same time, I want to know the answer. Because she's the reason I was at home alone on a Saturday night when I could have been out exploring a new town with Ava—or anyone, really, but I haven't bothered to try doing anything with anyone since I moved here. Even though I really should.

Her gaze comes back to mine with a new intensity. "Maybe?"

She's not making it easy to resist her when she makes it so obvious that she wants more. I pushed and got the answer I wanted, but really, what can I do with that anyway? Nothing. It just makes me feel worse. I need to shut this down before I cross the line. She has made it very clear she won't cross it.

"Come on, let's get you home. You must be exhausted."

"I am, thanks."

The drive to her place is short, and she is unusually quiet. I keep glancing over to her, wanting to ask her if she's okay.

My eyes drop down her body. Her legs go on for days in that short bodysuit thingy she's in, paired with thigh-high boots. It's a teenage dream come true. I always did have a thing for Wonder Woman. Peeling her out of that thing would be sexy as fuck. And after what she went through tonight, it makes me feel like a total creep for even thinking it.

I pull into the driveway of the address she gave me and stop my car, hopping out to walk her in and say goodnight. Not what I want, but that's really all I can do. I'm her coach. Even the thoughts I'm having about her are totally inappropriate. As much as I want to, I can't act on it.

When she makes it to her door, she turns to me and smiles. "Thank you so much for coming to save me. It's probably just a stupid prank or something, but it rattled me, and it's nice to know I can count on you."

"You always can, Andy. Any time of the day or night, if you need me, call, and I will be here. Okay? And please report this to the police. I know you might feel silly doing that, but they need to know what's going on. And block that number so he can't contact you again."

"Thanks, Brad. Yeah, I already blocked it when I was in the diner, that's why I wasn't getting any more messages."

"Good girl."

We stand in silence for a bit. I don't want to let her go. She looks at me like she wants to say something else, but she doesn't. It's her birthday—well, it was, but it's well past midnight now. But I just want to be able to spend it with her. Make her feel better after the shit that went down tonight. She'll never say it, but I bet she's scared to be alone.

"Night, Andy. I hope you had a nice birthday, apart from the weirdness," I offer, not knowing what else to say, when all I want to do is scoop her up, carry her to her bed, and make her birthday one she will never forget, for all the right reasons.

My eyes drop to her lips. I'm so tempted to kiss her. She reaches out and takes my hand. Standing up on her tippy toes, she kisses my cheek. Her hand stays in mine a little longer than it probably should, then she pulls away. "Thanks, Brad. See you on Monday," she whispers, turning toward the door and letting herself in.

I don't follow her in like I want to. I watch her go inside safely, then sigh. Home to my empty house, again.

I walk toward my car reluctantly. I wish I could just go back there and spend the night with her. I know it's what she wants as well. I could see it, every time we've been together over the past few weeks, the chemistry is there buzzing between us. It's not just the fact that we've slept together in the past. There is something here, a connection that you don't just have every day. But for now, we have a major roadblock stopping anything more from happening.

Just as I go to get in my car, I hear her scream. What the fuck? I run back up the driveway and pound on the door for her to let me in.

# CHAPTER NINE

### ANDY

I close the door sadly. Leaning my forehead against it, wanting so badly to go out there and tell him how desperate I am for him.

This is not how I want my birthday to end. I should be in the arms of the man I literally can't stop thinking about, Brad Swift. He is so close but so far. He was very sweet tonight. I feel terrible he had to come and get me to drive me home, but those messages really freaked me out.

I have been wracking my brain since it started tonight. Who could it be? I've never had any trouble like this before. I'm not like Brad, with fans everywhere I go. Most people have no clue who I am, unless they're a real diehard fan of the Angels, but there aren't many, so until now, I've gone fairly unnoticed.

I dump my bag at the front and head straight for my bedroom. I'm tired as fuck. I just want to cuddle into my nice comfy bed and block out the day I've had. Enjoy the lingering smell of Brad's aftershave or body wash that still clings to me.

Flicking on my bedroom light, I feel it instantly. Something's not right.

I take in my room and a blood-curdling scream leaves my mouth before I have the chance to stop it. My room is completely trashed. I hear banging at the door and jump, my nerves on complete edge.

"Andy, let me in!" Brad's voice calls out to me.

I remember he was just leaving. He probably heard me scream. I run back to the front door and check through the peephole to make sure it's him. Of course it is, but now I'm super freaking out.

His eyes are wide and he looks panicked. "What was that? Did you scream?" He must see my face and he pulls me toward him, hugging me to his chest. "What's going on, Andy?"

"My room," I splutter into his chest.

He pulls back to look at me. "Can you show me?"

I nod and he takes my hand, and we walk back up the hall to stand in the doorway of my room.

"Fuck, Andy, this is bad. You're not staying here tonight."

The wall has been graffitied with... red paint—let's go with that, because I don't even want to contemplate what else it could be. The words *you're mine* in messy brush strokes. The contents of my drawers have been emptied out and spread over the room. The strangest part, though, are the twelve shriveled rose heads that are lying on my bed. They must be the missing ones from the bunch I received this morning.

A hot flush washes over me, and I feel like I could get sick. This creep has been in my room, rummaging through my belongings. This is too much. "I don't have anywhere else to go," I say, turning away from the sight to look at Brad.

He takes my hands in his. "You're coming back to my place with me. Text Luna, Darcy, and your sister and let them know not to come home either, not until we make sure it's safe. None of you should be here."

"I can't come back to your place," I whisper, trying to fight his suggestion when it's the only thing I want to do. I don't want to stay here alone, that's for sure, and right now, I don't want to be alone at all. All I can think of is how nice it would be to have his protective arms wrapped safely around me. But we can't. If anyone found out, it could mean him losing his job.

He runs his hands up my arms in a comforting gesture. "You're not staying here. I won't allow it. And right now, at this time of night, there aren't really any other options, are there? Grab some of your things and let's get out of here."

"Shouldn't I call the cops now?"

"We can do that in the morning once you've had some sleep. Nothing is going to change now."

He's right. There is no way I could deal with filling in some report right now. "Yeah, okay." I glance into my room again and I feel the roll of nausea wash over me. Nope. "I can't go in there to grab anything. Let's just go."

I grab his hand and we head for the front door, just stopping to pick up my bag and locking the door. Don't really know what the point is anyway, because clearly any fucker can just let themselves in.

Once I'm in his car, I shoot off a text to Darcy and Luna. Then decide I need to call Jasmine. I know it's really late, but I need to hear my sister's voice. She answers quickly.

"Andy, what's wrong?" Her voice is sleepy like I just woke her up, and I feel bad.

I nearly burst into tears when I hear her voice but stop

myself. "I'm sorry to call you so late but I needed to talk to you. Our place has been broken into."

I can hear movement on her end, she must be sitting up. "What? While you were there? Are you okay?" she asks, panicked.

"No, I only just got home. I'm fine, just a bit shaken. It's been a weird night."

"Are you there now by yourself? Oh my God, Andy. I'm coming home." I hear a male voice in the background asking her what's going on.

"No, stay where you are. I'm okay, I'm going to stay with a friend."

"Brad?" How the fuck did she work that out by me saying friend?

I glance over to him, hoping it's okay she knows. He smiles like he doesn't mind. "Yes, he has a spare room I can stay in." I'm talking through my ass. I have no idea if there's a spare room or not, but that's what she can know. And that's the only explanation I can come up with right now, and it's probably correct. There is no way he's thinking for us to share his bed, is he? He wouldn't be.

"Be careful, Andy," she says in her mom voice, and I know she's not talking about my actual safety. She's worried because I'm with him.

"Yes, I know, Jasmine. I'll talk to you in the morning."

"Love you, little sister."

"Love you too." I disconnect the call, and a tear escapes. I don't know why but her telling me she loves me makes me feel vulnerable.

I'm glad I called her. She is the person I'm closest to, and even though she can drive me nuts at times, she knows all my deep dark secrets, and I know hers.

The ride to Brad's place is quiet after the events of

today. I don't have any words left. I'm freaked out and fucking pissed that someone thinks they can mess with me like this. The other girls both message back quite quickly, surprisingly. I thought they would have been asleep or busy, but they agree to stay out for the night. So at least I don't have to worry about them. Just myself now, left with Brad, alone in his house.

THE DRIVE IS FAST; TOO QUICK, REALLY. HE LIVES JUST around the corner from me, and it hasn't given me enough time to prepare myself for all of this. I feel like I'm on the edge of losing it completely, but I'm trying my best to hold it together.

He pulls into his driveway, and we both sit in silence. Then he turns to me, resting a hand on my leg, and I jump at the sudden touch.

"Are you okay?" he asks softly.

"No." I burst into tears. "I'm not." I was trying to hold it together, not wanting to lose it in front of him, but I'm tired and can't hold back the tears anymore. Especially when he's being so nice to me.

He jumps out of the car and comes around to my side, pulling me into him as I ugly cry into his chest, too exhausted to care what I look like anymore.

"Hey, it's going to be okay. We'll work this out, get the police onto it. It's all going to be fine." He runs his hands up my arms, trying to soothe me. "Come on, you're covered in goosebumps. Let's get you inside."

"I'm so sorry. I'm just being silly because I'm overtired. I never cry normally," I say, trying to redeem myself. I hate whiney girls. I'm not a crier, and I'm embarrassed that I just did that in front of Brad.

I pull back from him enough so he can close the car door and lead me inside. His arm snakes around me and he pulls me close into him as he leads me down a hall, passing various rooms I'm too exhausted to notice much detail of. I need a shower and sleep. That's if I even can sleep after everything tonight.

The closeness between us is so comforting and just what I need when I feel so vulnerable. I'm still in total disbelief that someone broke into my home, my bedroom. Who knows what else they did while they were in there. The thought makes me feel nauseous all over again.

"Why don't you have a shower, warm yourself up a bit. I can give you something to change into if you like? You're a fine sight dressed as Wonder Woman, but that doesn't look too comfortable to sleep in." He smiles kindly.

I had completely forgotten about what I was wearing. I take his hand in mine and look up into his beautiful brown eyes. "Thank you so much, Brad. I'm sorry about tonight."

"Andy, it's fine, I'm happy to be here for you." He gives my hand a squeeze then breaks the eye contact, heading toward the back of the house, and I follow him like a lost little puppy. I don't want to admit it, but for the first time in my life, I'm scared to be left alone, even if it's just for a second.

We enter the spacious bedroom. It's pretty obvious from the decor that it's his room. It's very masculine, with dark gray walls and navy-blue bedding. Other than that, it's devoid of any real personality at all. I guess he hasn't lived here that long, so that's probably why. He enters a large walk-in closet with a frosted-glass door and returns with a pale blue T-shirt and a pair of cotton plaid boxer shorts. "I know these are going to be too big but it's the best I can do."

I take the clothes from him. "Seriously, it's fine. Right

now, I really don't care what I sleep in." The fabric feels soft and smells like him. I'm tempted to bring it up to my nose and inhale deeply but that would just be embarrassing.

He slides open another frosted-glass door, and this one reveals a large en-suite, with double shower and freestanding tub. "Bathroom is through here if you want to take a shower, maybe warm up. You look cold."

"Thank you." I want to ask him to join me, partly because I would love the distraction of seeing his gorgeous body again. I'm sure he would look super-hot with water running over those toned muscles of his. The other part of me just doesn't want to be alone. But I won't overstep that boundary. He's just trying to help me tonight; it would be selfish of me.

He gives me a look like he wants to say something, then heads toward the bedroom door as if to leave the room.

"Where are you going?" I say, panic in my voice.

"I'll give you some privacy and wait in the living room while you shower," he offers.

"You don't have to. I feel so bad I got you out of bed in the middle of the night. You can just hop back into bed. I won't be long," I say, quickly trying to assure him I'm fine with him in the room.

"Okay, I'll just watch telly for a bit."

He's still unsure of what to do here, and so am I. I'm insanely attracted to him, and the adrenaline of all the events from today is wearing off, and all I want is for him to hold me and tell me everything is going to be okay.

I offer him a small smile, pleased that he's staying close by. I slide the door to the bathroom closed. I turn on the shower and wait for the water to heat up, as I get to work removing my costume. First the gold belt, then the bodysuit.

As I step out of it, a thought crosses my mind. I'm right

in front of the glass door, and I wonder if Brad can see me. I wonder if he even cares that I'm in his bathroom, just a wall separating him from my naked body. He might be preoccupied watching the TV, a good coach would be, doing his best not to even think of what is taking place in his bathroom right now, but I hope he's not. I hope he's watching my every move, seeing my naked silhouette and remembering what it felt like to touch me.

Just in case he is, I run my hands up my body slowly, from my butt to my breasts, then up to my hair that I flick over my shoulder before I tie it in a loose messy bun on top of my head, before stepping into the shower. If he did watch me, I'm a total tease, and I don't even care. This situation is hard.

I have never not been able to get something I want, and right now, I want the swoony Brad Swift so badly it hurts.

---

### BRAD

I prop myself up in bed, flicking on the TV. My line of sight drifts to the bathroom where Andy is, the light from the room illuminating the frosted glass against the contrast of the darkened bedroom—meaning I can see her silhouette.

I should look away, respect her privacy like I said I would, but I can't. I don't want to. The attraction between us is driving me nuts, and I know I can no longer act on it, but man, I want to. The events of tonight have just amplified my feelings toward her. I want to protect her. Not only that, but I want to take away her fear, tell her I can take care of her, but I can't even do that, really. She shouldn't even be here tonight, but there was no way I was letting her stay at her place, and it's too late to call around and work out where else she could stay. This was the best option.

I watch as she takes off her belt, then shimmies out of her costume. She looks back over her shoulder, and I wonder if she knows I'm watching her, but I don't look away. She slides her hands up her body from her ass to her tits then plays with her hair, styling it on top of her head.

My cock is rock hard at the sight of her naked and in my bathroom. She's a total knockout and looked sexy as sin in that costume, but the sight of her curvy body right now is doing things to me it shouldn't. I should have better control than this. That's why I went to leave the room while she showered, but the look she gave me... I couldn't leave her. She's still freaked out from tonight.

There's no way she didn't know I could see her, and she put on that little show just for me. Resisting the temptation of her is becoming more and more difficult.

I keep thinking back to the night we had together, how comfortable she was in her own skin. She let me fuck her on the balcony of my hotel without a care in the world, and it was the hottest night I have ever had. What would it be like to be with a woman like her all the time? Fuck, we could have some fun, push each other's boundaries.

The shower shuts off and I have no idea how long she was in there for. Her perfect shape appears again in the glass panel. She runs the towel over her body, slowly drying herself, then I watch as she slips into the shirt and shorts I gave her, and the door slowly opens.

I flick my eyesight back to the TV, pretending that's what I was doing all along.

She makes her way over to where I'm sitting on my bed, looking adorable in my oversized clothes. "Enjoying the show?" She tilts her head toward the telly. "I wouldn't have picked you for someone who watches old re-runs of Friends," she says with a brow raised.

I glance at what's on and she's right, it's Friends. I really hadn't paid it any attention when I turned it on, I was too busy watching her, but she already knows that. "Yeah, it's my guilty pleasure," I say, acting innocent.

She smirks at me, hands on her hips. Even after everything she has been through tonight, the snarky smartass is still there. "Why do I feel like that's not true and it was a different show you were watching?"

"I have no idea what you're talking about, Andy." I slide off the bed, giving her nothing to go off of, because if I do, I won't stop at just telling her how fucking hot the show she put on for me was. I'll drag her back to my bed and do what I want with her. "Come on, I'll get you set up in my guest room. It's just down the hall."

She follows me to the room I have made up with a queen bed. She looks around at her surroundings, and I can see how uncomfortable she is. She's probably still freaked out; I know I would be. I roll back the covers for her, wanting to do so much more but keeping myself in check. I'm a fucking grown male, I can control my urges toward her no matter how cute and vulnerable she looks right now.

"Thank you. I guess I will see you in the morning," she says sweetly as she sits on the side of the bed, her hand stroking over the soft coverings.

"Night, Andy, hope you sleep well. You know where I am if you need me." *Or if you want me like I want you.*

"I do," she says quietly, climbing into bed. She looks like she's in a daze; I guess she would be really tired.

I flick out the light and reluctantly make my way back to my empty bed. It feels so wrong to be going in the opposite direction to where I want to be. I should be in bed with her, pulling her into me, showing her exactly how I feel about her. Instead, I have to go back to my empty bed and pretend like it's what I want. Keep my distance because I have to.

I flick off the TV and pull up the covers, closing my eyes and trying to get comfortable, even though I know I'm not going to be able to.

And I was right. I toss and turn for what feels like hours. How am I supposed to sleep knowing someone is trying to mess with her? I keep seeing the sight of her upturned room and what that guy wrote in the text messages. It's all so disturbing. Right now, she is in my house, and I know I can protect her here, but what happens tomorrow? Or any other day, for that matter, when I'm not with her?

I hear the sound of footsteps and I flick on the bedside light to see Andy standing in my doorway. It's obvious she's been crying, and my instincts take over.

"I can't sleep alone. I keep seeing my bedroom."

I gesture for her to come into my bed, pulling back the covers on the side closest to her, and she does. I hug her into my chest and stroke her silky hair. "It's okay, stay here with me. I can't sleep either."

"Your friend that was stalked... did they ever catch the person doing it?" she asks me. I know she's looking for reassurance, but that's not what I can give her if she wants the truth.

"No, they didn't. He moved addresses a few times and constantly had to change his phone number, but he never really got to the bottom of what was going on. One day it all just stopped."

"That's odd."

"Yeah, but he was just so happy he didn't have to deal with it anymore, he didn't ask any questions, just moved on with his life."

"Do you think that's what this is? Someone is stalking me?"

I don't want to lie to her, she needs to know how serious this could actually be. "I don't want to scare you, but it looks like it could be."

"Yeah, that's what I thought. I don't normally let anything affect me, but this has me scared. Your home is meant to be your safe place. How am I supposed to go back there and ever really feel safe again?"

I pull her in tighter to me. "It's understandable, anyone would feel the same in this situation. Try and get some sleep. We'll work it all out in the morning, okay? I'm here to protect you tonight, so you don't have to worry about anything." She rolls over so I'm spooning her from behind, and I stroke her hair and hug her into my chest.

Having her this close in my bed is sweet torture, but I have already blurred lines I shouldn't have tonight. And this is just to make her feel safe, I tell myself, as I try and drift off to sleep.

## CHAPTER TEN

ANDY

I feel warm arms wrapped around me. One hand skates slowly up and down my hip, playing with the boxer shorts I have on. I press my ass back into his crotch, enjoying the closeness we're sharing.

The events of yesterday start coming back to me and play back through my head. Realization dawns on me. I'm in Brad's bed but not how I want to be. I'm here because he came to my rescue. I go to move out of his clasp. Letting him hold me like this is too dangerous, but he grips me into him tighter.

"Just a few minutes more, I'm not ready to let you go," he murmurs into my hair. And for a minute, I think he must still be sleeping. Fantasizing about a different reality.

As his hand slips up under my shirt and brushes over my breast, I know he must be asleep. If he were fully conscious, there is no way he would be touching me like this. He cups it, rolling my nipple in his fingers. It sends a shiver of pleasure through my body, and I feel the hardness of his cock pressed into my ass.

Man, I want this with him. But I can't, *we* can't. He'll

lose his job and I can't be responsible for that. "Brad, as much as I want you to wake me up with your morning wood, we really can't," I whisper to him.

As if realizing what he's doing, he pulls his hand back from me, quickly rolling over to his side of the bed. "Shit, I'm so sorry, Andy, I shouldn't have done that. I was half asleep and not thinking."

"It's okay. It's my fault, I shouldn't have blurred the lines by staying in your bed last night. I was being a silly scaredy cat." I slip out of his bed, letting my legs hang over the side. "I'm just going to get myself dressed, then I better get home and work out what to do about what happened yesterday," I say, reluctant to leave but knowing I have to. Reality awaits.

He reaches out for my arm to stop me. "Andy, this isn't your fault. I overstepped the mark, and I'm really sorry. It won't happen again. Okay?"

I focus on him, my gaze locked with his. He's so handsome, even first thing in the morning and all sleepy. "Don't be sorry. I would do just about anything to fuck you again. But I'm not going to be the reason you lose your job. That's the only reason I'm walking away right now."

I slip out of bed and pad across the plush carpet to the en-suite in search of the clothes I came here in last night. I find my costume where I left it, crumpled in a pile on the floor. I shimmy out of Brad's boxers and pull the costume on under the pale blue T-shirt of his, I tie it in the front so it looks like I'm wearing it as a dress. I wash my face and try and wrangle my hair into a braid off to one side that sits over my shoulder. That will have to do. Zipping the knee-high boots back on, I step out of the bathroom.

Brad is sitting on the edge of his bed, dressed as well, in worn jeans and an old faded soccer jersey. He looks mighty fine for someone who has just woken up. "Hope it's okay if I borrow your shirt? I ask. "I don't want to show up at home in just this."

He looks me up and down. He seems upset or angry. "Andy, you make controlling myself almost impossible." Nope, he's frustrated. He's just as sexually wound up as I am. We both want to act on it, but we know we can't.

"So do you, Brad. Let's go before we do something we will both regret," I whisper, getting the words out with difficulty.

He takes my hand, and I gaze at his handsome face. He is so intense right now, his eyes dark with desire. "I won't regret it." He looks like his mind is made up. He wants this, fuck the consequences.

I look at him, confused. "You will when you lose your job." I swallow, my line of sight dropping to his lips.

"I won't lose my job unless I get caught," he says, his other hand coming to my hip and tugging me down on top of him so I'm straddling his lap on the edge of the bed.

Oh man, why does he have to say stuff like that? He's laying his cards on the table, and he knows I want this just as much as he does. A moment of stupidity comes over me, and I can't resist him a moment longer. I lean in and press my lips to his.

His hand rises to my neck, pulling me deeper into him, our kiss intensifying quickly, and it's everything I remember from that night and more. Deep, passionate, and intense. My hands roam up and under his shirt, touching his muscular chest.

He pulls back from me, sucking on my bottom lip, his intense gaze locked with mine. I'm already breathless. He's filled with fire and looks like he could eat me alive.

I feel my nipples harden, and the wetness between my legs increases. My body is begging for him to take me and do everything his eyes promise. I lean up to kiss him again, my eyes fluttering closed as I get lost in the moment.

Only to be interrupted by the sound of my ringtone echoing through his quiet bedroom.

I pull back from him. "I should get that, it might be one of the girls," I say reluctantly.

I slide off his lap and reach for my phone, seeing the name Jasmine. "Hey, Jassie."

Brad pulls me back to sit on the bed between his legs. He places kisses down my neck. How can something so wrong feel so right with him?

"Where are you, Andy? You need to get home. Dad just got here and saw your room. He's pissed, says he's going to kill whoever is doing this to his baby. The police are on their way." She sounds panicked, and I know what my dad can be like, and she's been left to deal with him. She's right, I better get over there and quick.

Brad's still kissing down my neck, trying to distract me, and God, do I want that distraction. "How does he know already?" I ask her.

"I talked to Mom this morning. Sorry, I was worried. Dad must have got in the car and left straight away. You know how he is, especially when it comes to you."

I let out a sigh, knowing this moment is over. "It's okay, I'm on my way home now. See you in ten."

"See you then."

I disconnect the call and turn to Brad. "I'm sorry, I need to get home. My dad is losing it and the cops are on their way to check it all out."

"Of course, I'll take you. Your dad, he sounds protective. Should I be worried?"

"Only if he knows what we just did. Don't worry, you should be fine." I fake a smile cause this situation is not ideal. Dad isn't going to be happy if he thinks something is going on here, and it looks sus as hell.

---

My place is only a short drive, but neither of us say a thing about the kiss. The car is just filled with awkward tension. As we pull up, the high I was on from finally sharing a kiss with Brad has faded away, and the uneasy feeling comes back. I don't want to enter my own house.

There's a cop car parked in the driveway, along with my dad's SUV. Two officers stand out front of my house talking to Dad. His expression is serious. His attention comes to us, and I feel about five years old. I only saw him just last night, but there is something about my dad that reduces me to a little girl that has me wanting to run to him and be sheltered from the world in his big strong arms.

I jump out of the car and go to him, and he wraps his arms around me in a comforting hug then pulls back to look at me. "Andrea, are you okay? Your mother and I came as soon as your sister told us what happened."

"We're just going to take a look around, get some prints," says the nice-looking female officer, "then we will need to get a statement, Miss Harper."

"Thank you," I say as the two officers disappear inside my house.

I notice my dad's attention shift to Brad who has made his way out of the car and comes up the driveway to where we're standing. He narrows his eyes to me. "Where did you stay last night, Andrea?"

"Dad, this is Brad Swift," I say, changing the subject quickly. "Brad, this is my dad, William.

"I know who he is." My dad holds out his hand to Brad and they exchange a glance between them I don't like the look of.

"Mr. Harper."

"Nice to meet you, Brad. You're a fine soccer player and I hear coach." His words are kind, but the glare he gives Brad has me nervous all over again.

His focus comes back to me. "I'll ask you again, Andrea, where did you stay last night?" His face is so serious, but I know how to play him. I've been doing this shit since I was fourteen.

I smile at him sweetly. "Brad kindly took me in for the night. I was too freaked out to stay here, so I stayed in his spare room. So nice of him, wasn't it, Daddy? I feel so bad I was such an inconvenience on him."

Dad rises a brow, as though he isn't convinced. "Going above and beyond for the girls on your team then, are you, Brad?"

"Mr. Harper, the safety of the girls on my team is very important to me. When Andy called, scared because she was being followed, I was just trying to make sure she got home safely, but when we got back here, well... I'm sure you've seen the state of her room. She couldn't stay here. It was late, and she slept in the spare room." Brad looks like he would get into it with my dad no problem, but he's trying to be on his best behavior.

I need to get these two away from each other before this becomes another problem I have to deal with. "Dad, don't we need to go and talk to the police?"

"Yes, you're right, they need a statement from you. Let's go find them."

I offer a small smile to Brad to say sorry. I thought he would have taken off straight away when he dropped me off, but instead, he follows us inside, where the police have cleared the kitchen and living area.

My mom is standing in the kitchen with Jasmine, both with a cup of tea in hand. I introduce Mom to Brad. She's more impressed than Dad was, but that wouldn't be hard.

Jasmine gives me a knowing look and I know the interrogation from her will come later.

Brad and I both give our statements about what happened last night to the police officers. They want Brad's perspective of what happened as well and need to see the texts on my phone. They spend the better part of an hour taking prints of my room and assure me they will try their best to track this guy down. The rest of the house is totally untouched. Whoever the intruder was, they only went in my room. It's so strange and definitely points to it being some kind of stalker or someone who is just out to mess with me, not a robbery.

Brad has been here the entire time, and he and Mom have been chatting in the kitchen while Dad has been around the house with a locksmith to have all the locks changed and a state-of-the-art security system installed. His main concern and that of the police is that there was no sign of forced entry, so either one of us four girls left a door unlocked and the person took the opportunity... or they had a key.

The security system will monitor the house from the front door and the backyard and is pretty obvious, so it will hopefully deter any further chance of someone breaking in. Dad also organized a cleaner to come and scrub the walls for me. I haven't been able to enter my room again yet. I'm waiting for it to be clean and back to normal before I do. I still keep seeing the image of the red writing on the wall. Yuck.

I sit at the outdoor dining table with my mom, Jasmine, Luna, and Brad. Darcy hasn't made it home yet, must have been a good night for her. Mom made us all lunch, and while I haven't been able to have a second alone with Brad since we got home, just the fact that he has stayed, to be here with me and my family through today, speaks volumes about the type of guy he is.

I'm in deep trouble when it comes to him, I know that much already.

He smiles at me warmly. "I better take off. I have some stuff to organize for tomorrow," he says, standing.

"So nice to meet you, Brad," says Mom, hopping up to offer him a warm hug.

"It was very nice indeed, shame about the circumstances."

"You look out for my girl, won't you?" Mom whispers to him, but loud enough that I hear her.

"I look out for all the girls on my team, Mrs. Harper. Jasmine." He nods in her direction, and she smiles. "See you tomorrow at training, Luna."

She offers a small wave. She looks exhausted. I'm interested to hear what the rest of them got up to last night. Looks like it must have been good, by how tired both she and Jasmine are today.

"I'll walk you out." I follow him out to the car, not wanting him to go at all. "Thank you so much for everything. Sorry about my dad."

He smiles with a tilt of his head. "He's just trying to look out for his little girl. I understand, I would be the same."

"Yeah, he's a little overprotective of us all."

He goes to get into his car, and I can't help myself, I have to know where I stand with him. I'm falling for him and his charm. And I don't want the awkwardness tomorrow at training. "Brad, about what happened this morning. I know it can't happen again, but I wish it could."

"Yeah, so do I, Andy." I take a step back from his car and he closes the door. His eyes are still on me, like he can't take them away. I begin to walk back up the driveway and hear the engine start, and I turn to watch as he drives away.

I can still feel his lips on mine. I run my fingers over them, wishing this morning ended differently. What a tease to be so close to what we both want, but really, we're fucking miles away because it's never going to happen again.

Darcy pulls into the driveway. She hops out of her car, still in her costume from last night. I laugh at her. "Walk of shame, baby."

She giggles back. "You know it. Look at you, babe, you're just as bad."

"I know, right, but I'm not ready to go back in my room just yet, so I have a good excuse." Truth be told, I could have changed into something of Jasmine's if I wanted, we're the same size, but I didn't want to take off Brad's shirt. I have one small part of him with me, and I know I said I was just borrowing it, but he ain't getting this back.

"What are you doing hanging out in the driveway?" she asks as we walk into the house.

"Just saying goodbye to Brad."

She wraps her arm around my waist, pulling me into her. "Ohh, I bet you were. What the fuck happened with you two last night?"

"Nothing happened, Darcy. I was freaked out, just stayed in his spare room." Well, maybe a little, but that is now my little secret with Brad. I don't need any of my big-mouth friends knowing what really took place, not even if they're my best friends.

She pouts. "Lucked out then, babes, I can see how much you like him."

"I don't. He's just a good coach and was looking out for me. That's all, Darcy."

"Keep telling yourself that, cause you're not fooling anyone else. I know you better than anyone, and you have a total boner for him."

I just roll my eyes at her. What else can I do? She's right. I do. But I can't admit it out loud, because that would be really bad.

"What happened to you last night?" I ask to change the subject.

"Met a cute girl at the bar, went home with her and her boyfriend."

I widen my eyes at her, but I'm not sure why I'm surprised. She would jump on anything that moves. Male, female, she doesn't care. And I can't talk cause that used to be me as well. Not too long ago, Darcy and I had a crazy night together. But that's not me anymore, a little voice says inside of me.

There is only one person I want, and it's the fine male specimen, Brad Swift.

## CHAPTER ELEVEN

### BRAD

It's early Monday morning and I'm at the clubhouse, setting up the training schedule for this week. I'm finding it hard to concentrate with the events of the weekend playing over in my head.

Leaving Andy yesterday was harder than I thought it would be. We had shared less than twenty-four hours together, but the connection we have when we're together is so strong, it felt wrong driving away from her. Especially when it's pretty clear she has someone stalking her, and no one is any closer to working out who it could be. I know she has her sister and two friends in that house with her, but I still feel uneasy about her being there after what happened.

Meeting her family was an unexpected development, but her mother is lovely. Her dad, on the other hand, is scary as fuck and is clearly protective of his little girl. I'm kind of glad they live over an hour away.

On top of all the weirdness was that kiss. I shouldn't have, *we* shouldn't have, but I'm not sorry we did. I have been wanting to kiss her since she had a go at me the night I was announced as the new coach.

I feel a hand rest on my shoulder and turn quickly to see Ava. She smiles and sits on the desk next to me, crossing her long, toned legs one over the other. She has on black workout tights, runners, and a team shirt. "So, tell me what was so important that you ditched my fabulous tour of the city yesterday?"

Shit, I knew this question was coming. She has been so sweet to me since I started here, and I finally agreed to spend the day with her, only to have to cancel because of what happened with Andy. I knew she would be disappointed, and I felt terrible, but Andy needed me. Dealing with a stalker situation was more important than a tour of the city. "I'm so sorry, Ava, how about we try again for this weekend?"

She rises a brow. "Not this weekend. We're in Kansas City for a game on Sunday, remember?" She looks at me like I'm losing my marbles.

"Yeah, of course, the following one then." I smile.

The back door swings open loudly, and we both turn to look at who's coming in so early. Andy, Luna, and Darcy walk in chatting and laughing. "Hey, Coach," calls Darcy with a wave.

I offer them a wave and a smile. Andy's eyes come to me, and a smile plays on her lips sending signals to parts of my body I need to have under control right now. She's cute in her training uniform and her hair in those adorable braids.

What happened between us yesterday was not a one-off kiss. I know we both got caught up in the moment and we shouldn't have done it... but I want it again. Screw the consequences. No more of this trying to suppress the feelings I know we both have for each other because of our work situation. If things were different and I'd met her after

I had become the coach, it might be different, but I met her first, and that night we had together was something I want again. I reckon I can have her and keep this job, no worries, we just have to be careful about it.

The girls continue on to the change room and I watch her for longer than I probably should, wondering what she's wearing under that uniform.

Ava clears her throat. "What was that, Brad?" she asks, glaring at me.

"What?" I say, giving her my full attention. Might need to be a little more careful around Ava as well.

"Brad, is there something going on between the two of you that I need to be aware of?" she says in a hushed tone, knowing other team members are now making their way through the building. But she is pissed, and she wants me to know it.

"With Darcy? I'm not sure what you're talking about. Now come on, we have a lot of work to do if we're going to win this game against Kansas City this weekend." Yep, definitely need to be more careful around her if just a smile has her picking up on the vibes between me and Andy.

The morning session runs smoothly. The team have taken better to my new schedule than I thought they would, but when we have won our first three games, it's easy to convince them that my way is better.

It's midday now and we're all sitting outside having a break for lunch. I want to check on how Andy is after what happened, but I haven't had a chance to yet. It's too hard with the rest of the team around, and Ava has stuck to me like glue all morning. I need an excuse to talk to Andy so it doesn't look suspect. But I've got nothing.

While eating my lunch, Ava has been talking my ear off about some show she binge-watched over the weekend, and

I listen as intently as I can. My attention is being drawn to Andy every time I hear that adorable laugh of hers. She's sitting on the table with her two pals Luna and Darcy who are sitting on the chairs in front of her. The three of them seem very close. It's rare to see them not all huddled together laughing or chatting about something.

Andy glances up and catches me checking her out. She winks at me, and I smirk back at her. I decide not to wait any longer but to text her. It could be the end of the day before I get her alone.

**Me:** How are you after the weekend?

I watch her as she receives the text and looks my way with a small smile.

**Andy:** Pretty shitty. I didn't sleep a wink last night. No big strong arms around me to protect me from the big bad world.

That goes straight to my heart and my primal need to protect her. I knew when I was leaving yesterday that she was feeling the same as me. She didn't want to be away from me. And to hear she didn't sleep. I feel torn up because I want to be there for her, but I can't.

**Me:** I would have been there if I could have been.

**Andy:** You would?

I wonder why she's surprised by that. I thought I made it obvious yesterday morning that I wanted her.

**Me:** Absolutely! I want a redo. We got interrupted yesterday when it was just getting good.

Darcy grabs her hand and tries to take the phone off her, but Andy keeps hold of it and gets up, walking away from her mates to stand under a tree alone.

**Andy:** You're a bad boy, Mr. Swift, you know we can't do that.

She smirks as she sends it.

**Andy:** But if we could... what would you have in mind?

She looks up to me and bites into her bottom lip. It's sexy as fuck, and I wish I could type out what I had in mind to do to her.

"Who are you texting with that stupid grin on your face?" asks Ava, bringing my attention back to her.

"Just one of the guys from my old team," I lie to get her off my case.

She looks a bit confused. "Are you still close with them?"

"Some more than others."

"Yeah, true. That's nice."

"I was on that team for most of my adult life."

"Do you miss it?"

I don't even know how to answer that. I feel like a completely different person now. I might still be involved in the game but not how I want to be, and it's not the same. "I feel like a part of me is missing. I would give anything to be able to play again, but it's just not possible." I look down to my knee, where there are scars from the multiple operations I had to have it reconstructed. You can hardly tell, there's nothing wrong to look at it, beyond the scars.

"Least you have us. Must be nice to know how much of a difference you're making here."

I smile. I guess it is, but it's not the same. Maybe that's why I'm self-sabotaging, letting myself get involved with a player, because as much as I want this job to give me some purpose, I don't need it. I have money, plenty of it. And the distraction Andy creates is much more tempting than it should be.

I quickly send off one last text and wait for Andy's reaction. It's fun to watch her as she reads my words.

**Me:** My place, tonight, 6pm. Tell the girls you have a date or something, just don't tell them who it's with!

She reads it and smirks into her phone as she types out a reply.

**Andy:** So we're going to play this game, are we?

**Me:** No game. I want you, and I'm not waiting any longer. My place and I'll show you what I have in mind.

Her eyes rise to meet mine. The blush that colors her cheeks is the reaction I was hoping for. She licks her bottom lip, and I don't know if she's doing it on purpose or not, but she has to know how crazy she's driving me right now. She types out a reply.

**Andy:** I'll be there X

Good, tonight we will sort out what is going on here, and hopefully the night ends better than yesterday morning did. Because I'm not going to get through another of these training days watching her run around looking all fucking cute and out of reach.

---

ANDY

I knock on Brad's door and wait. I feel bad lying to the girls about where I was going tonight. I told them I was reconnecting with an old friend from school. Kept the details vague so I wasn't lying too much. I had to say I was going out somewhere, because I'm more dressed up than I normally would be, in a three-quarter fitted skirt with a split at the side and a vintage tank, a faded denim jacket over the top.

I was all over the place at practice this afternoon; it

didn't help that I had no sleep last night, but mostly I was just thinking about Brad. And what his plans might be for this evening. He is risking so much doing this with me, but he doesn't seem to care.

He answers the door in relaxed-style jeans and a shirt. He smells freshly showered and looks totally yum. I give him a little sidewise grin, still not sure if this is the best idea or not. I'm going to take his lead.

I don't have to wait long to find out what he wants, as he pounces on me, pulling me into his arms and turning me so I'm up against the open door, his lips pressed to mine, his tongue invading my mouth hungrily.

My hands run through his hair, and his hands roam down my body and settle on my ass. He squeezes it roughly, and I feel my need for him throb through my body and go straight to my lady parts. As we kiss, he pulls me into him hard, so we're as close as we can be. His kiss is desperate, and I love knowing just how badly he wants me. Knowing the crazy attraction I have toward him isn't one way.

I pull back, trying to catch my breath. "We should go inside," I suggest, knowing the last thing we need is to be caught like this. By who, I don't know, but it still feels like a bad idea when we're trying to sneak around that we don't go inside first.

He looks around. "We should. I just couldn't wait." He takes my hand and leads me inside his home.

"Your house is so lovely." I walk around the living spaces, checking it out properly. The other night when I was here, I wasn't in the right frame of mind to notice anything much. The rooms are large, the walls in a warm gray, the floor light timber. There's a comfy-looking navy sofa in the center of the room with a rattan armchair off to the side and an oversized shaggy rug. The windows are to the ceiling and show a nice-looking yard with manicured lawns and a pool. On the walls are stunning black-and-white images, some of people, maybe family, others are clearly him playing soccer.

He comes up behind me and wraps his arms around my waist, kissing my neck, just how he did yesterday morning. "You're so lovely," he murmurs into my neck.

"We both know that's not true. I'm a badass, there is nothing lovely about me," I sass, pushing away from him to look more closely at the photos on the wall. "Is this your family?" I point to one of the photos, an older couple, a girl in her thirties, and two kids.

"Yeah, they're all back in Australia, so every year they send me a new family pic to have on my wall. This one is taken just down the road from the house I grew up in. My mum Carol, dad Terry, and sister Amy, and her two boys, Zac is six and Jay four."

I turn in his arms so I'm looking at his gorgeous face. Those eyes kill me, I want to get lost in them. Drift away from the real world for just a little bit. "They're cute kids. Bet you miss them, not being able to see them much. My family are everything to me. They all live back in Palm Springs, except for Jasmine, and I miss them so much when I don't see them for a few weeks. I feel like every time I see my niece and nephew, they've changed."

"I guess I'm used to it. I have been living away from home for so long that it just feels normal to see them only once or twice a year."

There is the most delicious smell wafting through the house. "Are you cooking something? It smells insanely good."

He smiles as if he's happy with himself. "That's dinner for us. Should be ready in about thirty minutes."

# THE COACH

I rest my hands on his chest, a little surprised that he was so thoughtful. "You made me dinner?"

He runs his hands down my body, pulling me into him closer and placing a small kiss to my lips. "You didn't think this was a booty call, did you?"

I shrug. "Honestly, I had no idea what this was. But I'm very impressed. No guy has ever made me dinner before."

"And you came anyway? Not knowing what this was."

"I'm here to find out what exactly you want," I say, poking him in the chest.

His eyes sparkle with desire, and I swallow, my throat all of a sudden going dry. "I want you, Andy. But since that's a little tricky in our current situation, I wanted to know where your head was at and see what you're interested in. I'm in the middle of a divorce. I can't handle anything serious, and as you know, because of my job, this is against all the rules. This would just be..."

"Fucking, with no strings attached. All good. I don't want anything more than that anyway. Relationships are not my thing." I finish his sentence for him because I know what he wants from me, and I'm okay with that. I want him for the same reason. The memory of that night we shared stays with me, and if I can have me a little more of that, I'll be more than happy. No strings attached is even better. I hate relationships, and I'm not the clingy type, so if he's telling me he's the same, then this is going to be a match made in orgasmic heaven. We can do it for a while, get it out of our systems.

He places kisses from my earlobe down my neck. "You won't be able to tell anyone. Are you comfortable lying to your friends and teammates? Seriously, Andy, no one can find out," he gets out between distracting me, planting slow measured kisses down my chest as he says it.

"Do you think I want anyone to find out? I know you'll lose your job, but it looks bad on me as well." I already deal with enough from the bitches on the team. "Trust me, this is just between us," I whisper, because although I want to sound strong and confident right now, he has me weak. I'm falling under the spell of his magic lips touching my bare skin. He drops the straps of my tank one at a time and pulls my top down, exposing my breasts to the cool air.

"No bra?" He takes a hardened nipple in his mouth, sucking.

"All my nice ones were stolen on Saturday night," I admit.

He pulls back to look at me. "Are you for fucking real?"

"Yeah, creepy as hell, all my panties too."

His hand slides down under my skirt and he groans as he feels my bare ass. "No panties either. You're so fucking hot, Andy. You drive me crazy." He takes the sides of my skirt in his hands and tugs it down, running his hands over my skin.

I wriggle out of my top as well, so I'm standing in front of him totally naked. He pushes me down on to the recliner. He removes his shirt as I watch.

I sit on the end of the chair and pull him toward me, undoing his jeans zipper. His pants drop to the floor, and I drag his boxer briefs down as well. His massive cock jumps free, and I take it in my hand, stroking. "So fucking hard for me, aren't you, baby." I lick the bead of pre-cum off the tip and he hisses. "You taste so good. I have been waiting weeks to suck your big, hard cock," I tease, taking his length in my mouth, sucking, rolling my tongue over the tip as I go up and down his length. I watch as his eyes roll back in pleasure. I suck back and forth, showing him just how much I want him.

His hands go to the back of my head, and he pulls me onto him harder. I take him in as far as I can, giving him the control, letting him fuck my mouth. My hand digs into his rock-hard ass as he picks up the speed, really giving it to me. I love his cock in my mouth, him coming undone because of something I'm doing to him.

"Fuck, Andy, I'm going to come." He loosens his grip on my head so I can pull away if I want to.

But I keep going. Two more pumps and I feel the jerk of his cock as he groans my name and fills my mouth. I drink it down. He pulls out, and I swipe the back of my hand over my lips. And give him a sexy smile. "Was that good, baby?" I ask, already knowing the answer.

"Fuck, you have no idea just how good." He drops to his knees in front of me and pushes me back to lying down on the recliner. "Now I'm going to devour you." He grabs my ass and pulls me toward him, spreading my legs as wide as they will go.

He studies me, his fingers running over my dripping-wet pussy. He bows his head to taste me. The warmth of his tongue against my most sensitive spot almost bringing me undone at first touch. My body is hypersensitive and needy, wanting his touch everywhere.

As he eats my pussy, his hand skates up my body, landing on my breast. He squeezes my nipple and rolls it between in his fingers. A moan escapes my lips. Everything he's doing is so good. My back arches off the chair as I rise to meet his mouth. Greedy for more. He sucks harder and flicks his tongue over my clit, sending goosebumps over my skin. His fingers find my core and push in, filling me. He pumps me in precise movements, hitting right at the spot I crave. More incoherent mumbles leave my lips.

He's not just a skilled soccer player; he fucking knows

what he's doing with his mouth. I'm in heaven, one controlled by sex-god Brad Swift.

"Oh God!" I cry and cover my eyes as my orgasm ripples through my body, but he doesn't stop. He continues to lap me up until my body relaxes again.

He pulls back to look at me, and I prop myself up on my elbows. There is total satisfaction in his eyes; he knows how good he is. "Roll over," he demands, taking my hands to help me up so I can do what he asks.

I prop the cushions up under my tummy and watch as he goes to his wallet and retrieves a foil packet, rolling the condom down his length, then he's back behind me. His hands slide down my body and land on my ass, and he slaps me. And I love the way it sends a thrill through my body.

"Fuck, your body is scorching hot, Andy."

The sting is still there, but I like it. I look over my shoulder at him. "Do it again."

He smirks. "You like it a little rough, don't you, naughty girl?" He slaps me again.

"Yes," I hiss.

"That's why we're so fucking good together." He pulls my legs farther apart and lines himself up with my entrance. The anticipation while I wait for him is almost too much. Then he slams into me, pushing me forward on the chair. I grab hold of the side, and he grips my hips in his hands, holding me in place as he moves again, plunging into me so deep. So good, the way he fills me up. He moves in fast, deep thrusts, and I push back into him so our bodies slap together, the tension building again so quickly. I'm so close already. Then a buzzer sounds from somewhere else in the house. In my sex haze, it takes me a second to register that's what it is.

"Fuck, the dinner." He groans, disappointed. He pulls

out and makes a run for the kitchen. I watch his fine ass as he leaves the room.

"Don't burn yourself," I call to him, laughing to myself at the bad timing of his dinner. I sit back on the chair and wait for him to return.

The sight of him walking back through the doors—rippling chest, tensed legs, chiseled jaw, and piercing eyes—but it's his cock I can't take my eyes off. Fuck, he's hung. No wonder sex with him is like no other.

"What are you looking at?" He grins cheekily. He knows how fucking good his body is.

"Just thinking that you're one lucky boy, so blessed with what Mother Nature gave you."

"I think it's you who's lucky, my dear." He strokes himself as he closes the gap between us, kneeling down on the chair. I part my legs, giving him access to my body again.

"What about the dinner?" I ask, not really caring much for food right now.

"It's better if it rests for a bit anyway," he says, slamming into me again.

"Fuck!" I cry. His lips cover mine, drowning out my call with a passionate kiss. I forget about anything else and just focus on what he's doing to me. Raising my hips to meet his violent thrusts. I want it all. Every pump fills me with pure satisfaction. The rhythm we're building together.

His kiss is rough, and paired with the way he's rolling his hips into me, it's pure perfection. I could stay like this all night.

He pulls back to look at me, his gaze so intense I can't stand it. Why does he have to look at me like that while we're doing this? Like he sees me, all of me. That's not what this is. So I let my eyes roll closed to block it out. I can't handle the way it makes me feel. So deeply emotional.

His lips return to mine, our tongues battling, as my body begins to tremble with the euphoria taking over. He calls out my name as I feel the telling jerk, and he fills me. His body collapsing onto the chair with me.

My heart races and my breathing is ragged. That was insane. Life-changing, even. No other will ever compete with what he can do to me. But it's the look in his eyes, the moment we just shared, that will stay with me. It was too intimate, too real. And I don't understand how it could be. This is just fucking between two people who share an attraction to each other, that's all. He said it himself. That's what tonight was supposed to be about, a chat to clarify what this is.

Now I'm more confused than ever. I wanted this to be simple, but something tells me that was the start of something we couldn't stop, even if we wanted to.

## CHAPTER TWELVE

### BRAD

We lie together while we regain our breath. That was... I don't even know what that was. But I know I want to do it again. I think I'm addicted to her. She's sassy and naughty and a total vixen in bed. If I lie here too long with her, I might never want to leave her side.

"Come on," I say, dragging her by the hands to stand with me. "Dinner awaits."

I pull my jeans and shirt on and wait for her to wriggle back into her skirt and tank. Then I take her hand and lead her to the kitchen where the lasagna that I pulled out of the oven earlier waits for us. I don't know why I feel the need to lead her everywhere with me, but I just can't keep my hands off her.

"Wow, this is what smelled so good earlier. I love Italian food. I can't believe you made this for me." She beams, excited. I didn't think she would be so easy to impress, but if a home-cooked meal is all it takes, then this is going to be easy.

"From scratch, and there's a salad as well," I brag, pulling the salad from the fridge as Andy searches the cupboards. "Top right for plates," I point her in the direction.

"Thanks." She takes out two large white plates, placing them on the counter for me.

I serve up the dinner and we carry our plates to the dining room. "Do you want something to drink? Wine?" I offer.

She shakes her head. "Nah, I try not to drink during the week. I find it way too hard to train if I do. I learned that one the hard way in college. I'll have a water, though."

I place her water on the table and take a seat across from her. She chugs the entire glass and grins at me. "This all looks so good. I still can't believe you made it for me, I'm so impressed." She takes a bite. "It's amazing. You can really cook. Lucky, cause I really can't." She scoops up another mouthful.

"Oh, really? Who does all the cooking at your place?"

"Mostly Jasmine, she's good in the kitchen. The rest of us try and help out when it's something simple. I don't eat a heap of full meals, normally just something easy like a salad and tuna or chicken."

I nod, knowing that all too well. "That's me normally too. I don't see much point in going to the trouble just for myself."

She narrows her eyes at me, as if trying to read me. "Where did you learn to cook?"

I smile, remembering my cooking lessons as a teen. "My mum is incredible in the kitchen. She thought it was important for me to be able to cook at least seven meals, one for every night of the week, so before my sister and I left home, she made sure we both could."

Andy's smile matches mine. I can see she's imagining

me and my mum and sister in the kitchen. "Your mom sounds wonderful."

"She is. Your mum didn't teach you to cook?" I ask, a little surprised. I only met her mom once, but she seemed like the type who would be very invested in teaching her girls to cook.

She laughs. "Oh, she tried! But she gave up on me; worked out pretty quickly that my sisters held the talents in that area. She was wasting her time with me."

I grin, imaging her in the kitchen as a kid. She would have been covered in the ingredients, distracted by anything else, while her sisters listened intently.

"Fair enough. What are your other sisters like? There are four of you, right?"

"Yeah, I'm the third. My oldest sister, Amelia, is the creative one, not so lucky in love, though. She's going through a divorce. Her asshole husband came home one day and told her he had gotten his girlfriend pregnant and he was leaving her for the girl. Left her with two little kids on her own."

I can feel my blood boil for her poor sister. I have been in that situation, and it's awful, but at least I didn't have kids to worry about. And for him to just leave his kids, what kind of a dad does that? When I'm a father, nothing will keep me from my family. "Are you fucking kidding me?"

"Nope, wish I was. She is the sweetest, totally the last person who deserved for that to happen. She didn't see it coming at all either. And the worst part is he has been with this other chick pretty much their whole marriage. How fucked up is that. If I ever see him again, he will know what pain is." The anger she has toward this guy is intense. I can only imagine what she was like that morning when she thought I had cheated on my wife. I'm lucky she didn't attack me in the bed while I was asleep.

I shake my head in disbelief. "You're scary when you're angry. But I get it, I know that feeling."

She gives me a sympathetic smile and takes my hand across the table, interlacing our hands together. The small gesture is so comforting coming from her. "Yeah, you do. I'm sorry you had to go through that. Makes me seem less crazy for the way I reacted when we first met and I thought you were doing the same, though, doesn't it? If there's one thing I really hate, it's a cheater. If you're not happy, just be up front and honest about it. Don't drag some other poor person through all of that."

"I totally agree with you. I'm not sure why people find it so hard to be honest about the way they feel."

She gives me a sideways look. "You're always honest about your feelings?"

"I try to be."

"Good to know. Anyway, Amelia is a beautiful soul. Runs her own fashion brand back in Palm Springs. She's getting really successful and I'm so proud of her. My second sister is Jasmine, who you met yesterday. She's the smart one and works as a psychologist, with kids mostly. My little sister Cassie is just finishing up her education to become a primary teacher. She's also super smart. At the moment she is teaching dance classes at the local dance studio while she gets through her education degree. She still lives at home with Mom and Dad and is giving them a run for their money at the moment. I guess she is the most like me in that way. They should have stopped at two." She laughs.

I love the way she talks about her sisters. You can see how much she adores them and how important they are to her. It's so nice to see. I get a flashback of her father and the look in his eyes when he shook my hand yesterday. He definitely thought something was going on between us. He's not stupid, and he's not happy about it. Can't say I blame him. "Your dad hates me," I say as a statement, wondering what she thinks about it.

She nibbles on her lip. "It's not hate. He is just very protective of his girls."

"He would hate me if he knew what we were doing behind everyone's backs, though, wouldn't he?" I'm pretty sure he would fucking kill me if he knew for sure what we were doing.

She smirks at me. "That's just another good reason to keep this just between us. I haven't ever been one to follow the rules. I was hardly my parents' favorite kid, so nothing is new, but if I can avoid pissing him off, it's probably for the best. My mom definitely liked you, though. She was giving me little looks all day."

"She did? Your mom was lovely. You and Jasmine take after her so much in the way you look." I finish the last of my meal and push my plate aside. "You would have been so much trouble as a kid."

"What do you mean would have been? I *am* trouble. That's why you like me so much." She grins over to me.

She's got me. There's something about her I-don't-give-a-fuck attitude I find so enticing. Maybe cause that's how I used to be when I was younger and she brings it back out in me, makes me feel young again.

She finishes her dinner, placing her knife and fork together neatly on the plate. "Thank you so much for dinner. You're hot, good in bed, and can cook. You're a catch, Mr. Swift, you really shouldn't be wasting your time with me."

"I want to waste my time with you. You're fun and just what I need right now."

"You're just what I need right now as well." She yawns. "But I think I need to get home to bed. I'm seriously wrecked after the last couple of nights with no sleep."

"Yeah, you said you didn't sleep last night. Are you okay?"

Her expression changes and I can see just how much this is all really affecting her. "I'm kind of creeped out in my own house. It's not a nice feeling. I want to put it all behind me, and I keep trying to convince myself that it won't happen again and that I'm safe, but I'm not going to lie. The fear is creeping in. What if this guy comes back when I'm there? I doubt the security cameras and alarm will stop him if he really wants to mess with me." She looks down to her lap and plays with her hands.

This is really bothering her, and I wish I could do something about it. I would like to invite her to stay here again, but it really is too risky.

"They would be a pretty good deterrent, though, and give you time to get away if the alarm is going nuts. I don't like that you feel unsafe, though. I wish there was something I could do to help."

"Thanks, I think it's just going to take a bit of time to get over it." She collects both our plates from the table and walks through to the kitchen, placing them in the sink. "Did you want a hand with the dishes?" she offers, but I can see just how tired she is, and as much as I'm not ready for her to leave, I can see she needs to.

"No, I've got them. I just want you to go home and get a good night's sleep. I can't have my best striker too tired to score." I pull her into my arms, holding her close. I kiss her lips, wishing even more I could just take her to my bed for the night. I know I could help her fall asleep easily. She would feel safe here with me. But that's not how this is going to work. I need to let her go home to her own bed. I'll have to come up with another way I can help her to feel safe.

"Message me when you get home. I need to know you get there safely."

"Thank you for looking out for me, I appreciate it."

---

ANDY

I arrive at practice even more exhausted than I was yesterday after another completely sleepless night, tossing and turning, unable to settle my mind enough so I could drift off to sleep. Between how uncomfortable I now feel in my room and the desire to be with Brad, knowing how good the rest of the night would have been if I stayed with him, I just laid there thinking.

We all gather in the main room of the training shed, and I try to listen intently to what Ava is saying about our corner plays, but it's all going over my head today. I can barely keep my eyes open. Hopefully, once I start running around with our warm-up, I'll perk up a bit. I cover my mouth to stifle yet another yawn. I wish she would stop talking so I can just go train.

Finally, after what feels like forever, the meeting is over. I go to make my way out the door when the sexy Australian accent calls my name. I turn back to him as the rest of the room empties out, the other girls eager to get on the field. My tummy twists. I want so badly to see him again, but I need to play it cool here around everyone else. I had kind of hoped he would ignore me to make it easier on the both of us.

He makes his way over to me. "Andy, are you okay?" he asks, looking concerned.

I shake my head. "I'm so tired. I just can't sleep. I've never had problems sleeping before, I don't even know what to do."

"Have you talked to Jasmine about it? I'm sure she has some ideas for you."

"She thinks I'm anxious. She gave me some exercises to do before I go to bed, but they don't work. My mind won't stop. I just feel too creeped out."

"Maybe you could talk to Beth, our psychologist, she might be able to help?"

I give him a wide-eyed worried look. That is the last thing I want to do. "I'll be okay. I'm sure in a few days I will be back to normal."

"Alright, just do your best out there today. Hopefully tonight will be better." He looks at me like he wants to say something more, and maybe he does, but he can't, not here. So he heads out to where the others are running around, and I follow him, hoping he's right. Tonight has to be better.

I'M BACK AT HOME IN MY BED WATCHING NETFLIX, trying to keep my eyes open so I can hopefully sleep when the time comes tonight. Today was my worst practice I think ever. I was hopeless, with two left feet. I'm hoping tonight I'm just so exhausted I sleep no matter how crazy my head is going over all of this.

We heard back from the police today, and they have nothing from the fingerprints in my room, and the phone he was texting me on they traced to a garbage can on the street

I was walking on. So it was all a dead end, and they said there's really nothing they can do for now unless he actually hurts me or they can find evidence to pin against him. So that's just great. They will basically wait until I'm dead to do anything more. I'm being dramatic, but it feels so stupid that I have to just sit here and take it. There's nothing more that can be done. It could literally be anyone who did it, and I hate it.

There's a knock at the front door, and I hop out of bed to go and check who it is. I can see in the security screen it's a guy holding something. He looks harmless enough. I answer the door to see a young guy holding an adorable little black bull terrier puppy.

"Hi, can I help you?" I ask, thinking this guy must have the wrong house or something.

"Are you Andrea Harper?" he asks, looking unsure.

I nod. "Yes, that's me."

"Oh, good. This is for you." He passes me the cute little dog and takes a step back. "A belated birthday present. There's everything you will need to take care of her in here." He points to the box, and I look down at it then back at him. What is he talking about? Is this for me, a present? I look at the little puppy, and her big eyes melt me instantly, she's so cute.

"Really, who's it from?" I ask before he leaves.

"The dude said he will text you with the details, just paid me to deliver the pup. Have a nice day, ma'am. She is a cutie."

"Thanks," I say, waving him off and looking at the pup in my arms. This is interesting.

I close the front door and wander back to my room, not quite sure what to do with her. When I hear my phone ping, I'm not surprised to see the name when it comes up.

**Brad:** I sent her to protect you and keep you company when I can't x

She's from Brad. Of course she is. He's so thoughtful. He can't be here when he wants to be, so he sent a little friend for me. This is the sweetest thing someone has ever done for me. I place her on my bed, and I sit next to her. She rolls on her back, and I rub her tummy and giggle at her.

**Me:** OMG thank you so much! She is adorable, I just love her!

I take a selfie of me holding the pup as she squirms to try and get out of my arms. I send it to him.

**Brad:** You make a cute pair. I was hoping you would be allowed to have a dog at your place? Now I hope you can get some sleep tonight with her there to look after you.

I'm sure I'm going to be up all night taking care of her, but I don't care, because she is so cute. And he's right, even though she is a puppy now, I feel better just knowing she will be here with me. She'll let me know if someone breaks in.

**Me**: It's my parents' place, and if I explain to my dad that she's to make me feel safer, he'll understand. Thank you so much xx

I place her on the floor and walk with her out to the living area to show the other girls. Jasmine is the first to see her and comes running over, ecstatic. She loves dogs and has wanted one for ages.

"Oh my God, Andy, where did you get her? She is so cute." She snuggles the pup up into her lap, talking to the pup in a cutesy baby voice.

I need to think quick. I can't tell the other girls she was a gift from Brad, that looks super weird. Why would my coach be buying me a dog? "I called around today and found a breeder . You know how unsafe I've been feeling lately, and I thought she might help." Good cover-up, Andy.

"Dogs are a big responsibility, Andy," she tuts. I love her but she drives me crazy thinking she is so much older and more responsible than I am.

I roll my eyes at her. "I know, but I'm pretty sure I can handle it. I'm not a kid anymore."

She looks me over. "Yeah, I guess you're right. We couldn't get rid of her now anyway, I'm already in love." She giggles as the puppy licks her.

"I know, right. And that's good, cause I'm going to need your help on the nights I have to travel for work."

She smiles, not bothered by the inconvenience at all. "True. It's okay, she can keep me company. I've been feeling a little scared myself this week. I think you're right, having a dog around will make us feel safer. What are you going to name her?"

I pat her on the head and think on it. "Hmm, I'm thinking Nala."

"Like from the lion king? That's perfect."

Darcy and Luna come in the back door from an afternoon swim in our pool and squeal when they see her. They come running excitedly over. I think this little pup is going to fit in here with us girls just fine.

Brad has done yet another thing to make my heart flip-flop. He's getting under my skin, I can feel it. He's too sweet and caring. I'm waiting for the reality check when I realize he's just like all the rest of them, not worth my time. But for now, what we have is a fun little secret and the perfect distraction from everything else that's going on.

And the feelings that keep creeping up when he does something so nice for me, well, I have them under control. They don't mean anything at all.

## CHAPTER THIRTEEN

BRAD

I haven't had much of a chance to catch Andy alone this week. She's been busy with her new puppy. And during the days, we've been working hard all week with our training schedule. The game this week with be the hardest yet, as this team is also unbeaten and the reigning champions from last year.

I have also had a few after-work appointments with my attorney, trying to get all the paperwork sorted for when Madeline's in town in a couple of weeks. I want it all signed and finalized. I'm prepared to pretty much give her everything she's asking for, just so it can be done and I never have to see her again. Every time I think about it, all I can think is how glad I am we didn't have kids like Andy's poor sister. We had been trying to start a family, but it didn't happen, and at the time I was devastated. I was ready for a family and thought she was the one to do it with. But now I see just how much it was for the best. Being permanently attached to that woman would have been awful.

It also makes me doubt myself for the future. I want to settle down and have a family, but I can't trust myself to find the right person when I was so off with her. I was warned by my parents and friends to get a prenup, but I truly didn't ever think we would end up like this.

My mind wanders to Andy. She is the polar opposite to Madeline in every way. But Andy is just a fling, and an irresponsible one at that. She's fun and naughty and everything I need right now to distract me from the fact that the life I had mapped out is nowhere to be seen. One kick to the back of the knee sent a domino effect, and everything fell apart.

The whole team has just arrived in Kansas City for tomorrow's game. We will be staying at the same hotel, and I intend to make sure Andy and I get to see each other. The girls take the field for training before dinner tonight. They're all in high spirits now, but I know if we lose this game, that could change quickly.

"You think they're ready for tomorrow's game?" asks Ava who has been at my side watching the team.

"I hope so." I remember what it's like when you come up against *that team*, the one you just can't beat no matter how well you play, and for these girls, it's Kansas City. We haven't beaten them in three years.

My attention gravitates to Andy, and I watch her practice her goal shooting. She is so determined when she's on the field. The fun-loving girl I know is nowhere to be seen, replaced by the look of focus on her face, and you know she has blocked out the rest of the world. She's in the zone. And she's impressive to watch.

Ava places her hand on my arm, getting my attention. I flinch because I have just been caught watching Andy. She smiles to me sweetly. "Brad, after tonight's dinner with the team, I was hoping you might like to join me in my room for a drink?" She blinks up at me, and I'm at a loss for what to say to her. "You know, just to go over the last-minute game plan," she adds. Probably because I'm staring at her with no words coming out of my mouth.

I can't meet her in her room. Since the last away trip, she has been making her feelings toward me more obvious and that's just asking for trouble. She's a great girl but not my type at all. "Oh, um, let's do that in the morning over breakfast. We could meet in the hotel restaurant if you like." Public places are the best I can offer her, so she doesn't get the wrong idea.

She looks a bit hurt, and I feel bad, but I know it's for the best. "Yeah, of course, why didn't I think of that? An early night would be better anyway."

"Yeah, good night's sleep with the big game tomorrow, that's what I'll be doing." She eyes me suspiciously, and I offer her a smile. Hoping things between us aren't about to get super awkward.

After wrapping up our training session, the team and coaching staff are out to dinner in the hotel restaurant. We have separated out at a few different tables. Not all the players have come tonight; some have chosen to stay in and get mentally prepared. I'm sitting with our coaching staff: Ava, our team manager, our goalkeeping coach, physical trainer, nutritionist, physiotherapist, and psychologist.

Andy and her two friends are sitting together with a couple of the other players. I can't help but notice she has gone to more effort than usual for one of these dinners. Her long hair is out and she's in a silky-looking cami with dark skinny jeans and those boots with the heels. She's the hottest girl in the restaurant by far, and I can't help but wonder if every other guy in the room is checking her out as well as me. It's the most difficult part of this arrangement we have going on. We're in such close proximity all the time, but I can't be with her, when that's all I want to do.

As the night goes on, our meals are served and I listen to the small talk around the table, mostly about tomorrow's game. I'm not paying that much attention. I would much prefer to be at Andy's table.

As I thought, her table attracts the attention of a group of guys. They pull up their chairs, and the conversation looks flirty. I don't like the jealousy that washes over me at the sight of another man talking to her, but it does, and I find myself wracking my brain for any excuse to get her away from them. They look to be more her age too, probably the kind of guy she would normally hook up with. She said she doesn't do relationships, so I guess that means she does do random hook-ups, and I hate the thought of it. I know I have no right to want ownership of her, but I do.

Every now and then she glances my way, but it doesn't last long before she is drawn back into the conversation of the group. Her friend Darcy goes to sit on Andy's lap, wrapping her arm around her. They tell a story to the group and crack up laughing.

One of the guys leans in and whispers something to the two of them and that's it for me. My imagination is running wild with what he has said to them. Did he just offer them a threesome or something? I can't sit here and watch this any longer. Or I'm going to blow a fuse and storm over there and deck him. I type out a text to her.

**Me:** My room 203 in 5 minutes or else!

She reaches for her back pocket and takes out the phone, reading the text, then looks my way with a little sexy smirk playing on her face when she types her response.

**Andy:** Or else what, Brad?

**Me:** Or else I cause a scene in front of everyone and

blow our cover because I can't stand to watch you with them any longer.

She reads my reply and her eyes come back to me, and she looks worried. She should be. I'm serious. Well, I'm not, but I'm calling her bluff.

She says something to the group. Darcy kisses her cheek then slips off her lap. She takes her bag from the table and walks out of the restaurant with a flick of her long hair over her shoulder.

I wait another two minutes then excuse myself from my table, saying I need an early night, and make my way out of the restaurant after her. When I arrive at my room, there's no sign of her, so I go inside and wait. Within minutes, there's a knock at the door. When I open it, she is dressed in a coat, a pair of sexy black pumps, and a hat. I grab her by the waist and pull her into the room quickly, laughing at her. "What's with the change of clothing?"

"It's my disguise. I didn't want anyone to see me coming to your room." She laughs back, obviously realizing how funny she must look.

She was worried someone would see us. I'm glad she's being careful. "I'm purposely on a different floor to the rest of you. I knew I wanted you in my room tonight, and I wasn't taking my chances that someone would see us, so I got them to move me."

"Ahh, smart plan. Guess that means I'm a sure thing then, hey." She places her hands on her hips, the movement exposing a peek of lace from her bra. She is a naughty girl in just a coat and her sexy lingerie, walking around our hotel.

"Not what I was thinking. I do want to know what else makes up this disguise, though," I say, playing with the lapel and showing off more of her breasts.

She unties the belt at the waist, letting the coat open,

showing off her beautiful body. "Not a lot. You only gave me five minutes to prepare."

"Looks like I gave you the perfect amount of time then." I slide the coat off her shoulders so I can get a better look at her. "I see the second part of your birthday gift arrived."

"Yes, do you like?" She offers me a slow spin. I run my hands up her body, feeling the silky lingerie.

"I do." I pull her into me, kissing her luscious lips. Her body presses into mine and her hands roam under my shirt, bunching it up then pulling back so she can tug it off. Her hands skate over my chest. She has that naughty sparkle in her eyes.

"Thought you would have preferred me totally nude, but these are very pretty. Thank you."

"Oh, I like that look on you as well, but sometimes it's nice to have something to unwrap, and you did say all your nice ones were stolen. I couldn't have you going around in no underwear all the time. Could I now?"

She gives me a sassy smirk. Her fingers still dancing across my chest. "So, this present was as much for you as it was for me."

"Maybe a little for me." I pull her into me roughly, my fingers digging into her ass as I lift her and kiss her more aggressively. I've missed her this week. I need to feel her body under mine and show her just how much.

---

ANDY

Brad throws me down on the bed as I stare back up at him; he's so nice to look at. All night I've been trying to control myself and not look his way, but man, it's hard. Having distance between us because we're not supposed to have an intimate relationship and we're the only ones in the room who know there is something going on between us somehow makes him even more desirable.

His kisses are everywhere, my lips then my neck and down my chest, breasts, stomach, all the way down my legs. He places light kisses then nips and bites on his way back up my legs. His hands lightly running over my calves then my thighs, until he makes his way up to where my sexy panties sit. He spreads my legs and places a kiss on the inside of my thigh.

I could hardly believe my eyes when I unwrapped the parcel waiting at my front door to find three beautiful sets of silk and fine lace lingerie. I don't know how he knew what size I was, and I don't care. They're stunning. This set is my favorite, in a nude silk with black lace appliqué. How could I resist wearing them for him tonight? And by the way he's worshiping my body right now, I think I made the correct choice.

He runs his nose over the silky fabric of my thong, inhaling deeply. "Fuck, you smell good."

"That's because watching you from afar all night and imagining what you're going to do to me when we're alone totally turns me on." My back arches off the bed, greedy for more contact from him.

He grins. "What do you want from me, pretty girl?"

"I want you to eat my pussy, Mr. Swift."

"Oh God, Andy, you can't call me that when you're asking me to go down on you."

I bat my lashes at him and pout. "Why not, Mr. Swift? Does it make what we're doing here so much worse?"

He groans, then dips his head back to my panties, taking one side in his teeth and dragging them down my legs. He goes straight to my pussy, licking me, and the contact where I want it is everything. My hands reach for him, finding his hair, and I tug at the ends as he works his magic with his tongue, bringing me undone, one slow measured stroke at a time. I moan loudly, unable to stop myself.

He stops, glaring up at me sexily. "Shhh, pretty girl, we're in a hotel. Don't want to disturb the neighbors."

I bite my lip. "Sorry. Don't control yourself, I'll be quiet, I promise."

He starts devouring me again, and I take a pillow and bury my face in it, knowing I won't be able to keep my promise. This is too good, and I can feel the telltale tingles running through my body. I cry out loudly into the pillow as I let go, and the orgasm is pulled from my body, waves of pleasure rippling through me. He is so good at this. My body responds differently to him than anyone else. It's addictive, the way he makes me feel, I can't get enough of it.

He removes the pillow and smirks back at me. "You promised to be quiet."

"I was. The pillow muffled it, no one else would have heard." I grin.

His mouth meets with mine as he kisses me deeply, his tongue sweeping through my mouth, and I melt into him, loving the dominance he shows when he kisses me like this. He rolls me on top of him and I realize he's still wearing his pants. I pull away from his kiss and travel down his body to his waistband, undoing his pants and discarding them off the bed, followed by his boxer briefs. I take his large length in my hand and stroke him. He feels too good, so hard.

"Protection?" I ask.

"In my wallet on the dresser."

I reach for it, pulling out a foil packet and rolling the

condom on. Then I move up his body so I'm straddling him, legs spread wide, and lower myself down on to him.

"Fuck, yes. You're so hot like this, Andy." His hands reach up my body, cupping my breasts roughly through the fancy bra. As I start to move, rolling my hips back and forth, he drops the straps off my shoulders and pushes the fabric down, exposing my nipples. His thumb brushes over them, sending thrills through me.

He reaches up, taking one in his mouth, and sucks hard. I continue to rock on him, my clit loving the friction of our bodies so close together as I grind back and forth on him. He pulls his mouth back with a pop. He runs his hands down my back until he reaches my ass. He grips me, pulling me onto him harder as he moves position to sitting upright against the headboard. His hands dig into my ass, guiding me in a perfect rhythm, faster as he gets closer.

His mouth covers mine as I fall apart in his arms again, the pleasure so good it's almost too much to take. He pumps into me harder, and my body hangs slack, leaning my head on his shoulder, letting him take what he needs while I ride out my orgasm. Moments later, he moans, his own release taking over.

After we regain our breath, he cups my face, bringing it up to his. Our foreheads lean on one another, our eyes closed as we embrace. I don't even know what that was. I feel like I just had some sort of out-of-body experience, something so insanely good it can't even be explained in words.

He lifts me, carrying me to the shower, and we stand under the hot water together while he washes my body. I'm totally out of it. My body is still trembling, and he takes the advantage of my placation to wash me. His hands run everywhere, massaging and caressing me in a soft and tender way.

"I wish you could stay here with me tonight," he says quietly.

His words are enough to break me from my trance. I turn around in his arms and hug my body close to his. "So do I, but it's too risky. I think we've taken enough of a chance for tonight, don't you?" I kiss his lips tenderly, showing him just how much I wish things were different. And I really do. I don't know who I even become with him, but he brings out a softer side of me, one that wants to stay and cuddle.

"Probably. Come lie with me for a bit before you go." His eyes plead with me, and I wonder if everything is okay with him. He's not acting himself tonight, or maybe he felt the same shift I just felt, because staying with a guy after sex isn't normally my thing, but with him, I never want to leave. I would love nothing more than to stay in his arms tonight, but it's just not our reality. It's not what this is meant to be.

He shuts off the water and wraps me in a big, fluffy white towel then grabs one for himself. He dries off then makes his way back into his bed. I follow him, snuggling down into the covers, and his arms wrap around me. I'm comfy and tired enough that I could very happily just drift off to sleep.

"Andy, can you tell me something?"

"Anything," I answer sleepily.

"Why do you hate the idea of relationships so much? Did you get burned in the past or something?"

I'm surprised by his choice of topic. He wants to discuss why I don't date? I didn't think that was even an issue here. He was the one who told me how this was going to be between us. "I guess you could say that."

"What happened?" he pushes, and I wonder how much

I really want to tell him about all of this and why he cares so much in the first place.

I pull away from him and prop myself up on one arm, so I can see him. His warm brown eyes have nothing but comfort and reassurance for me. I should be able to talk to him about my past. He's told me about what happened with his wife, and really, that was so much worse. "The person I trusted the most in this world let me down. I was totally blindsided by the whole thing. I don't want to go through that again."

"Who was it?" He reaches for my hand, lacing his fingers with mine, kissing the back of my hand.

I let out a big sigh, not really wanting to talk in detail about it, but it's not like I need to hide it from him either. "He was my best friend throughout school. He lived on our street just a couple of houses down, so we spent all our spare time together. We were inseparable. The last year of high school, we took it further than friendship. That was probably the first mistake."

"He was your first?"

"Yep, he was. We were really good together. I know it's silly, because I was young, we both were. But I honestly thought we would graduate college and get married. I thought he was it for me."

"So what happened then?"

I raise a brow. "You can probably already see where this is going."

"I think I can, but why don't you tell me anyway. I want to understand you better."

"Fine. We went to different colleges. I had my scholarship to UCLA, and he went to college locally. I thought I could trust him. It was only an hour-and-a-half trip so we saw each other as much as we could, and we talked every day. It all seemed like it was going well. Least, that's what I thought. Then one weekend I wanted to surprise him and took a trip home, arrived at his house all excited, only to walk in on him with some bitch from our high school." I can feel my muscles tense even just reliving the scene in my head. "At the time, it was devastating, life-altering. But now I see it for what it was—a life lesson I had to learn."

He looks at me like he finally gets me and why I am the way I am. "That's why you hate cheaters so much."

"Well, I could just hate all men and be done with it, but you know I like sex too much so that was never an option." I laugh to try and lighten the mood that has become too heavy. I hate talking about real shit. But the way Brad looks at me, like he needs this to understand me better, I decide I'd better answer his question properly. "But yeah. I hate that anyone could lie to someone they are supposed to care about. He was my friend my whole life and I couldn't even trust him. That's when I decided I didn't need that shit in my life. I do what I want, when I want, with whoever I want, no strings attached, and that has worked really well for me ever since."

He tilts his head to the side, assessing me. And I wish he would just come out and say what he's really thinking right now. Because he's giving me nothing, just asking about my past, but I know there's a reason behind all of this and I want to know what it is. "Cause you can't get hurt again," he says finally.

I nod my head. "Damn straight! This way I'm in control of my life." And I mean that, it's not just some shit I say.

"But you don't ever really get to share anything special with anyone, anything real."

I'm a little surprised by his comment. He wants something real? "Don't tell me you want that after what you went through with your wife. I thought you would feel the same as me."

He sits a bit farther up in bed, his back against the headboard, and I look up at him. He's like a different person tonight, all deep and broody. What is going on with him?

"Yeah, but I don't. It makes me want the real thing even more. See, I don't think everyone is like my ex or yours. I know there is something real out there waiting for me, and when I'm ready, I hope I find it." His eyes gaze longingly at me, and I know what he's saying. He thinks something real is happening here between us, and maybe it is. But if that's the case, it's a whole other level of fucked up that I just can't deal with, because we literally can't be together. Not at this point in time, anyway.

"I'm surprised, Brad. I wouldn't have pegged you for a hopeless romantic." I smile cheekily, trying to make a bit of a joke about it. This conversation has become too serious too quickly, and it makes me uncomfortable.

"I'm not so sure I'm that, but I know I don't want to be alone forever. Do you?"

"I don't know what I want for the future yet. I'm twenty-four. All I know is I have plenty of time to work it out. Right now, I'm concentrating on my career while I can. You understand that, right?" I plead with my eyes for him to agree with me because I don't want this all to end. I'm having fun here, but I can't give him anything else. That's why I thought this arrangement was so perfect.

He nods and offers me his charming smile. "Yeah, better than most. And that's what you should do as well. You're a great player. You have the chance to be one of the best."

"Thank you, I hope so. Speaking of, I need to get to bed. I need my beauty sleep for tomorrow if I'm going to kick ass out there." I slip out of bed and search the floor for the clothing I came in wearing, finding my bra and panties and pulling them on, then throwing the large coat over the top. I can feel his eyes on me as I dress. I go back to where he's sitting. "I'll let myself out. Thank you for a fun night. See you in the morning, Mr. Swift." I put emphasis on his name.

I reach down to kiss him, and he pulls me into him, kissing me passionately. It's so good I don't want to let go. I want so badly to stay here with him and continue, but as I said to him, my career is the most important thing, and I need to go back to my room tonight. I need sleep if I'm going to be the best, and if I stay here, there will be no sleep. I pull back from him. "See you tomorrow."

"Night, pretty girl."

I smirk at him. I have no idea why he calls me that, but he has since the first night when we hooked up, and I secretly love it.

## CHAPTER FOURTEEN

ANDY

I walk through the front door with Luna and Darcy in total silence. We haven't said a word to each other in half an hour. I dump my bag in my room and go in search of Nala. I missed her and need some squishy puppy cuddles. I don't have to look for long; she comes bounding up the hall. I drop to my knees, and she jumps into my lap, cuddling in. Jasmine follows close behind her.

"What's with the faces? The other two walked straight past me and went into their rooms." Her eyes are wide with concern.

"Yeah, we lost our game. For some reason, Darcy is blaming me. We nearly got into it on the cab ride home, but Luna stopped us. Now Luna's pissed because she feels like she's always in the middle and just wants everyone to get along." I throw my hands up dramatically.

"Oh." Jasmine comes to sit on the floor beside me, patting Nala.

"How did you two get along, anyway? Did you miss me?" I say, nudging my sister on the arm, hoping to change the subject.

"We were just fine without you. She was a good girl. We even went for a little walk today. I think she likes me better," she teases.

"Thank you for looking after her. I owe you."

"Sorry you guys lost." She gives me a sympathetic smile.

"Can't win them all, I guess," I say with a shrug. It was shitty to lose, especially to Kansas City, but I'm not going to sulk about it.

Darcy enters the room and glares at me. I have no idea what her problem is. I got a goal today, not my fault she didn't. But I'm not blaming her. "Yeah, especially when Andy spends half the night in some random guy's room so she's too tired to play," she mutters under her breath on her way to the kitchen.

I whip my head around to stare at her quickly. Did she just say what I think she did? How the fuck does she know what I was doing last night? We weren't in the same room. No one saw me come in—at least I don't think they did. If she wants a fight, she's going to get one. She should know better than anyone I don't put up with bitchy comments being fired at me. "What are you going on about, Darcy? You got something to say, say it to my face. Don't go making snippy remarks under your breath," I call back to her.

She spins around, glaring at me. "Alright, I will. I'm sick of you sneaking round and being all secretive. There, I said it." She puts her hands on her hips, all defensive.

"I'm not," I snap back.

"Andy, I know you really fucking well. We have been friends for a long time, and when you left early last night *to sleep,* it was obvious what you were doing. I came looking for you later and you didn't answer your door, I kinda worked it out. You stayed with someone else."

I stand up, ready to defend myself. "I could have been

asleep with my earphones in and didn't hear you. Why do you assume—?"

She comes closer to me and gets up in my face. "Don't lie to me. I know you. I wouldn't care, except when you let the team down because you're so tired, it starts to piss me off."

I see red. How dare she blame me for this? "I didn't let the team down. I played my heart out today. We lost, yes, but not because of me. And you know I'm tired at the moment because I can't sleep properly from what happened on my birthday. It has nothing to do with anyone else."

Jasmine rests her hand on my shoulder, and I jump and glare at her. "Andy, let's go out for a walk, cool off a bit. This isn't going to get either of you anywhere."

She offers me a knowing smile. She wants me out of here and cooling off before I lose my shit completely and say something we will all regret later. I take a deep breath, trying to calm the crazy raging bitch inside. "Thanks, Jas, that's a good idea." I throw a look at Darcy. She better be over her foul mood by the time I get home, cause I'm not putting up with her moody shit. I've got enough going on.

I fasten the lead on Nala and she follows along happily. "She's a lucky dog, two walks today," says Jasmine. I can see she's trying to break the awkward tension. She's such a people-pleaser, she hates it when people fight. She was the same when we were kids, always having to step in and break up our fights.

"She is." We stride down the street, and I try to get my anger under control by using the breathing exercise Jasmine has taught me.

"What's going on? You guys never fight. You lost plenty of games last year and nothing like this came from it."

I look at her, trying to understand what is going on

myself. "I don't know, she's the one with the problem." I shrug.

"She has a bit of a point, though, doesn't she? You're sneaking around, Sis. Is something still going on between you and Brad? Is that what happened last night, you were in his room?"

I stare at her. Trust Jasmine to have it all worked out. I want so badly to talk to her about it all because I hate keeping secrets, it's driving me nuts. I know I shouldn't admit to anything but I'm bursting at the seams. I can't keep it from her any longer. "Oh my God, Jasmine, you can't tell anyone. You have to promise me."

She gives me a small knowing smile. "Of course I won't. Who am I going to tell? Anyway, I can't. Client-therapist privilege."

"You're not my therapist." I laugh at her for being silly.

"I kind of am, though." She laughs as well. "I wouldn't say anything. So, are you okay? Cause you seem off lately. Since your birthday."

I sigh. "Yeah, I'm alright. I just... well, things are different between us than I thought they would be. When I got into it, I thought it was just a bit of fun, you know. Exploring a mutual attraction for one another, made a bit more exciting by the fact he was off limits."

"You've never been one to follow the rules." She shakes her head.

I give her a look. I'm trying to have a serious conversation with her. She could be less judgmental and snarky about it. "Anyway. Things are getting complicated. He's my coach and in the middle of a messy divorce and way older than me. But I really like him. Like, stupidly so. To the point I can't stop thinking about him. He is so sweet. He's the one who got me Nala because he wanted me to have someone with me at night to make me feel safe when he isn't around. I think he feels the same as well. Last night he told me he is looking for his right person and he won't let the bad things that happened in the past stop him from finding her. I felt that he was talking about me. What am I going to do, Jasmine?"

She blinks back at me, her expression blank, like she's thinking it all over. "Okay, that is a lot to take in. What are the actual rules here? If you want to see him?"

"I can't. He'll get fired. It is literally against club policy."

"Shit, Andrea." She gives me wide eyes.

"Yeah, I know. My team loves him as well, so I will be the bad guy. Plus, he is such a good coach. I don't want to lose him, I have learned so much from him already."

"I bet you have." She eyes me suspiciously.

I throw her a dirty look. "You're supposed to be helping me," I whine.

"I'm sorry, Andy. I have to make a joke about it, it's crazy. Here I am, desperately searching for the perfect guy to steal my heart away, and you don't want anything of the sort, yet you found it, but you two can't be together. I really do think the Harper sisters are cursed."

I grab her arms. Her nonsense is making so much sense. "I never thought about it like that. You're right, we are. Destined to be alone forever." I laugh to cover how much it actually terrifies me. "Jasmine, you will find him, you know. Probably when you least expect it."

"What, like you?"

"Maybe? So, sister with all the answers, what do I do now, then, hey?"

"That I don't know the answer to. Only you can work it out, baby. Maybe it's one of those things that just needs time to play out. Like you tell him how you feel but you need to wait until the end of the playing season because you don't want your team to lose him as a coach." She shrugs. "Or something like that."

"Jasmine, I can't stay away from the guy, though. I'm like obsessed and so is he. I know I shouldn't be doing this, but I want him so much I can't help myself."

"Well, you better figure that out. Lock that pussy up for the year, cause you know the consequences." We make our way back up the street toward our house. I know my sister is right, but that doesn't mean I'm going to be able to stop what is going on between us. I'm too lost in him. I think it's already too late.

As soon as we walk in the door, Darcy comes sheepishly over to me. "Can we talk?"

I let Nala off the lead and she runs for my room. "Yes, of course," I say a little reluctantly, not knowing what I'm going to get from her.

We go into my bedroom and sit on the bed. I wait for her to go first.

"I'm sorry about before, I overstepped the mark. Whatever you do in your personal time is up to you."

I glance at her sad features; she looks really upset, and I don't get it. I mean, I know we lost, and it sucks, but it wasn't the finals or anything. "Darcy, what's really going on? It's never bothered you before what I do or who I sleep with. Normally you're all like, *you go, girl, give me all the juicy details*. Why are you so upset now?"

She nibbles her lip nervously. "I don't know. I think I just don't feel as close to you at the moment. We normally share everything, but you're being all secretive. I miss our chats. Have I done something wrong? Is that why you're pulling away from me?"

I didn't even realize I was distant from her. I guess I was

so wrapped up in everything that's happening, and because I can't really talk about it, I was maybe avoiding certain conversations lately. "I'm so sorry, Darcy. I'm not pulling away from you. Ahh, it's just, I can't say what's going on. But that's not because of you or anything."

She grabs my hand. "You can tell me anything, you know you can trust me." She laces her hand with mine, and I know I can. She and Luna have been my closest friends since we started at college together, and I hate lying to them.

"Okay, but you have to promise me this won't leave the room. Seriously, babe, this could cause so much shit if people found out."

She looks pleased that I trust her. "I swear, I won't say a thing, you know you can rely on me."

"Alright then." I cover my eyes. "I'm sleeping with Brad."

She hits me across the arm playfully. "I knew it! You little minx, hooking up with the coach. I can't believe you kept this from me." She shakes my arms, and I glance at her.

"It's just a bit of fun, Darcy, that's why no one can find out. He'll get fired, you know, and he is like the best thing that has happened to our team in ages."

She nods in agreement. "He is. Don't worry, your secret is safe with me. Thank you for telling me." She wraps her arms around me in an embrace, and I know things between us are going to be okay.

There's a small knock at the door, and Luna pops her head around. "You two all good yet?"

I motion for her to come over and join us, and she runs over, hugging us both. Then she pulls back. "So, are one of you going to tell me what's going on here?"

"I'll let Andy do that, it's her story to tell," says Darcy.

I fill Luna in on what has been going on, and just like

Darcy, she promises not to say anything, saying she already knew anyway but was just waiting for me to admit it. It feels good to get it off my chest and not be lying to my friends, but now I have the small problem that I probably need to tell Brad that they know. He's going to be pissed, for sure.

---

BRAD

I exit my bathroom, freshly showered with a towel wrapped around my waist, hair still dripping wet. After the disappointing loss today, I'm ready to relax for the night and tune out from reality, when I hear a knock at the door. It's just after eight. Who could it be at this hour on a Sunday? I throw on a T-shirt and check the peephole to find a fidgety-looking Andy leaning up against the wall. Since it's just her, I open the door.

"Hey, pretty girl, this is a pleasant surprise." I smile, surprisingly happy to see her. We didn't speak a word to each other after the game today. Neither of us happy with the result, we went our own separate ways. But I'm glad she's here now.

"Sorry, yeah, I should have called or something. Do you normally answer the door in a towel?" She smirks.

"Not unless there is a really pretty girl waiting on the other side of it."

She offers me a small smile, then drops her head. "I have to talk to you about something." She wrings her hands in front of her. "But you might have to put clothes on or I won't be able to concentrate."

"Okay, this sounds interesting." I stand back so she can come in. She looks worried, and I wonder what could be the matter. It's only been a few hours since we landed back in LA. What has happened in that time? "Make yourself at home, I'll just get dressed." I rush into my room and throw on a pair of pants.

When I come back, I take a seat on my couch next to Andy, and she tucks her legs up under her, getting comfy. "Okay, so I have to just tell you because my tummy is in knots."

"What is it, Andy? You're starting to worry me."

"The girls know." She looks at me, her eyes all wide and scared.

"They know what?"

She motions between us. "About what's going on here."

I sit up in my seat a bit straighter. "Which girls, like the whole team?" I ask, the concern more obvious in my voice than I want it to be. But fuck, if the entire team knows, that's it for me.

"No, just the ones I live with." She nibbles her bottom lip. "I'm so sorry, I know we agreed to keep this just between us. But after we got back today, Darcy and I had a big fight. She was super pissed at me, said I was being all secretive and that's why we lost. I had to tell her. We're usually really close, we tell each other everything, and it was starting to cause a problem with our relationship, and I don't want that. I love those girls, they mean everything to me. I'm so sorry, though, because I know it puts you in a shitty situation, and if you want whatever this is to stop because of it, it's okay. I just can't sneak around behind my friends' backs anymore."

I feel relief wash over me. This situation we can handle. I pull her closer to me so she's sitting on my lap. She gazes up at me with pretty pale blue eyes, and I find myself getting even more sucked under her spell by the second. "Andy, this is far from over. It's not ideal that your roommates know, but I was pretty sure they already had a good idea about it after the night we met. Then, of course, your birthday. Just as long as they know not to tell anyone else, I'm sure this will all be fine."

"They do. They won't say a thing. They don't want to lose you as a coach either."

I run my hand up the side of her face, my fingers threading through her hair and pulling her toward me, our lips meeting. She kisses me like her life depends on it, wrapping her arms around me and hugging her body close to mine. I get the impression she thought I was going to tell her this was over.

"There is one good thing about all your roommates knowing."

"Oh yeah, what's that?" She smirks.

"You won't have to rush off tonight."

I see the sparkle in her eyes. She wants this just as much as I do. "You want me to stay?" Her voice is happy, excited even.

"Only if you want to."

Her lips are back on mine, and that's all the answer I need. I scoop her up and carry her into my bedroom. Throwing her down on the mattress, she giggles loudly.

I WAKE UP WITH ANDY IN MY ARMS, HER SOFT PALE blonde hair tickling my chin, her chest rising and falling with shallow breaths under my hold, and it feels like this is where she should be. In my home, in my life. This girl was made for me and me for her.

After everything I went through with Madeline, I really didn't think I would be able to move on this quickly and start to have real feelings for someone, but I do. Andy is refreshingly honest, fun, and sexy as hell. How could I not be falling for her? She says she doesn't want anything real or permanent, that she made that choice after having her heart broken by her high school boyfriend, but she's not acting that way with me. She's opening up to me and letting me in. It didn't take anything at all to persuade her to stay last night. She is here with me because she wants this just as much as I do, and now that her friends and sister know about us, it's going to make it easier for us to spend time together.

She rolls over in my arms and smiles up at me sleepily.

"Morning, my beautiful girl." I kiss her forehead.

"Morning. Do you know what the time is?" she asks.

I check my phone. "Six."

She goes to roll out of my grip, and I pull her on top of me. "Where do you think you're going?"

She giggles, sitting up, her legs coming to either side of me. How anyone could look this perfect when they just wake up, I will never know, but she is stunning. Her long hair falling over her shoulders and framing her face. Her pale blue eyes bright, a light blush over her cheeks. She runs her hand through my hair playfully. "Brad, I have to go home and get ready for practice. I don't have any of my gear here, remember. And I don't want to be late, my coach is a real asshole when I am."

She's such a smartass. "Is he?"

"Yes, total hard-ass. Made me run laps last time." She smirks.

"How about I talk to him, get him to let you off the hook this time. We can tell him there was a very important job that needed taking care of."

She rolls her hips over my hard cock and grins. "A very

important job, huh?" She rolls them again, and I pull her down to me, kissing her.

Before I know what's happening, she escapes my grip and jumps from the bed. "Nope, I can't, he won't listen. He's super mean when he's angry too. Better go." She laughs, grabbing her clothes and pulling them on as she runs for the door.

"You're a tease," I call after her.

She blows me a kiss. "See you at practice." She walks from the room. I could just stay here, but I decide to follow her so I can say goodbye properly. Who knows when I'll have her like this again. The rest of the week will be back to our training schedule and our professional relationship.

I throw on some pants and hurry to the front door so I don't miss her. When I get to my driveway, she's standing by her car. Holding a red envelope. The happy smile from before is gone.

"Andy, what's wrong?"

She holds it up. "This was under my windshield wipers."

I join her, taking the envelope from her. Opening it, my heart sinks. She hasn't heard anything from her stalker since her birthday, and I was starting to think maybe it was all over. I think she was as well. But this shows very clearly that it's not.

"What is it?" She nibbles her bottom lip. She knows what it is before she even sees it. "It's from him, isn't it?"

"I'm sorry, Andy, I think so."

She snatches it from me, and I see her eyes go wide as she reads it.

> *I see you're dancing with the devil, beautiful. Naughty, naughty, I have eyes everywhere, and you need to be careful before you get burned. Breaking the rules might have been your thing in the past, but this time, it will catch up with you. Stop what you're doing or else I will notify Angels management of what has been going on!*

"What the fuck even is this?" she snaps angrily. "Is this a threat?"

"Sounds like your stalker has been watching us and is getting jealous. Is there anyone who could be doing this to you? An ex or hook-up that you jaded? Someone who thought there was more going on than there was?"

"I honestly can't think of anyone. Brad, they're going to report you." She looks concerned.

She's right, it looks like that's what they're saying, but I don't think they will. For some reason, I think this is more about messing with Andy than anything else. "It's okay, I don't think that's what they're going to do. And if they do, I'll deal with it. I came into this knowing the consequences, Andy, and I'm okay with it. It's just a job, okay? What we have going on here means more to me than that. It's your safety I'm worried about. If this person is watching you, we need to be more careful."

"I'm not okay with you losing your job because of me, I'm not worth it."

I pull her into me and hold her close. "Well, I think you are. But it's going to be okay. I really don't think they'll say anything about me, and what proof would they have anyway? Anything we've done has been behind closed doors. We just deny all of it. Okay? Trust me, this will all be fine."

That's what I tell her, anyway. On the inside, I'm more worried. I think it's time I look into fixing this so no one has anything to hold against her.

## CHAPTER FIFTEEN

### BRAD

An hour after our Friday-night game, I pull up at Andy's place. She must have been waiting by the door, because she comes running down the driveway so fast and jumps in my car. Jasmine is standing at the door cuddling Nala. Her gaze is narrowed on me with an expression that tells me she's not a hundred percent happy with me taking her sister away for the weekend.

I offer her a wave and turn my attention to Andy. "Are you ready to go?"

"Sure am, let's ditch this town." She laughs. She is glowing from the win and her two goals. I give her a quick kiss then start the car.

I love seeing her like this, all pumped up, still running on the adrenaline. I remember the high well. It's still exciting watching your team win as a coach, but the rush isn't the same.

Andy and I decided this week that we needed to head out of town for a little bit, so we could spend some time together without all the angst of wondering if we're being watched by Andy's stalker or the worry of getting caught by someone on the team. I have seen her anxiety about the situation escalate this week; she needs some downtime where she can relax.

"I'm so excited to have the weekend away. I love San Diego, and the weather is supposed to be perfect." She squeals and claps her hands.

"Amazing, two days at the beach sounds like just what we need," I agree.

I'm watching the road, but I can feel her eyes on me. "Aren't you a little worried that someone will see us together? I know it's nearly two hours away, but you never know."

"Andy, no one in San Diego gives a crap about us. The media stopped following me around when I couldn't play anymore, so they won't care. We're safe to be ourselves."

"Why am I more worried about you losing your job than you are?"

I run my hand up her bare thigh. I love this short skirt she has on, and I don't even want to think about this anymore. This weekend is supposed to be an escape from reality. "I guess I just think the benefit outweighs the risk. I need more time with you outside of the four walls of my house, and you need to chill out, pretty girl."

"Do I?" I can feel the smirk on her lips without even looking at her. She sees that comment as a challenge.

The next thing I know, her hand is cupping my cock through my pants. "Let me think... how do I chill out on a mini road trip, when I'm on a high from playing soccer? I think I might need something else to play with," she purrs, undoing her seat belt, and she faces her body toward me. She locates the zipper of my pants and slides it down. Her hand finding my cock. I slide down a bit farther in my seat, giving her easier access to free my already-hardened length.

"Mmm, this looks like it could help." She wraps her hand around my shaft and strokes me, the movement sending a thrill through my body.

I want her touching me. It's been a few days and I'm craving her like crazy, but it's going to make it very hard to concentrate on the road.

"I'm not sure it will help us get there in one piece if the driver is too distracted to drive," I encourage her, knowing she loves a challenge.

"Shh, you just concentrate on the road, baby. You're a good driver, I trust you to get us there safely. Let me have my fun." She dips her head and I feel the warmth of her mouth as she makes contact with my cock, and fuck, it feels so good. I'm not fighting her on this. It takes everything I have not to take my eyes off the road to look down at her. She would look hot as hell right now, taking me in her mouth.

I pull onto the highway and shift my car into gear as I speed up the road. She bobs in my lap, licking up my length, swirling her tongue around the tip then taking me in her mouth and sucking. With one hand on the steering wheel, I reach for her ass with my free one, slipping it down the length of her short skirt. I'm rewarded with bare skin. "No panties... you really are a naughty girl tonight, aren't you, Andy?"

She pulls back. "Yes, and you love it," she hisses before taking me in her mouth again, working her magic with her mouth.

My fingers feel their way to her dripping-wet pussy. She's so ready for me to play with her. I dip a finger in, and she sucks harder, the pressure almost bringing me undone. I focus on the road in front of me. It's surprisingly quiet for a Friday night, and I'm glad there are no cars close enough to see what we're getting up to. Not that it would worry Andy; she would probably like it more.

I push another finger into her tight little pussy and she moans. I fuck her with my fingers, trying to focus on what I'm doing to her but knowing I'm not going to last much longer, with the way her skilled mouth is working me. "Fuck, Andy." I grip the steering wheel tighter. "I'm going to come," I groan.

She doesn't budge from her task, just keeps going, and I release into her mouth, hot bursts of liquid pumping into her throat. She pulls back, and I drop my hand from her as she slips back into her seat next to me. "Fuck, Andy."

"I know, right, how hot was that?" She smirks.

"I don't see how that would make you more relaxed, but I know I am."

"Alright then, how can I relax?"

"I think you should take that skirt off and play with yourself for me." I glance at her.

She gives me a sassy look. "You need to keep your eyes on the road, mister, so we arrive safely. I'm pretty chill now, I can wait." She leans her chair back and makes herself comfortable.

My gaze returns to the darkened road in front of me, and I wonder if I should pull over so I can finish her off how I would like to right now. My hand runs up the smooth skin of her thigh. It's only forty-five minutes more until we make it to the hotel room, then I'm going to make her fall apart, just like she did me.

## ANDY

Yesterday was exactly what I needed. I had the best sleep I've had in what feels like months, not even pulling ourselves from bed until after ten this morning. Then we spent hours swimming in the ocean and lazing on the sand. The sun was out, and my skin now looks more golden. Best of all, we've been able to just relax and be ourselves—well, for the most part, anyway. I still can't shake the thought that there might be someone watching me. I can feel his eyes on me. It's so strange. Or is that just my paranoia? I've never felt the need to look over my shoulder or pay better attention to who passes me by. But now I'm constantly on edge. The person stalking me could be anyone, and I know Brad said they wouldn't follow us here, but why wouldn't they? If they really are watching me with some sort of crazy obsession, I'm not silly enough to believe that they wouldn't travel two hours to keep it up.

We have to drive back this afternoon, so this morning, Brad has organized a surprise for us. I'm told I need a hat and comfy clothing that can get wet. I'm so excited. It really doesn't matter what we're doing, I'm just happy to be spending the day with him. Again, who the fuck have I even become, all blissfully happy to be spending the day with some guy? But whatever, I am.

"You ready to go?" Brad calls to me from the bedroom of our hotel.

I enter the room from the bathroom. "I guess, is this okay?" I do a little spin for him, just because I love his eyes on me. Yes, I'm a bit of an attention seeker when it comes to his focus being on me. I'm wearing denim cutoffs, my string bikini, with a loose-fitting tank over the top.

# THE COACH

"Yeah, and you look cute." He smirks, pulling me into him for a kiss.

"Thanks." Brad looks mighty fine himself in board shorts and a white T-shirt. His hair is a little longer on the top at the moment and looks all kinds of sexy in that I-don't-give-a-fuck-what-I-look-like kind of a way. It's hot. I could easily stay here all day with him. I'm so attracted to him, I just want my body on his all the time.

He laces his hand in mine, and we leave our room and head in the direction of the water. "So where are you taking me?" I ask.

"You will see soon enough." He smiles smugly.

I narrow my eyes at him, but he seems unaffected, just enjoying the walk. It's a nice walk to wherever he's taking us. The weather is perfect again, sunny and warm. As we get closer to the pier, I see a line-up of speedboats and a large promotional sign with the words *Dolphin Adventures* printed on it. I glance at Brad with a grin. "Dolphin adventures?"

"You want to? You don't get seasick or anything, do you?"

I squeal. "No, and yes, I want to. This is awesome! I have always wanted to do something like this." I place an excited kiss on his lips, then practically drag him down toward the boats. I absolutely love dolphins, they're my favorite animal. I'm pretty sure I never told him that, so for him to have picked this as a surprise for me is so unexpected but amazing.

We're introduced to the guy who will be driving the boat, Stefan. He then gives some safety instructions, and we're told we can jump on board. It's a speedboat with enough seats for about eight, but other than our driver, we're the only two on board. Brad said he wanted privacy, so he booked it just for the two of us. He is ticking all the sweetness boxes today.

We take the seats at the front. Brad places his hand on my leg and gives it a squeeze. "You find it hard to sit still, don't you?"

"When I'm excited, yeah."

"I'm glad I picked the right surprise for you. I was thinking skydiving, but I had a suspicion you might like dolphins."

"Ooh, yes, we should do skydiving next time, I want to try that as well. But you're right, I love dolphins. Thank you, this is the best surprise." I kiss him again.

"Is there anything you wouldn't do?"

"Not really. I mean, I have to be careful, I can't injure myself doing anything reckless, but I like the thrill of trying new things, feeling the adrenaline pump, you know."

"Yeah, I do. Madeline wouldn't do anything. She was so afraid to try anything new or get out of her comfort zone. It's so refreshing being with you."

"She sounds boring, Brad. I can't see you two together. How did you end up marrying her, anyway? You don't seem very well matched." He gives me an uncomfortable look, and I wonder if I have overstepped the mark by asking. "Sorry, that was... I mean, you don't have to talk about her or anything."

"I don't really know now. I mean, at the time, I thought I was in love with her. She's very beautiful, and we knew a lot of the same people. It was just an easy match."

He still thinks she's beautiful. That's interesting. I'm not jealous by his comment but more intrigued, because I know very little about her, really. "Convenient?" I ask, wanting to know more about their situation.

"I guess. I think if I'm really honest, she chased me for a

while, and in the end, I gave in to her. She's very persistent. Once we started dating, things progressed quickly. We bought a place together, then she was talking about marriage all the time, so I proposed. We were trying for kids. I could have been stuck with her forever."

"Yeah, I guess you could have."

"When I look back now, I know I was just giving her what she wanted because I think I had no idea what I wanted myself, and at the time, it seemed like the right thing at that point in my life, to just move along to the next phase like a lot of our friends were."

What a scary thought, to just go along with the flow because it was expected of him. "I'm never going to be like that."

"You wouldn't sacrifice your own happiness for someone you care about?"

"If it's the right person you shouldn't have to. It should all just feel right. Shouldn't it?"

"I guess. So, you think there's a right person now?" He smiles at me cheekily.

I shrug, trying to play it down. "I'm starting to think there might be. Maybe?" I say quietly, looking out over the water so I don't have to look into his intense stare anymore. I don't want to give too much away about how I'm really feeling for him, but it's getting harder to hide. I'm sure every time I look at him it's written all over my face.

"I think we have our first pod of dolphins," calls Stefan from behind the wheel.

I turn my head to where he's pointing, and sure enough, there are dolphins popping up out of the water and playing about. We both move over closer to where they are. They're almost close enough for us to touch and they don't seem to be bothered by the presence of our boat at all.

Stefan kills the engine, and we bob about in the water, watching them. They are majestic creatures. There's something so grounding about watching animals in their own habitat.

Once they swim away, Brad takes my face in his hands and his lips meet mine. The salt spray from the wind splatters my face, but I don't care. I'm lost in this moment with him. In this perfect kiss.

His arms wrap around me, pulling me in closer, and my fingers trace lines over his back. My heart hammers in my chest with a rush of something I don't really understand.

The boat starts up again, and we're pulled from our moment as we move along to tour around slowly for the better part of an hour, seeing more playful pods and even some sea lions.

ON THE RIDE BACK TOWARD SHORE, I FLIP MY LEGS over Brad's lap and cuddle into him. The breeze over the open water is cooler than I thought it would be, and I have goosebumps running up my bare arms. He wraps his arm around me and hugs me close to him. His smell is so comforting to me. It's the strangest thing, like that wonderful feeling you get when you go home for Christmas and everyone you love is there sharing good food and laughs. To me that's what he feels like. Like coming home for Christmas. Is that what love feels like? Am I seriously falling in love with this man? That kiss we just had, it was something else, something I've never even come close to experiencing before.

"Hey, I know you, don't I?" calls Stefan, breaking me from my thoughts. He looks Brad over, assessing him, clicking his fingers together. "Yeah, that's it, you played for

Chelsea. You're like a soccer legend. Brad Swift. What are you doing here in America?"

Brad glances at me, and I can tell he's wondering how much he should say. We've been all over each other the entire boat ride, we don't need this guy knowing who we are.

"Just here for pleasure. I don't play anymore," he answers with a half-truth.

Stefan nods. Then he looks at me. "Nope, I know why I recognized you. I read that article about you not long ago. You're coaching our women's team, the Angels."

I break into a hot sweat, thinking he's about to recognize me as well. I tug my hat down a little farther and thank God I decided to wear my big dark sunglasses today. "Awesome work too, they're winning more than ever since you jumped on board," Stefan continues.

"Yeah, thanks, mate. They're a good team."

We pull up at the docks, and I can't get myself off the boat fast enough. The last thing I need is this guy recognizing me as well and talking to the tabloids about the unlikely couple he had on his boat, all in the name of five minutes of fame.

I wait for Brad to finish up his chat and walk up to me. I'm feeling slightly irritated. So typical, he's the one who gets noticed. Not that I care, because I don't want Stefan to know who I am right now anyway. But Brad hasn't even played for two years and I'm literally the best striker for this dude's state's team. Just goes to show we have come a long way in women's sports but we're still not considered as good as the men, no matter how incredibly we play.

I roll my eyes at Brad, and without me even saying a word he knows exactly what I'm getting at. "I would have recognized your pretty face. We're lucky this guy is an idiot." He wraps his arms around me as we make our way back.

"Yeah, I guess."

"Come on, let's get you home."

I offer him a small smile, but I don't really want to go home, I'm not ready yet. This weekend away has been just what I needed, and I feel like I've gotten to know Brad better than all the last month combined. He has been so open and honest with me. And when we go back, we have to deal with the realities of our situation all over again.

Maybe I should just ditch my career and run away with him. Seriously, has this dude got me brainwashed? Cause I have no idea where the old Andy has gone. I'm completely screwed when it comes to him. So much for having a bit of fun and not getting too involved because I don't do that. Apparently, all it took was a sexy soccer superstar to make me cave.

## CHAPTER SIXTEEN

ANDY

This weekend was bliss, but it's now Monday morning and it's time to get back to reality. I shower and dress in my training uniform before Brad is even out of bed. Then help myself to some granola and fruit for breakfast and sit at his kitchen counter, eating and scrolling through my phone.

I hear the shower. He must be up. That's good, I was about to go and wake him so he wasn't late for practice. I stayed here last night because I couldn't bring myself to go home. I needed one more night in my happy Brad bubble before I had to deal with it all.

Five minutes later, I'm washing my plate in the sink when I hear a knock at the door. In this situation I would normally answer it, but I can't do that. It could be anyone and I'm not supposed to be here. I race into Brad's room. He's just in a towel, all glistening and gorgeous, freshly showered.

"There's someone at your door," I tell him.

His forehead creases and he throws on some pants and a shirt. "At this time of the morning?"

I shrug.

He makes his way for whomever is at the door. I stand in the hallway and wait to see who it could be.

"Brad, darling, I thought you were never going to answer." I stiffen as I hear a woman's voice purr. Who is she?

"Madeline, why are you here?" he snaps. By his tone, I'm going to assume this is the wife—or ex, rather—and he is less than impressed to see her. For a second, I was worried he might have been seeing someone else, but I push that thought away and listen.

"I told you I was coming to town this week and I wanted to see you. I dropped in yesterday, but you weren't here. I wanted to catch you before you left for work today, so here I am." Her voice is getting closer, and I realize she must have let herself into the house.

Fuck, what should I do? I don't really want her to know I'm here, but at the same time, I want her to know Brad has moved on from her cheating ass and is happy with me. Her heels click on the floor, and I don't have time to decide because she's already standing in front of me.

I blink back at her a bit like a deer in the headlights. She looks me up and down, assessing me, a snobby pout on her lips. She's stunning, of course she is, even better than in her pictures. She's tall and slim, with long dark hair that sits perfectly straight down her back. Her nails are manicured, and her make-up is perfect, fake lashes and all. She is the most beautiful woman I have ever seen in real life. Fuck, and this is his ex. What on earth must he see in me?

"And you are?" She flicks her long hair over her shoulder, looking back over to Brad.

"None of your business," I sass at her. She wants to give

me attitude, I'll give it straight back and better. I already hate her for what she did to him.

Brad comes to stand by my side, wrapping an arm around me in a protective gesture—or at least that's what I think he's doing until he opens his mouth. "This is Andrea, my girlfriend." No, that was more of a fuck-you to his ex.

My gaze snaps to him, and so does hers. Why did he just call me his girlfriend? That is not something we have talked about. But of course, he could just be saying it to piss her off, and I would totally get it if he was. Not the best idea, though, Brad, when no one is supposed to know about us.

Her face turns sour, and she looks at him with pity in her eyes. "She's a child. What is she, one of the girls you're coaching?" She laughs as if it's a joke, then she must see the look on his face. She widens her eyes at him. "She is, isn't she? Oh, Brad, I knew you had hit rock bottom, but this is really bad," she tuts, shaking her head.

How dare she talk to him like that. Who the fuck does this stupid bitch think she is? "He hasn't hit rock bottom, far from it. He's having the time of his life now. He got rid of your cheating ass," I snap at her with venom in my words and daggers in my eyes. If looks could kill, she would be pinned against the wall behind me with knives.

Brad gives me a look like he wants me to stop before I make it worse. But she needs to be put in her place. I hate stuck-up bitches like her—they think they can just say whatever the hell they want and get away with it because the world falls at their pretty feet.

"I'll ask again, Madeline, why are you here? You said you would let me know when you were coming so we can organize a time to sort out some things. My house at this time of the morning isn't going to work for me. I'm busy and I need to get to work."

"I can see that." She glares at me, and I feel about five years old. This woman is a total bitch.

"Wait here." Brad disappears into his office, leaving me alone with her. Oh, fuck, he knows I might try and fight her, right?

She closes the gap between us, and I stand a little taller, trying to show her I'm not intimidated by her. Just because she is super-model tall and towering over me. In fact, I could knock her flat on her perfect little ass if I wanted to, and I just might. "Shouldn't you be running around with someone your own age, not a married man who is way out of your league?" She glares at me.

"Shouldn't you be off with Brad's best friend? Clearly marriage vows don't mean fuck all to you. Don't try to claim him as your husband when you were the one who destroyed all of that," I throw back at her in just the same condescending tone she used on me.

She laughs sarcastically, and I know I have hit a major nerve. She is now aware of just how close me and Brad are and that he's confiding in me what she did to him. "Cute that you think you understand anything at all about marriage. You need to be very careful, sweetie. I have a lot more influence over Brad than you think. Whatever this is between the two of you, it's just a distraction for him. Don't go deluding yourself that there is something real going on."

What the fuck would she even know about what's going on between us? Nothing at all! She's just jealous because she thought she could show up here and he would be sucking up to her ass, desperate to have her back. But he's not. "You're the delusional one if you think there is any chance he would take you back." I turn to walk away from her. I've had enough of this shit, and if she says something else, I'm likely to fly through the air and attack her pretty face.

"Andrea," she calls.

I flick my head back to glare at her.

"I'm not stupid, I know whatever is going on here would be against club policy. One call to your general manager and I would get exactly what I wanted: Brad back with me. He would leave his job here in America and have to come crawling back, and it would be all your fault." She says it with a sickly sweet smile.

I storm toward her. "You know nothing." I poke her in the chest, and she takes a step back, looking like I hurt her. "You force him to leave the job he loves and you're the bad guy, not me." I stare angrily at her, so ready for a fight. I hate people like her, entitled stuck-up bitches who always get what they want. Not this time.

I feel Brad's arm wrap around me, pulling me back from her and closer to him. "Andy, don't let her worry you." His voice is cool and calm. I wonder how much of that conversation he just heard. I hope all of it, then he knows just how awful his ex really is. "Here, this is what you're here for, isn't it? Everything your lawyer asked for is in there. Just sign them. I want this over with." He shoves the papers toward her.

She looks down at them then back to Brad. She looks wounded. She does have a heart after all. "I... I'm not here for this. I just want to see if we can talk." Her voice is shaking, and realization must be dawning on her. She can't just snap her manicured fingers and get what she wants this time.

"I don't have anything left to say to you."

She glances at me, and I smile smugly at her. Her eyes

flick back to Brad, and she looks like she might cry. "Well, maybe I have something to say to you, and if you hear me out, you might be more understanding."

This is getting mighty awkward, and I'm just standing here in the middle of them, and I don't need to hear any more of what she has to say. "I'm just going to pack my stuff. I have practice soon so I need to get out of here," I say, pulling from his grip, quickly exiting the room. I'm not sure if either of them even heard me; they're still having some sort of a silent staring match that I don't understand. I can't believe that's his wife. Even worse, she wants him back, that much is for sure. Over my dead body.

I throw my stuff in my overnight bag a little more aggressively than I probably should, then slump down on the edge of his bed to wait for him. I'm not going back out there, I don't want to see her again. And I don't want to leave the house while she's still here with him.

I hear the front door slam and I wait. Brad storms back in the room. He is livid. I have never seen him so angry before. Understandable, she would make anyone fuming mad.

"What did she say?" I ask quietly. It's not really any of my business but I still want to know.

"She won't sign the papers until I hear her out. She wants to have dinner this week." He huffs, walking into his wardrobe, slamming stuff around.

"Oh." I pause. That's the last thing I want him to have, dinner with his stunning ex that he is still technically married to. But he needs those papers signed so he can move on. He sits on the bed next to me. I run my hand up his leg and give it a squeeze. "I guess having dinner with her couldn't be all that bad if it means you get her to sign the divorce papers and you get to be rid of her, could it?" I ask, trying to be supportive but hating every word that comes out of my mouth. I shouldn't care this much about him having a meal with her. But I do.

He cups my face, turning me so I'm looking at him. "Thank you for being so understanding, Andy. But dinner with her is the last thing I want to do. She is a manipulative witch, and if she wants to have a meal with me, it's for a reason she is yet to reveal."

"You probably need to find that out, though, Brad. Just go and see what she wants. You don't have to give her anything, she is the one who fucked up here, not you. Just stick to your guns."

He places a small kiss on my lips. "Thank you. I'll see how I feel about it later. Right now, we need to get to training."

"Can I ask you one thing first?" I ask, unsure if I even should, but I need to know the answer.

"Anything?"

"When you introduced me, you said I was your girlfriend. Was that for show to make her jealous or is that what you want?"

His eyes drop down and I see the flash of guilt. "I wanted to make her jealous." He pauses. "But honestly, if we could be in a proper relationship, that's what I would want. I hope that doesn't scare you off, make it too serious. But I can't stand the thought of you with someone else."

I blink back at him, and I can tell he is completely genuine. The thought should have me running out of here as fast as my legs will take me, but it doesn't. "If I could have anyone as my boyfriend, Brad, it would be you, there is never going to be anyone else," I say sadly, the reality of the situation washing over me. We won't ever be able to be that to each other, at least not while we're both a part of the same team. And I don't want that to change.

A really big part of me wishes things were different. This thing that started out as a bit of fun, both of us guarding our hearts so we didn't get hurt, can now only end one way—with total heartache, because we really can't be together in the way we want to be. And I see this going one of two ways. One, someone reports us, either his ex, my stalker, or one of the girls I live with fucks up and accidentally says it.

Or one of us lets the other go to avoid the inevitable.

I thought I would be strong enough to be that person, but I'm not. I couldn't say goodbye to him now even if I wanted to. I'm completely in love with him, and for the first time in my adult life, I know I'm not going to get what I want. And it actually hurts my heart.

---

BRAD

Somehow, we both arrive at training on time, after the run-in with Madeline this morning. I can't believe she had the hide to just show up at my house like that. I don't even understand what she was there about. She was so upset when I handed her the divorce papers, but she knew this was coming. We have been separated for months now, and other than the one phone call she made to tell me she was going to be in town, she's made no attempt to contact me.

I head straight for my office and gather everything I need to go over with Ava today. There's a knock at the door behind me and I turn to see Ava's smiling face. I motion for her to come in and she enters, leaning up against my desk.

"Did you hear management are on the lookout for a coach for the men's team for next year?" She smiles largely, knowing I had no idea.

It takes me a second to process what she's saying and why she's grinning at me like that. Is she for real? "Are you serious?"

"Uh-huh. Sure am."

This is the opportunity I have been waiting for. A chance to still stay with the club and close to Andy but not be her coach. If I could get this job, we would just have to get through the rest of the season, then we could actually be together like we talked about this morning. "Have they started interviewing yet?" I ask, a little more desperation in my voice than I intended.

"No, they're looking for expressions of interest at this point. You going to throw your hat in the ring? It would be perfect for you, get you out of the predicament you're in." She smirks.

I give her a look, wondering what exactly she's talking about. "And what would that be?"

"That you're hot for Andrea."

I frown at her. "What?"

She pats me on the arm. "Don't deny it, just put in a good word for me when you talk to Hamish. I want the women's head coach job, and you know I deserve it."

I blink back at her, wondering how much I should say right now. She is very observant if she has just worked this all out. Also, how did she hear about this before me? But she is right, she would be the right person to take over from me. "You do, you would be perfect for it. Let me see what I can do. This might just work out really well for both of us."

"I hope so. That's why I came to you as soon as I heard.

See you on the field." She pushes off from my desk and makes her way out of the room.

My head is spinning. This would be a good solution, and after Madeline showing up this morning, I know for sure this meeting is the best thing for everyone. I don't want to flake out on the team, but I can't keep being their coach, not when I have real feelings for Andy, and I know I want to explore what's going on between us. It's only going to cause a hell of a lot of trouble for both of us if I stay with this team. It would also put a stop to the blackmail messages she's getting from her stalker and anyone else who has already found out about us from holding it against us for their own personal gain. It would mean another big change for the team, but they will adjust, and Ava will make it work.

I need to work out how to make this happen.

Surprisingly, the day after I called for a meeting with the general manager, I have one. I have decided not to tell Andy anything about all of this until I know if I even have a chance at getting the job. For a start, I know she won't be happy about me leaving the Angels, but I'm hoping if I can explain to her that this is the best outcome for both of us, she will understand I'm doing it so I can be with her.

I arrive right on time, more nervous than I should be. I would be ideal for this job, and I sat in this office not long ago and went through the same process. But the stakes are higher this time because now I know what I want with my life and that's to be with Andy. I know this is probably the only way that will happen unless I leave the club completely, and she's not going to let me do that. For so many reasons, it would be really difficult if I did. It would also mean that if we both worked for different teams, in between all the travel we would both be doing, I would never get to see her. This is the best solution and has to work.

"Brad, come in and take a seat." Hamish, our general manager, grins from behind his desk. He's wearing a dark suit, his light brown hair short. He's in his late fifties now but was a top player in his day.

I make my way through his spacious office and sit opposite him in the plush leather chair. "Thank you for seeing me."

"I must say, I wasn't surprised you wanted to talk about this opportunity, you would be perfect for the job. Your name had already been suggested. But I need to ask, is there a reason you want to leave the women's team not long after starting with them? They've been playing so well since you jumped on board this year, and when you took over you assured me you were the perfect fit for them."

I want to say the real reason, I have feelings for one of the players and I can't keep on coaching her if it means we can't really be together, but that would just cause all sorts of trouble for us both, so I stick with the simplest answer I can come up with. "I think I would be just as good a fit for the men's team, and now that the opportunity has come up, I wasn't going to miss the chance to show my interest. I'm sure you understand that."

He nods, pleased with my answer. "You would be a good fit, and with the progress you've made with the Angels, I'm sure you could do some wonderful things here as well. We would have loved to have you as a player if it weren't for your injury."

"Yeah, life sometimes throws us a curve ball. But you

know that, you were also shot down in your prime with an injury."

"That's right, and my skills have been invaluable for this club. Just like yours will be. You made the right choice when you decided to join our coaching staff, Brad."

"I know. I miss playing like crazy, but I'm glad to be a part of the game. If you do consider me for this job, rather than going outside the club for my replacement, I want to recommend Ava for the head coach position of the Angels. She is very deserving of it and has been with the girls for a long time."

He rubs his chin and thinks on it. "Ava has been on our radar for a while, and I'm impressed by her dedication to the team. I will definitely keep her in mind. Thanks for your input."

I feel like I need to push a little harder for her. I'm not sure why she wasn't offered the job before I started, and what Andy said to me about women having it harder is so true. I want to make sure she really has a chance here. "She has been the key playmaker all year. She knows that team inside and out, she would be perfect," I add. I wouldn't be sitting here if it wasn't for her, and she deserves this just as much as I do, probably more.

He gives me a nod, and I feel like I have just swayed his decision. "I agree. I'll call her in tomorrow for a chat. Brad, if you want the job, it's yours. We don't need to look any further." He holds out his hand for me to shake.

Just like that, he's offering me the position. I'm a little shocked; I thought it would be a long process, with other people I was up against. I shake his hand. "I want the job," I confirm.

"Good. It's done then. Brad, this is between us for now, alright? We'll tell the Angels after we make the semis, I don't want anything to disrupt the killer year they're having."

"Totally understood." I had thought he might say something like that but hoped he wouldn't, because that means me lying to Andy. I could risk it and tell her, but I know there is no way I can tell her without her friends finding out, they're just too close. So for now, I won't. But we're one step closer to being together. I just hope when I finally get to tell her, she doesn't kill me for keeping this from her for so long. I caught a glimpse of her really angry yesterday with Madeline and think back to what she was like when I first took over. I don't want to be on the receiving end of that again.

## CHAPTER SEVENTEEN

### ANDY

I'M LYING ON MY BED STARING AT MY PHONE, NOT SURE how I feel about the text I just received from Brad. My response was *that's fine, see you tomorrow*. But it's anything but fine. He can't see me tonight, because apparently, he has decided to go for dinner with his ex-wife after all. Which is *fine*. I'm the one who told him to. Except it's not fine. I don't want him anywhere near that manipulative witch—his words.

I'm glad he was up front with me and told me that's what he was going tonight instead of hiding it, but it pisses me off even more that he's seeing her instead of me. We had plans to see each other tonight, now all of a sudden, he has to meet up with her. I know I'm overreacting. I have spent every night over the last two weeks with him, and ordinarily, after that much time with another human, I would be feeling smothered. I should be grateful for the evening to myself, but I'm not. All I want to do is spend it with him.

I don't even know who I am anymore, the annoyingly clingy girl hung up on some guy. Geez, I sound like my sisters when they're dating. This is not me at all.

I think the thing that is worrying me the most is that I know something is off with him, and it has been since he saw his ex on Monday morning, but I can't quite work out what it is. Is he thinking about getting back with her? Would he really do that to me, to himself?

On the surface, everything between us is the same as it has been. In public we act like nothing more than acquaintances because he's my soccer coach, and behind closed doors, the wild chemistry is still there, but something has shifted. He's hiding something from me, I can feel it.

He couldn't be thinking about getting back with her. I mean, I know she is still technically his wife, but she's a stuck-up bitch! I can't even see those two together at all. I can't believe he ever married her.

I decide it's probably not that, but it's something, and I want to know what.

There's a knock at my door.

"Come in," I call.

Darcy pops her head around the door. "Hey, babe, we're all going to catch a movie, you want to join? If you're not too busy with lover boy?"

I roll my eyes at her mention of Brad like that. "Why not. I'll just get changed." Distraction with my friends is exactly what I need tonight. Plus, I've been a bad friend lately, too focused on Brad, and I miss spending time with them.

"We're leaving in ten," she says, lingering, her eyes still fixed on me, and I wonder if there is anything else she wants to discuss?

"You all good? I'm going to get changed."

"Yeah, sorry, I'll leave you to it." She disappears, closing the door behind her.

That was odd. I turn to my wardrobe. What to wear? I

chuck on a baggy off-the-shoulder sweater and a pair of cutoff shorts. Twirl my hair into two buns and grab my converse high-tops. I meet the others in the kitchen.

"So glad you're joining us tonight, Andy. Brad needs to learn how to share," says Luna, wrapping me in a hug.

"I have been neglecting you guys, haven't I? Well, tonight it's my treat to make up for it."

We arrive downtown at the movie theater and make our way inside. The girls are really taking advantage of my generous offer and have selected the reclining chairs and a mountain of snacks. We settle in at the movie theater with a box of popcorn and Maltesers that Jasmine insisted we needed, to watch The Suicide Squad—also Jasmine's choice, she loves Harley Quinn.

I relax back in my chair and take a handful of popcorn. This is nice, hanging out with my friends and big sissy. Who needs Brad Swift, anyway. I try to push aside the thoughts of what he and his wife are getting up to. If I think on it too much, my imagination runs away with me.

An hour into the movie, I feel a message ping on my phone. I would normally just ignore it, but it might be Brad filling me in on what happened with Madeline, so the temptation to check is too strong.

I pull it out of my pocket and regret checking it immediately. It's an unknown number, and my stomach sinks. I open the text to see a photo. I instantly break into a hot sweat when I see what it's of. The location is my bedroom, and it's a photo of me changing this afternoon. I'm in just my bra and panties. Another pops through. It's Brad in my bed with me from earlier in the week. I'm straddling him, the sheets wrapped around my ass and legs. From the angle of the photo, it's very obvious it's him and me.

Suddenly, the room feels about a thousand degrees, and I feel like I can't breathe. I jump up from my seat and squeeze past Jasmine.

"Where are you going?" she whispers.

"I need to get some air," I call. Moving quickly up the stairs and out the front door of the theater, I lean against the wall and try to catch my breath. My chest is tight, and I feel like I might have a heart attack. Someone can see me in my bedroom. How is this even happening? How long has this been going on for? Oh my God, now they actually do have proof of me and Brad. Something they can use against us if they want him to get fired. Another text pings in and I check it.

**Unknown number:** You're not safe anywhere, beautiful. Wherever you go, I'm watching. Is this proof enough?

**Unknown number:** Break it off with the coach or I send this to the general manager. You're all mine and you need to remember that.

Tears prick in my eyes. Why is this happening? Who the fuck is watching me? I glance up and down the hallway to see if anyone is here watching me right now, but there's no sign of anyone. All the other doors are closed, with movie sessions running. I'm alone out here, and I don't know if I'm comforted by that or more scared that he might just appear out of the shadows. If he's watching me in my room, who knows what else he is capable of?

Jasmine rushes out the door, running to me. "Andy, what's going on with you?"

I glance at my sister, wanting to tell her, but I can't get the words out over my panic. I hand her my phone so she can see for herself as I continue to suck in air.

"Oh, shit. Not again!" She takes one look at my face and wraps an arm around my shoulders, trying to comfort me. "Hey, it's okay, just breathe. I think you're having a panic attack." We sink to the ground and she talks me through the calm breathing she has been trying to teach me. It takes a few minutes, but sure enough, my breath starts to return to normal and the feeling of overheating cools down.

I glance at her. "Jas, oh my God, those cameras must be in my bedroom. Someone has put cameras in my room." I cry, my shaky hands covering my face as my breathing shortens again. I try to relax and breathe like she said. Almost impossible through the flashing alarm going off in my head. The one that tells me this situation is so much worse than we thought. This guy is not giving up until he gets what he wants, and for some reason, he wants me and Brad to be over.

"Try and just focus on your breathing for now, slow and steady. In for four then out for four. We can work the rest of this out. You're safe, Andy, I've got you." She pulls me to her and hugs me as I try to do what she's saying and concentrate on my breathing. It's so hard while my mind is racing with thoughts of everything this creep has watched me do over the who knows how long since they had cameras watching me.

She hops up and holds out her hands. "Come and sit down with me." She leads me over to a small table and chairs and we sit down. "Wait here." She runs to the candy shop and then back. "Here, have something to drink." She hands me a bottle of water.

I open it and take some small sips. "I can't even wrap my head around what this means. How long has he been watching me?"

"I don't know. We'll call the police when we get home, see if they can work it all out."

The police again. It was bad enough last time having to give statements, and they'll just say they can't do anything anyway. Then there are my parents. My dad is going to freak. I turn to Jasmine. "Don't tell Mum and Dad this time, okay? It only worries them, and I don't want them to know the full extent of what's going on."

"What, like it looks like someone is trying to blackmail you because of your relationship with Brad?"

"Well, yeah. But I have no idea why. Who would care so much that I'm with Brad that they're doing this?"

"I'm not sure." She pauses for a moment, thinking. "His ex-wife or an acquaintance... what about that assistant coach, what's her name, Ava? You said you think she has a thing for Brad. Maybe she's worked it out and is pissed? Or it could be another player? You're not the favorite of some of the other girls; maybe this is one of them?"

I think about what she's saying, but it doesn't add up. "Nah, his ex has only just arrived here from England, and I don't think Ava is that type of person. And when I was getting those messages on my birthday, I got the impression it was a guy. They keep saying I'm theirs. Like they have some sort of ownership over me."

"Maybe a jealous ex of yours?" Her eyes go wide. "That might be more like it."

"I don't have any exes, well, not really, anyway. No one who would bother to do something like this. Jamie was years ago, and I haven't heard from him since. And anyone else has only just been a one-night thing." I dismiss her comment. I really can't think of anyone who would want to do this to me.

"Maybe it's not someone you know or have actually been with, like a fan who's obsessed with you and they think you should be with them or something? Shit like that happens, Andy. It's scary and can escalate really quickly."

"You sound like Brad, that's what he thinks. The idea of that scenario is even worse. This could literally be anyone, Jas." I look at her, even more scared. This is too much.

"Yeah, it could, Sis. I'm sorry this is happening to you. We'll talk with the police, and I really think you should be talking to your team psychologist as well. They might be able to give you some better ways to deal with your anxiety over it all."

I bury my head in my hands. "That's what Brad says as well." I look back to her. "But I don't need to talk to anyone else, I have you. Besides, I can't really go in there and tell them the full story now, can I?"

"I guess not. That's okay, you can talk to me." She takes my hand across the table.

People start to filter out of the theater. The movie must be over. "I'm so sorry you missed it. I know you were looking forward to this one."

"It's okay, Sis, this is more important than some movie. We can try again next week."

Darcy and Luna find us through the crowd. "What happened to you two?" asks Darcy.

I give Jasmine a look. I don't want to have to go over all of this again with them. "I just needed some air. I was feeling a bit sick. It was too hot in there."

She gives me a look like I'm bullshitting her. And I know I should just tell them, but I'm so exhausted by it all. "Oh, okay. Well, you missed a good movie."

We hop up from our seats and make our way out through the front of the building toward our car. I can't help but keep glancing around. Am I being followed now? My mind is racing. How am I even supposed to go home right now, to my room, knowing there is a hidden camera somewhere? I feel sick to my stomach over all of this.

---

BRAD

I sit across the table from the woman I used to love. At least I think I loved her, now it all seems so hard to believe I could ever have loved someone like her. She is beautiful, yes, stunningly so, with her perfect hair, face made up, and designer clothes, but as the saying goes, it's what's on the inside that counts, and in this case, that is manipulation, deceit, adultery—none of it pretty.

She has been making small talk for over an hour while we ate our meal, and I'm beginning to wonder if there was any real reason she even wanted to meet up tonight at all. Or if this was all just a ploy to spend time with me and try to manipulate me again.

"So, as I was saying, I have decided to move to LA. What do you think?"

"I think it has nothing to do with me where you decide to live, Madeline. We're not together anymore, and after you sign the papers, we won't have any reason to see each other again."

She tries to take my hand across the table, and I pull away. There is that flash of wounding in her eyes again, but she recovers quickly. "Brad. We have been through so much, are we really going to let what happened back in England tear our marriage apart? I thought our vows meant more to you than that. I mean, it was just one little slip-up, and it will never happen again."

I stare back at her in disbelief. I can't even believe the words she's saying. How could she possibly think I would just forgive her over this and take her back? She's delusional. "What? Um, screwing my best mate behind my back for over a year is not one little slip-up. And the only one who needs to think about what our marriage vows meant is you. I stuck to mine."

Tears well in her eyes. She always did know how to turn it on when she wanted things to go her way. But her waterworks no longer work on me. I cross my arms over my chest and wait for the sob story to start. "What happened back there was just a stupid mistake. I was so stressed and worried about you after you got hurt, and you were distant. I needed reassurance, but you were going through your own stuff. If you could see it in your heart to forgive me, nothing like that will ever happen again. I want what we had in the beginning back, Brad. I want to start a family with you like we planned. Together, we could have it all."

I glare at her, not giving her anything. "Did Byron end it with you or something? Last I heard you had moved in with him and the two of you were living the high life."

She gives me a look like I shouldn't have brought up his name. But she was the one messing around with him. "He didn't dump me. I regretted what happened as soon as you left and wanted you back."

More bullshit. Something obviously happened there, or she wouldn't be here begging me for forgiveness. "Too late, Madeline. I have moved on. And so should you. We are never getting back together."

She scowls at me. "What, with that teeny bopper I met at your place? I'm happy for you to get it out of your system, whatever this is you have going on with her, but, Brad, we both know you will end up back with me. You can't have a real future with her. She's just a kid, you are in completely different stages in your lives. She's probably out partying and having fun. She also has a soccer career to think about. Do you really think she would be ready to have a child any time soon? Even if she wanted to, you would have to wait years for all of that. We're at the stage where it's time for us to settle down and start a family. I know how badly you wanted to have a baby. Now is our chance to do this together."

She's unbelievable. Making this all about what she can offer me over Andy. "No, our chance was before you fucked it all up. That's over now, and that's on you." I push back from the table, take the papers from my pocket, and throw them down in front of her. "This is over. Sign the papers. I won't be meeting up with you again," I say angrily, making it as crystal clear as I can.

I take out enough cash to cover the bill for dinner, toss it on the table, and storm away from her and don't look back. I can't even believe she had the nerve to bring up the fact that I wanted a baby. She's messed up, using that against me. And to say that Andy and I aren't right for each other because we are in different stages of our lives. What the fuck would she know about what I even want anymore. She makes me fucking furious.

I storm angrily up the busy street. It's Friday night and there are a lot of people around this part of town with all the restaurants and nightlife entertainment. I make it to my car, and as I go to jump in, I hear someone call out from across the street.

"Hey, Coach Swift." One of the girls from my team.

I look over to where the voice came from and see Luna

and Darcy. They wave from outside a small bakery. Darcy is leaning up against the wall and she motions for me to come over to them. I'm not really in the mood to deal with them, but I wonder if Andy is around as well. I know she's pissed at me for going to dinner with Madeline. She said it was fine, but I know it wasn't. But it was also something I needed to do. I close my car door and cross the street in the direction of the girls.

Andy and her sister come out of the store with brown paper bags. She's smiling at something Jasmine has said, but I can tell instantly something is not right with her. Her usual sparkle is gone, and it looks like she has been crying.

"Brad, what are you doing here? I thought you had that dinner," she says, looking confused.

"I did, but it's over now. I was just about to head home when your friends called me over." I motion to my car across the road.

"Oh, okay," she says sadly, and I can't tell if she is just ticked off with me or if something more is going on. But I know she's not her usually sassy smartass self.

"Are you alright?" I ask, rubbing her arm.

She shakes her head, and I take her in my arms as she cries. I look to Jasmine for an explanation. "She got some more messages. It's not good, Brad," says Jasmine, the worry for her sister etched on her face.

I knew it was just a matter of time before it happened again. Andy keeps thinking it's just pranks, but I think tonight she may actually realize how serious this is. "Hey, you're safe, I have you now. Let's get you home and we can work this all out. I won't let anyone hurt you. Andy, you're safe."

"There are cameras," she mumbles into my chest.

# THE COACH

"Cameras?" I mouth to Jasmine, and she nods. Shit, where? "Jas, I'll take Andy with me, we'll see you at home."

"Alright," she says, leaving with the other girls.

I wrap my arm around Andy's shoulders and lead her across the street. "It's going to be okay, Andy. I promise I won't let anything happen to you, okay?" She doesn't respond, just hugs me closer to her.

## CHAPTER EIGHTEEN

### ANDY

We pull into the driveway of my place and I know what I have to do. The drive here was quiet, with us both in our own thoughts. But his hand never left my leg; he needed the contact as much as I did.

"This is all going to be fine, Andy. I'll come in with you and search your room, get rid of these cameras, or we can just get your things and you can come back to my place."

I give him a look, like what the fuck. "Did you not read the message? This person is watching me, watching us. I can't come home with you. We need to end it. It's the only way for it to stop, and I need this fear to end. If we keep seeing each other, you will lose your job and I'm going to lose my mind." I'm babbling, the words tumbling out of my mouth quickly as tears roll down my face. But he has to be able to see where I'm coming from. I look out the front of the car, searching, wondering if we're being watched right now.

He flicks his eyes back to me. "Leave you to deal with this by yourself when you need me the most? I don't think so, Andy. It's just a job. It's more important that I protect you from this asshole." He's livid, and I can see his protective side is taking over. He thinks he can save me from all of this, but he can't, not if we're together. This all started after he was on the scene, and that's the only thing consistent about all of these messages. This person wants us not to be together.

It's not what I want at all. That's why I'm so upset right now. This relationship I have with him is the first time in my life I actually wanted so much more, but not like this, looking over my shoulder, worried what their next move will be. If this person is as crazy and possessive as it seems, who knows how far they will go to keep us apart?

I take his hand in mine and our fingers lace. "Maybe we just cool it for a bit, so it looks like we've broken it off. I can't deal with this, it's all too much for me, and I need to focus on playing, not all this shit." Tears threaten to fall again. Part frustration, part because I'm so sad by all of this. The way he looks at me, so wounded, kills me. I only want to make this man happy, especially after all he's been through with his wife. But it's just not meant to be right now.

"If you break it off with me, this person wins, they get what they want," he says sadly, looking defeated.

"I'm not breaking it off with you. Don't make this harder than it already is. This isn't what I want at all, but what else can we do? What if this person hurts you because of me? I couldn't live with myself. Let's just cool it for a bit, see if they back off. Please, Brad, I'm starting to get really freaked out here. We don't know how far they'll go to keep us apart."

"If that's really what you want."

"It's not what I want. But we can't be together anyway, can we! Not really the way we want to. And now with all of these threats, we have to at least try. Maybe when the season is over, we can work all this out between us, but for now, this is for the best for us both. Don't you think?"

He doesn't say anything, and I feel like a total bitch because this isn't what I want either, but what else am I supposed to do right now? We've gotten ourselves into an impossible situation and now the consequences are going to catch up with us. "I'm just trying to stop this from becoming something you regret. I'm not worth it, Brad. And you already have so many other things to worry about. You're in the middle of a divorce, you need to time to deal with all of that as well. Maybe this will be a good thing, some time to get all this shit figured out."

"You're worth it all, Andy. But I don't want to add any more pressure to you. I get what you're saying. This is messy, and if we appear to have called it off, it might stop him. But I don't want to be apart from you."

"I know. I'm sorry. This is hard for me too, but it's what we have to do." I kiss him on the cheek. "Bye, Brad."

I turn to get out of the car, and he grabs my wrist. "Andy, how am I supposed to keep you safe if you're not with me?" His eyes plead with me not to walk away, but I know I have to for both of us. This isn't forever, this is just for now. At least, I really hope that's the case, and once this is all worked out, we can be together.

I give him a small smile, trying to show how tough I am, when I'm really not right now. "It's not your job to protect me, Brad. I have Nala and the girls, I'll be fine."

He pulls me toward him, placing a kiss on my lips. It quickly turns desperate, making it almost impossible to leave him. When we kiss, the rest of the world fades away and I forget about anything else. God, I don't want to leave. This is what I want, to be with him. But I can't, not right now anyway. His grip on me loosens, and I pull away from his lips. And slowly slip from the car without another word.

Once in my bedroom, I hear his tires screech and his car scream down the road. I throw my bag against the wall in frustration. This is fucked up. I'm devastated by this whole situation.

My eyes dart around the room, looking for the fucking hidden cameras. From the direction the images were set, they have to be toward my headboard. No sign on the ceiling or by my window. I start throwing things around my room in my mad search for it. I empty my bookshelves, bedside tables, every fucking damn drawer in the place, and still nothing. Where are they?

My gaze focuses in on the plant behind my bed. It's the only thing left in here high enough. I jump on my bed and reach for it. Sure enough, there is a little white circular device just sitting there, hidden by the leaves. I hurl it across the room, and it smashes into pieces against the wall. But I'm not satisfied. What if there's another one?

I turn around in a rush to see the girls all standing in my doorway. I drop to the floor and the tears I have been trying to hold back break free again, and I melt into a puddle on my floor. Sobs escape me.

"It's okay, I'll talk to her," I hear one of them say.

Then Darcy is next to me, sitting on the floor, her hand on my knee. She pulls me into her, and I completely lose it. I feel completely out of control of my whole life. This stalker is messing with my mind. It's what they wanted, and they win, because I'm a total mess and I have just told the only man I ever wanted to leave.

"Hey, it's going to be okay, baby. Shh."

But it's not going to be okay. I have stupidly gone and fallen for him. Someone I should have stayed away from, and I knew it right from the start, but I had myself convinced it was just a bit of fun. I didn't want anything more, so I should've been able to walk away when I needed to, but I can't without it breaking my heart, and worse, his.

---

BRAD

I slam my keys and phone down on the side table as I enter my place. I'm fucking pissed off. Tonight went from bad to worse. First, having to deal with Madeline, and then messages from Andy's stalker. She thinks by pulling away she is saving me from losing my job and stopping her stalker from contacting her, but that's not how these things work. Whoever it is, he will still be watching her, except now I won't be around to protect her. That's probably his plan, get her alone.

I know Andy is fiercely independent, and until now, she's dealt with everything on her own. But she doesn't have to anymore, she has me. And I'm ready to change my life for her because I can see a future with her, one that is worth fighting for.

I take in the sight of my empty house. Nope, I can't do it tonight. I feel like I have been holding all this in for too long. I need to talk to someone about the shit that is my life. I dial the only real friend I've made since moving here and organize to meet her at the pub round the corner.

When I walk in, Ava is already at a table. Her face lights up and she offers me a small wave when she sees me. I hope I'm not making a big mistake by telling her all of this, but I figure she knows most of it as it is. She's worked it out. And we have gotten quite close since I moved here.

She has been confiding in me, and I feel like I can trust her.

I order a whiskey from the bar and slide into the seat across from her. "Thanks for meeting up with me, I know it's late."

"It's okay, I didn't have anything else going on, so it was nice to get the call. Are you okay? You didn't sound right on the phone." I can see the concern on her face, and it's nice to know she cares so much. She's a really sweet girl.

"Not really. It's a whole big fucked-up mess, Ava," I say, talking a large gulp of my drink.

"What is?"

"My life," I huff.

"That's a bit dramatic, isn't it? Have you been hanging around a team of girls for too long?" She laughs. "Why don't you start at the beginning and tell me what's going on."

I run my fingers through my hair, the frustration and anger from tonight almost overwhelming. "I wish I was being dramatic. Okay, well, you were right. There is something going on with Andy, and it's not quite what you think." She raises a brow and sips on her drink, waiting for me to elaborate. "I met her the night I came for my interview, out at a club, and we connected. I had no idea who she was, that she would be one of the girls on my team. Fuck, at the time I thought she didn't even like soccer. I had no idea who she was. We hooked up. And then that was it until I saw her again that first night I came to training. I was shocked as shit to see it was her."

Ava's eyes are now wide as she takes in what I just told her. "I bet you were."

"Fuck, I mean, what are the chances? There are nearly four million people that live here and I slept with one of the twenty-odd on the team I'm about to start coaching."

She nods, agreeing. "Yeah, that's pretty crazy. So, what happened when you both worked it out?"

"We agreed it was a one-time thing and that we would just forget about it and stay away from each other. I thought it would be easy. But every training session got harder to stay away from her, and then one night, she was being followed and called me for help. She has like a crazy stalker or something. We're still trying to work it all out. But someone was following her, and when I dropped her home that night, she walked into her bedroom to see it had been trashed, items stolen... it was a whole thing. It wasn't safe for her to stay there alone so I invited her to stay at my place."

Her eyes look like they're going to pop out of her head. "Shit, Brad, you didn't."

"Not that night. She was scared, and I just wanted to help her. Ava, I have this crazy connection with her. Unlike anything I have ever had with anyone else."

She drops her head, looking into the glass she's drinking from. "I can see why I never stood a chance with you," she says softly.

"I'm sorry, Ava."

She looks back to me and smiles. "Brad, it's okay. I was just joking, trying to lighten the mood. We've been friends for a long time. We're okay. So, I can only assume what happened next. You found yourself falling for her and you have the moral dilemma that you're her coach. What do you do?"

"It's so much worse than that now. We crossed the line and now her stalker has photographic evidence and he's trying to blackmail her. Saying she has to break it off with me, and if she doesn't, he'll go to the club and tell them."

"Shit, are you serious?"

"Deadly. She broke it off with me tonight. She doesn't

want me to lose my job because of her. The worst part is now I'm really worried we're playing right into his hands. She's now alone all the time instead of with me. He can take his fucked-up opportunity to get to her."

"This is messed up, Brad."

"I told you I wasn't being dramatic."

"Yeah, you're right about that. This is probably obvious, but have you called the authorities?"

I give her a look like is she kidding? Of course we have. "Yes, but they're doing fuck all. Her dad has installed a security system and better locks and she has a dog now, but I just really feel like she shouldn't be alone." We both go quiet, and I sit looking into my drink, hoping for some answers. I have just overloaded her with information. "Seriously, Ava, what am I supposed to do?" I feel like I have lost total control of all of this.

"I have no idea. I thought when you called me tonight it was to tell me how it went with Madeline."

"Oh, that is another whole level of fucked up. She wants to get back together so is refusing to sign the divorce papers."

She tilts her head and raises her brow. "After what she did, are you kidding me?"

I shake my head, still in disbelief after our dinner. I don't understand her at all or what she's thinking this time. "I wish I was."

She finishes her drink and places it back down on the table heavily. "Okay, well, let's look at it all logically. You told Madeline that it's over and she has to sign the papers, so I'm sure she will realize it's over soon enough and just sign them. I wouldn't worry too much about her, she'll move on to something new and shiny soon enough and won't be your problem anymore. And Andy wants to cool it for a bit.

Honestly, that can't be such a bad thing for now, Brad. You have such a good opportunity coming your way with the men's team. Maybe this is for the best. Just have a break for a bit until you're not her coach anymore, then there's no need for her to be blackmailed by this crazy stalker dude."

Everything she's saying makes sense. I knew she would be logical about it all and able to calm me down. But I still feel unsettled. I swirl my drink around one more time, then throw it back. "That's what she thinks, but what if he hurts her while I'm not around to protect her? I'd never forgive myself."

She offers me a knowing smile. "You're really smitten with her, aren't you?"

"Do you think I would be risking my career otherwise? I fell for her that first night I met her. This is just an impossible situation."

"What has this guy done so far? Just taken some photos from afar, sent some texts?"

Ava's trying to make it seem not so bad, but she doesn't know the half of it. I wouldn't be reacting like this if it were nothing. I start listing it off on my hand. "He followed her when she was walking home one night. He broke into her house and trashed her room, sent photos of us together in her bed. He even messed with her car. Oh, and I'm pretty sure he turned the lights out at the club when she was there one night alone."

"Okay, that is all pretty fucked up. But he's never approached her or physically threatened her. From what we can tell, he just wants you to stay away from her, so for now, maybe that's the best thing to do. Give her a little space and maybe make sure she has a friend with her when she's out of the house just to be careful."

"Yeah, maybe you're right." Hopefully she is and me

staying away will stop him from contacting her while we play out the last few games of the season. Then his threats will no longer matter. "And this conversation..."

"It stays between us, Brad, I get it. I don't won't you losing your job either." She wraps her arms around me in an embrace. I trust her, I know she won't tell anyone. I wouldn't have called her otherwise. And it does feel good to finally be able to talk it all through with someone, it puts things into perspective.

"Thanks, Ava, you're a good friend."

## CHAPTER NINETEEN

### BRAD

As much as it's killed me, I've given Andy her space all week. I've only seen her every day at training, and my beautiful girl looks lost. She's not herself at all. She is missing her usual sparkle. I know how she feels because I'm the same. I hate being without her. I agree with what both she and Ava said last weekend, but this situation is starting to take a real toll on both of us.

And I know I shouldn't be feeling like this really, we hardly know each other, but this thing between us has taken me by surprise. I went into it just thinking it would be some fun. A bit of a distraction from all the shit I have been through in the last few years, but things changed so quickly between us, and I know this is more than just a physical attraction, an itch that I want scratched. She is under my skin in a way that feels very much like it could be something permanent.

I thought when I married Madeline that was it for me, the way I felt about her I could never feel for another, but with Andy, it's so much more intense. I can't even explain the way I feel about her, only that I know I want more of her. It's becoming an obsession, a need that only she can fulfill. Being with her is like the high I have when my team used to win a big game, but I feel like it all the time when we're together, and being away from her this week, just watching her from afar, is like torture to my soul. I feel empty, and there is nothing that can fill the void but her. And after a week of it, I can't stay away from her any longer.

So, I wait.

I have given her the space she asked for, but now she needs to listen to me. After watching her play our game tonight in North Carolina, I know I have to talk to her. We won but only just, with Darcy scoring both our goals. Andy didn't play the way she normally would and fouled a player, earning her a red card and the rest of the game on the sidelines, as well as next week off. I can see how much all of this is messing with her game, and we need to come up with a better solution to it all. So, I wait out in front of the changerooms until I know everyone else has left. She is always the last out, and tonight that works in my favor. As soon as she walks around the corner, I grab her arm, pulling her toward me in the darkness behind the building.

She squeals then realizes it's just me and relaxes. "Shit, Brad, you scared the life out of me." A hand goes to her pounding chest.

It was a stupid move on my behalf when I know she's already jumpy. "Sorry, not what I was trying to do. I just didn't want anyone to see I was talking to you." I pull her toward me, pinning her against the wall, so close I can feel the rapid pound of her heart, probably from the scare I just gave her. She blinks up at me. Her stare is intense, baby-blue eyes bringing me undone. My lips meet hers, showing her just how much I can't be without her. She needs to know what she means to me.

She pulls her lips back. "Brad, you know we can't. Especially not in public," she whispers, but her body is betraying her words. Her hands cling to my shirt, her tits pressed to my chest. Her eyes search mine, like she is desperate for me to persuade her she's wrong.

"We're in another city, no one knows us here. There is no way your stalker is here. We're safe, and I'm not waiting."

"Only the entire rest of our team and training staff, yeah, no one," she sasses, rolling her eyes at me with a little smile. But her eyes drop to my lips then slowly rise back up.

I take her pretty face in my hands, so she is focusing on me and only me. I wish I knew how to get through to her. I really don't give a flying fuck about anyone else. All I care about is this moment right now. "They're all gone to dinner already, it's just us." My lips move to her neck as I place kisses down to her shoulder, hoping I can convince her that she can't be without me either, the only way I know how. And to my surprise she lets me, with each kiss her body softening more. She feels this pull, this need to be with me, just as much as I feel it toward her. We're made for each other, that's why we can't stay away.

"I don't know how to be without you anymore," she whispers into the night.

And I thank the gods that she is right there with me. I sweep my gaze up to look at her. Her eyes are glassy, and I know she is torn because she's scared of the consequences us being together holds. But I'm right there with her. I know I can't be without her. "I know, baby, you won't have to be for much longer. One more game, then it's the semis. The season is nearly over, then I have a plan."

Her hands roam up under my shirt and she holds me close. "What plan, Brad? I'm so done with all of this. I feel like I'm falling apart. I don't even know who I am anymore. I'm constantly looking over my shoulder. I hate it."

"You let me worry about all of that." I kiss her. "Just trust me, I have it all sorted." My hands roam down her body to her ass, and I scoop her up, her long legs wrapping around my waist. Our lips are hungrily back on each other. My tongue taking control of her mouth. I'm so desperate for her I could take her here against the harsh wall of the building. I need to devour her, show her she's mine and that what we have developing here can't pause even for a few weeks because I won't let it.

"God, I want you so badly after this week," she murmurs, and I take pleasure knowing she feels the same.

"You're not the only one." I thrust my hips towards her so she can feel my need for her.

She pushes my chest, trying to create distance between us, but I won't let her. "We shouldn't be doing this. What if someone finds us?"

"Stop trying to be a good girl. We both know you're not the kind of girl who does what someone else tells you to, so stop letting this creepy guy get to you. And let me take care of your needs."

She gives me a look of surprise, and I think for a second maybe I overstepped the mark. She is clearly not in a great frame of mind at the moment. But then the twinkle of desire is back in her gaze and that sexy smirk returns to her lips. "You're right. Fuck me right here, up against this cold, hard concrete wall. It's what I need. Show me how much you missed me. I need to be reminded just how bad I can be."

Music to my ears. "Good girl." I scrunch her short skirt up higher around her waist and pull her panties to the side, giving me access to her soaking-wet pussy. I knew she would be drenched and ready, she always is.

I stroke her, feeling her warmth as I explore. I can't see her beautiful body very well in the shadowy dark, but the scent of her arousal is in the air and it's lethal for my senses. I slip two fingers in deep, filling her tight little pussy. She arches her back, grinding herself toward the pulse of my movement.

"Yes," she moans. "God, this is what I need."

As I pump her, she reaches for my pants, tugging and pulling them down enough for my hard dick to be released. I slide my hand out of her, grabbing her ass to reposition her so I can push straight in.

"Fuck, yes," I hiss. This is what I've needed since she left me sitting in my car in her driveway last week. To know we're okay. I move back and forth slowly, looking straight into her pretty blue eyes. I was craving her raw and ready for me, nothing between us, our two bodies connected. Fuck, realization dawns. "Please tell me you're on birth control, because I don't want to stop what we're doing right now."

She grinds toward me, not liking that I've stopped. "Keep going. I am, we're covered. Don't fucking stop now."

That's all I need to hear. I don't think I could stop now even if I wanted to. "Thank fuck." I pick up the speed, thrusting into her with all the pent-up frustration I've had toward this situation all week. I know I'm taking it out on her, and I shouldn't be, but she really doesn't seem to mind like this. My free hand palms her tits through her shirt. Her body feels so fucking good under my touch.

"That's it, Brad. Screw me so hard. I need it, I need you." Her voice is hoarse and desperate, and I love that I do that to her. Her hand goes to the back of my neck, and she pulls my lips back to hers with force, kissing me hungrily. Her nails dig into my back as she grips on through every hard pump. She's getting close, I can feel it.

I drown out her load moans of pleasure with my mouth as her body convulses around me, ripping my own orgasm from my body as I fill her. I can feel the beads of sweat dripping down my back. That was fast and hot. And everything we both needed right now.

I hold her in my arms, and she drops her head to my shoulder. "Brad, I think..."

Someone calls out Andy's name. She jumps up quickly. Then another person calls for her. Her friends must have come looking for her. Damn it, I wasn't done here. I still need to talk to her properly.

"Shit, Darcy and Luna." She cringes, already wiggling out of my grip on her. "I'm so sorry, but I better go before they find us like this." She stands, tugging her skirt down and fixing her shirt.

I pull her face toward me and kiss her once more. "See you at dinner," I say quietly so her friends don't hear, then she takes off around the corner and into the night. I hear them talking and I know she's safe with them so I can leave. I better get to the team dinner that I'm now late for.

Not exactly where I was going when I wanted to see her tonight. I wanted to talk, but with Andy, that's where it always seems to end up. We need each other. I need her more than I have ever needed anything before in my life.

# CHAPTER TWENTY

## ANDY

I sprint around the corner to find where their voices are coming from. My friends are walking together, and they look pissed. At me. "We came back for you when you didn't arrive at the restaurant. You had us worried," snaps Luna angrily, hands crossed over her chest. "You know you're not the only one worried about this stalker that's following you, right, Andy? Your friends are scared as hell for your safety."

I give her an apologetic smile. "Sorry. I'm fine, though, just caught up in my own little world having a long shower after the game," I lie, feeling the slippery ooze of what I was just doing roll down my legs.

They both give me a filthy look, and I know I'm the shittiest liar in the world so they can see right through me. "What? I was!" I protest, probably too hard. "I was pissed off with myself, so I needed it," I lie again. But it's half true. That is the reason I was here late before I ran into Brad. And I feel bad because these girls are my best friends, and I normally would tell them everything. But in this situation, I know I can't, not anymore.

"Brad wasn't at dinner yet either..." says Luna, raising a brow. "I thought you two broke it off." Damn, they're too smart, they know me too well.

Darcy takes my hand; she's not as pissed as Luna. "We're just worried about you, Andy, you're not yourself lately. He has you doing things you wouldn't normally. Don't you think?"

"Not really," I say with an eye roll. I get it, they care, but I'm pretty sure I can handle this on my own.

"Babe, you know you're not yourself. What happened tonight out on the field, that wasn't you. We have been your friends a long time, and we can see you changing for this guy. Your head is in the clouds, you're distracted, you're not sleeping or eating properly. Even your sister is worried about you."

Jasmine hasn't said anything to me about any of this, and she would normally be the first to. I give them both a hard assessing glare. "I'm not changing for him. This has just been a shitty week. If anything, I played so terribly because I miss being with him. Breaking it off with him was really hard, especially when I didn't want to. This whole thing is fucked up. I finally find a guy I like enough to want to try something with and he's out of reach. Not only that but I'm being watched. You two have no idea how much that shit messes with your head. I'm fucking over it. I want my life to go back to normal." Good thing no one else is around because I'm practically yelling at them.

Now it's Darcy who rolls her eyes in Luna's direction. Why are they hating on him so much? I thought they liked him. Can't they see he makes me happy? I'm only off my game this week because we've been apart. "Ahh, you two wouldn't understand," I say, throwing my arms up in frustration and stalking up the road faster. I finally find a guy worth having something with and my two best friends are trying to warn me away from him.

They jog to catch up with me. Luna grabs my arm, stopping me, and I spin around abruptly. "Hey, Andy, don't be like that. We just care about you, and we're a little worried for your safety. See, Darcy has a theory."

I glance at Darcy, and she gives me a tight smile. A theory? What is she talking about? "On what?" I snap. I have almost had enough of this shit for tonight.

"Just hear her out, Andy, I think she might be on to something." Why am I not surprised that Darcy is the one behind this? She probably wanted him for herself and is all jealous.

I glare at her, waiting for this wonderful moment of clarity she's about to enlighten me with. The two of them take a seat on a park bench. I stay standing, not wanting to completely commit to the conversation when I have no idea what she's going on about.

"Andy, don't you think it's a little odd that all the strange things that have been happening to you started just after you met Brad?"

I hadn't really looked into the timeline before. Now that I think about it, what she's saying is correct, but what has that got to do with anything?

"And every time something happens, it ends up in Brad's favor. Like, when the lights went out in the changerooms, who was conveniently there to save you and take you for dinner? After your birthday party, who magically came to your rescue and let you stay the night at his place? The other night when you were upset after the movie, who turned up at the exact right time to comfort you? It's all a pretty big coincidence, don't you think?"

I blink back at them, not really finding words to argue

the point. My mind is racing as I try and think about all the times she's talking about. At the time, I never even considered Brad could be the one doing this to me. What would he stand to gain from any of it? He's gorgeous, wealthy, charming, he could get any girl he wanted. He wouldn't need to resort to pulling stunts like this so I took notice of him. There is no way he would do anything like this. He wouldn't need to.

I look between my friends. They both look so serious. They're worried about me, and I appreciate their concern, but they're wrong on this. "Sorry, Darcy, I know you're just trying to help, but what you're saying makes no sense at all."

Her eyebrows shoot up. "Really? Well, what happened tonight then, Andy? You tell the boy you need space, that you need to break it off so all the stalking shit will stop. Right? Did he respect your wishes? My bet is he waited for everyone else to leave then he approached you, said something you couldn't resist, and you melted. He has you right where he wants you. You're scared and running to him for comfort, you know I'm right here."

I glance to Luna. Is she really thinking this is all true as well? She gives me a small sympathetic smile that tells me all I need to know. They both think Brad is my stalker, a wolf in sheep's clothing. I shake my head slowly from side to side, trying to get rid of the thought she just planted there. I can't even process what my friends are saying, I don't want to. "There is no way this is him. He has no reason to do any of this, why would he?"

"I think it's pretty obvious. He is used to getting what he wants, and you, my girl, play hard to get better than anyone I know. He was obsessed with you after that night you met at the club, so he worked out a way to get you. It's probably the whole reason he took the job as our coach. He's a predator, Andy."

I don't want to hear any more. I turn away from my so-called friends and stride up the street. I need to get away from them, from their silly accusations. I can't believe they would think all of this about him.

"Where are you going? We have to get to dinner," calls Luna.

"Back to my hotel room. I'm not hungry," I yell back, swiping the angry tears that have started rolling down my cheeks. This is bullshit. My best friends think the guy I'm in *love* with is my stalker. Fuck, I just admitted to myself that I'm in love with Brad. I am, I know I am. This is so messed up.

I make it to my room somehow, my eyes blurry, my head thumping, and let myself in, then slam the door, throwing myself on my bed and burying my head in my pillow.

I want to cry so hard I wash away all the uncertainty, all the shitty thoughts that have now burrowed their way into my brain. I can't unhear what my friends said. All the events of the last few months are spinning by. Yes, some of it adds up, but that doesn't mean it's true... does it? He wouldn't do this to me. He knows how much it's messing with my head. There is just no way it's him. There has to be another explanation.

But the more I think about it, the more it all makes sense. Every time something happened, he was the hero, strategically placed, waiting to rescue me. And if two of the people who love me and I trust completely could be thinking this, then maybe there is something to it.

I have no idea how long I lie on my hotel bed feeling sorry for myself, but I'm pulled from my self-pity party by the buzz of a text on my phone.

**Brad:** Where are you?

He is probably wondering why I never showed up at dinner. I don't feel like having to talk to him, so I ignore his message and decide to change into my pajamas and go to bed instead. My head has been pumping since I started crying, and I just need to sleep it off.

I pull the pale blue shirt I have been sleeping in this week from my bag and slip it on. It's the one I borrowed of Brad's on my birthday. I never gave it back, and somehow, wearing it brings me comfort. Even tonight when I'm full of so much uncertainly about him. I turn off the lights and get comfy in bed, trying to quieten the thoughts.

My phone lights up and I glance to see who's calling. Brad. I ignore it and close my eyes. It vibrates on the side table next to me then stops. Then starts up again. He's not giving up easily.

My head fucking hurts. Why am I not surprised? Stress always has that effect on me, and at the moment, everything feels all too much. I'm completely overwhelmed with my life. My first red card ever, all because I was tired and frustrated at myself. It was a stupid mistake, and it shouldn't have happened.

Then there is the other mess, all the warning messages to stay away from Brad, and Luna and Darcy hating on him. Is he my stalker? Am I that dense that I have fallen for my own enemy?

---

BRAD

Why the fuck won't she answer her fucking phone? Both her friends turned up at dinner not too long after me, but she was nowhere to be seen. She knows how worried I get about her. If she wasn't going to bother turning up, the least she could have done is let me know.

I try her again.

Nothing.

I start to panic, all the thoughts of what could have gone wrong flicking through my head. Fuck it, I'm going to find her. I'm standing out front of the restaurant and the meal is practically over by now anyway, so I don't bother going back in. I stalk straight for the hotel we're staying in tonight, praying that she's in her room sulking, not taken by this crazy guy.

I arrive at her room and pound on the door. She'd better be in there. I'm praying to whoever will listen, please let her be okay.

I hear movement inside the room, and I start to relax a little knowing she's at least safe. But clearly ignoring my calls. She cracks open the door enough that I can see her long blonde hair and pretty pale blue eyes staring back at me. She looks tired and upset, like she's been crying. She's dressed for bed in just an oversized T-shirt, one I recognize as mine, the one I lent her the morning after her birthday.

"What are you doing here?" she whispers, looking irritated by my presence. She hangs onto the door handle, almost hiding behind the door and keeping distance between us.

"Making sure you're alright. You didn't turn up at dinner," I say back, just as irritated. What is going on with her? I close the gap, nudging the door open a little more, forcing her to have to take a step back and let me in. I don't want to be standing in the hallway where just anyone could walk past at any moment. I close the door behind me and face her. "What happened to you tonight?"

She looks to the ground, tracing a line with her big toe. Something is up. Something has changed since I saw her only a couple of hours ago.

"I just didn't feel like coming out. I wanted an early night," she mutters without making eye contact, and that's enough for me to know she's lying to me. She won't even look at me. What the actual fuck is going on?

"Really? What happened since I last saw you tonight, Andy? Something is wrong, I can tell." I put my finger under her chin, forcing her to look up at me. I don't like that she is avoiding my gaze.

She blinks back. "Nothing happened. I'm just tired and ashamed at how badly I played today. I just needed a quiet night."

"So why not reply to my calls, then? At least let me know you were home safe. You must have known I would be worried."

A flash of something I don't recognize goes through her eyes. "Brad, I need some space, you're acting crazy right now," she says quietly.

It would have hurt less if she had slapped me. "I'm acting crazy? What are you talking about? I was worried about you when you didn't turn up. I don't see how that is me acting crazy." I drop her face and take a step back.

"I'm sorry, this is all just too much for me. I need to get my head around everything. I need some space," she says quietly.

She's pulling away from me again. And I don't get it. "What about tonight then, Andy? What was that? You wanted every bit of me then. You can't deny it, I could feel it."

"You're right, I did. But Brad, I can't think straight when you're around. That's half the problem. Everything has happened so fast with us, it's overwhelming for me. Between everything that is happening with you and the stalker." She looks me over and I really have to wonder what on earth is going through her head. Whatever it is, I don't like it. "I feel like I'm starting to lose my mind. I can't concentrate on playing, and I fucked up tonight because of it. If you really cared about me like you say you do, you would give me some space to get myself figured out."

I stare back at her, her words cutting straight through me. She's acting so cold, like a different person completely. I don't get what could have changed so much from when I saw her just a few hours ago. I'm not going to stand here begging. "I'll leave you to it then, if that's what you want," I say, glaring at her, waiting for her response.

Her hands cross over her body protectively and she straightens up. "That's what I want," she says with quiet determination.

I take a step back, not even sure what else to do or say to convince her not to block me out. It looks like she has already made up her mind. Somehow, I'm the reason she is messed up? She's blaming me for all of this. I knew right from the start that getting involved with her was going to be a bad idea, but I couldn't help myself. Somehow, I thought I could see something more with her, and I thought that was worth not only fighting for but losing my career as well.

I thought she was worth it, but I guess I don't mean the same to her.

I look back once more and she appears lost, devastated, broken. And it finally dawns on me. She's right, I have to leave her alone to work through all of this. Without another word, I walk away.

## CHAPTER TWENTY-ONE

ANDY

I DROVE TO PALM SPRINGS LAST NIGHT AFTER PRACTICE and stayed at my parents' place. The home I grew up in. It's beautiful here, and I can already feel myself relaxing knowing I'm out of LA and away from all the drama of the last few weeks.

On Monday when I got back from our away game, I finally sat down and talked with the team psychologist. It was Jasmine's idea, after I told her everything that happened while we were away. Jasmine's not entirely sure the girls are right about Brad. She says it doesn't add up. Like, why would he be sending me messages asking me to stay away from him if it was him? She's right, that part makes no sense at all, so I have to agree with her. It couldn't be him. Thank God.

In the light of day, I knew all of that. And I probably should have gone and talked to him about what Darcy and Luna had said straight away, but the truth is, I needed this time for myself. To process my feelings. So I have kept my distance this week, because someone is still out there trying to keep us apart, and if they are a total nutjob, I don't want them escalating anything. Brad could end up fired, or they could be a real psycho and he could end up hurt or worse. I can't stand the thought that anything could happen to him because of me.

I was more than grateful when Beth, our psychologist, said I should take the weekend off. I'm suspended anyway, but she thinks I need some space from everything. And she doesn't even know the half of it, only that I have a creepy stalker invading my privacy, not the whole sleeping-with-my-coach thing. I couldn't go into all of that with her, because I don't want the club to know and for Brad to get in any trouble.

Jasmine came home with me. She has an exciting interview near here anyway and needed to come to Palm Springs for it.

"Bacon and scrambled eggs?" asks Mom with a warm smile. She dips her head into the fridge, inspecting its contents. And I realize I've been staring out the window to our yard for quite some time.

"Sounds perfect, thanks," I reply.

My parents live on a large property with a stable and my dad's pride and joy, his horses. It's a stunning mid-century modern home with five bedrooms, three bathrooms, and gardens framing the house. There is also a large pool out back. You couldn't have a house here in Palm Springs without one; it's so hot in the summer. It's way more than my parents need now, it's just them and Cassie living here, but they love it and have no plans to leave any time soon.

Dad is out feeding the horses, like he is every morning. They have been his main focus since he retired from the entertainment industry ten years ago.

Mom pulls the items she needs from the fridge, and I hop up to help her, deciding not to be a lazy bitch just because I'm sulking about my life. I crack the eggs into a bowl, add milk, and whisk. The bacon is soon sizzling in the pan, and the delicious smell wafts through the house, bringing my little sister Cassie out of her bedroom.

"Smells like breakfast," she says. She's still in her pajamas, hair like a bird's nest, and the remnants of last night's make-up smudged under her eyes. She takes a seat at the kitchen island. I didn't get to catch up with her last night because she was out with some of her friends from college. She could have lived on campus with them, but she has a casual job as a ballet teacher that she loves here close to home so decided to stay with Mom and Dad until she has completed her studies and gets a full-time job as a teacher.

I give her a smug smile; seeing her hungover is just funny. "Looks like you had a big night, Sis?"

"Let's just say I need whatever you're cooking in that pan to bring me back to life." She drops her head to the counter and rests it on her arms as her eyes close.

I smirk at her. I'm sure she's having the time of her life, and why not? Because I'm such a nice big sister, I fill a glass of orange juice for her and place it alongside some painkillers on the counter in front of her.

"Don't you have an assignment due Monday?" asks Mom.

"It's under control," she murmurs, not opening her eyes or lifting her head.

I look over at Mom and shrug.

"You okay?" she asks me quietly.

I let out a long sigh. "Yeah, I guess." I want to talk to Mom about it all, but she tells Dad everything, and I don't want him to get all protective and shit, so I keep it at that.

"How is that lovely soccer coach of yours doing? Brad. I could hardly believe my eyes when I saw how handsome he was." She smirks, that glint in her eyes she gets when she knows what's going on in one of our lives without us even telling her. I don't know how she does it, but she has always had a knack for reading our minds. That's why I always used to end up in so much trouble in high school; she knew what I was up to before I did half the time.

"He's fine, Mom, probably stressing about today's game right now. Just your typical soccer coach," I huff, trying to throw her off the scent.

She flips the bacon and it sizzles away. She gives me a knowing look. "Probably, without the best player on the team."

I give her a look like whatever. "I'm not the best player."

"They need you playing, though, not on the sidelines because of a silly tackle."

"I know that," I snap. I know I fucked up majorly. It was stupid, but once it was done, it was too late. It's one of those mistakes I just have to live with now.

"How on earth did you get the weekend off, anyway? I thought even when you were suspended you had to show up and watch. You're the captain."

"Normally you do. I'm on leave this week. The team psychologist thinks I need it. They are having one of the other girls fill in as captain."

She looks me over, assessing me, and I know I'm worrying her by saying that. "I knew there was something wrong with you. What's going on?"

I let out a long sigh. "It's just been a stressful year. I was frustrated last week. It was a mistake, shit happens sometimes, Mom."

"Andrea," she reprimands.

"Sorry, but it does."

She wraps an arm around me in a side hug. "Well, I'm

glad you're not too old to come home when you need a time-out from it all. We've missed you."

I smile at her. It's nice to be home, to be in the kitchen where my mom cooked all our meals as kids, and just nice to be in an environment where I feel safe for the first time in weeks. Last night was the first proper night's sleep I've had in a while.

"It's nice to have you home. And you want to know what I think?" she says with a small smirk.

I give her a look that tells her I don't, but I know she's going to say it anyway.

"I think you're in love."

"What?!" I squeak, my voice way more high-pitched than I intended it to be. That was the last thing I expected her to say. Cassie has now lifted her head from the kitchen counter and is listening intently to what our mother has to say about the whole thing. Jasmine also picks this moment to enter the kitchen, fresh from a shower. She's wearing a smug smirk, much like our mother's, and I know she just heard Mom's comment.

"You are. I saw it that day after your birthday, when the two of you were together. I know what that look was the two of you gave each other. I might be getting on in years now, but I still remember what it was like when I fell for your father. That's why I moved across the other side of the world for him. I knew right from the start that he was my person. And I think you might have just found yours."

I'm in utter shock. How on earth could she have gotten that from a look between me and Brad all those weeks ago? I didn't even know how I felt about him back then. I choose to ignore her and instead open the kitchen cupboards, grabbing five plates and serving the eggs I have been cooking, Mom follows with the bacon.

I take my plate over to the table and dig in, not waiting for the rest of them. I can't believe she just said that. Could it really have been that obvious back then? We didn't even know we were all that into each other. Is he my person? I'm sure after this week he's done with me completely. And so he should be, I've been such a bitch to him. I know I hurt him last weekend by freezing him out. I wouldn't be surprised if he never spoke to me again other than to yell instructions at me from the side of the soccer field.

Jasmine sits beside me, leaning in so only I can hear. "You know she's right, I've seen it as well. I'm so jealous, I would give anything for a guy to look at me the way Brad does with you."

Dad enters the kitchen through the back door, removing his work boots and leaving them by the door. I throw Jasmine a look, telling her to shut her mouth before he hears.

"Something smells amazing. How lucky am I to have this beautiful lady make me breakfast every morning," he says, wrapping his arms around Mom and kissing her cheek. They still seem so in love, even after four kids. She hands him a plate, and he takes his place at the table with us. "Three of my girls back home with me. How did I get so fortunate to have such beautiful and talented daughters? I couldn't be more proud of all your achievements." He smiles at us proudly, and I wonder if he would still feel that way if he knew what I had been getting up to this year.

"Thanks, Daddy," says Jasmine, giving his arm a squeeze. She always was a suck-up.

I offer a smile, and Cassie digs into her food, looking like if she doesn't get it down soon, she might just puke all over the table. Don't think he would be too happy about that, either.

I turn to Jasmine, trying to take the heat off me. "So, what time is that meeting you have lined up for today?" Jasmine has been offered an amazing opportunity for someone her age, to go into a private practice with another couple of psychologists. Instead of working for someone else, she would be her own boss.

She nibbles her bottom lip. "It's a lunch thing. I'm still not sure what I'm going to do about it, though, and they want my decision by today."

"I think it's a good opportunity for you. What is there to think about?" I ask.

"It would be moving back here. And it's a bit of an investment to start with," she says sadly, and I get it. We have a good thing going in LA, but the truth is, Jasmine hasn't been that happy there this year, and I think she's just staying because she thinks I need her.

"You could stay with us. What's the problem?" huffs Dad.

"No offense, Dad, but I need my own space, I'm nearly twenty-seven. I'm just worried about leaving Andy by herself in LA." She gives me a wide-eyed look, and I know what she means. She's talking about at the moment with everything that's going on. But I'm not her problem. She still thinks I need my big sister looking out for me.

"Don't be. I'm a big girl, I can take care of myself. You need to do this, Sis. It's perfect for you," I try to convince her. There is no way she is missing out on a good opportunity for me.

"Andrea is right, and besides, she has her own things going on. The two of you aren't going to be living together forever," says Mom with a wink. She's not going to let this go. She thinks she has me all worked out. And maybe she does, but I'm not telling her that.

"What has Andy got going on?" Dad glares at me with a questioning gaze. Why did Mom have to say that? I feel like a little kid in big trouble when he uses that voice with me.

"Just my soccer. And I have the other girls, I'm all good," I say a little too quickly.

He looks happy enough with that answer. And his attention returns to Jasmine. I'm glad, because the last thing I want to do is explain to my father what is actually going on, even if my mother has somehow worked it all out.

---

BRAD

I'm waiting at my local Thai takeout. It's Saturday night, and we lost our game today. The team needed Andy, and because of her fuck-up last week, she was banned for a game.

I shouldn't be so annoyed with her; I know last week she was going through all sorts of shit and that's why it happened, but we can't afford not to have her with us. This is just another reason why I know I have made the correct choice by moving to the men's team for next year. It's too messy when you mix business with pleasure. I want to protect her and support her, but also, she let the team down, and as a coach it fucking pisses me off.

After a week of her completely avoiding me, I was told on Friday by Beth our team psychologist that she's been given stress leave and is having a weekend away back home. I'm glad that she's finally talking to Beth. She'll be able to help her through what is going on, but I wish she would talk to me about it as well.

My order is called, and I go to the counter to collect it.

As I leave, I nearly walk straight into someone because she's blocking my path. One of the last people I want to see tonight—or ever, really.

"Brad, darling, it's you," she purrs, as if surprised.

I groan inwardly. All I want to do is take my greasy dinner home and watch the game on my oversized flatscreen. Try not to think about the fact that Andy is probably out having fun with her sisters. "Madeline, what are you doing here?" I huff. After I saw her last time, I thought she had left the country, and I couldn't have been happier about it.

She pulls in close, kissing my cheek, and my entire body tenses at her touch. What the fuck is she doing? "I have decided to stay."

My eyes go wide. Stay? "What, in LA?"

"Yes." She beams, her face lighting up. "After you left me that night in the restaurant, I met someone. A nice man, and well, I thought I might give it a go in a new town. You know, start over like you have."

I'm not sure why I need to know any of this, but I guess if she's with someone else then she's not going to be bothering me. That's exactly what Ava had said would happen with her, and I guess she was right. "Good for you. Guess I will see you around then," I say, preparing to continue my walk up the street, done with the conversation. What else is there to say here?

She touches my arm lightly. Stopping me, her gaze holding mine. "Oh, I hope so, Brad. I would love nothing more than to see a whole lot more of you. Actually, I was thinking we should do a little double date or something? Since I don't know that many people in this town and all. You could bring your teenager." She smiles that bitchy stuck-up smile I hate.

She has got to be fucking kidding, acting all sweet with me, but there it is, the dig she just had to make. "She's not a teenager," I reply.

"Just joking with you, darling." She hits me playfully. "We should, though. I want to see you again. I'm not doing anything tonight, and it looks like you're alone. I could come back to your place? We could catch up, for old time's sake. We used to have so much fun together. You remember that, don't you, Brad?"

I hear a voice call to me from across the street and look over to see Andy's two friends, Darcy and Luna. They give me a wave and a smile. I offer a small wave and a tense smile back, then turn my attention back to Madeline. I need to get rid of her.

"You have them all after you, don't you, Brad, darling? All the young ones love you, but they don't know you like I do. You need a real woman to take care of your needs." She gives her head a little shake as she watches the girls disappear up the street. Then her eyes are back on me. "You made me feel so bad for sleeping with Byron, and I'm sure you would have been doing the same, I just didn't walk in on you. It's okay, though, I'm alright with that. I'm very good at sharing." She bites her bottom lip, I'm assuming because she is trying to be cute. She just comes across as pathetic. Here she is telling me she has met a nice man and she is still trying to get with me. I really have no idea what I ever saw in her. She disgusts me.

"Well, I'm not! I never cheated on you. I could never have done anything that would hurt you like that. You're the only one here with no morals. Not me. If you're finished with whatever it is you're trying to do here tonight, I need to go, my food is getting cold."

"If you change your mind and get lonely tonight, call

me." She gives me her version of a sexy smile, and I take that as my cue to walk away from her. She's not listening to me at all.

"Bye, Madeline," I say, not waiting for her reply.

The woman is completely deluded. She has convinced some other poor sucker to take her in and she is still trying to look for something with me, when it couldn't be any more obvious that it's over. I can't believe she has decided to stay here. I was hoping when I saw her for dinner the other week it would be the last time I ever had to, but apparently, I'm not that lucky.

When I get home, I throw off my shoes and get comfy on my leather lounge chair with my takeout food and a beer. I'm still pissed off about running into Madeline. I feel like she has an ulterior motive here or something. Running into her tonight felt weird. I don't know what she's playing at, but I don't like it, and I don't want her anywhere near Andy.

When I'm done with my food, I pull out my phone to scroll through my social apps. A photo of Andy and her sisters comes up. The four of them are at some club in Palm Springs. She's dressed in a short fitted black dress, and she looks sexy as fuck. I instantly feel possessive of her and want to take off for Palm Springs, go find her and drag her back here with me, where she should be. But I'm not a psycho, and I trust her. We might be in a weird space right now, and she's icing me out, but I know that's just the panic she has going on because of her stalker and the whole threats situation. I know we have something real going on, and I just have to give her time to work it all out. A night out with her sisters is probably exactly what she needs.

The image also highlights just how young she is, and while it's not something I have put a lot of thought into before, having Madeline bring it up again tonight, it makes me wonder... once this is no longer a fun game where we're hiding it from everyone, will she still be that keen to explore what this is?

I am at the age where I'm ready to settle down and start a family, and I know for her she's years away from that. She has to focus on her soccer career while her body is up to it. I know that better than most, it won't last forever. I don't know why I still let what Madeline says get to me so much. I can wait for those things with the right person, and I know Andy is. I just hope she's on the same page as me.

Just as I go to put my phone down, another text pops in from a number I don't recognize.

**Unknown number**: While the cat's away the mice will play. Better be careful, Brad. Andy hates a cheater. She won't forgive you even if you are on a break.

What the fuck? Before I have time to process what is even going on, another text comes in, and this one is a photo. It's me and Madeline from earlier tonight outside the restaurant. From the angle of the image, it looks like we're standing in an embrace. It must have been when she kissed my cheek. I wrack my brain. Madeline is manipulative as hell, and when things don't go her way, she doesn't like it, but I don't think she would stoop so low as to actually set this shit up just to break Andy and me up. Would she? We've been thinking the whole time this is some guy that's into Andy, but maybe it's not. Maybe it's Madeline, jealous as hell and out for revenge on me.

Another message follows.

**Unknown number:** Andy deserves so much better than you. Lucky she has me looking out for her tonight. Don't worry, Brad, I'll keep her safe.

Then another image. This one is Andy on the dance floor with her sisters. This isn't Madeline.

Panic hits me. This fucking creep is at the same club as her. How is he even in Palm Springs already? I guess it has been a couple of hours since I was out front of the restaurant with Madeline. He could have made the drive if he took the photo of us then drove straight to the club where Andy is—or maybe it's two people working together? The thought of that makes this even worse.

I grab my keys and jacket and take off for my car, madly trying to dial Andy's number as I walk. But nothing, no answer. I try her sister Jasmine and get the same result. They probably can't hear over the music. Fuck, I need to go and find her. This is exactly what I was afraid would happen while I wasn't around. That it would give him an opportunity to get to her.

# CHAPTER TWENTY-TWO

### ANDY

I MOVE TO THE BEAT OF THE MUSIC AS IT PUMPS through the club. This isn't the trendiest club here, but it's where all the locals come. It has low light and is kinda dingy, with only the bar area lit up. But that's the appeal, I guess; dark places for getting up to no good. It's busy, mostly people in their early twenties, here to get wasted and either pick up or spend the night on the dance floor. That's my plan; my sisters and I love to dance, and tonight, I really need the escape.

I have consumed more than my fair share of drinks, and I'm feeling good. Really good, actually. A nice warm buzz flowing through me has me feeling more relaxed than I have in weeks. This is what I needed, some time with my sisters. Away from all the shit of LA. I have to admit, though, being a little tipsy makes me think of Brad and how much I miss him. I wonder what he's doing tonight.

Jasmine accepted the job at her meeting today and starts in two months, giving her time to move and get herself set up. I'm excited for her, if not a bit disappointed that she's leaving me and we won't be living together anymore. But

# THE COACH

this is the decision she needs to make for her life, and I get it. We had to grow up sometime and do our own thing. So the four of us sisters are out tonight celebrating. Amelia has left her kids with Mom and Dad for a movie night and Cassie has ditched the books to have some fun.

We're all glammed up, even me. I'm wearing a cute little dress for the occasion. It's one of Cassie's, because when I packed to come home, I wasn't expecting to be coming out. It's black, of course, but it's figure-hugging and I look sexy as hell. I have to admit, it actual feels nice to get dressed up all pretty.

I move to the rhythm of the music and try to clock out of reality, but the guilt from missing today's game keeps biting at me. This afternoon, not long after our game finished, I got a text from Brad saying we lost, and he said nothing else. I feel bad enough about missing the game, but I know what that message was. He was disappointed, and I feel the weight of my own actions. But I'm not fucking perfect. What does he want from me? This is where the coach and boyfriend line blurs—not that he has ever been officially my boyfriend, but it's where it gets messy.

Like the bitch I am, I didn't even respond to him. What am I going to say, *Sorry*? Weak, I know, but I didn't really know what to say. I'll sort it all out with him when I get back. There is actually a lot I need to talk to him about.

I feel a tap on the shoulder and spin round to see a face I haven't seen in years. Jamie Hall. Not since I slapped his pretty-boy face so hard I left a red mark. That was after finding him sleeping with that fucking slut from our school, Erica.

He smirks cheekily, clearly happy to see me. "Look at this, the soccer star Andrea Harper has decided to grace the

Palms with her presence," he says, but it's in a friendly, smartass way. Not an arrogant way.

I look him up and down, taking him in. There's a nervous flutter inside. Not because I still feel anything for him, more I think because of how it all ended with us and I haven't seen him since to deal with how it would feel. "Just home to see my family, Jamie." I motion to my sisters. Not sure what else I'm supposed to say to him.

Seeing him again is weird. I thought I would still feel really angry and hurt because I have been carrying that all around with me for so long. But I think over time, he has lost the emotional hold he had on me. He has no power over my feelings anymore. He's just someone from my past who hurt me. I think what has happened with Brad over the last few months has really helped with that as well.

"You want to go somewhere to chat?" he asks, and I have to say I'm thrown off guard a little. What could we possibly have to chat about?

"Not really," I say back with ease. So much so that I even surprise myself. When I was younger, I was so obsessed with this guy, would have done anything for him. Guess I really have changed. He did that to me. He made me harden the fuck up and stop being a doormat.

He brushes his hand over my arm, and I glare at him for having the nerve to touch me. "Come on, Andy. I know it was a long time ago, but I feel like such a dick for how things ended between us. Can we just talk for a bit?" He's practically begging me, and I feel a little smug satisfaction at that.

"Okay, fine," I say with an eye roll. I start walking from the dance floor, looking for a quiet spot to talk. I see a table along the back and head straight for it, making him follow me through the club.

"Do you want a drink?" he offers, gesturing to the bar.

"Nah, I'm pretty sure I've had enough." I have no idea why I just told him that.

"Alright." He looks down at the table then back to me. His features look older, more weathered, for someone who is still so young. He isn't aging well. And part of me, the bitchy part, takes a bit of satisfaction out of that. There's also a very noticeable wedding band on his ring finger. My eyes flick back up to his face, trying to act like seeing that he's now married doesn't bother me.

"Andy, I'm so sorry for how things ended. I didn't mean it all to happen that way," he mutters, looking genuinely sorry. Bit late for apologies, but I guess better late than never.

"No, I bet you didn't! No one intends for the girlfriend to walk in on them fucking another girl. You were just thinking with your dick instead of your head." God, I should shut up, but I can't help myself. I have gone over this conversation with him so many times in my head. All the good comebacks I would say to him if I ever got the chance.

"Something like that," he admits. "Anyway, I never wanted to hurt you, and I'm sorry I did." He pauses, giving me a once-over, and I almost cringe. He thinks he has some sort of a chance with me because he just apologized. Is that what this is? "You look like you're doing well, though?" He smirks, and just like that, his apology is over and he's trying to chat me up. Is this dude for real?

"Sure am. Living my dream playing soccer, what more could I want."

"You're still smoking hot, Andy. I really fucked up cheating on you."

My eyes narrow in on him. Is he seriously thinking this is going to go somewhere? Cause it's fucking not. "Um, thanks, I guess. So, looks like you got married," I ask, changing the subject. Cause if he says one more thing to me that he shouldn't, I might just drop-kick him right here in the club.

He glances down to his hand like he forgot the wedding band was there. I bet he's pissed at himself for not taking it off before he came out tonight. A leopard never changes his spots, and I'm sure in this case, he was looking to hook up or something. Never going to fucking happen, douche.

"Yeah, we did. About a month after we broke up, Erica found out she was pregnant and her dad insisted I marry her before the baby was born."

I blink back at him. Shit! There is a God, and she answered my prayers to screw him over. Should I be smiling smugly? Probably not, he looks sad about it. I try not to act so happy. "Fuck, that's... an interesting turn of events for you, I guess? So, you have a kid?"

"Yeah, two."

Two. So he fucked up again? Why am I not shocked? "Lucky you, sounds like you have the perfect little family then." I don't know why but knowing this pisses me off more than I thought it would. I don't really need to hear anything more from him. He has apologized, and now I know I dodged a really big bullet with him. That's good enough for me. So I stand up, ready to finish up the conversation. "I'm going to get back to my sisters," I say, turning to leave.

He grabs my arm to stop me. "Andy."

I turn back to him.

"It was the biggest fuck-up of my life. I'm trapped in a fucking living hell with a woman who hates me because she feels just as caged and kids who I love but I'm not ready to be responsible for. You were the love of my life, I knew that from when we were really young. I miss you every day, and I will always regret what I did to you. I should have never let you walk away." His hand loosens its grip on my wrist, and I just stand there in shock, blinking back at him.

The bitch inside of me wants to drop him a line, like, *karma's a bitch,* and just walk away, but this guy was my childhood best friend, and at one point in my life, the most important person to me. I actually feel kind of sorry for him. He looks truly miserable. "You broke my heart that day, and it has taken me years to build up my trust in other people again. I'm sorry your life isn't what you planned it out to be, that sucks."

"But you're happy in your life now?" he asks.

Except for my fucking stalker. But he doesn't need to hear about that shit. I smile. "I really am. Sorry, but I have a man in my life who would never treat me the way you did." And I really do. My friends may have made me doubt Brad, but I know he's a good man, and he really likes me. Or he did before I was such an ice queen to him. I need to fix this, tell him how I really feel about him before I get in my own way and fuck it up for good.

He nods his head as if understanding. "And that's what you deserve. I'm happy for you."

"Thanks. Good luck, with everything. Give Erica my best," I offer, not really meaning it, but I guess she got hers as well. I slip out of his grip. And turning, I walk straight into a hard wall of muscle.

---

BRAD

I can hardly believe I got here as fast as I did. This was the club it said they checked in at on her socials, and I glance around, frantically searching for any sign of her. I find her sister instead and head straight over to her. "Jasmine, where's Andy?" I call over the music.

Her face breaks into a massive smile, obviously happy to see me. "Hey, Brad's here. Girls, this is Brad, Andy's..."—she tilts her head, looking at me with a questioning gaze—"coach." It's pretty obvious she's had too much to drink. And right now, she is loving life and would be happy to see anyone.

I offer a short smile at the other girls, obviously her sisters. They all look so much alike except for the hair color. I turn my attention back to Jasmine. If the three of them are here, where is Andy? "Jasmine, where's Andy?" I say, with desperation in my voice. I need to know she's safe.

"She went off over that way. She's okay, Brad, just chill. She's out having fun. Come have a drink with us."

"Jasmine. Stop for a sec. This is serious. Her stalker contacted me tonight. I think he's here watching her."

Her face falls and she looks like she might be sick. "What? Okay, I'll help you find her. Girls, spread out. We need to find Andy right now."

She leads me through the club in the direction she thinks Andy went in and my heart starts to beat normally as soon as I spot her. She's talking to some guy who has his hand on her wrist. I stalk toward her. What the fuck is going on between them? I don't like the way he's touching her. I'm about to rip his arm off her when she pulls out of his grip and spins right into me. I catch her before she falls backward in the impossibly high heels she has on.

She blinks up at me. "Brad, what are you doing here?" she asks, straightening herself up. I glare at the guy, and he takes off into the crowd.

"What are you doing here? Who is this guy?" I throw the question back, trying to work out what the hell is going on.

"My ex." Her ex? The one who cheated on her? What is she doing here with him? He could be the fucker who took the photo.

I glance in the direction he took off in but he has already disappeared in to the haze of people.. "Why were you talking to him?"

"Why are you here?" she asks me again.

"He's here somewhere. I had to come and make sure you were alright."

The fear is back in her eyes instantly. "Who?" she asks, even though she already knows the answer.

"Your stalker. He started messaging me tonight. He sent a picture of you dancing with your sisters. He must be here somewhere." I scan the room as I'm saying it, but it would be impossible to see anyone in this place if they didn't want to be seen. It's so dark in here.

She glances around, her eyes going wide. "He's here? Get me out of here, Brad, please."

I can see the panic take over. I wrap my arm around her shoulder and usher her out of the club as quickly as I can and straight to my car.

Jasmine follows us and jumps in the back seat. "I'll message the others, let them know where we are."

Andy's panicked face looks over to me. "What the hell is going on? Brad, how do you know he's here?"

I hand her my phone, I have nothing to hide. If whoever this is thinks they can fuck up my chances with Andy by showing her shit like this, then they're wrong. She's a smart girl and will see it for what it is. She scrolls through the messages, then looks up at me, accusation and hurt in her eyes. "What is this? Did you have dinner with your ex-wife tonight or something?" she snaps angrily.

I can see her trying to process what she's seeing. "No," I

assure her. "I ran into her out the front while I was getting takeaway tonight. I haven't seen her since the dinner I told you about, I swear, but whoever this is must have been watching me tonight and took the opportunity to take a photo to make it look like something more than what was there."

She looks at the image then back to me and I know she's not totally convinced. She has been burned in the past and this is bringing up her trust issues, I can tell. "There is another image from tonight as well." I point to the next photo. "He must have taken the photo of me then driven straight here to watch you."

"Show me, Andy." She hands my phone to Jasmine. "Yeah, that's us from tonight alright. Shit, I just got goosebumps, this is creeping me out, guys. Who the hell is it?"

"I thought if I didn't see you anymore, they would leave us alone," Andy says sadly, almost to herself.

I take her hand. "It's not that simple, Andy. I would say this guy is to the point where he is obsessed with you. He's not going to leave you alone until he gets what he wants. That's half of what I was so worried about last weekend. He gets me out of the picture and it's easier to get to you when you're alone."

"I'm not alone, though, I'm here with my sisters."

"You weren't when I found you."

"I was just talking to Jamie, he wanted to apologize. I didn't even think about the stalker." She glares at me. "You think I'm stupid, don't you? That this is my fault that he was able to get so close to me tonight." I can see how upset she's getting, her voice trembling, and I know she's on the verge of tears.

"No, that's not what I'm saying at all. I just think that we need to be really careful from now on, and that's why I want to be with you, so I can take care of you and make sure he can't get anywhere near you."

I hear Jasmine say, "Aww," in the back of the car, and I remember that she's there.

"I am stupid. I keep thinking this will just go away, but it won't. I really thought if I broke it off with you, they would leave me alone, but it doesn't matter what I do. They're not going to give up, are they? What does he even want from me?" She starts to cry, and I grab her, pulling her toward me.

"Hey, it's all going to be okay, you're safe with me." I look at Jasmine as I say it, and she knows my words mean nothing, just as I do, but what else can I do right now? Some sicko is trying to mess with Andy, and it's working.

"Have you guys maybe thought that it's not some guy who's obsessed with Andy but a female who's still in love with you, Brad?" asks Jasmine. "That's why they started messaging you tonight, Brad."

I look at her. "You think it's Madeline?"

She shrugs. "I don't know. This could have all been set up by her tonight. I'm just thinking out loud. Who stands to gain anything with you two breaking up? Maybe she figures if Andy's out of the picture, you'll take her back or something?"

"She did come on to me pretty heavy tonight."

"The bitch did what?" Andy looks up at me, anger flashing through her teary eyes.

"Don't worry, I turned her down. Obviously. She means nothing to me anymore. It's you I want to be with."

Her face softens a little. But I can tell she's still pissed, and if given the chance, she would show Madeline just what she thinks of her.

"So this could be her?" Jasmine suggests. "You turned her down tonight, maybe that was her plan. She would try and win you back, and if she didn't succeed, she retaliates by sending these threats to make sure you two stay away from each other."

"Yeah, the thought did cross my mind. I'm so sorry, beautiful. The whole thing tonight did feel weird, though, bumping into her like it was some kind of a set-up. She was acting all strange as well, saying she's staying in town now and she wants us to go on a double date or something. I don't know, I just didn't like the sound of it all. I don't trust her."

Andy looks between me and her sister. "So you think she might be the one messing with us?"

"I don't know. It sounds ridiculous when I say it out loud, but I mean, it could literally be anyone. She would have as good a reason as anyone to try and split us up, and she can be fucking crazy and manipulative when she wants things to go her way."

"Fuck, it could be her!" She turns to look at her sister, her eyes wide, and it's like a silent message is passed between them.

"What?" I ask.

"But the night of my birthday, it felt like it was a dude, or at least a chick who was into other girls. Darcy and Luna actually tried to convince me it might have been you." She laughs and it comes out nervous, like she's not fully convinced that they're wrong. This is the first I'm hearing about her friends thinking it was me. How fucked up do they think I am to pull such a stunt?

"I hope they were kidding."

Jasmine shakes her head. "They were pretty serious, Brad, but Andy and I knew it wouldn't have been you. For a start, why would you? It's pretty obvious how much you like

Andy, and what would you stand to gain by threatening her to stay away from you? It makes no sense at all."

I look at Andy, shocked that she might have actually thought I could do this to her. "This was last weekend that they came to you with this idea that it was me? That's what happened to you, wasn't it? Your friends came to find you and tell you they suspected me. That's what had you all freaked out."

She looks down at her hands, guilty. "Ah, yeah, it was. I'm so sorry."

I lift her face so she's looking at me. I need to see her eyes, I need to know she doesn't still think this could be me. "Why didn't you ask me then and there?"

"Because I thought about it and what they were saying didn't make any sense. They thought you were making me feel unsafe so you could swoop in and protect me, look like the hero. But it was always me who came to you, not the other way around. And besides, whoever this is, they want to break us up. But you're doing everything for us to stay together, so it doesn't make any sense. I knew it wasn't you. I didn't need to ask you about it. I was just exhausted last weekend after the game, and then I had a fight with my two best friends. I couldn't deal with going over it all with you as well."

"Well, good. I wouldn't do anything like what they are saying. Why would they even think it was me?"

"I don't know. I guess they're just being protective of me. We're really close and they don't want to see me get hurt. It still doesn't bring us any closer to knowing who it is, and now they have your number as well."

"This is getting out of hand, Andy," says Jasmine. "We need to talk to someone else about it, get some help. You don't know how dangerous this person could get if they don't get what they want."

"Jasmine's right, we need to talk to your parents. The guy with his hand on you from inside, you said he was your ex?"

"Just my boyfriend from high school, he's harmless. He was actually apologizing for cheating on me. It was weird, but it's the first time I have bumped into him since, so I guess that's why."

"Are you for real?" I give her a serious look. She shakes her head, trying to signal that she knows what I'm thinking and that I'm wrong. She looks at Jasmine in the back.

"He's got two kids and is married to some chick he hates. Karma," she tells Jasmine, and she smirks.

She might think he is harmless, but for all we know, he could be the one we're looking for. "You sure he's harmless, not someone who is still holding a claim to you, and now that he sees you happy with someone else, he's jealous?" I raise a questioning brow. He was here tonight as well. Bit of a coincidence. He could have taken the photo, and he has motive; they dated and she left him when he cheated. He might want her back.

She shakes her head. "There's no way it's him," she says, definite in her answer. But how can she know for sure?

Her other two sisters come out of the club, and Jasmine pops open the door. "We're in here," she calls to them, and they come over, jumping in the back seat.

"You driving us all home, Brad?" slurs the younger one.

"Looks like it. Someone needs to tell me directions," I call as they all strap themselves in.

I glance over to Andy who is now staring out the front windshield. She looks so sad, and I hate the fact I had to come in and ruin her night out when she was having fun, but she had to know what was going on. And the list of possible suspects just keeps getting longer. Madeline, Andy's ex-boyfriend, some crazed fan, and if I'm being really honest, I don't trust her friends anymore. I know she says they're just looking out for her, but to throw me under the bus when I have done nothing but look after her, they seem suspicious to me now too.

# CHAPTER TWENTY-THREE

### ANDY

I don't know how I let my sisters and Brad talk me into this, but somehow, I did. Brad drove us all home, back to my parents' house. And well, since he's here, I guess we had to tell them something, because I wasn't letting him drive all the way home tonight. Now, I think it's time to tell my parents what is going on. But I'm shitting myself. My dad is going to go ape when he hears what's going on between us. I just know it.

Before getting out of the car, I turn to my sisters in the back. "You sure we need to tell them? They're going to freak. I think they'll be better off kept in the dark."

Amelia gives me her best don't-fuck-with-me look. The one she normally uses on her kids when they're playing up. "Andy, you know that's not true. You're a grown woman who can make her own decisions about who she chooses to date. Right now, it's more important to tell them everything else that's going on."

I sigh. "Yeah, okay." So much for a fun night out with my sisters. Well, it was fun for a bit, anyway. Now I'm slammed back to reality.

Brad comes around to my side of the car, opening the door for me. He gives me a tight smile. He is shitting himself as well, I can tell. "We can do it together. I'm sure they're not as scary as you're making them out to be."

"Ha, that's where you're wrong. You're about to learn that the hard way."

He holds out a hand for me to take and I do, walking to the house with our hands intertwined. I can't believe I ever let my friends put doubt in my mind about him. I find it so hard to trust men, and when they gave me a reason to doubt him, I did. He is a genuinely good guy who cares about me. I saw the look of fear in his eyes tonight when he found me. He must have been thinking the worst the entire drive here from LA after seeing that photo. I never should have pushed him away.

"It's all going to be okay. We just need to tell your parents the truth about what's going on so we can keep you safe," he says, and I hope he's right.

"It's *your* safety I'm worried about right now," I sass, leaning in to give him a quick kiss before we enter the house.

It's just past midnight, so I'm not surprised that the house is quiet when we push open the front door. Mom and Dad would be in bed. Before I have a chance to say, *oh well, I guess we tell them in the morning,* the hall light flicks on and Dad's heavy footsteps come down the hall. I drop Brad's hand immediately.

"Just checking that my girls got home safely," says Dad, stopping when he sees all of us. "Andrea, why is your coach here?" He looks between the two of us.

Amelia gives me a smile. "I'm going to go and check on my kids," she says, slipping out of the room.

"Yeah, and I can hear my pillow calling my name."

Cassie turns to me. She mouths, "Good luck," as she scurries off to her room. Some help they are.

"Dad, why don't you take a seat. We all need to talk to you about something," says Jasmine, taking his hand, and I'm grateful that she is at least staying to mediate the situation. If we need a mediator, that is.

"Alright. But something tells me I'm not going to like where this is going," he grumbles, taking a seat. Jasmine sits next to him.

"What's going on?" Mom comes sleepily into the room, and I silently thank God she's here, because if anyone can calm down Dad, it will be her, and she is already on to this. She takes a seat beside me. She smiles over to Brad, and he offers her a quick smile back.

"Sorry, guys, we didn't mean to wake you. It's just, well... I'll let these two tell you," Jasmine says, handing it over to us.

I look at Brad, hoping he will do the talking, because I don't even know where to start.

"Mr. Harper, Mrs. Harper, sorry to intrude at this time of the night. But there have been some further developments with Andy's stalker, and your daughters and I felt that it was time you knew what was going on. I'm starting to really worry about Andy's safety."

The way he says it is so formal, and if this weren't such a shitty situation, I would have laughed at him.

Dad's face changes immediately, his brow furrowing and his lips forming a thin line. "What new developments? I thought that was just a one-time thing on her birthday." He looks at me, then Brad, getting impatient for answers.

"It wasn't, Dad, it's been going on since my car was tampered with. Different things have been happening. It's really starting to mess with my head," I admit, feeling pathetic for letting it all get to me so much.

Mom rests her hand on my knee. "That's why you came home on stress leave. What exactly is happening, love?"

I look at her and wonder just how much to say. She offers me a warm, comforting smile, and I just want to curl up on her lap and get consoled from her like I used to when I was a kid. "Um, I'm getting text messages, some with threats, some with photos. My bedroom was bugged with a camera and there were images taken of me."

"What are the threats?" snaps Dad.

"That's why I'm here. They're to do with me," admits Brad.

Dad raises an accusatory brow, and I can see he's getting ready to lose his shit. "Why? What do you have to do with it?"

"Andy and I have been seeing each other for a few months now, and this person is trying to split us up with threats of telling the club what we have been doing. It's not an ideal situation, and I can see how bad it looks, but we met before all of this, when neither of us had any idea I would end up her coach." Brad is talking fast, trying to make it sound less suspect than it already does, but this is bad. We both knew what we were doing, and now we're going to have to deal with it.

Dad doesn't say anything, and I'm not sure what else to add to make any of it better.

"The photos they have taken are all of us together," I say awkwardly, in case they didn't get it already.

"It seems as though the person is obsessed with Andy," adds Jasmine, trying to explain it to them as well. "They're watching her every movement, and they don't like that she and Brad are seeing each other. They feel like they have some claim to her, like an ex who is still hanging on or a fan who is obsessed."

"Right. Do we have any idea who this person could be?" asks Dad, and yet again, I'm surprised that he hasn't blown up about the whole Brad-and-me-together thing. Did he hear what we said?

"We have a couple of ideas, Dad, but nothing really seems to add up."

"What happened tonight?" asks Mom. She looks so worried, and this is one of the reasons I was putting off telling them. I don't want to worry her unnecessarily.

"He took a photo of Andy and her sisters at the club they were dancing at and sent it to me, saying he was watching her."

Dad's eyes narrow, and I can already see he is murdering this stalker in his head right now.

"When Brad got the threat sent to him, he drove here from LA to make sure I got home safely," I add, trying to make sure Dad knows what kind of guy he is.

"Thank you, Brad, I appreciate you looking after our Andrea," says Mom. "I think it's best we all sit down and work this out in the morning. It's late and everyone is tired now. We're not going to get anywhere," she says, looking in Dad's direction.

"Your mother's right. Let's get some sleep. I'll put the alarm on," Dad says, standing.

I look at Brad and wonder what we're supposed to do next. He can't go home now, so I guess my parents are okay with him staying with me. We all get up and start to walk toward our rooms.

Dad turns back to us. "We haven't finished this conversation about your relationship with my daughter yet either, Brad. You can stay with her tonight, but only because I know she's scared after what happened. If I hear any funny business under my roof, there will be hell to pay in the morning." He turns and stalks for his room.

That's more what I was expecting from him. I'm surprised he's letting Brad stay with me at all.

As soon as my parents are back in their room, I grab his hands and drag him into my room. It's so strange having him here in this house. My childhood bedroom. Lucky for him, my parents made some upgrades a few years back and there's a queen bed in here now. Once inside my room with the door closed firmly behind us, he pulls me to his chest, wrapping his arms around me. He places a light kiss on my hair. And I enjoy the way it feels to be so close to him again. He smells so good. I really missed him the last couple of weeks. I hate to admit it—because I hate to admit anyone is right but me—but my mom is right. I have fallen for him hard.

"Come on, let's get you into bed," he says, pulling away. I watch as he removes his pants and shirt and pulls back the covers, slipping into my bed. I had forgotten just how hot he is with his shirt off.

"Can you help me with the zipper?" I ask, standing by the side of the bed, my back turned to him. It's a back zipper, and I can't quite reach. Well, that's my excuse, anyway. Really, I just want his hands on me.

He slides the zip down my back and the dress falls to the floor, pooling at my feet. I step out of it and turn round to face him. Waiting for his reaction to me in just my black bra and panties.

"Are you trying to tease me?" He smirks. "You heard your dad, didn't you?"

"I'm not trying to tease. I just missed you, that's all," I say, running my hands up my body, loving his eyes on my bare skin. He looks like he could eat me alive, and I want him to so badly.

"I may have missed you too, my beautiful girl. But I don't have a death wish." He reaches under my pillow and pulls out the pale blue shirt of his that I have been sleeping in and throws it to me.

I drop my bra with him watching and shimmy into the shirt with a pout, then flick off the light and join him in bed. His arms snake around me protectively, and it feels so good to be back here with him again in this comfortable place.

"You have to let me look after you. Until all this stuff with the stalker is sorted out, I'm not letting you out of my sight. Tonight scared me, I can't even tell you all the thoughts I had running through my head when I couldn't contact you and I was so far away."

I knew that's what he was thinking, I could see it all over his face. Normally that type of protective stuff would make me angry and totally turn me off a guy, but not with him. He really cares about me, and I kinda love it. "Alright. I don't want to be apart from you ever again, anyway."

"Is this Andy admitting that she wants a committed relationship? Who are you and what have you done with the girl I was seeing?" He laughs, and I feel it vibrate through my entire body.

"You've changed me, Brad. I can't see my future without you in it, and this is what I want. I have no idea who I am anymore, but all I know is that when I'm with you it just feels right."

"That's how I feel as well. I know you thought I was acting crazy. But Andy, I'm in love with you. That's why the last few weeks have killed me so much. I couldn't stand being without you, and more than that, I was worried that something would happen to you and I wouldn't be there to keep you safe."

I turn in his arms so I'm glancing up at him, with only the light from the moon shining through my window and illuminating his face. He's so handsome and he just told me he loves me. "I love you too," I admit. Saying it out loud for the first time doesn't feel strange like I thought it would, it just feels right. I'm totally in love with this beautiful man.

He strokes the hair out of my face and our lips meet in a slow passionate kiss. My hands curl around his body as I cling to him. Now that I have finally given into my feelings for him, I'm never going to want to let go.

Our kiss deepens and becomes more hurried and desperate, and I grind my body against his now-hardened length, not caring where we are anymore, I just want him. My body won't be happy until I feel him inside of me.

He pulls back from our kiss and smiles at me. Then in one movement I'm spun around, facing away from him. He pulls my back close into his chest, his large arms wrapping around me. He places kisses down my neck. "Not tonight. There will be time for all of this tomorrow when I get you back to my place."

"Are you serious? You're going to deny me when I'm dying to have you inside of me?"

"Just delaying it, that's all, beautiful girl. Now close your eyes and get some sleep. You're going to need it with what I have planned for you tomorrow night."

"You're scared of my dad." I laugh.

"Fuck yeah, that dude is all kinds of scary."

I giggle again. "Okay, I'll let you get away with it then. Night, Brad. I love you."

"I love you too, beautiful." He kisses my hair, and I

snuggle into him, my eyes fluttering closed, and I fall into a deep sleep.

---

ANDY

It's first thing Monday morning and the entire Angels squad is gathered in the main building. Waiting on our general manager Hamish to show up. No one knows what's going on, but I don't like it. He very rarely comes to a training session, so something big is about to happen.

My gaze flicks to Brad, trying to read him. Does he know what's going on? He gives me a brief smile, nothing anyone else would notice, but I know it was supposed to make me feel more at ease, even though I don't. He knows what's going on, I can see that now for sure. And a small part of me thinks, thank fuck, at least it's not that someone has turned us in or something like that.

After Saturday night, I feel so much better about things between us. Telling my parents what's going on was the right choice, and to my surprise, my dad and Brad sat down together and worked out a plan to keep me safe until we work out who is doing all of this. I'm pretty sure he gave Brad the "hurt my daughter and I will kill you" speech, but all in all, he seemed to be on board with us dating. The hard part now is we have to return to our normal lives, pretending we're not together, and after the weekend we had and knowing how he really feels about me, it's even more difficult.

Hamish arrives and the attention of the room shifts to him. "Angels, I wanted to talk with you all today because we have some very important and exciting news that I would like to share. As of the start of next season, Brad will be taking the head coach with our men's team, and Ava will be stepping into the head coaching role for the Angels. So as of today, Ava will be taking more of a coaching role, assisted by Brad."

My eyes focus on him. He's leaving us? Something like this, he must have known for a while, how could he not have? I'm sure he would have been sworn to secrecy because the club wouldn't have wanted the information leaked too early, but he could have trusted me. I feel a little blindsided.

The other girls on my team look around at each other, trying to process what we've just been told. Darcy and Luna both look to me, and I know what they're thinking. This is my fault. He's taken this job because of me. This must have been the solution he was talking about, the plan he had so we could be together. I feel so guilty. I look at Brad and his expression is hard to read, but he isn't giving me any eye contact either. He's purposely avoiding me.

Hamish finishes up talking then dismisses everyone. Just as I'm about to leave, he calls my name. I walk over to him tentatively, feeling very unsure of what is going on.

"Andrea and Brad, I need to see you both in my office briefly before you start training for the day," he says before taking off in the direction of his office.

My gaze flicks to Brad, my heart pumping. Fuck, Hamish knows for sure. Brad's eyes are just as wide, so this is news to him. Fuck, fuck, fuck. I don't even know what to think right now. Someone has turned us in and we're both in deep shit.

We both follow Hamish to his office, and I tentatively take a seat. I feel like a naughty kid at school in the principal's office, waiting to hear the words I know are coming.

His face is stern as he eyes us both. "There has been a complaint about the two of you. This morning an anonymous person came forward and said you're in some sort of romantic relationship. I really hope this is just a slanderous rumor, but I wanted to come to you both first. Is there something I need to be worried about getting out to the media?"

Brad stays silent, and I rack my brain for what to say. I know there are photos of us, there is proof, so if we lie now and they surface, we're even more screwed.

"Yes, we have," says Brad before I have a chance to make my mind up as to what to tell Hamish.

Fuck, he said it. Now what?

I can see Hamish's face turning bright red. This is bad, really fucking bad. He is angry. His whole job is to make sure the club looks good to our investors, and this looks really bad. "You've been sleeping together all year?"

"What Brad is saying is yes, we have, in the past. It was just one night before I knew he was going to be the new coach, and he had no idea who I was because I lied to him about my identity. As soon as we worked it all out, he has been nothing more than my coach. None of this is his fault either, I came on to him that night," I lie to save his ass.

He glares at Brad. "Is this true, Brad?"

"Yes, what she is saying is true."

He looks us over as he rubs his chin, and I'm sure he's deciding exactly what to do with this information. He is about to speak when Brad interrupts him.

"It's true, but also, there is something else I think you need to be aware of."

"Go on?"

"I wanted the job with the men's team because I have feelings for Andrea, and I know I couldn't continue on as her coach. If I stay here next season, I intend to date her, and if that's not going to work then I need to know now so I can resign."

Hamish actually looks shocked. I'm shocked. "You're telling me you would give up your dream job to coach the LA men's team to be with Andrea?"

"No, that's not what he's saying," I interrupt, surprised by what he has just said. What is he doing? He's about to fuck it all up over me, I'm not worth it.

"Yes, that is exactly what I'm saying." Brad gives me a stern look. He is serious about this. Ready to lose his job for me.

"Brad, can you wait outside? I need to speak to Andrea alone."

"Okay," he says, getting up to leave and closing the door behind him.

"Andrea, I know you're trying to protect your coach because you don't want to come off like the one who's doing the wrong thing, but you're not going to get in trouble here. You haven't done anything wrong. Brad is your coach and in a position of power over you, this all falls on him. If he did anything to hurt you or make you feel pressured in any way, you can tell me. I'll have it all dealt with discreetly. This is a safe space, feel free to tell me anything."

Oh God, could this get any worse? I want to sink down in my chair and hide, but I don't. I sit up tall and do my best to convince him I'm not some victim, not at all. God, if anything, this is all my fault. "Brad hasn't done anything wrong, I'm not trying to protect him by saying that. I was the one who came on to him, and I had no idea he would end up as my coach. This is all just a messed-up coincidence."

"And you agree with him changing to the men's team next year?"

"I had no idea that was even happening until today," I say honestly.

He looks surprised but nods his head. "Okay, you can tell Brad to come back in now. You better get to practice. Andrea, if you ever need to see me about anything, my door is always open. Okay?"

"Thank you."

"You can go." What? Fuck, I don't want to go now, I want to know what is going to happen to Brad. But I decide today isn't the day to piss Hamish off even more, so I slip from my seat and make my way out into the hall.

Brad is leaning up against the wall. He looks cool and calm, unaffected by the entire situation. "He wants to see you again," I say. He nods and makes his way back inside his office, closing the door without another word to me.

I wait just outside the door. I can't hear a thing they're talking about, but I can't bring myself to leave either. Why did he have to say all of that? If it gets out, he is screwed, and so am I by default. There are already haters on my team who would gladly see me branded as a slut who sleeps with her coach.

I pull my hair out of the high ponytail it was in and run my hands through my long hair. I have a stress headache starting again. I try to massage my scalp, telling myself everything is going to be fine. But the truth is, this is what you get when you can't control your urges. It's all my own fault, and if it gets out, I will just have to own it like every other time I have fucked up in my life.

I flick my hair back up into a high ponytail and lean against the wall. Just when we start to think we have this situation under control, something else happens. No need to guess who told Hamish about Brad and me. My stalker must have seen me with him yesterday. He knows we're back on and has followed through on his threat to out us. Everything here is about to explode, I can feel it. God, what are they talking about for so long? I should go, get to practice like Hamish said, but I can't move without knowing. Just when I'm about to give up, Brad walks from the office. He gives me a look that I can't read then closes the door behind him. Taking me by the arm, he sweeps me around the corner.

"Oh my God, what happened? Why did you say that?" I whisper.

"Whoever told him might be the one with photos of us. Do you really want to risk that? Better to come clean now than lie and get found out later."

"You didn't have to tell him you have feelings for me," I say, frustrated.

"Yes, I did, because I do, and I'm not lying about it anymore. It's causing too many problems."

"What did he say? Do you still have your job?" I ask, panicked.

"Kind of. I won't be coaching you girls again this year. That's why he made the announcement today, about me taking over the men's team. I was surprised myself, because originally, he wanted to wait until we made the semis, but I think after the anonymous tip-off this morning, he's trying to protect the club and distance me from the team before anything gets out. Ava will take over immediately, and they'll bring in someone to help her. Hamish thinks it's for the best. But I will be back next year to take over the men's team. That is as long as the media doesn't get wind of it. If they do, he may not be able to protect me."

"What about the rest of our season? Our team needs you." I'm almost crying I'm so frustrated at this situation with him. He can't leave us now.

"I'll be around, but Ava will lead you through the last few games. Andy, look at the positives here. This means we don't have to be held hostage by your stalker's threats. This is all for the best. Come on, we need to get you back to practice. And I need to talk to Ava."

"She probably did all of this just so she could get your job. She's wanted it all along," I say under my breath. Ava has never liked me very much, and she has a major crush on Brad. She would be the one who stands to gain the most from all of this. It all makes sense now. I bet that's true. "Actually, I bet this *is* her doing. She was pissed she didn't get the job in the first place, this makes sense," I say louder, looking at Brad, waiting for his reaction. He thinks on it, then shakes his head.

"I don't think so, Andy. She was the one who recommended me for the job. She has been nothing but supportive."

I narrow my eyes at him. I don't know if I'm quite as convinced as he is. I know they're friends and all, but I don't trust her. "Well, someone did this," I huff, deciding to keep how I really feel about her to myself. She has just become my new coach.

"Yes, they did. I'm about to deal with it."

He's going to deal with it? I look at him, trying to work out where he's going with this. Something clicks and I see what he's thinking. "You think it's your ex-wife, don't you? And she set up the photo of you and her together as well so that I might dump you and she could get you back?"

"I know nothing for sure, but I'm going to see what she knows. It would be just like her to pull a stunt like this and turn us in because she didn't get her own way. I don't know that she's the one sending us messages and threats, but I could see her calling the club and letting them know about our relationship."

It better not be her. I already hate that bitch for what she did to Brad and thinking she is better than me. If he finds out this is all her, I'm going to lose my fucking shit.

# CHAPTER TWENTY-FOUR

### ANDY

I'M THE LAST ONE AT THE FIELD TONIGHT. SURPRISE, surprise. When we have the semis tomorrow, I need all the mental preparation I can get. I just need to have a quick shower before I get out of here for the night.

I texted Brad, and he's already in the parking lot waiting for me. He hasn't been around much this week for practice, as he has been told to keep his distance for now, but he has dropped me off and picked me up every day. Just to make sure I'm safe. I'm not taking any stupid risks.

My team has recovered from his shocking exit on Monday, and so far, no blame has landed on me. The club made some bullshit excuse, and that seemed to keep everyone happy enough. We also haven't received any further threats or communication at all from my stalker. What is there to threaten us with now, anyway? Brad's convinced it's his ex-wife trying to get revenge, but she's disappeared, he hasn't been able to get hold of her all week. That in itself is strange. So maybe it really was her.

I turn off the water, dry myself, and pack my bag. I push open the door, and as I do, the lights flicker off. Fuck, not

## THE COACH

again. My heart kicks up a notch instantly. I'm already on edge with everything that has happened lately and the game tomorrow. *It's probably nothing*, I try to tell myself so I can calm down and don't start having another panic attack. I'm sure it's just a power outage, but my body still reacts with the panicky feeling. My chest tightening, my breathing becoming harder. I'm thankful I at least have clothes on this time. I cling my bag to my chest and dash for the door. Just as I get there, someone switches the light back on. I stop dead when I see who...

"Darcy, are you okay? You scared the shit out of me," I stammer, clutching my chest.

She stands in front of me, staring straight through me. She looks weird. Her eyes are all glazed over, and she is staring just past me in a daze. I take a step closer to her because she hasn't answered me. I reach out to her arm and give it a squeeze. "Everything alright?" I ask her again. "You gave me a fright." I laugh.

She shakes her head slowly from side to side. "No, Andy, I'm not okay."

"What's going on? Has something happened?" I try to comfort her, but she shrugs me off.

"Don't you touch me."

"Okay," I say, hurt by her animosity. I have no idea what I've done to piss her off. She has been so moody lately, it's hard to know what exactly it is this time. "You know you can talk to me about anything, right. If something's not good for you at the moment, I can try and help you."

"You don't get it, do you, Andy."

"Get what? What's going on with you, honey?"

She reaches out for me, cupping my face. I blink back at her, not sure what she's doing. She pushes my hair over my shoulder and stares back at me, her eyes glassy. "I'm in love with you, Andy," she whispers.

I blink back at her in total astonishment. I don't believe the words coming from her mouth. None of this is making any sense at all. What do I even say back to her? "You're in love with me?" I stutter, the words hard to get out. We all have a lot of love for each other, but I'm not *in* love with her.

"Yes, and I thought by breaking you and Brad up I would be able to have you all to myself, but you're still in love with him, I can see it every time the two of you look at each other."

She's right, we are. But right now, I need to focus on her and getting her to a better place. This Darcy is scaring me. "I care about you so much, Darcy, I don't like seeing you hurting like this, but I had no idea that this is how you felt."

She looks at me, her expression angry. "You did. We've been super close this year, you knew where it was going. Every time you hugged me or looked my way, you knew what I was thinking. You had to."

I shake my head in total shock. Does she think we've had something going on all year? "I..."

She interrupts me. "You did this to me. You constantly led me on, made me fall for you. Now what am I supposed to do? You're going to go off and live your life with him. And I'll be left here with a broken heart, and you don't even care."

I want to help her, but I'm not standing here while she abuses me for something I knew nothing about. "I don't understand your anger toward me."

"Yes, you do. The weekend before you and Brad hooked up, you were in my bed. After years of being so into you, I thought you were finally into me as well."

Oh, my God. That night she's talking about was just a

fun weekend for me. I thought it was the same for her. She hasn't brought it up since. I really should have known better than to get involved intimately with a friend, but I thought we agreed. We had way too much to drink after a game and it all kind of just happened. I've been with other girls before and so had Darcy. We both knew this about each other, so it was just a bit of drunken fun.

"That was a fun night, but it was months ago." And then there was the night in the club when I met Brad. She picked him for me. It was the week after. This makes no sense at all. "Darcy, it was your idea for me to go after Brad that night. Why would you even suggest him if you felt like this?"

She runs a hand through her hair, then pulls on the ends. "I didn't think you would actually end up together. It was just supposed to be a fun game. And now I've had to stand by and watch you two fall for each other. It makes me sick. He's not your type. He's too cocky, too conceited."

"You said nothing to me. All this time, I didn't know."

She glares at me. "You knew, you had to. I want you to break it off with Brad so we can be together."

I blink back at her. She's now asking me to end it with him for her. "I can't do that, Darcy."

"Yes, you can, you just won't."

I reach for my phone. This is way beyond what I know how to deal with. I need to talk to Luna or Jasmine. Or someone else who can help me get through to her. She's acting all crazy.

"What are you doing? Can't handle a good dose of reality, Andy, so you going to call your sister to therapize me? Like she does you."

"I just thought... You know what? Fuck you, Darcy. You can't just come in here all pissy with me over this. I didn't know what you were thinking, and that's on you. At any time, you could have come and talked to me about this, and you didn't. This isn't my fault. I'm outta here. See you at home when you've cooled down and we can talk properly." I spin and walk for the door.

"Don't walk out that door, Andy. I need to talk to you now," she calls, her voice desperate.

"Not when you're like this," I say over my shoulder.

"You're going to regret it," she mumbles, but I keep walking. I can't hear any more of this tonight.

I can't believe her. First, she scared the living shit out of me standing there all creepy when the lights came back on, then she tells me she's in love with me. As if I don't have enough shit to worry about at the moment. I mean, I love the girl as a friend, and I care about her, but this is too much. I wonder if Luna knew anything about this. They have been super close lately.

I'm nearly at the parking lot when I hear her behind me. I turn around slowly to see her holding a knife. Panic takes over. She's lost it and is going to kill me because I won't be with her. Reality hits me—it all must have been her all along. And I feel stupid for not seeing it.

But then she stumbles forward, and I see the blood dripping from her arms. I scream and run to her. *Fuck, she's cut her wrists!* Blood drips from them like water out of a leaking tap. "I wouldn't have had to do this if you had just broken it off with him," she says, her words slurring.

She's scaring the shit out of me, but she's still my friend. I need to help her. She drops the knife to the ground and falls to her knees. What do I do? There is so much blood. I feel sick to my stomach. I get down and cradle her in my arms.

"Jesus, Darcy, you didn't have to do this," I cry. I search

around in my bag, frantically trying to find something that might help. I pull out a shirt, ripping it into strips I can use as bandages. I have no idea what to do here, but something is telling me I need to wrap her arms to stop the bleeding. My shaky hands wrap the strands around and tie them. One arm at a time. Then I dial 9-1-1. I don't know if I have time to get her to the hospital or not, and I need help. I'm freaking the fuck out.

I explain our location and what has happened, and the lady on the other end of the phone tells me what I need to do while I wait for help to arrive. The whole time I keep hold of Darcy. Trying to talk to her and tell her she'll be fine and I'm sorry. She has her eyes closed and keeps murmuring something, but I'm not sure what it is. I have never been so scared in my life. My friend could die tonight, and it will all be my fault. Why didn't I just stay and talk to her for a bit longer? In the parking lot, I notice some headlights and remember Brad is here waiting for me. "Brad!" I scream out, hoping he'll hear me from where we're sitting on the ground.

I hear a car door open then he comes running down the hill toward us. "Andy, what's happened?" He leans down next to me.

"We had a fight, she cut herself," is all I can tell him before the sirens of the ambulance scream up the road, and before I know it, there are people everywhere. Brad pulls me out of the way as they take over. A gurney is wheeled out of the vehicle, and they lift her onto it. I stand back and watch in disbelief as an IV is inserted into her arm and they call instructions to each other.

His worried eyes find mine. "What happened, Andy?"

I shake my head, trying to process what just happened. "She was furious with me. I came out of the shower and the lights flicked off like last time. But when they came back on, Darcy was standing there. She looked weird, kind of out of it. I tried to talk to her, but she was so angry with me."

"What was she angry about?" He looks confused, and I try to find the words to explain what happened.

"She said she's in love with me," I whisper, still finding it hard to process myself.

He blinks back at me. I've shocked him. I was surprised myself. "Like..."

I cut him off, needing to explain. "Like we slept together this one time, and ever since she has apparently been in love with me, and I had no idea."

He gives me a weird look, and I can tell he is trying to wrap his head around what I just admitted. "You slept with Darcy?"

"Ahh, yeah, it was before you. The weekend before. She only told me tonight, but she has been hung up on me ever since."

"We're leaving now. Are you coming with us or driving in?" asks the paramedic, approaching us.

I look at Brad and he gives me a nod. "I'll go with her," I call.

"I'll follow you there." Brad kisses me quickly, and I take off for the ambulance. What he must be thinking... I just dropped a lot on him. Not things I was trying to hide from him or anything, but just things we never talked about, I didn't really even consider important to bring up until now. But I guess I was wrong.

## BRAD

I follow them in the hospital's direction. I'm not sure how to process what Andy just told me. I knew she and Darcy were really close friends, but I had no idea she was even into girls like that. It's not a conversation we have had, and now, to hear Darcy is in love with her. I'm thrown completely. Actually, it explains a lot, like why she was trying to warn Andy off me.

It all clicks into place.

Andy said that she and Darcy were together right before she met me, and all of the stalker things started when she met me... The kind of girl who pulls a stunt like slitting her wrist in front of her best friend could be the very same person who has been watching her and sending threats all this time. I don't want to believe it, because I know how much Andy cares about her, but it makes so much sense now with this new information. She had access to the house, to Andy's car, to the soccer changerooms. She would have had both our phone numbers, and I did find it strange how she would just turn up in the places I was. Now I know why.

I think Andy's stalker is Darcy. It has to be.

I park my car in the hospital lot and take off in the direction of the emergency room. When I run through the doors, I see Luna and Jasmine have already made it here. They're huddled together on the plastic waiting chairs, Jasmine's arm wrapped around her friend. They're understandably distraught. A soon as Jasmine notices me coming toward them, she runs to me.

"Brad, do you know anything else? Andy called, she said there was an accident and we had to get down here right away. She was crying hysterically, and I couldn't really understand what she was saying. What's happened?"

"Let's take a seat, I'll tell you what I know." I follow her back to where Luna is sitting, and she glances up at me. Her knees are up to her chest, with her arms wrapped protectively around them, her eyes wet with tears. Jasmine sits next to her, and I take a seat across from them. How do you tell someone their best friend just tried to take her own life? "Girls, Darcy's not doing so well. The accident that happened... she tried to take her own life tonight."

Jasmine's hand goes straight to her mouth in absolute shock.

Luna starts to cry harder, covering her eyes.

They're both already devastated, understandably, and I'm not sure if I should tell them what Andy told me about their fight or not.

"Is she going to be alright, Brad?" asks Jasmine, tears falling from her eyes.

"I hope so. They couldn't tell us a lot. She has lost quite a bit of blood and her body went into shock. Andy's with her. I'm sure she will let us know whenever she knows more."

Luna uncovers her teary face. "I don't understand. Why would she do this?"

"I don't know the full story, but she confronted Andy tonight. She was really angry with her. Darcy told her she's in love with her."

Jasmine looks at me, confused. "She's what?"

"Apparently, she's in love with her. I don't really know the entire story, but Andy said they shared a night together a while an ago and it all stems from that. I really don't know anything else."

The girls both look at each other and a silent message is

shared. And I take it by their expression they must have known about this night. "I thought... I thought that was just them playing around. Neither of them are the fall-in-love type of people." Luna looks at me. "Well, Andy wasn't until she found you, anyway."

So she has told them how she feels about me. Maybe that's why Darcy did this tonight. She knew there was no way to blackmail her friend anymore. Now I'm not their coach, and Andy admitted how she felt about me to them, really solidifying the situation. Darcy would have known it was too late.

"I should have seen this coming," Luna sobs. "I'm her closest friend and I had no idea she would do anything like this. How could I not know?"

"People don't show you what they don't want you to see, Luna. You couldn't have known this would happen, none of us could."

Luna sits up straighter in her chair, her face turning white.

"What is it?"

"This is why she wanted Andy to believe you were her stalker, isn't it? Because it was her all along."

"It might have been," I say.

"Oh my God, Luna is right," gasps Jasmine. "This all makes sense. It was her."

A text pings on my phone and I pull it out of my pocket to check it.

**Andy:** They're giving her a blood transfusion. She is stabilizing but still out of it.

**Brad:** Okay, thanks for the update. I'm in the ER waiting room with Luna and Jasmine.

"Andy says she's stable, and they're giving her a blood transfusion."

"Oh shit, she lost so much blood," Luna says.

"She did," I say, remembering the sight of her in the parking lot.

"She really could have died. What will happen to her now?"

Jasmine takes Luna's hand, trying to comfort her. "Once she is awake and stable, they will have a psychiatric nurse visit her and she will be put on psychiatric watch for at least forty-eight hours. She will be in the hospital for a while; they have to make sure she's up to it physically and mentally before she will be able to leave. I worked in a hospital for a bit when I was doing my training. It's standard practice, but it will depend on how she handles her recovery."

After half an hour, I go in search of something to eat. We have all missed dinner, and the truth is, I'm finding it hard to sit still. My mind is racing with what-ifs. What if Darcy had been so mad she turned the knife on Andy instead of herself? What if I had gotten there earlier tonight? I might have been able to stop the whole thing from even happening, or I could have been the target of Darcy's anger. What if we had worked it all out sooner? We could have avoided this whole mess and got Darcy the help she needed, but none of us saw this coming. We had no idea at all.

I find a coffee shop and order some toasted sandwiches along with extra-strong coffee and snacks for later. We might be in for a long wait. I wish I could see Andy. I hate the thought of her sitting there by Darcy's bed all alone, just waiting for her friend to wake up. I make my way back to our seats and hand out the food and coffee.

"Thanks, Brad, this looks amazing."

I give Jasmine a nod and sit and sip on my coffee.

Luna has been silent, and really, what else can she say?

This is a fucked-up situation for them all. We're just finished with our sandwiches when Andy comes through the doors. She is a mess, her tear-stained face pale, so much pain in her eyes. I run over to her and pull her into a hug against my chest.

"Has something happened?"

"She's awake, but she wouldn't stop screaming until I got out of the room. She doesn't want to see me."

"Hey, it's okay. She'll come around, and she is just processing what happened. Give her time."

I usher her back over to her sister and friend. They hop up, wrapping their arms around each other. "You guys can go in and see her. She doesn't want me in there."

They pull back, looking at her, unsure. "Okay."

"She's in room 212. Just down that way." She points.

The girls walk tentatively through the doors. I'm sure they're both scared of what they will see once there.

"Do you want something to eat?"

"I can't eat. My friend nearly died tonight because of me." I pull her into me again as she breaks down.

"Shh, baby, I've got you."

## CHAPTER TWENTY-FIVE

### ANDY

I'M SITTING IN THE ER WAITING ROOM IN A DAZE. What the actual fuck happened tonight? This is not the friend I know, the one I went to college with and have been so close to for years. When I looked at her frightened face tonight, she looked like a complete stranger.

The last few months start to flash back through my memory. The night Darcy and I hooked up. The weekend after when she told me to go for Brad, then us finding out he was cheating on his wife—or at least we thought so from Jasmine's message that night. Darcy was the one adamant that he would be. *All men are cheats and liars*, she said to me, just like my high school boyfriend. She had joked I should just go for chicks from now on, and I laughed it off with her, not thinking she meant her.

Then all the strange things started happening. The stalker things. What was the first thing that happened? My car so I was late for practice on Brad's first day. Everything makes total sense now. All the things lead back to this, to her, I know it. She was the one with access to the house, to my car, my room, the changerooms. I have complete clarity of this whole messed-up situation. I'm no longer scared by this, I get it. "It was her all along, doing this stuff to me, wasn't it?"

"Probably," Brad says. "We don't really know anything for sure, but it all adds up to that being the case."

"I can't believe it. You think you know someone. But I didn't really know her at all. What makes a person so desperate that they do such awful things to someone they care about? Then try and kill themselves when they don't get what they want."

"I guess in this case it was love."

"She doesn't love me. If she did, she wouldn't do this to me."

"Andy, are you okay?"

"No, I'm not. I just sat there holding her limp hand for hours, for her to kick me out as soon as she came to. And now I have just worked this whole fucked-up situation out. I'm not okay. Not at all."

The girls are making their way back to us. They were quicker than I thought they would be.

"They're telling us to go home and get some rest," says Jasmine. "She'll be kept in here for a couple of days under suicide watch. She's tired and just needs to sleep."

"Okay, let's get home then," offers Brad, leading us out the door.

BRAD DRIVES ME HOME, AND JASMINE AND LUNA GO together in Jasmine's car. The entire way home, I just stare out the front window. I keep seeing her standing there in the dark, blood dripping from her wrists. I don't think I will ever be able to get the image out of my head. I scrub my hands over my face and try to take myself anywhere but back there. It's no use. I just see the blood and feel my fear when I realize I don't know what to do. I really thought she was going to die.

The car pulls up to a stop and I'm surprised to see we have arrived back at home already.

I look at Brad. He looks tired and worried, the lines on his forehead showing more than normal. "Can you stay tonight?"

"I'm not going anywhere."

"Thanks."

We make our way inside, and the girls arrive not long after. Brad heads straight for the kitchen and I follow him. "What are you doing?"

He pulls a box of cereal from the cupboard and a bowl and spoon, then goes to the fridge and gets the milk. "You need to eat something, and I know how much you like this stuff, so breakfast for dinner it is."

He pushes the bowl over to me, and I offer him a smile. "Thanks." I take a seat at the breakfast bar and slowly eat my cereal. Luna and Jasmine have already disappeared into their rooms. I think none of us knows how to deal with this. We're all shutting down.

"I'm just going to get ready for bed. I'll see you in there," says Brad.

I nod, not having the mental energy to come up with a reply. I concentrate on eating my food, scooping one mouthful at a time until it's all gone. I feel like a robot on auto pilot. I have no idea how Luna and I are supposed to get up in the morning and play our semi-final, but we'll already be down Darcy, so we have to. And somehow, I guess we will.

. . .

I WAKE EARLY WITH BRAD'S WARM ARMS CURLED around me. He likes to sleep like this, and originally, I thought I would hate it, get too hot or something, but it's wonderful. I have never felt so safe and protected as I do in his arms. And right now, this is where I want to stay. I don't want to go out there and deal with the real world. I don't even know how to today.

I close my eyes and try to drift back off to sleep. I hear a small tap at the door. I slip out of his arms and tiptoe over to my door, opening it to see Luna. She's in her pajamas and looks like she hasn't had a wink of sleep. I close my door behind me and walk up the hallway so we can talk.

"Hey, sorry to wake you."

"It's okay, I was awake. Kind of hard to sleep."

"Yeah, I know." She takes my hand. "Andy, I'm so sorry you had to go through that yesterday. It must have been awful."

She's right, it was the worst day of my life. I never want to experience anything like that again. And last night, I was angry with Darcy for it all. But in the light of day, I just feel sorry for her. "It was, but it's worse for Darcy. She's going through a lot. We need to be strong so we can help her."

"Okay. But I think there's something you need to see first. You need to know the whole story."

"Alright."

She leads me by the hand to Darcy's room, and I hesitate a little. I'm not sure if we should go in there without her being here. It feels wrong. "I couldn't sleep, so I came in here. I feel like we should have seen this all coming. We should have known it was happening."

"You couldn't have known, Luna, none of us could."

"No, I mean..." She pushes her door open. "Andy, she's the one who has been stalking you."

Luna walks into Darcy's room and pulls back the sliding door to her wardrobe. I gasp in shock. I don't know why seeing all the evidence surprises me, I had already worked out that she was the one stalking me. But seeing it like this...

All my pictures are pinned up on the wall inside her wardrobe. Brad's face is cut out of the ones where he's with me. Then there's the lingerie that was stolen. It's hanging in among the images nailed to the wall.

"I don't even know what to say." This is so disturbing. Her collection of me right here in our very house.

"There's more."

"What else could there possibly be?" I ask, not really wanting to know the answer.

She opens the bedside table drawer to reveal a collection of knives. "We have to tell them at the hospital. She's worse than we thought. This is really bad, Andy."

I look around the room, trying to take it all in without completely freaking out again. I can feel it, the tightness in my chest, the impending panic attack. *I am safe,* I say on repeat, the mantra Jasmine taught me, and I am, now that we know this was all Darcy's doing and she is in the hospital under watch. But I still don't feel it. I'm not sure I will ever truly feel safe again. "Yeah, it's bad."

Luna cries, and I pull her into me. "I only came in here this morning because I couldn't believe she could be capable of doing this, but this is all proof she did it. Where do we even go from here?" she asks me.

"We help her because she is our friend and she needs us."

"I don't know if I would feel the same if it was me in your shoes, Andy."

I offer her a sad smile because I don't even know how we help Darcy now. Part of me is so angry with her, the things she did to me. If it was anyone else, I would want them dead, but in the light of day, I don't feel like that. She is obviously very sick, and I just want her to get the help she needs.

# CHAPTER TWENTY-SIX

ANDY

I walk from the team psychologist's office, not feeling any lighter than I did when I went in there. I feel like I'm carrying the weight of the world around with me. Yesterday, we won our semi-final, so we progress to the final. But for once in my life, I don't even care. I don't even know how Luna and I showed up at the game yesterday, let alone played, but we did.

After the game, Luna and Jasmine went to the hospital to check up on Darcy during visiting hours. I wanted to go as well, but she doesn't want me there. She hates me—well, at least that's what it feels like to me. Jasmine says it's normal for her to need someone to blame. I don't know what's normal in this situation, but I tell you what, it's not very fair that her blame falls on me.

I keep trying to think back over the last six months to work out if I led her to believe that there was something more between us. But other than that night we shared, I can't think of a thing other than normal friendship. That night we shared wasn't even either of our ideas, it sort of happened because the guy Darcy had brought home that night said he didn't think we were the type. I think he was egging us on so he could watch or something, but he had way too much to drink and passed out, so we proved him wrong. Nothing like setting me a challenge. I wouldn't have done it if I had known things would turn out like this.

I wish we could all just go back to the way things were. But that's never going to happen now.

I jump in Brad's car, and he smiles over at me. "How did it go?"

I shrug, not sure what I'm supposed to say. "I told her what happened. We have another session booked for Tuesday."

He takes my hand, kissing the back of it. He has been acting so strange with me since it all happened. I think he doesn't know what to do. "Okay, it'll help, I'm sure. Beth is very good at what she does." He offers me a reassuring smile.

I stare out the window as he starts the car. I know Brad is just trying to help in the best way he can, but right now, nothing is going to help. I feel sick to my stomach with guilt. I just want to see Darcy, talk to her, then maybe we could work this all out. It's not fair that she is blocking me out. I still keep seeing her standing there, face pale, blood dripping from her wrists. I don't even want to close my eyes, because every time I do, that's what I see. I think if I could talk to her now, see that she is still actually alive, that vision might go away.

Beth said the same thing as Jasmine. With time, it will fade. I don't believe either of them. It feels permanently etched into my eyes.

Brad's dashboard lights up with an incoming call and he presses the button to answer.

"Hello?"

"Hey, it's Jasmine. Is Andy with you?"

"You're on speaker."

"Oh great, thanks. Andy, Darcy wants to see you." Jasmine sounds a little more upbeat than she has been. Maybe they had a good chat with her today and she's looking a lot better. I can only hope.

"Really? Okay, when can we go?"

"It's visiting hours now if you can come straight away. Otherwise, not until tomorrow at ten."

I look at Brad. "We're on our way there now, Jasmine," he says for me.

"Thanks, Jas."

"Good luck. Remember to be gentle with her. She's not well."

What the fuck does she think I'm going to do? I know that. "Okay. Bye."

Twenty minutes later we pull up at the hospital. Brad's hand strokes my thigh, and I realize I must have been staring out the front of the car again. I'm trying to work out what on earth to say to her.

"Do you want me to come in with you?"

I glance up at him. He's trying so hard to be supportive. "Thank you. Probably not the best idea, though."

"Yeah, you're right. I'll wait just outside for you."

We walk in quietly, and just as I get to the doors, he kisses my cheek. "I'll see you soon." He looks nervous about letting me go in by myself, and I guess I can't say I blame him after everything that has happened. He knows how she feels about me and what we did together. He doesn't want to leave me alone with her.

I offer him a small smile, take a deep breath, and slip inside her room. She's in bed facing the other wall, and for a moment I think she might be asleep, but then she rolls over to face me and I stay stuck in the doorway, frozen.

She looks terrible. Not as bad as when I left her here, but her skin is pale, and she looks like she hasn't slept in days, with black circles framing her eyes.

"Andy, you came." She sits herself up in bed.

"Yes, I wanted to see how you were doing." I smile softly.

"Like you care." For a moment I thought she might be happy to see me, but no.

"Of course I care, you mean a lot to me," I say, coming closer to her bedside. She is still hooked up to a drip, her arms bandaged up tightly, so I'm careful not to bump anything.

"Luna says you won."

"We did win. It was a tough game without you."

"Yeah, right. I knew you didn't need me." She rolls her eyes. She's so negative, so down on herself. I knew she wasn't right mentally, but I wasn't quite prepared for this. It's such a change from her normal personality.

"Darcy, you know that's not true. Every single person on that team missed the fact you weren't there. You're so important to all of us."

"I bet Brad didn't miss me," she huffs, looking out the window.

I ignore her comment and instead slide a chair over to sit by her. "Darcy, I need to understand. Why?"

She turns back to look at me. "Why what?"

When everything clicked into place for me, there was one question I still had, and I have to ask her. Even if it pisses her off. Because I don't get it. If she loves me like she says, she wouldn't have done this. "Why did you mess with my car?"

She blinks back at me. "I didn't," she lies. She doesn't know what we've all seen, that we have worked it all out.

"Yes, you did. Why did you do it?" I ask as nicely as I can. Even though knowing she did this to me hurts. She is too fragile to deal with my real feelings about it all.

She drops her head, knowing I've caught her out. "I saw the look on your face when you came home. After finding out Brad was our new coach, you were smitten with him. And you had already let him convince you he wasn't a cheating scumbag. I could see the writing on the wall."

"So you fucked up my car so I would be late and he would think I was a slacker. If my car conked out on the highway instead of our driveway, you could have killed me," I whisper angrily, my temper slipping.

Her eyes go wide. "No, I knew what I was doing." A slow smile crosses her face, and I have the realization that I don't know this girl at all. I have only seen the side of her she was willing to share, but there is a whole other personality in there, and she is one scary motherfucker. "I could see what was going to happen between the two of you before it even began. That's how well I know you, Andy. I saw you talking that night at the club, and I instantly regretted setting it up. Originally, I thought you wouldn't have gone for such a cocky guy like him. He's not your type at all. But I was wrong. I could see the chemistry, so when you left together, I followed you. I watched him fuck you on the balcony of his hotel room."

I have to cover my mouth to hide the gasp. She was there that night? I look at her, shocked. "You what?" I ask, hoping I heard her wrong.

She smiles smugly. "I followed the two of you. It was fucking hot. I watched him fuck your brains out on that balcony. I was just an innocent bystander on the street below. You really do need to rein in your need to fuck publicly, Andy. You make it easy to watch. Anyone could have seen you, you're lucky it was just me."

I stare at her in disbelief. "You realize how messed up this is all sounding, don't you?"

"Loving someone enough to make sure they're safe and not making bad choices isn't messed up, Andy. It's true love."

I blink back at her. She says it like it's so obvious. She thinks she is the one in the right here. She's delusional.

"Anyway. After I followed you, I knew I needed to make sure you never saw him again, so I made sure you found out he had a wife. It was easy, I just had to tell Jasmine, and I knew she would message you right away. I thought the problem was dealt with. Until I found out he was our new coach, and I had to rethink, so I messed with your car." She shrugs like it was no big deal.

It's so hard to hear what she's telling me. I trusted this girl with my life, and it has been her all along. Not only that, but the way she talks about it is like she is completely disconnected from the situation, like I am as well. It's as if she's talking about a book she read or show she watched, not our lives. "And all the other stuff that happened, did you really do that to me as well?" I ask, already knowing the answer, but for some reason I need to hear it from her mouth that it was her.

She shrugs again like it was no big deal. "I just did whatever it took to stop you two from seeing each other, but you kept going back for more." She rolls her eyes. "Why can't you just see I did it so we can be together. You're just playing around with Brad. What we have, this could be real."

"But my birthday, we weren't together then. All of that

stuff was so creepy. I was really scared; you must have known I would be."

"Honestly, Andy. I wanted to scare you. That way you would stop being so stupid, so reckless with your life. Who walks home by themselves at that time of the night dressed like Wonder Woman? And you might not have been together yet, but I could see it coming. I didn't even know for sure you would run straight to him. I had a hunch you might, and you did. You're quite predictable."

I'm done with her shit. She might be in a bad place, but she is fucking pure evil, and she is aiming that at me. I see red. I push my chair back and stand. I need distance from her. "How could you possibly think all of this would make me want to start some sort of relationship with you? You never even told me how you felt. You have spent months making my life a living hell. Seeing me fall apart. Why would I now turn around and want anything from you? You know above anything else honesty is the most important thing for me. Friends don't do this to each other," I cry angrily.

"We're not just friends, Andy, you know that. That's why I did this." She touches her wrists. "I needed you to see what you mean to me." Her gaze is locked with mine, and the intensity of it sends a chill straight through me. "I will kill myself if we can't be together."

It's a threat, and I feel it right through to my core. She is deadly serious. She needs help, but how am I supposed to get her the help she needs? And for the first time since all of this happened, I'm glad she's in the hospital under psychiatric watch. She needs the help they can give her.

I look at her sadly. "You can't say things like that, Darcy, you know how much Luna, Jasmine, and I all love you. We would be devastated if you did something like that."

There's a knock at the door, and we both turn to see who it is. A young man probably in his late twenties, with dark hair. He's well dressed and has a nice smile. "Sorry to interrupt, I just needed to see Darcy quickly before visiting hours close," he says.

"Oh, sorry, of course." Looking back to Darcy, I try and regain some calm. "Remember what I said. We all really care about you, Darc, and we just want to see you get better. I'll come and see you tomorrow."

She stares at me, a blank expression on her face. I turn and walk toward the door, not quite knowing what else to do. "Andy," she calls. "Don't bother coming tomorrow." Her words are cold, and they hurt. I wanted to help her, but maybe it's for the best we have some distance if she really hates me this much.

I head for the door quickly before the tears I've been holding back erupt, but the man stops me. "You're Andy?" he asks.

"Yes," I whisper.

"Can you hang around for a bit? I need to talk to you," he says with a sympathetic smile. I wonder who he is.

"Okay," I say, then leave the room hastily.

I find Brad waiting for me across the hall, and as soon as he makes eye contact with me, I burst into tears. That was too much. She is more messed up than I even realized.

---

BRAD

I take Andy in my arms and hold her as close as I can, hoping that will ease her pain. The sobs wrack her body. I have no idea what they talked about, but I can only imagine how hard it must have been for her. I hate seeing her like this, in so much pain. Anyone else would walk away from a person that had done this to them, but not her. Andy wants to help her friend, she thinks she can somehow save her.

After some time, she pulls back from me. Her breathing has settled, and her tears have dried up. "Come on, let's get out of here," I offer, hoping I can take her away from here and distract her for a bit with something, anything. I just wish I knew what to do at the moment, but I haven't got a clue.

She looks up at me. "I can't. Did you see that guy that went into her room? He wants to talk to me."

I didn't notice any guy. "Do you know who he is?"

"No idea. But I guess we're about to find out. That's him coming toward us now." She looks in his direction. He's young and nicely dressed, with an air of confidence in the way he moves. But there is something about him that looks familiar.

He smiles toward us. "Andy, thanks for waiting. I'm Darcy's brother, Dylan."

She looks at me, surprised. "Oh, hi, sorry, I didn't know she had a brother."

This is news to all of us. But that would be the familiarity; he has Darcy's eyes, and there is something about his overall look that is similar to her as well. "Dylan, hi, I'm Brad. I coached Darcy this year." I hold out my hand, and he gives it a firm shake.

He assesses me. The look on his face says he's not impressed. "Yeah, I know who you are. Darcy has filled me in." And I'm left to wonder what exactly that means. If it's her version of events, it could be anything. By the look he gives me, I'm positive it's not great. He turns his attention back to Andy. "I'm not very close with my sister, but the hospital called me. I'm down as her next of kin, so here I am."

"Oh, okay. Thanks for coming to help her. She needs all the support she can get at the moment."

"I'm sorry for what she did to you, scaring you like that. No friend should ever have to see someone they care about go through that. I know the last time she did this still haunts me," he says sadly.

"She's done this before?" I ask. From what I can remember, there is no record of any mental health issues with her. The club would know if there was.

"Not this bad, but yes. Andy, can we go somewhere to talk for a bit? It feels weird standing in the hall talking about all of this."

"Yes, of course." She looks up the hall for somewhere to go.

"There is a cafeteria on the next floor down," I suggest.

"Can we talk in private?" he asks her, completely dismissing me.

I give him a look like no way in hell, buddy. He has to be fucking kidding. We don't know him at all. There is no way I'm letting her talk to him by herself, especially in the state she's in.

Andy takes my hand and laces it with hers. "Ah, Brad can come. He's my boyfriend, anything you have to say you can with him there."

Thank fuck she said that. He gives me another glance. Then huffs out, "Okay."

As we walk, I give her hand a squeeze; she curls her fingers around mine, gripping on tightly. It's a slight gesture, but it's nice to know she needs me and isn't still pushing me away to deal with it all on her own. A situation like this could see a new relationship fall apart, but it's only making us stronger. She is opening up to me and letting me in.

We take a seat and I grab coffee for the three of us, placing the tray of crappy cafeteria coffee down in front of them.

"So, as I was saying, she did this once before, when she was sixteen. I'm a couple of years older than her, and it was right before I was about to leave for college. Darcy and I don't come from a wealthy family. Our mom was an addict, and our dad took off and left her when Darcy was only a baby, so we grew up poor. When we were young, we got by helping each other. I was smart, and Darcy, she had the personality. She could manipulate anyone to give her just about anything. She was also fantastic at sports, but you guys know that already. Anyway, we grew up with very little, and at eighteen, I got offered a scholarship to Stanford. It was too good not to take up the offer. It promised to change my life, and it has.

"But Darcy didn't cope well when I told her. She felt like I was abandoning her, leaving the responsibility of our mom on her shoulders. So the night after I told her, she tried to cut her wrists with a razor blade. Luckily, I walked in on her while she was doing it, so I could stop her before she had gone too far. I took her to the ER and we played it off like an accident, one where she had slipped and fallen on a broken window. I don't know if they really believed our story, but that's what it was recorded as. It's also why I feel so terrible now.

"I'm so sorry. I knew she wasn't right mentally, but after that, she assured me it had scared her and she would never do anything like it again. I believed her."

"You were just a kid yourself," Andy says. "How could you know what she would do now? Dylan, what I don't understand is why I have never heard of you before? I've known Darcy since college, and she never mentioned you or her mom. I obviously knew she had some family, but it must have been a sore point, because she never brought you up."

"Yeah, she wouldn't have. After I went to college, I tried to keep in contact with her. I would send her money and try and call her, but she blocked me out. She felt abandoned, so she shut down from me and wouldn't let me back in."

"I'm so sorry, that must have been awful for you."

"It was, but I'm here now, and she's talking to me, so it's a start. When they release her, she'll come home to San Francisco with me. I'm doing alright for myself now and have the means to help take care of her."

Andy looks at me, lost as for what to do. I know it must be breaking Andy's heart to hear that Darcy will have to move away, but it's for the best. For all of us. Andy needs a fresh start without Darcy around, and Darcy is going to need time to heal and move on with her own life.

And I know I will feel safer knowing she's a few hours away.

# CHAPTER TWENTY-SEVEN

## ANDY

My sleep is restless again. I toss and turn, trying to get comfortable, but it's just not happening. I fall asleep for half an hour then I'm awake again. I try and at least keep my eyes closed so I'm getting some rest, but when I wake for the millionth time of the night, something tells me to open them this time.

When I do, the cold fingers of someone's hand press into my skin, covering my mouth so I can't scream. My eyes go wide as I try to focus in the dark, and when I do, I see Darcy sitting at the side of my bed, dressed in her white hospital gown. Her hair is wild and out, curling around her face, and her expression is blank.

And she's holding a knife in a silent threat.

I want to scream to tell Brad who is in the bed next to me, but I don't make a peep, I'm too worried about what she intends to do with that knife. I have no idea what she's capable of anymore.

She leans into my ear and the touch of her hair on my skin sends goosebumps down my arms. "Don't make a sound. I need you to come with me," is all she whispers.

I slip from the bed, and I curse Brad for being such a deep sleeper; he doesn't move a muscle. My only hope is that Nala might wake up when she hears movement. But then I remember she was sleeping in with Luna tonight because she needed the company.

Darcy drags me along with her into her room. Once inside, she drops her hand from my mouth and flicks the lock on the door. She rests her back so she's leaning against the door. And a slow smile creeps over her lips.

"We need to pack a bag. We're going on a trip," she says calmly.

The panic inside me increases. I'm not leaving this house with her. "To where?" I squeak.

She tilts her head to the side, assessing me. "Somewhere nice. I feel like a holiday, don't you, Andy? Maybe the beach?" She lowers the knife to her side.

Do they have her drugged up on something? She is acting so bizarre, loopy even. So not like her. Or maybe this is her and I just haven't seen this side of her before. "Darcy, we can't go anywhere. Your brother will worry about you."

She laughs and it's dark and tortured. She grabs my face. "My brother dearest couldn't give a flying fuck about me. He didn't when I was a kid, and he won't now. You're all I have left, Andy."

"I talked to him yesterday. He cares about you a lot. He wants to help you. And what about Luna and Jasmine and the other girls on the team? There are a lot of people who care about you." I mutter the words, hoping they'll help.

"You're the only one I care about." She drops my face. "Now we need to pack. Sit down, and just do what I say, it won't take me long." I plop down on the bed like I'm told, and she turns to her wardrobe, pulling out a bag and throwing items of clothing in.

My eyes flicker to the bedside table. I know what's in there, Luna showed me yesterday. I could make a grab for a knife. I'm not sure what I would do once I got it, but I also don't want to wait around here to see how this fucked-up scenario plays out.

I wait until she is looking away and I pull open the drawer, grabbing the first weapon I find. My hands shake as I hold it in her direction. Her eyes go wide when she turns around and works out what I have. "I'm not coming on this trip with you, Darcy. I'm walking out of here now, and you're going to let me." I say it as calmly as I can, but on the inside, I'm shitting myself. What if she doesn't care? She did try to take her own life this week; maybe threatening her with a knife is a stupid thing to do. But I don't have a lot of options. She seems to be stunned enough that it gives me time to move quickly across the room, flick the lock and open her door, running swiftly out.

I don't know why but I sprint for the back door. I should run back to my room, wake up Brad, but I don't want him caught up in this mess. She has a knife and I'm scared she will threaten him or one of the other girls with it. If I at least get outside and run, then hopefully she will come after me and I can hide somewhere and call for help.

But the blood-curdling scream of rage I hear echoing through the house stops me dead in my tracks. Then Nala's barking starts. Part of me wants to stay and try and help Darcy, the others will be awake and find her soon, but I don't know how anymore. Nope, I have to get out of here. Get help for the rest of us. I'm too scared Darcy has flipped a switch in her brain and she's someone none of us even understand anymore.

I go for the door handle, flicking the dead bolt and turning the knob. I dart out the back of the house into the dark of the night. Past the pool and down the back of the yard. I can hear her not far behind me, but I don't want to stop. I can't handle this anymore. I'm close to another panic attack, I can tell by how tight my chest is feeling.

"You leave, you'll never see me again," her cold voice calls from behind me and sends shivers of fear over my skin.

I stop running immediately. Fuck, I know she's serious. What she did this week was a cry for help, but after what she's told me today and what I found out from her brother, it's painting a picture of just how unstable she is. I slowly turn around to a furious Darcy. Her nostrils flaring, a knife in her hand.

I hear the others calling my name from inside the house; her scream would have woken them. "Darcy, we need to get you back to the hospital. They can help you there." I don't know what else to do so I start trying to negotiate with her.

Her eyes bore through me. "I'm not going back there. This ends one of two ways tonight. Either you tell Brad it's over for good and come with me, or you don't... and you will have my blood on your hands. I'm ready to end it, Andy. I'm done with feeling like this. You're the only one who can stop me."

My heart is pounding. What am I supposed to do? I believe every word she says. But I don't like either of those options. How has everything spun out of control so quickly? I stare at her, hoping something will soften. "Okay, Darcy. Let's just talk then. This is all just a misunderstanding, I'm sure. I'm your friend, remember? We've been through so much together. You can trust me. Let's just talk about it." I plead with my eyes for her not to do anything stupid.

"Why did you run if you care so much then, Andy? Are you making this all about you again?"

"You had me a little freaked out, Darc. That's all."

She takes a few steps closer to me, running the knife up and down the length of one of her bandages. It sends the hairs on the back of my neck standing on end. I don't want to see her cut herself again. "I want to talk to you properly, and this might be the only way I can get you to see things from my perspective. You are very good at manipulating me, Andy, you know how to get me to do what you want, but not this time. Now it's my turn for you to listen to me. You have no idea how hard the last few months have been on me. Watching you and Brad together, making love right here in the same house as me. It was so hard for me. You must have known that, knowing what we had, but you don't care about anyone but yourself, do you?"

I cringe at the words she's saying, knowing that she was the one taking the photos of us in compromising positions, watching us. The things she would have seen. It's so disturbing to think about. "That's not true at all. I care about you and your feelings, I just didn't realize this is the way you felt."

She glares at me, her eyes now glassy. "How could you not know? Because you only think about yourself. Andy, the superstar. Andy, the pretty one. Andy, the team hero. Andy, the one with the loving family. You have it all, and now you have our coach as well."

Is she right? I can be pretty self-centered at times. Maybe if I had paid more attention to what was happening with her, I would have seen this all for what it was. But if I think back, all I remember is her saying things like she had a hot date with this guy or that. She made it look like she was out having fun all the time. "But you've been dating like crazy all year, Darcy. You're always out partying with someone."

"Maybe that's what I said to you. But most of the time,

my hot date was spying on you and Brad while I ate takeout food in my car."

"Oh." That is so creepy. We can hear Jasmine's, Luna's, and Brad's voices getting closer, and I can see how on edge it makes her. She looks over her shoulder at the back door.

"Enough. You need to go back inside and break it off with him for good. I'll be able to hear every word you say so don't fuck this up."

I nod and walk slowly into the house. I can feel Darcy behind me, but she stops in the doorway. Probably doesn't want them to see her like this or they will know there is something wrong instantly. I see Jasmine first, and I can't help it, a tear runs down my face. I want to hold it together, do what Darcy has said so I can help her, but I can't. I'm not strong enough. I'm losing it. My hands tremble even though I will them not to.

"Andy, what's wrong?" she asks, looking toward Luna who's standing in the doorway of her room with Nala in her arms.

I shake my head, trying to signal to her not to say anything. "I'm fine, nothing's wrong," I say as confidently as I can.

She looks at me, confused, and I tilt my head to the back door. Realization dawns on her and she nods her head as if understanding what I'm trying to say.

"Oh good, sorry, we were just worried, we heard a scream," says Luna.

"Sorry to have worried you both. I'm fine, though," I say like a computer.

Brad arrives in the room. I can tell from the look on his face he already knows this is bad. He doesn't say anything, just walks right up to me and drops his head to my ear. "I saw the security footage. I know Darcy is out back with a knife. The police are on their way."

I look at him, scared. Oh fuck, at the first sound of sirens she's going to freak. Another tear slips from my eye and rolls down my cheek because I think it's too late. I can't help her anymore.

"Tell him it's over, Andy. Tell him now," she demands in a harsh voice, slowly emerging from her hiding spot.

"Brad," I start to say. Their faces show the shock when they see her. Darcy looks like death with pale sunken skin and a knife held to her wrists. She has removed the bandages, and the sight of her stitched-up wrists makes my stomach turn.

I look at Brad. I know what I have to say, what she needs me to say to stop what she is about to do to herself, but I can't get the words out, not even if they're fake. The fear has taken my voice.

"Tell him!" she yells angrily. Her eyes are wild as she stares at me with all her focus. Her hands tremble, the blood dripping like a leaky tap from her thin wrists.

Brad walks toward her and stands in front of me, so he's in between us. No fear at all that she's holding a knife. "Darcy, you need to put the knife down so we can get you some help, okay?"

She shakes her head. "You're not in charge here, Coach."

"I'm not, you're right. But look at the scared faces of your friends. They love you and don't want to see you do this to yourself. Don't do this to them."

She glances at us and it's as if she has a moment of clarity or a realization. She looks back at him. "You're right." She goes to hand him the knife. Just before it reaches his hand, she moves and plunges it toward him. "You're right, Coach, I don't want to die today. I just need you out of the picture to get what I want." He drops to the floor, gripping his chest. And I realize she's stabbed him.

The three of us scream and I run to him, holding him in my arms. Jasmine pulls Darcy away from us, as the police erupt through the front door.

I clutch at him, trying to work out where all the blood is coming from. At first, I think she got his chest, but on closer inspection, the knife has hit his shoulder. Someone pulls me out of the way, then I feel Jasmine's arms wrap around me and Luna's hand slide into mine. The emergency services rush to help him.

Please let him be okay. I can't lose him.

---

BRAD

I wake up and gasp for air. Pain radiates down my side, and I clutch my shoulder. For a brief moment before I was awake properly, I had hope that was all just a terrible nightmare I was having. But now I know it wasn't, with the throb of pain.

My memory is a little foggy as I try and piece together what exactly happened for me to end up in here. Like this. First there was Darcy screaming, that's what woke me, then Nala's barking. Then I realized Andy wasn't in bed with me anymore. I thought the worst. That she was gone, that Darcy had done something to her. Then I found Jasmine and Luna searching the house, just as frantic, trying to work out what was happening, just like me.

I knew I had to put a stop to Darcy's craziness. I didn't want the girls to see their friend brutalize herself again, so I had to step in and stop her. I just wasn't expecting her to turn on me like she did, or I would have gone about it differently.

"Andy, he's awake." I hear Jasmine's voice fill the room.

Then I see her. My beautiful girl. It might be the painkillers they have me on, but she looks just like an angel with light illuminating her. Her long golden locks falling around her pretty face. She squeezes my hand, and her lips turn into a smile.

"I've been staring at you, waiting for you to wake up, for the last hour. You scared us," she says shakily.

"I'm sorry, I really didn't think she would stab me."

"You're not the only one," says Jasmine with a smile.

Andy looks down at me and touches my face. "Are you in a lot of pain?"

"It's not comfortable, but I'll be fine."

"Are you in too much pain for me to kiss you?" She smirks.

"Never." With my good arm, I pull her down to me so our lips meet, and I kiss her with everything I have. When Darcy flew at me with the knife, Andy was the one I was thinking about. How awful it would be to leave her now when things were only just starting with us.

Jasmine's chair scrapes along the floor. "Okay, I'm going for a walk," she says, leaving the room.

Andy giggles, pulling back from me a little. "The whole time you were in surgery I was so worried about you. No one would tell us anything."

"I'm going to be okay, Andy. No more worrying, it's all over now," I tell her, but really, I have no idea how bad my injury is.

She nods and offers a small smile. Like she still doesn't believe it fully.

"What's going to happened with Darcy?" I ask.

A sadness washes over her again. "I don't know, they haven't told us yet. The police still need to take a statement from you as to what happened. I talked to Dylan briefly this morning. He said he's trying to have her transferred to a psychiatric facility in San Francisco, so he can help her."

"That makes sense. How did she even get out of the hospital in the first place, she was supposed to be on psychiatric watch, wasn't she?"

"No one knows, or if they do, they're not saying. Brad, does it make me a bad person? That I don't think I can see her again?" She drops her head and tears fill her eyes. "I mean, I was her friend for a long time... and..."

"Andy, she did some awful things to you, to us. I think it's understandable."

"She's sick, though. She needs me, and I'm just going to abandon her."

I run my hand down the side of her face. "She is, and you might also feel differently in a few months when she's had some professional help and you have had time to heal. Don't beat yourself up. None of this is on you. She might be unwell, but she made all the choices to do everything she did." She snuggles in at my side and I wrap my arm around her, closing my eyes, suddenly feeling very tired again.

Nurses come in and out all day, checking different things, and Andy stays by my side. I'm told I will be in here for a couple of days, then I'll have months of physio to regain full movement in my arm. I hope that's as long as I'm stuck here, because the girls' final is on Sunday and I want to be there for it.

My arm is in a sling for now, my movement limited, so I sit on the end of my bed and watch her. Friday has finally rolled around. I will be released today. Andy is packing my bag for me.

She has been at training for most of the day and is starting to look more like herself again. She says it's really strange not having Darcy at practice with them. They've played together for a long time, and this is such an important week for the Angels.

Ava has been to visit a few times this week, and I know she's concerned about team morale and the changes. But they played last week without Darcy and won; I'm sure they can do it again this week. And that is what I keep assuring Ava. She's working well with her new assistant coach, and I know she can help them bring home the win.

Andy turns around, grinning at me. "What?" she asks with a smile.

"I don't know, I just never imagined you as the domestic goddess type of girlfriend. But here you are, fussing over me."

"Well, don't get used to anything. Cause as soon as you're out of that sling, I'll be returning to my very undomesticated self. And then you'll owe me."

She comes to stand between my legs, and I pull her in, kissing down her neck. My good hand comes down to rest on her ass, giving it a squeeze. "I'm sure I can come up with all sorts of wonderful ways to make it up to you." I'm dying to get my hands on her body again. Being cooped up in the hospital has made for a very long week without her body wrapped around mine. Just because my arm is out of action doesn't mean I'm not craving her like crazy.

She giggles. "I'm sure you can." She kisses me.

There's a tap at the door, then heels clicking along the vinyl floor. "Looks like you're going to live," says Madeline with a friendly smile.

I'm more than a little shocked to see her. "Madeline, what are you doing here?"

Andy takes a step back from me, glaring at her like she's ready to shove her back out the door she just walked through. Madeline looks her up and down, flicks her hair over her shoulder as if dismissing her, then returns her attention back to me.

"I'm glad you're okay, Brad. I was so scared when I heard the news. I just wanted to pop in and give you these before I fly out." She places some papers down on the table in front of me. I glance over at them, and sure enough, it's the divorce papers, signed. "And I wanted to make sure you were okay, of course."

"You signed them?" I asked, stunned she actually did.

"Sure did. It became a necessity. I'm getting married again." She grins and flashes me her hand with an enormous diamond ring on it. I can't say I'm surprised she has found some other sucker to marry her, but it was faster than I thought it would be. I really couldn't care less. But I'm happy she has signed the papers so at least I can move on from that part of my life. And I won't be the one having to deal with her anymore.

I can hear Andy laugh from behind her. "What a lucky guy he must be," she says under her breath, but loud enough for us all to hear.

Madeline ignores her comment. "Good luck with it all," she says, waving a hand in Andy's direction. "Hope you don't wait too long and miss out on what's really important to you." She spins on her impossibly tall heels and strides out the door, leaving Andy looking at me. I know what she's thinking before she says it.

She comes to sit on the bed beside me, pushing my hair out of my eyes, staring up at me like she wants to be able to read my mind. "What are you going to miss out on if you wait too long?" she asks me in a quiet voice, like she's scared of what my answer might be.

Not really a conversation I'm ready to have with her right now, but I'm not lying to her either. "Having kids," I blurt out. "She thinks she knows what I want, Andy, but things change."

"Oh," she says, looking a little taken aback. And I'm not surprised. She's only twenty-four, kids would be the last thing on her mind.

"Andy, I'm not worried about that with you, okay? I know you have your career, and we can talk about all of that later."

She looks worried. "But she said it because she knows that's something that is really important to you, and you said it yourself. You nearly ended up with kids with her. You're a little older than me. I get it if you need to live your life now. If you can't wait for me to catch up. I don't want to hold you back."

"You really think I could walk away now?"

She shrugs.

"Andy?"

"No, I don't, but I don't want you to miss out on anything for me."

"I'm not going to. Right now, I just want to concentrate on us getting to know each other properly. The rest of it will come in the future."

She smiles up at me and kisses my lips. "That's what I want too. But just so you know, when the timing is right, I want it all with you."

I knew it already. I see it when she looks at me, feel it when our skin connects, but to hear her say it is music to my ears.

## CHAPTER TWENTY-EIGHT

ANDY

"Hey, Andy," I hear Luna call as she walks into the kitchen from her bedroom.

"Yeah," I call over my shoulder, shutting the fridge. I don't really need to eat anything else, I shouldn't. I'm just so excited about today's final so I'm looking for a distraction.

"I wanted to talk to you about something." She looks nervous, and I wonder what it could be. There has been so much going on, and I've spent so much time at the hospital this week that we haven't had a lot of time to check in with each other since everything happened.

"Anything, babes. Spill." I smile.

"Well, you know how Jasmine is moving back to Palm Springs and, well, you have Brad now. I'm thinking of moving out."

"You are?" I ask, surprised.

"I can't live here anymore, not after what happened last week. I'm sorry."

"Oh God, don't be sorry. I've been feeling the same but didn't want to put you out. This place is haunted now. I get it if that's how you feel as well. Where are you going to go?"

She gives me a sly smile. "A friend's place?"

"A nice-looking male friend's place? I've seen you, girlfriend, sneaking around with him. He picked you up from practice yesterday, didn't he?"

"Maybe?" She smirks. Good for her. She has been seeing this guy for a while, and it looks like it's working out. I couldn't be happier for her. Even if she won't call him her boyfriend or anything. She's happy with him, whatever their arrangement is.

"Where does he live? You're not moving too far away, are you?"

"Not too far from here. We can catch up for dinner once a week or something, and I'll still see you at practice every day."

"True, dinner once a week sounds like a nice idea."

"Are you going to move in with Brad?"

I scrunch up my face. "I don't know. Do you think it's too soon?" I ask her. Cause I really don't know what the right thing is to do. He seems all in, and I know he's ready for more commitment. He's the kind of guy that once he has made up his mind, he goes for what he wants. But this is all so new for me.

"As if you do anything just because it's normal. The Andy I know just goes and gets what she wants." She smirks.

"I don't want to fuck this up, though, Luna. What if it's too soon? Then we're over it and decide we hate each other."

"The dude got stabbed for you. I don't think he will move in with you and decide he hates you." She must notice my jaw drop, a little surprised at what she just said. We haven't talked about it at all. She wasn't really making a joke of it. She said it more matter of fact, but still, it sounded wrong. "Sorry, is it too soon to say that?"

"Feels kind of weird, you haven't talked to me about it at all."

"I know. I don't know what to say. I feel guilty because I should have seen it all happening. Because I should have stopped Darcy. Do you think we'll ever feel normal again?"

"I'm not sure, honey. I don't think I will. But Jasmine says over time it will all hurt less and we will trust other people again." I wrap my arms around her. "Don't feel guilty about any of it. None of us saw it coming."

She hugs into me, and I feel so grateful to have her. "Come on, enough of the sappy shit. We have a game to win."

---

BRAD

We clink glasses and I take a sip of my scotch. "Congratulations, beautiful. You and the Angels did it."

"I think I'm still in shock." She grins, her entire face lighting up. The sparkle is back in her eyes tonight, and she's the most gorgeous I have ever seen her. She's glowing from her win. And she's wearing a sexy black dress, short and body-hugging, showing off her luscious, toned body. On her feet she has some sexy heeled ankle boots. Her legs are long and tanned. She looks good enough to eat.

I haven't fucked her since before I got stabbed because she has been too worried about me overdoing it. She won't let me even get close to her. It also might have to do with everything she's been through, so I haven't pushed it, but I don't think I can wait a minute longer. But there is something I need to talk to her about first, so I'm going to have to wait.

We're out on the terrace just off my bedroom, and I take a seat on one of the deck chairs. "Can I talk to you about something before we go to the after-party tonight?"

She takes a seat opposite me, crossing one long leg over the other and sipping her drink. "What do you need to talk to me about, Brad?" She is a temptress, and she knows it. The way she says each word, distracting me from my thoughts.

I look at her pretty eyes, trying to concentrate on what I want to ask her. "I know you're struggling to stay in your house. And with your sister moving to Palm Springs and now Luna moving in with her guy friend, you will be all alone in that big house."

She gives me a sassy look. "I have Nala, don't forget."

"How could I forget about her? What I was saying, though, is... you're here all the time, anyway. Why don't we make it permanent?"

Her face breaks into a full-on grin. "Are you asking me to move in with you, Mr. Swift?" She sits forward in her chair and pulls it closer to mine, leaning over so she is just inches from my face.

"Yes." I close the gap, devouring her luscious lips. Her hands come to the back of my head, and with my good arm, I pull her in closer to me. I need to feel her body against mine.

She pulls back from me. "We don't have time for any shenanigans, we have a party to attend." She giggles.

I give her a serious look. "I don't give a fuck about the party, baby. There are more urgent matters that need to be taken care of."

"Oh yeah? And what would they be?"

"You know exactly what I'm talking about, my beautiful

girl." I run my hand up my length, palming it through my pants.

Her face turns serious. "Are you sure you're really okay?"

"I won't be if you keep wrapping me in bubble wrap. I need to fuck you."

She smirks, her sexy, sassy smile. "Well, when you say it like that." She stands, unzipping her dress. It falls to the floor below her, revealing her sexy-as-fuck body—no underwear. "I guess we could be late. I think you should fuck me right here on your balcony. Prove to me how okay you are."

"That is my plan."

# EPILOGUE
## ANDY: SIX MONTHS LATER

Brad laces his fingers with mine as we walk into the ballroom Amelia has rented for her spring fashion show. The place looks insane. It's an opulent space, with decorative wallpaper in a smoky-charcoal, almost-black color lining the walls, and large drapes adorning the windows. In the center of the room hang three large chandeliers, and below them, a long runway down the length of the room. There are seats on either side of it. The lighting is dark and moody, with a large spotlight highlighting where the models will walk.

Until I walked in tonight, I hadn't realized just how big of a deal my sister and her fashion label had become. But this is unreal. There must be over five hundred of California's elite here. And my big sister is rubbing shoulders with each one of them, flitting from one group to the next. She fits in with this crowd. This is her scene, and you can tell how much she loves it. I have never seen her look more confident and comfortable in her own skin, and I couldn't be happier for her. She deserves this; she has worked so hard and dealt with so much to be here.

Brad gives my hand a little squeeze as we stop by the bar. "Are you going to tell them tonight?"

"Do you think I should? This is Amelia's night. I don't want to take anything away from celebrating her."

"You're wearing the ring. I think they might put two and two together." He smiles, and I know he's right, but there is no way I was taking it off.

I glance down at the stunning diamond engagement ring Brad proposed to me with last week. I can't help the stupid smile that appears on my face every time I look at it. It's so beautiful. But more than that, I'm just so blissfully happy. The past year has had its ups and downs, that's for sure, but right now, everything is perfect, and that's all I want to concentrate on. When I moved in with Brad, I was so worried it was too soon, that we hadn't had enough time to get to know each other properly before we just jumped in. But it has been the best decision I've ever made.

The lights flash to signal the show is starting, and we make our way to our chairs alongside my parents, Jasmine, and Cassie. Jasmine grins over at us with a cheeky, knowing smirk. I roll my eyes at her and signal for her to watch the show. I told her straight away, she would have killed me if I didn't, but I wanted to wait till I was in person to tell the rest of my family.

The models take to the catwalk one by one, and with each stunning design, I'm more and more impressed at how skilled my sister is. Her designs have a boho feel, with relaxed floral dresses, playsuits, maxi skirts with cute crop tops, and Aztec-looking jewelry. Her last design is a stunning eggshell-white gown with a fitted bodice and flowing lace skirt. My heart skips a beat, not because I love the dress or anything—it's beautiful and all, but fashion really isn't my thing—but because I'm getting married, and for some silly reason looking at a wedding dress makes me want to dress up for my man and get all girly.

The last model takes Amelia's hand and pulls her on to the stage, and she walks the catwalk with her hand in hand. The crowd celebrates her, and I look on with pride.

After the show, we mingle and have a few drinks with my family. "So, Cassie, you landed a teaching gig at our old school. That's going to be..."

"Weird?" She pulls a face like she's not that happy about it. When mom told me, I got the impression she was pumped, so I'm confused.

"I was going to say exciting, but yeah, I guess a bit strange."

"Yes, it's exciting. I think I'm just nervous to actually start teaching."

"Congratulations, Cassie," Brad says. "From what I hear, it's hard to land a permanent job your first year out of school." I give him a look. What would he know about the American school system?

"It's been my dream for so long. What if I hate it?"

"Then you try something else," I say.

Cassie grips my arm, looking me over. "Why are you so calm and relaxed all of a sudden? The Andy I know would have said then you suck it up and get on with it."

"She's too loved up to be a bitch," says Jasmine, glancing down at my hand, tipping her head to emphasize that Cassie should look.

I give her a death stare.

"You have got to be kidding me. You guys got engaged!" squeals Cassie, her eyes darting between me and Brad.

"We did," he says.

Cassie's excitement has drawn attention to us, and my parents make their way over to see what all the fuss is about.

She holds my hand up to them, showing off my new very special piece of jewelry.

"Congratulations, you two, we couldn't be more thrilled," says my mom with a gigantic grin, and I wait for Dad's reaction. He's the one I wasn't sure would be happy. He has warmed up to Brad over the last six months, but I'm not sure we're at the point of family yet.

"You did it, son," he says with a genuine simile. I look at him, surprised, then to Brad who is smiling, pleased with himself. He must have asked my dad's permission. I had no idea he did that. It's old-fashioned but so sweet and would have meant the world to my father.

"Oh my God, do I get to be a bridesmaid?" asks Cassie.

I look at Brad and shrug. We haven't really talked wedding plans. I don't think we even want to get married any time soon. "I guess all three of you will be? We haven't made any decisions yet."

"You don't get to choose whether we'll be your bridesmaids, Andy. We're your sisters and you can't get married without us," says Jasmine. She is being very bossy tonight and kind of a pain in the ass about all of this. What's her deal? I glare at her. "Sorry, I just mean, some of us might not get a wedding of their own. We might have to live through you."

She says it sadly, and I feel bad for being a bitch. She's the one who always wanted the wedding to the perfect man, the whole fairy tale love story, not me. Twelve months ago, I couldn't give a fuck about any of it. It just hasn't worked out for her yet, but it will. If I'm any proof, it will all happen for her when the timing is right.

Someone calls to my mother, and she takes Cassie's hand and leads her over to a group of people she was just talking with, and Dad and Brad head over to the bar, so I'm left with just Jasmine.

"Jas, it will happen, you know. He's out there. You just haven't met him yet."

"Yeah, I'm starting to believe that's all bullshit, Andy. Maybe it's just not going to happen for me, and you know what... I'm okay with that. Don't need some guy to control my life, anyway. I'm better off on my own."

"Um, who are you and what have you done with my sister? The one who has believed in true love since we were kids and she used to parade around the house in Mom's heels with a pillowcase attached to her head as a veil."

"She gave up. She grew up and realized that's not how it is for everyone."

Jasmine is acting strange. I don't believe her, she's not the type to give up on love. "What is really going on here, Jas? You're hiding something from me."

She looks at me, all sweet and innocent, but it's the blush that rises up over her chest and her face that confirms it for me.

"Spill."

"Okay, fine, you're right, I'm hiding something. Something huge, but you can't tell anyone. Not Luna or Brad, and especially not Amelia or Cassie. The last thing I need is for Mom and Dad to ever know about this."

"Alright, what has my perfect sister been up to?"

"I'm serious, Andy, not a soul. Ever."

I gesture that I'm crossing over my heart. "Your secret is safe with me."

"I wouldn't say I was so perfect anymore." She pauses, and by the look on her face, I'm not sure if she's going to change her mind about telling me or if she'll burst into tears.

"Oh my God, Andy, I think I have done something momentously stupid."

She leans in and whispers in my ear, and I glance at her in complete shock. Did I hear her correctly? I'm at a loss for words. My perfect goody-two-shoes sister is definitely not so perfect anymore, and I love it.

Her life just got a whole lot more exciting.

---

Stay tuned to find out what happens in Jasmine's story "The Escape" coming April 2022.

If you or someone you love is experiencing suicidal thoughts or tendencies, please seek assistance. The below website has international links to mental health resources
https://www.therapyroute.com/article/helplines-suicide-hotlines-and-crisis-lines-from-around-the-world

## ALSO BY A K STEEL

The Broken Point Series
Always Fraser — http://mybook.to/alwaysfraser
Eventually Blake — http://mybook.to/eventuallyblake
Only Theo — http://mybook.to/onlytheo
Forever Drew — http://mybook.to/foreverdrew

Secrets of the Harper Sisters Series
The Coach — http://mybook.to/thecoach
The Escape — (coming soon)

If you enjoyed The Coach, please leave me a review. Reviews really do make such a difference. Even a short one-liner is a big help.

## ACKNOWLEDGMENTS

My partner, Kiel, you have changed my life in so many wonderful ways. Thank you for pushing me to start writing. Without your encouragement and love, I never would have put pen to paper and started this fantastic journey in the first place. I feel like I found myself this year, and I'm finally where I'm supposed to be. Without you, this never would have happened.

My amazing mum, Kay, thank you for your constant love and support. You read every word I write and have always been my number-one fan. You put up with my meltdowns and endless questions, you are my best friend, and I'm grateful every day to have you in my life.

My dad, it's been seven long years since you left us, but the outlook you had on life still inspires me every day. It's the reason I believe that if you work hard enough, you can achieve any dream, no matter how impossible it seems.

My kids—Hamish, Marley, and Quinn—thank you for looking at me like I'm amazing and can do anything, even when I don't feel like I can. Everything I do is for you. And I hope I have shown you that with a bit of determination and hard work, your dreams really can come true.

Karen, my friend and mentor, you made this dream feel possible. Every time I thought I couldn't do it, you encouraged me to keep on going. I couldn't have done any of this without your knowledge and friendship.

T. L. Swan and the girls from the Cygnet Inkers group, I'm loving being on this journey with you all. You girls keep me positive and motivated, and I love you for it.

Lindsay, my editor, thank you for your patience with a new author. Your knowledge and expertise have made this book what it is.

Sarah, for my gorgeous cover design, and your patience with my indecisiveness. I love the cover you created for me.

Give Me Books Promotions, thank you for your help spreading the word about my books in the book community and helping me share my stories with the world.

My beta readers— Shelly, Kirstie, Bek, Francesca, Jemma, Patricia, Tobie and Anita—thank you for your time, honesty, and support. Without you lovely ladies I wouldn't have had the courage to publish and share my story.

My proofreader, Kay, thank you for double and triple-checking every word.

To my friends and family who have been so supportive along this journey—you have all been so amazing —thank you.

And lastly to my readers, thank you for taking the time to give a new author a chance, and making my dreams become a reality.

## ABOUT THE AUTHOR

I'm a contemporary romance author of books with swoony men, twists and turns, and always a happily ever after.

I'm a busy mother of three pre-teens, who lives on the beautiful South Coast of New South Wales, Australia. I have always been a creative soul, with a background in fashion design, interior decoration, and floristry. I currently run a business as a wedding florist and stylist but have always had a love for reading romance novels. There's just something about how the story can transport you to another world entirely.

So, in 2020, I decided to jot down some of my own ideas for romance stories—always with a happily ever after, of course —and from that came my debut novel, *Always Fraser*. From that moment, I haven't looked back. Writing has become a part of me. I have a long list of stories plotted, and I look forward to being able to share them all with you soon. I hope you enjoy reading them as much as I loved writing them.

XX

For all the news on upcoming books, visit A.K. Steel at:
   www.aksteelauthor.com

facebook.com/a.k.steelauthor
instagram.com/aksteelauthor

Printed in Great Britain
by Amazon